D0350788

CAGES

CAGES

David Mark

**SEVERN
HOUSE**

First world edition published in Great Britain and the USA in 2021
by Severn House, an imprint of Canongate Books Ltd,
14 High Street, Edinburgh EH1 1TE.

Trade paperback edition first published in Great Britain and the USA in 2022
by Severn House, an imprint of Canongate Books Ltd.

severnhouse.com

British Library Cataloguing-in-Publication Data
A CIP catalogue record for this title is available from the British Library.

ISBN-13: 978-0-7278-9091-7 (cased)
ISBN-13: 978-1-78029-780-4 (trade paper)
ISBN-13: 978-1-4483-0518-6 (e-book)

All Severn House titles are printed on acid-free paper.

MIX
Paper from
responsible sources
FSC
www.fsc.org   FSC® C013056

Typeset by Palimpsest Book Production Ltd.,
Falkirk, Stirlingshire, Scotland.
Printed and bound in Great Britain by
TJ Books Limited, Padstow, Cornwall.

For Kate L-G
Thanks for putting up with me

Frightened, he runs off to the silent fields
and howls aloud, attempting speech in vain;
foam gathers at the corners of his mouth;
he turns his lust for slaughter on the flocks,
and mangles them, rejoicing still in blood.
His garments now become a shaggy pelt;
his arms turn into legs, and he, to wolf
while still retaining traces of the man:
greyness the same, the same cruel visage,
the same cold eyes and bestial appearance.

The story of King Lycaon from Ovid's
Metamorphoses, Book I, ll. 321-331

PROLOGUE

Annabeth Harris.

On her knees again.

On her knees and looking up: a penitent receiving communion – staring at the heavens as if holding the gaze of God.

Look at her. Look down . . .

Nineteen next birthday and already gone to seed.

Careworn. Lived in. *Frayed.*

She's all sharp edges, under the bad skin and make-up. It's as if she's made up of teeth and elbows; of cheekbones and knees. She's all spots and burst blood vessels. Bleeding gums, behind the smile. Her mouth, all metal and meat.

Annabeth. Silver hoops and pink nails. Denim skirt and blue leggings. Baggy cardigan over too-tight top. Fox-fur hair in jaunty pigtails. Pinpricks and scabs in the crook of her arm.

Annabeth. In a room with a high roof and crumbling walls. A mottled ceiling rose; bare bulb hanging low. Mauve walls, chopped into rectangles by dado and picture rail. A rotting, unvarnished wooden floor; missing boards here and there, like teeth pulled from rotten gums.

Annabeth.

Breathing in . . .

Damp wood and dead flowers. Talcum powder. *Sex.*

She tries to keep clean, does Annabeth. Still has enough pride about her to want to prettify her surroundings. But her benefactor doesn't like it if she's too well groomed. Takes it personally if she starts scrubbing at the skirting boards or sponging down the walls. Tells her it makes him feel unappreciated. Tells her that if she thinks she deserves so much better than he provides for her, she can go back to where she was when he found her. And Annabeth doesn't want that. Even in her very worst moments, she knows she is better in here than out there. She knows herself to be safer in a cage than adrift among the wolves.

Better anywhere than out there, where the past is only ever half a step behind.

Annabeth. In her crappy room, at the top of the big old house. Splendid, once upon a time. Opulent, even. Three floors of Victorian grandeur. Double doors and a vestibule. Mosaic hallways and a fireplace fit for Santa. A home for merchants and bankers; their wives and children. Annabeth can picture them, when she tries. Can conceive of herself as a cheerful young nanny, wheeling a great black perambulator across to the gardens in the centre of the square. Can see bonnets, and parasols, and a fat cherub-faced baby with red curls and a cap, who won't settle for Mummy and will only cease his tantrums when Nanny sings her special song.

Annabeth can spend many an hour lost in such a daydream. When she was small she had dreams of becoming an author. Loved stories. Loved them so much she became a liar. Improved her reality with exaggerations and happy endings, until nobody believed a word she said. Sometimes, she couldn't tell where the truth ended and her imagination began. It was cute, when she was young. Ugly, by the time she hit her teens. By then, all she wanted was to be believed.

Annabeth still scribbles down the occasional diary entry. There's a loose floorboard beneath the bed, and she has taken to scribbling down memories on the wood, the nib of her stolen, catalogue-shop pen scoring impassioned inkless wheals into the grimy wood. There is nothing legible, but she finds the act briefly soothing.

Annabeth would very much like to tell her story. Explain how she came to be here. Chatsworth Square, Carlisle. Hundreds of miles from the last place she really called 'home'; sickeningly grateful to the man who feeds and houses her, and who takes payment from her flesh.

She imagines herself into a different reality. Tries to enact some form of metamorphosis upon her surroundings. Comes up against the impenetrable actuality of the rotting squat where she has been waking up these past weeks. The big Victorian house is all flats now. Bedsits. Temporary digs for student types and the perennially unemployed. Smokers. Drinkers. A bass player and his girlfriend in Flat 3. Always a stream of visitors. Hard to know who lives here and who is just passing by to smoke a joint and strum a guitar. A foreign family, for a while; exotic smells drifting from their flat on the second floor. They left after the third burglary.

Annabeth considers herself. Tries to identify the individual feelings within the complexities of her mood. She realizes she is at once excited and giddy and absolutely terrified. Feelings are returning like blood flooding into a dead limb. She's been numb for so long. Anaesthetized herself. Shut down all the parts capable of compassion. For hope.

And yet suddenly, that is what she feels.

Annabeth.

Goosepimples on her bare arms. The white lines she has carved into her skin seem to blur and pixelate. White lines, neat as train tracks, puckering closer together.

Wobbling now. Unsteady. Reaching out and putting her hand on the inflatable mattress. It sags. She'll have to blow it up again soon; smear lip gloss on the nozzle and exhale until she sees stars.

She lowers her head, her celestial beseeching briefly halted. Takes a quick inventory. Checks that everything is where it should be. She has few possessions, but those that she does possess are to be cherished. Her snow globes look cheerful. Six of them. *Stonehenge. Colchester. Edinburgh. London. Paris. Tunisia.* The last two were gifts. She has never been abroad. They form a fragile circle around her little CD player; dribbling some tinny pop, so quiet it sounds like a whispering from a distant room. A tangle of Christmas lights is woven through the slats, throwing a multi-coloured glow onto her sparse possessions. Make-up, in a sparkly bag. A stack of paperback books, retrieved from a pile dumped outside the charity shop where she had spent two cold, unmemorable nights. Three pairs of shoes, lined up neatly by the wall. Battered white trainers, a pair of Army-style boots, and her 'work' shoes. Four-inch heels; black and strappy. T-shirts, jeans and her bomber jacket spill from a rucksack.

She's barefoot now. Barefoot, kneeling down, staring at the ceiling; mascara brush to her eye, mouth open in concentration.

There's a pain at the back of her neck; a big fist of tension and gristle. She pictures a knot in a damp rope. A door opens in her mind. Something she's read. Sees nimble little fingers, pale and bloodied, picking at tangles of tarred thread. A line of poetry, long forgotten. Something about Satanic mills.

She blinks, and it's gone again. She's still on the floor in the empty flat. Still looking up, neck extended; a chick waiting for Mama to regurgitate some grubs. Still waiting for him. Her benefactor. The man who keeps her safe. Safe from everybody but him.

Annabeth.

Still doing her make-up. Still turning her eyelashes into spider legs. Still smearing greasy lip gloss onto lips that she has never liked. They're too thin; the top one barely there at all. She has to perform miracles with an eyebrow pencil to make them seem even vaguely alluring.

She lowers her head. Pulls a face. Steels herself, and flicks her head skywards again. Checks herself over. It's hard to tell, from the angle, but she knows she's done the best that she can. Not even the best make-up artist in the business could guarantee perfection if forced to use a mirrored ceiling to apply their slap. She's suggested to her benefactor that he bring her a little hand mirror with his weekly delivery. So far, he has paid her no heed, and she knows he does not like being pestered. She will ask him again, when the time is right. For now, she will continue to use the mirrored ceiling, installed long before Annabeth took up residence in the damp, dingy space. Walter has helped a lot of girls, over the years. Enjoys laying back and watching his waifs and strays show him their appreciation.

Annabeth rolls her head from left to right. Kisses the air. Kisses it again: a loud smacking together of her lips. So, this is it. This is the moment. This is when it will happen, or it won't. *Christ*, how she hopes she's got it right. She needs him to see her properly. To see more than the skinny, dead-eyed girl he picked up and decided to keep for himself. More than just his favourite place to release the tension after his difficult day. She wants him to think of her as a future; as somebody who could care for him; help him, support him. She needs to make him see that there is a soul worth loving inside the body that gives him such pleasure. She needs to make him see who she might have been, had things been different. Had life been kinder. Had she not made such terrible mistakes, or trusted the wrong people, or said yes when she should have said no.

She hears the sound of the fire door slamming shut one floor beneath. There's a tremble in her chest – a feeling that spider eggs are hatching under her skin. She hears footsteps. The quiet jangle of keys; chains hanging from the wrists of a ghost. She fancies for a moment that she can hear voices. Dismisses it. She is a squatter here. A trespasser. She is dug in deep; a tick in a dog's neck. Nobody knows she's here, save for him. And he guards his privacy so very jealously.

Metal on metal.

The rushing of blood and the desperate, absolute need for this to go right . . .

The door swings open. He waddles in the way he always does, pushing out a lungful of air; knackered from the journey up the stairs. He's a small man. Small, and round. Babyish, really, in his dimensions. Big head and fleshy limbs and a jolly round gut that he makes no effort to hide. Bald, save for the few strands of red he streaks across his gleaming red scalp. There's a waxiness to him. A sheen, as if he has just scrubbed off his top layer of skin. Small, deep-set eyes, seemingly pushed deep into his skull by the same hand which grabbed a fistful of face and pulled out a fat, bulbous nose. There's a harlequin pattern on his zip-up cardigan. A neat seam in his polyester trousers. Plastic sandals. He's got carrier bags in his hands. Annabeth sees tins and biscuits, long-life milk. Baby wipes. Toothpaste. Sees the telltale outline of a large bottle of vodka and a box of Maltesers. This is the man who has saved her. The man who keeps her safe. The man who has done terrible things to her, but kept her safe from anything worse.

'Walter,' she says, breathily. She makes sure her smile is so wide and welcoming it could belong to a housewife in an old US sitcom. She wishes she could hand him a cocktail. Perhaps kiss his cheek. Wishes she could have prepared him dinner. She needs him to see past the girl he comes here once a week to feed and fuck.

'Those bloody stairs,' he grumbles, pushing into the room. 'Be the death of me.'

'I'm sorry . . .'

'Not your fault, is it? What are you gonna do – carry me up?'

'I could try,' she smiles. 'Stronger than I look.'

'No you're not. Little arms like yours? Like satsumas in a sock.'

'Can I take your coat . . . I was hoping . . .'

He stops, still half in and half out of the room. He eyes her critically. 'What's this, then?'

'What's what, Walter?'

'You look a bit . . . I dunno. A bit . . . plain, I suppose. Mumsy. Were you not expecting me? It's Thursday, isn't it? I always come on a Thursday.' The jolly redness of his face darkens. He looks like uncooked beef. 'What have you done to your lips? And where are your shoes . . .?'

Her heart starts to beat faster. She's got it wrong. Made a mistake. Misjudged it horribly.

'I can dress however you need; I just wanted to tell you something . . .'

He waves a hand, dismissively, and then turns back to the door. 'Come away in, Mike. Don't stand there shivering.'

Annabeth takes a step back. He's never brought anybody with him. Has made her promise, time and again, that she will do all in her power to remain his secret. She clenches her fists. Remembers. A staircase in a little terraced house. A man she thought was her friend. The sudden, searing pain. The start of it all. Feels the hot, burning memory like a coal against her skin.

She watches as Walter shuffles out of the way. Mike has to stoop to make his way into the room. He's tall. Too tall. Stringy with it. Long black coat and fawn trousers; jet-black hair and a thick black beard. He looks like a match burned down to the grip.

'Here, love. This is Mike. Mike's my pal. Sorry about the state of her, she's obviously trying to make a point. You should see her in the high heels. Good calves on her. Proper little pit pony.'

Annabeth feels hummingbirds fighting in her chest. Feels light-headed. Guiltily, she glances at the bed. At her make-up. Lipstick. Mascara. Blusher. Nail varnish. A white plastic strip, laid across her nail file like a cross.

She looks at Walter. The thick mascara on her lashes makes her vision into a cage. She tries to make herself smile as she says it. 'This is a bit unexpected. I thought we were supposed to be ultra-secretive, weren't we? Not a peep, you said. Not a sound . . .'

'This is what I have to deal with,' says Walter, turning to his friend. He drops the shopping on the floor with a thump. Shakes his head. 'Close the door, lad, you're letting the smell out.'

Annabeth shoots a look at Mike. He seems a little shy, looking down at the floor like a bashful child receiving praise.

'Not much of a greeting, is it?' says Walter, churlishly. He dabs the sweat from his forehead with the sleeve of his cardigan. Leans against the wall. Glares a hole through Annabeth. 'Expecting somebody else, were you? Some lad who likes the librarian look? What's with the fucking cardigan?'

She twitches a smile, hoping he'll think it girlish and sweet. Points at him, her finger and thumb a pistol. 'You're wearing a cardigan, Walter.'

He laughs at that: an unpleasant, snorting sort of a noise. 'You've got some cheek, love. Some cheek to be waiting for me dressed like that. You know what I want. How this works . . .'

Annabeth takes a breath. Tries to calm herself. Makes her features soften. 'I wanted to talk to you, that's all. Wanted us to maybe chat about a few things.'

Walter's eyebrows shoot up. He shakes his head, neck and chins wobbling. 'Talk is it? And what do we have to talk about, girl? I give you a roof over your head. I feed you. I slip you a few quid as and when I can. And you keep your mouth shut apart from when I tell you to open it. Seems pretty straight-forward to me, love. I mean, you can show me your workings-out, if you like.'

'I'll go, Walt,' mumbles Mike. 'She doesn't seem like she's keen.'

Walter shakes his head, pissed off. 'No, lad, you've been promised a place to dip your wick and by God I deliver what

I promise.' He swivels to Annabeth. 'I was going to be sweet about this, love. Even brought you a box of chocolates and a magazine. But you're taking some liberties here. I've done myself a mischief, as it happens, so I won't be troubling you for a jump, but I hate seeing good meat go to waste so I told Mike here he's allowed a turn at the table. Got a few problems, has Mike. His marriage is suffering. Stuff he wants to do and the wife isn't in to it. Nor should she be, not really. But if he gets it out of his system, he'll go home a better husband. We're doing a kindness here, love. So, Mike, how do you want her . . .?'

Annabeth has already prepared the speech in her head. She's spent the day perfecting the delivery. She has imagined the scenario a dozen different ways. But here, in this moment, it just comes out. Erupts, like blood from a puncture wound.

'I'm having a baby, Walter. I'm pregnant.'

He doesn't say anything for a moment. Just stares at her, dark little eyes drilling holes into her forehead. Then he twitches his nostrils. Shakes his head.

'You said you can't,' he says, quietly. 'All messed up, you said.'

Annabeth feels tears pricking her eyes. She'd believed it when she said it. Had thought herself too damaged to ever conceive.

'I thought I was . . .'

'How do you know? My wife misses her periods all the fucking time . . .'

'I stole a test,' says Annabeth, her voice catching. 'Snuck out. I was weeks late. Feeling sick. I had to know. Don't worry, nobody saw . . .'

He barks a laugh. 'Not my prime concern, right now, lass. Not important, as it happens. Not when I've got some fucking slag telling me she's carrying my baby.'

Annabeth feels the tears spill. 'I'll be a good mum,' she says, softly. 'I'll try so hard.'

Through the mist she sees Mike turn his back on them both. Sees him pull the door open and stoop his way into the hallway. Hears hurried footsteps.

And then it's just Walter.

Just Walter, standing there.

Looking at her like she's rotten. Looking at her like she's filth and puke in a skin suit.

'You think you're going to keep it? You think I would allow that? No, love, we're drowning the little bastard.' He raises his hand to his forehead, dripping sweat, talking half to himself. 'I know somebody. Old doctor. Did some treatments in Ireland before they threw him out. I'll call him. Get him over. Pull the fucker out before they can take root . . .'

Later, Annabeth will remember little about what comes next. The pictures will be jerky and blurred, as if the reel of film in her mind has been exposed to sunlight. As if it has been shredded and stuck back together.

But she will recall fear. Anger. Will recollect the absolute and certain knowledge that she must protect her unborn child until the last breath.

Here, now, she tells him so. Tells him that whatever happens, this child will live.

She sees the cold rage take hold of his features. Sees him make the calculations. Sees him decide to do the only thing that can be done.

Later, she will remember fat, sweaty hands at her throat. Remember the rubber bed against her cheek. His spittle on her face. The word 'bitch, bitch, bitch' as he drags her to the floor and pounds her head off the wood.

And she will recall the cold smoothness of the snow globe in her hand. The impact of it against her skull. The sharp pain as the jagged glass cuts her palm. Then the hot blood as she thrusts the circle of lethal-looking stalactites into his fat neck and tears his flesh like the belly of a cod.

She will not remember it often. But when the memories do stir, she will stroke her child.

And though she will hate herself for it, she will permit herself to smile.

PART ONE

REWARD TO BE OFFERED TO HELP FIND MISSING LUCY

By *Swindon Courant* Chief Reporter, Daryl Corcoran

April 19, 2005

THE FAMILY of missing Swindon teenager Lucy Brett have made an emotional appeal for information regarding the whereabouts of their 'sweet, beautiful' girl.

15-year-old Lucy was last seen leaving the family home at around 8.15 a.m., for her morning walk to school. However, she did not arrive. A 'mystery man' made a call to the school shortly before 9.30 a.m. to say she would not be attending due to illness. Believing the man to be Lucy's father, the alarm was not raised until that evening, when she failed to return home from school and her older sister, Cameron, began to worry. Police were called in shortly before 10 p.m.

While police believe that Lucy may be with a friend or boyfriend, her family are urging witnesses to come forward and are trying to raise the money to offer a reward.

Lucy's father, Tim, 43, said: 'People might read this and think she's just another runaway, or that she's a bad girl who's gone off with her boyfriend. Certainly that seems to be the way the police reacted at first. But we know Lucy and she would never do this to us. She would do anything for anybody. She's a kind, sweet, beautiful, God-fearing girl who's never caused us any worry.

'Of course, nobody knows the whole truth about everyone, including their nearest and dearest, but we've asked her friends, schoolmates; people she hangs out with at her after-school clubs and her Rainbows group at church. Nobody has told us anything that would suggest she's been keeping secrets. There's nothing missing from her room – we've been through every scrap of paper in the house looking for a note or a sign she was planning to run away. We're putting up a reward with the help of some family friends. I am begging anybody who thinks they may have information to come forward at once.'

Detective Inspector Callum Hansen of Wiltshire Police defended the Force's handling of the inquiry. He said: 'We are taking Lucy's disappearance very seriously and are leaving no stone unturned. We're putting together a timeline of her last movements.

'As for this person who called the school, this is clearly a very compelling piece of information.'

Friends from Lucy's Rainbows group – a youth club set up for teens and run from a church hall in Gorse Hill – are still coming to terms with their friend's disappearance.

Colette Newbury, 14, told the *Courant*, 'She's always just been this big, bubbly ball of energy and happiness – always smiling, happy to help the younger members and listen to the older ones. People are saying all sorts of horrid things, like she had a secret boyfriend, or something, but that's not Lucy at all. She's just sweet, really. I don't think she's got any interest in boys. Honestly, she'd be giddy if you gave her a bar of chocolate so there's no way she would keep something like this to herself. I'm thinking all sorts of horrible things. I just want her to come home.'

HELP BRING 'PERFECT SON' HOME
By Roger Lytollis
June 12, 2006

A 14-YEAR-old boy missing from his Carlisle home has been called 'a perfect son' by his frantic parents.

Phillip Westoby was last seen leaving his home in Carlisle's Morton Park at a little before 9 a.m. on Sunday morning.

Five days on, his parents say they have 'done everything in their power' to try and contact him and now believe he may have been taken against his will.

Phillip's mother, Sue, a receptionist at a city centre

dental surgery, is urging anybody with information to
contact police.

She said: 'We know for an absolute fact that he left the
house early on Sunday because a neighbour saw him closing
the door and heading down the drive. We think he may have
been heading to the newsagent's to pick up some things.
There was very little milk in the fridge and he likes to start
the day with a good breakfast. That's the kind of lad he is.
Reliable. Decent. He'd see something missing from the
cupboards and would just go off and get a replacement. He
liked surprising us. Getting the papers – spending his pocket
money on little treats for his dad and me and his big brother.

'It sounds hard to believe but he's always been a perfect
son. His dad suffers with terrible back pains and Phil has
very much stepped up as the man of the house. I just want
him home.'

Police claim they take every missing persons case
seriously and have urged anybody with information to get
in touch.

HOPE FADING IN MISSING SCHOOLGIRL
INVESTIGATION
Durham Sentinel, April 2, 2005

A SENIOR detective has warned that the chances of
recovering missing schoolgirl Melanie Grazia are growing
slimmer with every day that goes by. The 14-year-old went
missing from boarding school in picturesque Barnard
Castle, Weardale, on Friday afternoon.

The 'star pupil' excused herself from lessons to return
to the boarding house, suffering from stomach cramps
and blurred vision. She was walked back by a fellow
classmate, who returned to lessons when Melanie was
still on the doorstep of the small property in the grounds
of the Victorian-built school.

The Head of Pastoral received a telephone message
around the time of the final school bell stating that

Melanie's parents had come to pick her up and that she would be away all weekend. As this is against school policy, the staff member called her parents to clarify. They claimed they had left no such telephone message. Police were called the following morning.

A spokesman for the school said: 'We are reviewing all of our safeguarding policies but for now all that matters is finding Melanie safe and well. She has been gone for over a week now and her friends are frantic with worry. She is a big part of this school, be it her integral part of the school's drama group; the orchestra, the choir, the sports team. She's an exceptional person and a true delight to have around. She's a big help with the younger pupils who struggle to readjust to life away from home.'

Inspector Simon Marsh, of Durham Constabulary Press Office, said: 'We all have our fingers crossed that Melanie is with a friend and is safe and well and ready to come home. Certainly the information we have suggests that she had been struggling with some emotional problems in recent weeks and had complained to her family of being overwhelmed by her workload and in need of some space to clear her head. But the statistics make for grim reading and with each day that goes by without us finding a firm lead, the chances of a happy ending to all this grow slimmer.'

Police are urging witnesses to come forward. Melanie is 5' 3", with olive skin, green eyes and black hair. She was wearing a blue jumper, pleated blue skirt and black shoes when she was last seen in the school grounds. Witnesses have reported seeing a girl matching her description sitting alone in the park near the town's historic ruined castle, though police have been unable to verify the sightings.

ONE

'OM actual G! Have you seen yourself? It's, like, super *awks*, seeing your dad all, y'know . . . cringe! Like, I can't see where you stop and the armchair begins.'

Rufus Orton opens one eye and immediately regrets it. Inside his skull, the movement makes a sound like a windscreen wiper screeching across icy glass. He manages a low groan, and angles the bloodshot eye down towards various parts of himself. He feels the same little flicker of surprise as he assesses the devastation of the vessel into which he has been poured. Not young any more. Not much to look at. Not the floppy-haired author whose books were going to change the world. He's middle-aged, provided he dies aged 104. Baggy around the middle, loose at the neck. He can smell himself: all mildew and bad wine.

'Are you awake? Have you, like, had a stroke? Because that's the last straw, Dad. I'm serious, if you've had a stroke that will be totes unacceptable, yeah?'

Rufus would like to offer Dorcas some words of reassurance, but his tongue won't unstick itself from the roof of his mouth. Barnacle-like, it clings to his soft palate, sucking the moisture from his mouth and no doubt getting itself pissed as a consequence. He doesn't think he's had a stroke, though he understands his daughter's concerns. He makes a somewhat pitiful spectacle. The shiny leather patches on the sleeves of his corduroy jacket are the same shade as the battered chair in which he sprawls, boneless and crumpled. His pyjama trousers are tangled around his knees, somewhere beneath the partition wall of his old laptop. He can't remember the colour, and can't be bothered to look.

'This is so crashy! Like, scuzz-central. Grossville. Have you eaten today? I don't see why you're like still so flabby – you like live on wine and paracetamol. Oh, and FYI, there's a dead mole on the mat. And a shrew's head, which is mad cause the cat's been dead since last Christmas. Anyway, whatever.

I don't suppose you've like bought any more credit for my phone, have you?'

There's a serrated edge to the way she asks, as if she already knows the answer but wants the reply to hurt. She's seventeen now, his darling Dorcas, and stopped being his daughter the moment she started peppering her sentences with the word 'like'. She's his wife's offspring now, and the very image of her mother, Shonagh. Startlingly attractive, but with a distinct nastiness around the eyes. Rufus had entertained hopes that by this age she would be a bohemian, a libertine: that they would attend rallies in Westminster and chain themselves to old oak trees together – maybe brew some potent scrumpy in one of the outbuildings and read one another selected passages by neglected poets. Had rather imagined she would become his assistant in some capacity: PA, researcher, a doting and dutiful companion and ever so slightly humbled to be the daughter of Rufus Orton, *modern great*.

She went the other way. There's a bit of a sneer about her now. Would swap him for an Amazon voucher if somebody put the offer on the table. She won't leave the house without make-up, watches pointless people saying pointless things on social media, and gets excited when imbecilic YouTubers release a new range of must-have merchandise. He hasn't seen her reading a book since she was twelve. Apparently she can't concentrate for long enough to get into novels. She'll watch the occasional movie on a streaming channel, but only if she's already heard of one of the actors. Rufus has lost interest in her, if he's honest. Loves her, out of habit, but doesn't see very much to admire. She doesn't suit the house anymore. It's old and crumbling, tucked away down the end of a long green tunnel of overgrown trees and backing on to a popular tourist trail, a couple of miles from Masham, North Yorkshire. It looks OK from the outside but the interior, and the kitchen in particular, look like the setting for a particularly grimy period drama about a morose farmer witnessing the death of a way of life.

'I'm back, anyways,' she says, and though his eyes are closed he's sure he can hear the scrape of her lacquered eyelashes unsticking as she rolls her eyes. 'I'll be leaving early. Millie wore my top for drama – I saw the post on Instagram – so if she pops in tell her she's a thieving cow-bag and I'm taking her Converse for the open day, right? You don't have to do anything else. Just sit there and look for people who think you're amazing. It'll keep you busy.'

Rufus, in counsel with his uncooperative tongue, decides that silence is the best option. He can feel half a dozen smart-arse replies lining up like bullets, but he has just enough pride not to fire them. He can't imagine feeling particularly good about himself if he made his eldest daughter cry by telling her that when her looks fade and she has to rely on her personality, she'll be royally screwed.

There are scrapes, bangs and the damp thud of an avalanche of papers sliding off the end of the long farmhouse table, then angry footsteps to the door. He gets a smell of her. Perfume, pizza, nail polish, sweat. He feels briefly better for it. The kitchen is all mould and spilled wine and damp paper. It's as if somebody has let in a sea breeze.

He stretches. Feels the headache in his shoulders. He rubs at the nape of his neck, trying to persuade the dull throb to push on to somewhere less important, like his legs. He has very little interest in his legs. They just sort of dangle there, occasionally propelling him to the car and from there to the village shop, where he and Dave, the long-suffering owner, have an 'arrangement'. Rufus passes on signed copies of his books, and Dave pays him in bottles of red wine.

There's a vibration, somewhere beneath him. He shifts, awkwardly, then makes a desperate lunge as the laptop slides off his knee and plunges down his bare legs to clatter onto the flagstone floor.

'Fiddlesticks,' he mumbles, out of habit. Then he catches himself. He's made a conscious decision to stop living by Shonagh's rules. He can damn well swear properly if he wants to. 'Bloody shit,' he manages, then winces at the inadequacy of the curse.

He retrieves his phone from under his left buttock, noting with some modicum of shame that he probably didn't make for a particularly inspiring sight when his daughter came home and saw her father was largely naked from the waist down, save for a pair of leather deck shoes.

He answers without looking at the number. 'Rufus Orton,' he says, in the voice he uses on the telephone. It's very English. Very 'Young Conservative'. Very Chipping Norton.

'Rufus, hi. Hi. Hi. How are you doing? Hi.'

He doesn't let himself sigh, though he feels it swell inside his chest. The multiple greetings are a dead giveaway – it's Harriet, his current book editor. She's only ten years older than his youngest daughter, but she is tasked with making his manuscripts fit for market. She's energetic, fizzy and full of mollifying synonyms, all designed to make an author feel better about the fact that their manuscripts have started becoming a little on the 'shit' side.

'Harriet,' he says, pulling himself out of the chair and feeling the earth sway a little beneath his feet. He looks around for some trousers, aware that he is about to have an important meeting. Spots a pair of soft cords dangling over the edge of the big Belfast sink. He recalls a vague incident with spilled wine and some attempt to sponge the crotch with the hem of the floral curtains, but doesn't want to follow the thought any further.

'Is it as awful up there as it is down here?' she asks, in her usual way. She always gives him a little weather report before launching into the actual purpose of the call. 'One of those horribly grey days in London. You could actually see the mist rising off the river when I jogged in this morning. Like an army of ghosts, I thought, and then I realized I'd probably cut that sentence if I spotted it in a submission.'

Rufus gives a dutiful laugh. 'I haven't seen much of the day. The windows in the kitchen make everything look dark – even on a gorgeous June day. But judging from the muddy footprints on the flagstones, it's been raining. Welcome to Yorkshire, eh?'

'I do miss it,' says Harriet, a note of whimsy in her voice. 'I hope to get home for the bank holiday, see the folks, maybe take a boat on the river at Knaresborough. If you're around, as always, it would be lovely to buy you lunch, meet the family. I haven't seen Shonagh since the launch before last . . .'

Rufus feels his heart clench. He doesn't need Harriet to see his life. These last couple of years he has managed to tell her just enough about his domestic set-up to stop her asking any more questions, but if she were to walk into the kitchen of his tumbledown house on the North Yorkshire moors, she would lose any lingering respect for a novelist once named as a rising star, and described by the *Telegraph* as 'the most exciting new literary voice for a generation'. He's been using that line on the covers of his books since 1998.

'I'm hoping there'll be some good news to share,' says Rufus, looking around the catastrophe of his kitchen and wondering if he should be looking for bin liners and rubber gloves, or just pulling the pin from a grenade and lobbing it into the fruit bowl. 'Can't say I'm feeling massively positive at the moment. I know *RedGreen* was a bit ambitious but that was the point, surely. I mean, readers are the clever ones, aren't they? The thinkers? Surely people buy books to think new thoughts, or at least to hold up a mirror . . .'

'Yes, I saw the blog piece you wrote,' says Harriet, reproachfully. 'Harsh.'

He winces, remembering the vitriol he had spewed at two a.m., his fingers hitting the keys on his laptop as if each letter drove a nail further into the forehead of the reviewers who had eviscerated his latest work. 'There were some good responses,' he mutters. 'My readers all liked it.'

She doesn't disguise the sigh. 'Rufus, your readers would buy your work if you just wrote your name over and over again on a blank manuscript. Your readers love you. What we need is new readers. I know this isn't news to you and we've had this conversation *ad nauseum* but unless we can get the supermarkets on board or reposition you as a name for the mass market, we should really be grateful for getting reviews at all. That's rather the reason for the call, actually. The marketing department think you'll be better positioned for the spring brochure rather than the autumn, so we'll push back the release date of the new one by six months, which will buy you some time on the deadline and obviously give us more time to think of a way to get the buzz out there . . .'

Rufus's head spins. Six more months to wait before the new book sees the light of day. Six more months until he receives another quarter share of his meagre advance. His money worries are all consuming. Not many bailiffs are able to find his house, but plenty do. He's behind on the rent, has maxed out every credit card and has to decide each week whether to put fuel in the car or food in himself. He usually finds a compromise by ignoring both concerns and just drinking wine until he finds the right frequency for optimism. He doesn't think it can go on like this much longer. Shonagh looks at him with true disgust. The children are rarely home. His book launches pass without so much as a 'congratulations' card from the publisher and the long-mooted screen adaptation of his first book remains trapped in 'development hell', which strikes Rufus as a synonym for 'the bin'.

'Whatever you think best,' says Rufus, trying to sound breezy. 'You know me, Harriet. Team player. Will it still be a five thousand print run on the *RedGreen* paperback, or do you think we should think big and go for ten?'

Harriet makes a noise he doesn't like. 'Oh no,' she says, as if this were truly absurd. 'No, I think it was a thousand, wasn't it? You know the situation – the independents will take your stuff but we can't offer the discounts to make you attractive alongside the established names, so . . .'

Rufus licks his lips. Feels a prickly heat all over his skin. He's not an established name, apparently. Can't help wondering what that makes him. He starts picking up empty bottles. Moves some dirty plates around on the floor by the dishwasher. Reaches up and picks at a cobweb that dangles from the dried herbs pinned to the dark oak timbers in the ceiling. Half trips on something sticking out from beneath the table, and falls out of his deck shoes. Treads in something wet. He feels like crying.

'. . . so we'll see if that has any impact and maybe take it from there, yes?'

He realizes he hasn't been listening. Pretends he has. Pretends he's fine.

'Anyway, stay safe tomorrow, yes? You never know, there might be a decent story to be found there. A big market, true crime. Never did Capote any harm. And hopefully it will lead to some more work.'

It takes him a moment, but he catches up. A firework of panic starts to spin in the centre of his chest. Was that this week? Tomorrow? The prison thing? Fuck!

'Oh yeah, yeah. Looking forward to it. Not sure what they'll be handing in after I help them unlock their imaginations, but it should certainly be interesting.'

Rufus wonders if he means it. He took the gig teaching creative writing to inmates at HMP Holderness, because the lady who approached him had said lovely things about his books, and because they were willing to pay the figure he plucked from the air. Six sessions in the education wing of a Category B prison that even the *Daily Mail* has likened to something from the nineteenth century. It's been the subject of endless damning reports and the governor has gone on record saying that he can no longer guarantee the safety of either staff or inmates. He supposes he would have been excited about the opportunity, had he even remembered he was meant to be doing it. He hopes they'll be happy listening to him prattle on about the same stuff he delivers to libraries, reading groups and Women's Institutes on the rare occasions when he is in demand. But how to stretch out a one-hour talk to six full days? He slips back into the chair, feeling as though he has been given a dustpan and brush and told to help clear up after an earthquake.

'Anyway, hope the weather picks up. Do keep your spirits up. We'll get there.'

And then she's gone, and he's a middle-aged man, half-dressed, in a kitchen full of unpaid bills and unsold books, trying to work out how to pay for the petrol that will get him out to East Yorkshire in the morning. He drags the laptop back onto his knee. Calls up the email correspondence he's enjoyed with the chatty prison officer who'd first contacted him through his website and told him how very much she loved his work. Types her name into the inbox of his cluttered email account. Annabeth Harris. Skims their conversations. Feels a little better for it. She's friendly, but not gushing. Sounds competent and thoughtful. He's no doubt she will hold his hand through any unpleasantness. He considers what the day may bring. Wonders if he will be chatting with murderers and rapists. Rather hopes so. East Yorkshire is a long way to go for the company of a low-level drug dealer or a cat burglar.

He types HMP Holderness into Google and is greeted with

a raft of critical news stories. Flicks through the various articles, focusing on 'controversial and outspoken' Governor Laicquet Hussain, who made the mistake of being honest with journalists when questioned on the state of British prisons. As a thank-you for that, the tabloids eviscerated him: turning HMP Holderness into the emblem of a system unfit for purpose. The same newspapers that gloried in likening British jails to holiday camps printed lengthy opinion pieces demanding that the outdated, understaffed and downright dangerous old prison be closed down at once. When three serving prisoners used mobile phones to post videos of themselves getting out of their minds on spice, the Home Secretary told the rabid press pack that the jail was 'on its last warning'.

Rufus fumbles around beside his chair until he finds a bottle that makes a pleasing splish when he shakes it. Takes a mouthful of vinegary red wine. Winces and swallows. Tries to make the best of it. There might be a book in it. Maybe he could get pally with Hussain and offer to ghostwrite his memoir when the poor bastard inevitably loses his job. Or there could be a good-lad-gone-wrong or a bad-lad-going-right that he could fictionalize and turn into something with mass market appeal. He shrugs. Doesn't really mind if it's just a day out and a new experience. He's rather looking forward to meeting Annabeth Harris. He hasn't been able to find very much about her online. Mid-thirties, new to the job, degree in Criminology and Psychology. Single mum, as far as he can recall. Worked for a couple of charities for a while. No pictures, much to his dismay. He lets himself imagine her. Sketches a picture in his mind. Feels his spirits fall. She'll see the truth of him at once, he knows that. Will be looking at him the same way that Shonagh does before the first session has reached its end.

He settles back in his chair. Calls up something soothing on the laptop: his ears filling with the tinny lullaby of Brahms dribbling out of broken speakers. Types 'HMP Holderness' and 'murder' into Google.

Starts to read the top story. Something about police digging up farmland in Lincolnshire. It doesn't grab him. He skips on. Skim-reads something about a teenager taken from a posh school in the north east. Feels a sudden surge of sadness as he considers his daughters. His wife. The pitiful specimen he has become. Closes the laptop and stares up at the ceiling.

Drifts off into a sleep filled with locked doors and cobwebs.

Feels more at home within the nightmare than he did when awake.

TWO

'You think he did all of them, then?'

'Best not to pre-judge, Andy. Preconceptions can muddy your thinking, the boss always says that.'

'Yeah, but she says lots of things then goes and does them herself, doesn't she?'

'She's allowed. She's the boss.'

'So it's one rule for her and one rule for the rest of us? How's that fair?'

'Privilege of being better than us.'

'Is she better than us?'

'Well, yes. She's got the Queen's Police Medal. She's Head of CID and she'd be chief constable if she didn't think the uniform made her hips look like two badly parked vans. And most importantly, she's not guarding a hole. That's the main thing, for me, Andy. She's not keeping a patch of mud from coming to harm.'

'You make a good point.'

There is a long pause. A light aircraft putters slowly overhead: a speck of white on a grey canvas. Detective Constable Ben Neilsen starts counting backwards from ten. Lets the cold, rain-speckled gale slap damply against his face. Smells the damp earth; the fusty reek of rotting wood and untended crops: potatoes and turnips turning to mulch beneath the churned earth. Gets to four before his colleague gives him a playful nudge in the ribs.

'Pre-judging apart . . . you think he did all of them, then?'

Neilsen smiles. Nods. 'Yeah, I think he did all of them.'

Beside him, Detective Constable Andy Daniells pulls a

shocked face: a perfect circular emoji of surprise. '*Ommm*,' he says, in a schoolboy voice. 'I'm telling.'

For the past half an hour they have been staring into a hole. They find themselves at Chappell's Farm: the nearest neighbour to Humberside Airport, near the tiny Lincolnshire village of Kirmington. It's a place of big skies and green fields: dotted with pretty little hamlets and old churches. A place of pitted country roads, where colossal tractors chug along at the head of mile-long tailbacks; the drivers making complex calculations about whether to risk their lives by overtaking, or stay where they are and lose their minds. There's a smell of industry in the air: the docks and the oil refinery conspiring to add a chemical tang to the forest-and-farmyard scents of the immediate locality. Both men have been here before. They are officers within the Serious and Organized Unit within Humberside Police, though they are currently working in concert with half a dozen other forces under the overall command of the National Crime Agency. Both are secretly rather thrilled at being able to introduce themselves as such, though DC Daniells went too far when he told the absentee owner of the abandoned farm that he and his colleague were with the FBI. It takes a lot to embarrass the portly, ever-cheerful DC, but his jolly round face did turn a school-sock grey when he replayed the sentence in his head.

'So, we just stand here, do we?'

Neilsen shrugs. He's not in the best of moods. He's a handsome, snappily-dressed thirty-something who prides himself on always looking freshly laundered and flatteringly photoshopped. He's wearing wellingtons, and he is wincing internally as he pictures what they are doing to his trouser legs. Beneath the bottle-green Crombie, his two-piece suit is a tailored woollen number from French designer Pal Zileri. It cost enough money that his boss had taken him aside and warned him that he ran the risk of catching the eye of the Independent Police Complaints Commission. He hadn't worried. Neilsen spends most of his salary on looking good, though he wouldn't consider himself vain. It's more a product of a thirst for self-improvement. He wants to be the best at everything he does – not in a spirit of competition, but more through a pathological need to be the ultimate version of himself. It makes him a very good police officer.

'And they said she's down there? Like, that exact spot?'

'Wouldn't be here if not, Andy,' says Neilsen, in the manner of somebody who has been repeatedly asked 'are we there yet?' by an infant. 'I didn't just wake up and think, you know what – let's pop over to Kirmo and look in a hole.'

Daniells turns and looks at him. Sticks out his lower lip. 'Cheer up, Buttercup.'

'I've told you about the Buttercup thing, Andy. Makes me sound like a cow.'

'You didn't like Sweetcheeks, either.'

Neilsen puts his hands in his pockets. Closes his palm around his phone and says something a little like a prayer. He wants it to ring. Wants to be told that the cadaver dogs have arrived with their handlers and that he and his colleague can go get in the van.

'Bronwen, yes?' asks Daniells, for what Neilsen reckons to be the ninth time.

'Bronwen Roberts. Last seen, April 4th, 1998. Known to have been a participant in a music contest attended by one Griffin Cox. Known to have become an object of affection for somebody in the weeks leading up to her disappearance. Somebody was sending her letters. Books. Pictures, posh soaps. Not the sort of thing a teenage lover would naturally send.'

'And a nightingale, you said . . .'

Neilsen nods, a smile on his face. 'Yeah, a bloody nightingale. I'm a romantic, Andy, but I've never sent anybody a nightingale.'

'And it was Cox?'

'Nobody thought so at the time. He was just a passing acquaintance. It was years before the family even thought he could be in any way connected. He came to the memorial service, you see. And then, when he was arrested for the abduction . . .'

'I can see how that might get them thinking, yeah.'

Daniells kicks at a long, damp thicket of grass and twisted crops. Makes a show of peering into the patch of exposed earth at their feet. 'What happened to the nightingale?' he asks, conversationally. 'And all the stuff? The letters, the books . . .'

'She burned them before she left the house. That's why the original team treated it more as a runaway than a potential crime. Like all the others.'

Daniells doesn't ask him to elaborate. For all that he plays the fool, the cheerful, middle-aged detective has a good mind. He knows the names of the other potential victims off by heart. All were bright, attractive and somewhat naïve. In the weeks before they were last seen alive, each began communicating in secret with somebody whose identity was unknown to friends or family. And each hid or destroyed their recent correspondence. A few scraps of paper were recovered from a brazier at the bottom of one missing teenager's garden. The paper was thick and creamy. Expensive. Possibly Italian. The fire had scorched most of the contents of the correspondence, but what was visible had been written with a quill, in a rich black ink. The only words that could still be made out were the final couplet of a work of ancient poetry. Daniells remembers it perfectly – had recognized it even before he finished the briefing notes from the NCA. It is a line from a translation of Ovid's *Metamorphoses*.

> . . . fix'd, she stands upon a bleakly hill,
> There yet her marble cheeks eternal distil.

'So we're going to see him, I suppose,' says Daniells, quietly.

'Be rude not to,' says Neilsen, staring into the blackness and not sure what to hope. He doesn't want her to be down there. Doesn't want any of them to have been deposited in the little sinkhole at the deep end of this field, not much more than half an hour from the home where her parents have kept her memory alive for more than two decades.

'It's all circumstantial,' says Daniells. 'He moved around. He was bound to have crossed paths with lots of people. He judged music competitions, gave talks at public schools. A decent defence barrister wouldn't even break a sweat.'

'That's why we need something concrete. And the source says we'll find it here.'

'And they're sure it's the stepfather?'

Neilsen doesn't feel able to answer accurately. All he knows is that three weeks ago, around the time Griffin Cox was being transferred to HMP Holderness, somebody left a post on a website set up by the family of Bronwen Roberts. It was at once a memorial, and a place for people to leave any information about her whereabouts. It had been sporadically maintained over the past few years but in the first week of March, this year, somebody instructed the family to dig in the sinkhole at Chappell's Farm. The post was ignored. Then *Crimestoppers* received an anonymous tip. The information was the same. Their source claimed that they had been the accomplice of one Griffin Cox on the night he killed Bronwen Roberts, and disposed of her body in a place he knew nobody would think to look. The information was duly passed to the team responsible for looking into the teenager's disappearance. It had already come to the attention of the Cold Case review team, under the auspices of the Serious and Organized Unit. It had then come to DC Daniells, who had made contact with the other investigative units who had all identified convicted child abductor Griffin Cox as a definite person of interest. All were of the same opinion: the tip-off had come from Cox's guardian, Wilson Iveson. Now eighty-six and recently diagnosed with stage four pancreatic cancer, the information was seen by many as being an attempt by a dying man to soothe his conscience. Three different sets of investigators have visited him at the old people's home where he now resides. All have come away unsure what to believe. As well as the cancer, Iveson has advanced dementia. According to the care assistants, he didn't even know how to use a computer.

'He's visited him every fortnight since he was locked up,' says Daniells, quietly. 'Regular correspondent. Only phone call he ever makes, save for his lawyer. And Iveson's looked after the sod's affairs for years. I don't see why he would just turn on him. I just hope it leads somewhere. For all the stuff he's linked to, he's not far off the end of his sentence. He's only got one black mark against him, and it's cost him eight years. A long way to fall for a guy used to the finer things. Grew up in all kinds of luxury, bosom buddies with the Bullingdon boys, if you believe the papers. You should see the photos of the grounds of his house! Statues and cypress trees and waterfalls – like something from the Renaissance. That's how him and Iveson met. He designed the gardens. Did the work in the 1960s when Cox's mother was barking mad and opening up her stately home to any passing hippy willing to share a joint and give a day's labour in the grounds. Weird environment for any kid. Not making excuses, but if Cox did go a bit bloody peculiar, you wouldn't need to be Sigmund Freud to trace it back. Still, the idea that he's done all of them . . . It's hard to imagine.'

Neilsen agrees. He finds it hard to imagine. And yet, as his boss can't resist telling him, stranger things have happened. He remembers her exact phrase. 'Outlandish shit is our bread and butter, Ben'. She has always had a way with words.

'He might not be wanting out,' says Daniells, picking the head off a length of grass and throwing it into the cool air. 'Not all the high-profile prisoners who get released from the vulnerable wing are going on to have much of a life. How many have been done, now? Eight? Nine? Questions in parliament, apparently.'

'I don't like vigilantes,' says Neilsen, and means it. 'It's mob justice, however well intentioned. But I do understand the motivation. It's that old question, isn't it? What do you do with predators who can't ever be rehabilitated? There's no cure for paedophilia, is there? But you can't lock people up forever and you can't tell people murder is wrong when the state is doing the same thing to people who kill. It makes my head spin.'

'Let's ask Cox what he thinks about it all,' smiles Daniells. 'See if he has any interesting theories on the matter . . .'

In his pocket, the phone vibrates. Grateful beyond measure, Neilsen retrieves it and answers with as much enthusiasm as he can muster. Within moments, his face is settling into a distinct glare. Beside him, Daniells mimes throwing himself into the hole. It doesn't get a laugh.

'Well?' asks Daniells, when he hangs up.

'No cadaver dogs available,' growls Neilsen. 'And the press office has had three calls from a freelancer who's got wind of it.'

'Male or female?' asks Daniells.

'Female.'

Daniells relaxes. 'I presume you're going to call her, yes? Do your thing?'

Neilsen flashes angry eyes. 'What's my thing?'

'Come on, Ben,' says Daniells, laughing. 'You know. Soft eyes, soft voice, syrupy voice, appealing to their better nature . . .'

'Oh,' says Neilsen, unable to argue. 'Yeah, probably.'

They stand in silence for a while. 'So we just keep guarding the hole?'

Daniells scowls. Chews his lip. Counts down from ten. Gets to three.

'So you reckon he did all of them, then?'

THREE

Key in the lock. *Turn.*
Step inside. *Half-pirouette.*
Close door. *Lock.*
Check handle.
Check again.

It's all about the routine. All about muscle memory. All about getting yourself so used to repeated actions that it becomes impossible to get it wrong. Annabeth Harris received this piece of advice on her first day of training, and has employed it every day since. She doesn't make mistakes. She remembers everything. She knows when to follow the rules and when to improvise. She likes being good at her job. She's been accredited by her governor with a veritable string of superlatives. 'Compassionate yet firm; professional and discerning – an asset to us all'. She's without doubt the very best of the fresh crop of prison officers at HMP Holderness. Would be even if the others hadn't all quit through stress.

Deposit key in the left-hand pocket of the waterproof that hangs on a hook in the hall.

Take off coat. Hang it over the waterproof.

Turn.

And . . . *home.*

Annabeth sees no reason to treat her home any differently to the corridors and cell blocks at work. Her little semi-detached in the waterfront hamlet of Paull, needs to be impenetrable. This is her fortress. This is where she and her son need to feel safe.

A pause, at the foot of the stairs, shouting up to the empty landing.

'I'm home!'

A muffled hello from the bedroom.

Sit on bottom step. Remove hefty black boots. Place them beneath the telephone table. Pick up the damp, discarded white trainers, and place neatly side by side . . .

Left, and into the living room.

A glance to the clock on the TV stand. Nine seventeen p.m. Two minutes earlier than yesterday. Not a record, but not far off.

Breathe in . . .

And 'stop'.

Annabeth gives a little growl of irritation. She should be able to smell cottage pie. Her nostrils should be full of meaty aromas: perhaps the acrid tang of burnt cheesy topping, if he's got distracted and let it dry out. But she should be able to smell something other than Singapore noodles and Chinese chicken curry.

She counts backwards from ten. Makes it to eight.

'Ethan!'

There's no response. She knows she won't get one either. He'll be in gaming mode, headphones on, controller in hand, blasting zombies or shooting spaceships or whatever the hell it is that takes up ninety-five per cent of his leisure time.

She looks at herself in the mirror above the fireplace, composing herself. She doesn't want to tell him off with a face like her own mum. Doesn't want to be an ogre, even though she has a nagging suspicion that she is painted as such despite her best efforts. The uniform doesn't help, of course. He hasn't got used to it yet. Two years as a prison officer and still he reacts as if she's wearing a Nazi uniform. She pulls off the black V-neck jumper and unbuttons her white shirt. Considers herself. Mid-thirties, now. A couple of jeans sizes bigger than she would like. Hair bleached-blonde and dark at the roots. No earrings. No jewellery. No make-up. Just a face, really. Nothing more or less. Tries a smile in the mirror. It lights her up. She passes inspection. Looks sufficiently unthreatening to tell her son off.

Up the stairs, careful not to stomp.

Three knocks on the door. The sound of laughter, excited teenage voices, the raucous crash of something exploding.

'Come in then.'

And she does. Enters her son's bedroom with the same trepidation that she opens the door of a high-risker on suicide watch at work.

'All right, Mum?'

Annabeth pauses in the doorway. Reminds herself that he is her son, her only son, and she loves him to his bones. Raises her eyebrows at him.

'Cottage pie, Ethan?'

He whips off his headphones. Spins his gaming chair so he's facing her. He'd look like a Bond villain if he had a cat in his lap instead of the giant box of Frosties that he grips with his knees. He's wearing his dressing gown over his school uniform. His forehead is damp, his fringe flopping forward like a dog's ear. He looks younger than his fifteen years. Cherubic, even. Dark eyes and a bit of puppy fat about him. He's nearly cute enough to distract her from the state of his room. Nearly, but not quite.

'I can smell the Chinese, Ethan.'

'That's a bit racist, Mum,' he says, hoping that cheek will pass for charm.

'It was simple enough. Put it in the oven. One hundred and ninety degrees. An hour. Make gravy if you want it . . .'

'Yeah, I saw that. Seemed really complicated.'

Annabeth looks past him. Three monitors: a triptych of technology, each a blur of multi-coloured computer code and screens, the central console given over to some cowboy shoot-'em-up that looks so lifelike it's eerie.

'Too complicated? Ethan, you can read binary code!'

'I figured the Chinese would be easier. I paid. It's OK, isn't it?'

'But that's my tea as well, Ethan,' says Annabeth, growing exasperated. 'I made it before I left for work so it would be ready as soon as I came in. You know how I need my routine.'

Ethan rolls his eyes. 'Mum, if cottage pie were as nice as Singapore noodles, there would be takeaway cottage pie shops all over, wouldn't there?'

'You've got an answer for everything, haven't you?'

'Not really. I get a bit lost on the existential questions. Some imponderables leave me stumped. I mean, are eyebrows facial hair? What do people who are born deaf hear when they think? Why doesn't glue stick to the inside of the bottle? Why can't we get mouse-flavoured cat food . . .?'

'Smart arse. What am I going to eat now?'

'You could try the sweet and sour chicken with egg fried rice. It's staying warm in the oven on a low heat. My treat.'

Annabeth pulls a face, a lovely golden warmth spreading through her. He's a good boy, is Ethan. Straight A student. No bother. Nice group of friends and not so much as a police caution between them. He's not great at keeping his room tidy and he has a tendency to forget things, but she's proud of him, and proud of herself for providing an environment in which he has been able to become more than the sum of his parts.

'You can come eat it with me, if you like. Sit on the bed. Grab a controller. We can play an ultimate fighting game. I'll create a character for you. You can be The Governess. Nineteen stone of pure muscle. Street fighter. Tattoos on your teeth. Finishing move is a headbutt to the groin.'

'Not much of a change from work, really,' muses Annabeth. She steps over a mound of discarded clothes and bends down to hug him. He doesn't smell like her little boy any more. His hair needs a wash and there's a little bit of musty sweat covered with body spray adhering to his clothes. Even so, she fills herself up with it. Her boy. Her young man. Her delight.

'Knock anybody out today?' he asks, turning back to his game. Annabeth follows his gaze and tries to make sense of the complex patterns scrolling down the different screens. She knows that he is renting 'server space' from another teen, but she isn't really sure what that means. She wants to ask him but doesn't like the idea of seeming so horribly old and ill-informed. Instead she gives vague parental lectures about the importance of not mistaking a fifty-year-old truck driver from Texas for a sweet sixteen from down the road.

'Bloke on his way to Seg tried to raze up Mr McDermid. Two blades in a toothbrush. Ended up just putting a hole in his fleece. Paid for it when the lads arrived. Left cheek looks like he's sucking an apple.'

Ethan pulls a face. He's at a funny age. Part of him still thinks it's kind of cool that his mum does a job that seems positively macho, but she knows he worries about her. There's always been just the two of them. She had to promise him when she first applied for the position that she wouldn't ever put herself in unnecessary danger. Even so, he likes to hear stories from work. Likes to tell his mates that his mum spent her shift trying to stop one inmate from opening another's throat with a shank they'd secreted somewhere horribly personal.

'Did anybody throw poop at anybody else?' he asks, and Annabeth notices how strange the childish phrase sounds in his recently deepened voice.

'We found a poop-and-pee canister in his cell. Shampoo bottle full of both, waiting to give whoever opened the hatch an eyeful.'

'Cool,' grins Ethan. 'Van Morrison would approve.'

'Sorry?' she asks, not getting it.

'You know – turning those blue eyes, brown.'

Annabeth can't help herself. She starts to laugh: a pleasing sound that adds light to her eyes despite the tiredness. He's always been able to make her laugh. Even in those early days, when they were moving between squats and bedsits, the two of them wrapped up in each other, waiting for the call from the Housing Association to tell them they had finally got a place of their own; even then he had been funny. He was quite the little actor: melodramatic to the extreme. At two years old he could turn the slightest disappointment into a catastrophe, flopping to the ground as if his strings had been cut and declaring that life was 'too much, too much'. The fact that the source of his dismay was the absence of Digestives in the biscuit tin, only served to make her laugh all the more. She owes Ethan every-thing, she knows that. She's been clean for fifteen years. No smack. No drink. No bad decisions, save for the occasional disastrous romantic entanglement. She's done OK, has Annabeth. Better than she ever thought she would. She owns this house, not far from the water's edge in the remote fishing village of Paull. Has nearly paid off the sofa, the bed and the giant plasma TV. Has bought all of Ethan's gadgets outright and her VW Golf has its MOT, insurance and road tax, which is far more than any of her colleagues can claim. She's got a degree in Criminology. It's from the Open University and she completed it while working full time for a charity specializing in helping ex-prisoners get back on their feet. They like her at work. She's got a future, according to her boss. Could be a boss within five years if she doesn't join the throng of new recruits packing it in and running to the papers carping about intolerable working conditions.

'You've had an email from the bloke you keep reading,' says Ethan, glancing at his screen.

'Ethan!' She shakes her head. 'Will you please stop hacking my email?'

'I'm keeping you safe,' he protests. 'You can't just keep adding a new digit to the end of your password. Some hackers can count your keystrokes and it doesn't take a genius to . . .'

'Fine, fine. Anyway, which bloke?'

'The author. The one you read like you're a diabetic and his books are made of insulin.'

'Shut up,' she says, smiling. She feels her cheeks begin to colour, and turns her back before he can tease her any more. 'I'll bring you up a hot chocolate in a bit, if you like.'

'You won't,' says Ethan, to her back. 'You'll forget. And you'll fall asleep on the sofa. But when I wake you up, I'll have made you a tea.'

'Love you.'

'Love you back.'

She closes the door behind him, feeling pretty good. She retrieves her phone from her trouser pocket and calls up her email. Sure enough, Rufus Orton messaged her half an hour ago when she was on the drive home. Subject: Help!

She plonks herself down on the sofa and starts to read, deciding that her food can most definitely wait. Rufus Orton is her favourite author. He's written eight books and a volume of poetry. He's been longlisted for the major literary awards on three occasions. One of his books was adapted for the screen, though it was an arthouse movie made in Belgium and unrecognizable from the source material. She's read each of his books twice. Just six months ago she felt giddy that he retweeted one of her funny little Tweets. Five months ago she was doing cartwheels that he had followed her back on Twitter and sent her a Facebook friend request. When he replied to her self-deprecating fan-girl missive, she thought she had got as close to her icon as the fates would ever allow. Now they are close to friends. They talk a lot online. She's helped him out with some research for a new book. And he's agreed to come to the prison, teach a class, and make her look pretty damn spectacular in the eyes of her bosses.

She reads the message twice, whispering to herself as she does so.

> Hey you. What a bloody day. Trying to do the American copyedit on the latest one. Oh my God, these people! It's good that there's a job that provides suitable employment for the severely autistic but they are so bloody picky! Apparently I used the phrase 'she flashed a smile' 14 times between chapters six and nine. So? I mean, can you picture it – me sitting here trying to think up 13 different ways to describe a flash of smile. Anyway, I'm digressing. Just wanted to check in to say hello and see how many we've got signed up for next week. Will feel a right prick if it's just you and me, though there are worse ways to spend a day, of course. Do I just ask for you at reception? Really appreciate this chance. As I said last time, if you could pull some strings and get the payroll people to pay me up front, it would really be a help. Wolves at the door, and all that. Anyway, give me a call if you like. Shonagh's working late, the teens are battling monsters, and I intend to be quite drunk soon. Take care. R.O. xx.

She sits back, feeling good. Looks at her hands and realizes they are sweating. She feels giddy and nervous. She wants things to go well, but more importantly, she wants Rufus to feel he made the right decision when he said 'yes' to teaching a six-week course in creative writing to the inmates at HMP Holderness.

She thinks about calling him. Imagines his voice, loquacious with drink. Realizes, at once, that she is still too shy to speak to him in person. Better to send a message. Better to keep things professional.

> Hi Rufus. Got your message. Course I did – that's why I'm writing! Anyway, nine signed up. Not bad at all, considering. The poet who came last year only got two, and that was because one of them had misread the poster and thought iambic pentameter was an Olympic sport that would allow him access to javelins. So, looking good. We actually got a request in from one of the prisoners on the Vulnerable wing, but I turned it down. Too many possibilities for things to go wrong. Really not a very popular chap, so best off saying 'no'. So yes, all systems go. Do just ask for me on reception and I'll be there quick as a flash. I've told you, haven't I? Bring a passport, and be careful what you bring in your satchel. Really looking forward to it. Very best, A.H.

She doesn't put a kiss on the end of the message. Doesn't notice she's used the word 'satchel' until after it's been sent. Cringes a little. He'll know at once that she's been stalking his social media profile. He has a battered leather satchel with him in a lot of his photographs. Has a professorial look about him, though there's enough rumbled bad boy about him to suggest he likes his port and stilton with a cocaine chaser.

She heads to the kitchen. Decants her food, heats it up, and sits down at the little round table. Eats it with a fork because nobody's watching. Tells her voice-activated virtual assistant to play some Irish folk, feeling like somebody from the future. The kitchen fills with plinky-plonky strings and heartfelt vocals that make her feel as though she should be supping Guinness and sitting on a sack of potatoes.

She plays with her phone. Slurps up bean sprouts and

water chestnuts. Gets up and drinks milk from the bottle, knowing she would tell Ethan off at once for doing any such thing.

Checks her phone. No reply yet.

Agitated, she turns her thoughts to today's shift. She'd been a bit surprised to receive the request from the Vulnerable Prisoner wing. Normally they would do anything in their power to avoid mixing with the general population. Holderness is a category B prison, and there are some very bad men within its walls. But it's the nonces – the sex offenders, the paedos and the grasses – that are considered lower than low. Only convicted coppers and former screws are given a harsher time inside. For Griffin Cox to request a place on the creative writing course, he must really be either a fan of Rufus Orton, or be up to something.

She wrinkles her nose. She knows his name, of course. When he transferred over from Wakefield in the summer, she was alerted during the Monday morning briefing that they had something of a celebrity joining them, and to be alert for any and all attendant problems. She's had nothing to do with him yet. Spotted a small man with a dark widow's peak wheeling a trolley of books in the library, but that has been the sum total of their interaction. She's tempted to allow him to participate in the course if only to see what sort of stories his mind will conjure up.

She shudders. Decides, on balance, that his mind needs no help in expressing itself.

Googles him, just for the hell of it.

Reads, as she eats her noodles.

Considers his image. Watches her own reflection swim in the colours and patterns on the screen.

Looks into the face of a killer.

And for the briefest moment, allows herself to remember.

The warm blood. The feeling of glass skewering flesh. The hot fear in her belly and the desperate fight to survive.

She looks up, through the ceiling, to where her son plays video games with his friends.

Closes her eyes.

Makes peace with it. Makes peace, as she has every night for fifteen fucking years.

Former Pupil at Elite School Jailed for Sick Abduction

By Jonathan Feasby

A FORMER classmate of two Cabinet ministers has been jailed for an indefinite period following the attempted abduction of a teenage girl.

His victim yesterday told this reporter that she believed he was 'truly evil' and did not believe herself to be his first victim.

Griffin Cox, 44, was sentenced by Judge Michael Marwood at York Crown Court yesterday. Earlier, a court had heard that Cox, a buyer for a boutique furniture company, had grabbed a 15-year-old girl from a quiet street, having previously posed online as a twenty-something music student in order to gain her trust.

Having made arrangements to take her to a performance at York Opera House, he then claimed to be the tutor of the young man she was due to meet, and talked her into getting into his car. At which point, his victim told the court that he 'turned into something from a horror film'.

Police who pulled Cox over for a minor motor vehicle infraction found the terrified student hog-tied and masked in the back of a rental car he hired for the sole purpose of abduction. At his lavish home, filled with expensive furniture, police later discovered a 'white room', adjacent to his well-stocked wine cellar. Painted perfectly white, it was entirely soundproofed and contained run-off channels transferring any spilled liquids into the drainage system.

Police last night refused to rule out the possibility that Cox may have been responsible for more abductions, and he was described by a senior detective as 'a truly evil man'.

Cox, raised in a 60-room stately home in rural Cambridgeshire, spends much of his time abroad. He is single and childless but is an esteemed patron of the arts and a globally renowned expert in stringed instruments. His defence team yesterday urged Judge Marwood to consider their client's previous good character, and provided dozens of character witnesses, including a letter from a retired Home Secretary who said that Cox was 'a decent man' who could have accomplished extraordinary things if not for his mental health problems and a traumatic childhood. His mother, Procne Henshaw-Cox, was an eccentric figure who transformed the grounds of the stately home into a replica of a Classical Italian palazzo and garden, before her death in 1974.

Speaking after the sentencing, Cox's victim, who cannot be named, told reporters: 'He was so charming. So believable. He made me feel that I was the centre of his universe and that I was safer with him than anybody else. But when he showed me the truth of himself, I glimpsed something that can only be described as "evil". I've started going to church again since this happened. There must be a god, because I know I've met the devil . . .'

FOUR

The hardest part of prison is the loss of silence.

Of all the privations and punishments thrust upon Griffin Cox these last years, it is the intrusion of other people's noise that he finds hardest to endure. He can stomach the smells: the lingering miasma of bleach and piss, of sweat and spice. He can convince himself there are fleeting elegances in the architecture and décor; ways to locate beauty in the damp green walls; to admire the workmanship in the cream-painted iron railings and staircases that wind up through the floors. He has even learned to value the nearness of violence: sharpening his senses to something lupine – his primal antennae neatly attuned to the petty hatreds and unspent frustrations that make the air of HMP Holderness sizzle like burning oil.

No, it is the intrusion of unsolicited noise that Griffin Cox cannot yet abide. Even after all these years of incarceration, it is the aural infringements that he considers his true punishment: his act of penance for a solitary mistake.

Outside, Cox took great steps to ensure a life filled with glorious spells of pure, perfect soundlessness. Here, now, he can conjure the acoustic memories. The tiny, private sounds.

His breath.

The sinewy rustle of shed garments.

The muffled screeching of the wriggling, terrified specimens who fought so hard against the gag.

The quiet acceptance: the giving up hope – the commencement of his glorious transformation from living and corruptible thing, to a truly immortal beauty.

Cox has always felt most comfortable in environments where the only sounds are those for which he is responsible: a conductor in a mute orchestra. Feels sanguine only when he is master of the song. Prison offers him no such peace. No such blessed isolation. His days and nights are filled with the raucous cacophony of countless men cat-calling and wailing, crying and pleading; hooted laughter and the crash of metal on metal; metal on brick, skin and metal and brick upon skin.

That is why Griffin Cox has decided that he has served sufficient time. Griffin Cox is going to release himself from incarceration. He does not like the word 'escape'. It implies some frantic, desperate flight: all chaos and baying dogs, search-lights and shots. He has simply decided to remove himself from this place. He's been here long enough. And of late, he has more pressing matters to attend to than marking time.

'. . . *fucking nonce, Cox! Gonna cut it off! Mail it to the mum of that lass!*'

'. . . *do it, Suggs. I'll hold him down for ya!*'

'*Don't deserve to live, Cox! Don't deserve to breathe the same air as us!*'

'*That'll do, Suggs. Off the landing. Back to your floor.*'

Cox pays no attention to the sudden eruption of noise. Does not allow any glimpse of dissatisfaction to show. He is well used to such threats. People have tried and failed to dish out their own punishments for his so-called crimes. All have learned the error of their ways. He would prefer them to come for him and try some brute physicality, rather than continuing to fill the still air of his cell with their crashing consonants and guttural threats. He has already spent seven years inside. Moved between jails four times: on each occasion bringing with him the wisdom hard won at the last. He knows now that to ask for something is to guarantee its opposite. Knows that those whose manner seems kindest are the ones to be distrusted. Knows that to tell a secret is to place oneself in another person's debt. Knows that boiling water and sugar form a syrup which can cause the skin to hiss and bubble: that peeling it off takes with it so much epidermis that a handsome face can be reduced to gristle, blood and bone.

He closes his eyes. Allows himself to see.

Cox's recall is uncanny. His memory is more than photographic. Cox can spot details in his recollections that he did not know he was a party to. He can remember a landscape and return to it later, picking out individual birds; the movements of trees; the shape and passage of the clouds. He can open a book, glance at it as if taking a mental picture, and read it later in the comfort of his own solitude. He has never consented to an IQ test and has deliberately refused to answer honestly when questioned by police, prison officers and countless psychiatrists. He does not want anybody to feel they know him. He prefers to be constantly underestimated. It has served him well. Behind his veiled eyes, his pupils contract, eyes twitching left and right as he scans the text of the newspaper article that has led to his recent change in circumstances. Led him here, to HMP Holderness.

MURDER SQUAD VISIT CAT-A PRISON TO QUIZ CONVICTED KIDNAPPER

By *Weardale Times* Senior Reporter, Val Aitchison

September 23, 2019

DETECTIVES probing the 2005 disappearance of Melanie Grazia have travelled to a maximum security prison to question a convicted sex offender.

Melanie, 14, disappeared from an elite boarding school in the middle of the afternoon. A mystery man left a voicemail telling staff at the boarding house she was going home with parents. She has not been seen since.

Serious Crime officers within Durham Constabulary have conducted a Cold Case review and believe there are sufficient similarities between Melanie's disappearance, and the abduction of a teenage girl from a busy street in York in 2013.

Although the identity of the inmate has not been revealed by police, this newspaper understands that police questioned Griffin Cox, 51, who was pulled over by police for a motoring offence and discovered to have a terrified schoolgirl in the boot of his hire car.

Cox was given an indefinite sentence following his trial at York Crown Court, when detectives described him as an 'evil man' whom they feared may well have struck before.

Police yesterday refused to comment on the outcome of the interview, but it is understood that the new developments are a direct result of work carried out by charity organization Missing People. Staff at the respected charity have been posing on internet forums and conspiracy sites to try and make contact with any one of the 300,000 teenagers who disappear from home each year. They found evidence that connected Cox to several missing persons cases.

A spokeswoman for the charity said: 'It's difficult to go into too much detail without adding to the pain of the families involved, but we've discovered several cases with similar circumstances and feel it is only right that the police take this seriously and ask Cox to account for himself.'

Cox's arrest stunned establishment friends who believed the 'gifted, intelligent' man innocent of the abduction and offered up character references to spare him jail. A former Cabinet member said Cox had been 'a victim of bullying' in his formative years but was a kind, gentle person who would never have intended to cause harm.

> The unmarried childless Cox lived a life of luxury
> having inherited his mother's property upon her death, and
> spent much of his time in Italy purchasing antique furniture.
> It is understood that authorities in Italy are also looking
> into Cox's activities while staying in luxurious accom-
> modation on the Amalfi coast.

Cox knows that he is not many steps ahead of those who would ensure he is never released. He has a few black marks on his prison record but release is still within his grasp – provided no more crimes are pinned to his name. And Cox has reason to believe that if he does not secure a very swift release and an opportunity to tidy up loose ends, that evidence will soon be dragged into the light.

Cox considers himself, and more, as he lies on the floor of his cell, still as death. He has his arms outstretched – Da Vinci's Vitruvian man. The tips of the fingers on his left hand stretch under his bunk to touch the wall. His right hand falls three inches short of the opposing brickwork. He spends twenty minutes in this position every morning and again before lights out. He suffers with a painful back, and despite repeated requests to see a physiotherapist or masseuse, he has so far been denied this most basic of human rights. Instead, he allows gravity to work on the knotted muscles and creaking vertebrae. Presses himself flat to the cold floor and waits for the series of flicks and cracks that inform him his bones are being inexorably pulled downwards: through three floors of institutional brickwork, and deftly rearranged by the magnetic pull of the earth. He enjoys such moments of communion. In his mind he is able to see the different layers of strata beneath the foundations of the old prison building. Can see bones and pottery shards, masonry; scattered remnants of the villagers that once made home on this flat, windswept land. Can see the multicoloured bands of rock and earth; make out minerals and sparkling seams of unmined rock. Can see all the way down to the earth's core.

It would be a meditation, of sorts, were Griffin Cox not reaching out with the eye of his mind to grasp the remains of the children he has left beneath the ground. Would be an act of mindfulness, of therapy, were he not remembering the sensation of their skin beneath him, and listening again to the memory of their screams.

FIVE

Annabeth dreams.

She sees her father: a five-penny piece atop a tuppence: pudgy arms, short fingers, fell-pony legs. Bald, with bottle-black strands teased backwards from what used to be a widow's peak. He's reading the big broadsheet newspaper, licking his thumb to turn the page. There's butter and a smear of marmalade on the bottom corner of the front page. And he's talking to her. Talking in that low, rumbly way of his, that means he's embarrassed and irritated and wishes somebody else could do this for him but that there's nobody he trusts to do the job properly.

'. . . *even if it did happen, what do you expect? Making all those moony eyes at him, sitting on his lap at the staff party, and that little top you wore, with your belly button out for everybody to see – we didn't know where to look. If it's there on a plate, people are going to eat, Annabeth. We never had this with your sisters. You're going to get yourself into all sorts of trouble and it's the poor chap who falls for it who gets in trouble. Your mother can't even stand to think about it. We want no more talk about this. No more. You'll be keeping your legs closed from now on, and I suggest we do the same with that bloody mouth of yours before it gets you into trouble . . .'*

The image flickers; distorts. She's eighteen. She's standing at a bus stop in a little tourist town in Cumbria. She's been kicked off the bus for having used a day-old ticket, scavenged from a bin and carelessly flashed at the driver ninety miles back. She'd hoped to make it as far as Dumfries, just over the border, where a girl she met in a hostel has told her she's secured a bedsit and that she'll be welcome on her sofa for a few days. The driver had demanded a second inspection of the ticket when he saw her scratching at her arms, shaking and wriggling, feverishly, way down the back of the coach. He'd kicked her off at the next stop, telling her he wasn't having some junkie slag puke up on the upholstery. And now she's sitting on her rucksack, wrapped up in her own arms, hoping that some late-night dog-walker will spot her and ask if she's OK – maybe direct her to a refuge or invite her home for the night. She'll adapt to the situation as it develops. If it's a man she'll play pitiful: let them be her knight in shining armour. She'll feign pride and self-sufficiency if it's a woman – repeatedly refuse offers of help until she hears the magic words 'I insist'. Something will turn up. She just needs to score, that's all. Needs to take something to shave the edge off . . .

And now she's getting in the car, with the darkish, plumpish man. And he's telling her he has a habit of picking up waifs and strays. And he's telling her he has a place she can stay, if she's quiet, and does as he asks.

In her sleep, Annabeth twists. Grimaces. Bites down so hard she can taste blood. And in the clutch of the dream she is beneath him. She can feel his blood hot and wet upon her skin. Can feel the weight of him. And she is sitting, caked in gore, shivering, crying, rocking back and forth, and then the door is opening, and the tall man is telling her to go, to just go, that he'll tidy everything up, she just needs to go before anyone sees . . .

And now she's a mother. She's holding Ethan close as she climbs in through the broken window at the rear of the aban-doned house. It's a fairy-tale cabin: a gingerbread house – big round logs and chipboard windows, thatched roof and birds in the eaves. And she's holding Ethan so close, so tight, that she fears crushing his fragile bones. Eight months old now, and still he doesn't look anything like his father. Still there's no sign of the dead man in his boy. And Annabeth knows she can keep doing this. She can keep moving from place to place, staying a step ahead of whatever's chasing her, and that she'll fight to her last breath to stop any harm coming to her baby.

She shifts in her sleep. Grabs at the bedclothes. Whimpers, like a child. Her brain is full of flickering images. She sees herself getting older; Ethan getting bigger. And now she's living in the little flat in Stockport, sharing the rent with a woman she met at the free childcare centre, and they're taking it in turns to watch each other's kids so they can both share a job as a cleaner at the office block by the canal. And Annabeth is thinking: they don't know. Nobody's looking for you. You can be somebody. You can stop running. You can stop being afraid.

And now the tears come. Still sleeping, she weeps – dribbling out from behind her closed, flickering lids. She's sitting at the kitchen table, staring at the unopened envelope, while Ethan, nine years old, tells her to just do it, that he believes in her; that he knows she's brilliant so they will too, and she's tearing open the gummed flap and reading the letter on the headed paper, telling her she's got the job – that they'll do all they can to help with childcare arrangements, and she's looking down and staring into Ethan's happy eyes, and she knows that she has to tell him. Knows, suddenly, that she can't carry it alone. Knows she has to tell him who his father was, and what she did.

And now she sees a prison. A visiting room. A tall man, shrunken by years. And she's telling him about who she is now. About what she is becoming. About the good she is trying to do in an ocean of bad . . .

Quietly, tenderly, Ethan comes and lies down beside his mother. He wraps the quilt tighter around her shoulders, and lies behind her, one arm around her. It is an inversion of his first memory, when she would hold him like this, in the dark, and whisper in his ear that whatever was coming for them, she would stop it. That he was her everything. That he was her reason for becoming more than she was. He snuggles up close, and holds her until her breathing begins to find a softer rhythm. Lies beside her until he knows that wherever her mind is, there is nothing trying to harm her. Then he retreats to his own bedroom, and opens up the computer screens. Navigates his way to a page he only visits when he knows there is no chance of interruption.

Angles his head, as the screen fills with images of convicted paedophiles, recently released: whereabouts unknown. He hopes they're dead. Hopes they're all dead. Hopes they died in agony. He revels in the thought of their pain. He knows that as long as he celebrates the suffering of those like his father, it means that he is not like him – that the evil died when his mother stuck a snow globe in his throat.

When Ethan falls asleep, his own dreams are of nothing but the dark.

SIX

A shape at the door. Black trousers, black boots.

'That helping, Cox? You look like you've fallen off the ceiling.'

He knows the voice at once. Mr Windsor. Declan, to his friends. Prison Officer HN 252. Plump. Beard. Spectacles and wonky teeth. He's one of the friendlies. Still new to the job and convinced he can make a positive difference to people's lives. Cox has met his type before. The younger ones always start out enthusiastic and compassionate. They believe that if they treat people fairly they will be treated fairly in return. That criminals are made by society and that all can be redeemed. Cox knows that within five years, Mr Windsor will be jaded beyond return. He will have been abused, spat upon, lied to, manipulated and physically assaulted by so many different inmates that he will no longer see individuals in need of a mentor, but as the accumulated scum of the earth. He will come to see himself not as a confidante and counsellor, but as a zookeeper. He will be the first to put the boot in whenever circumstances allow. He'll have heard so many lies that he will be blind to truth. But all of this is yet to come. Windsor seems still blissfully unaware of what the future holds. For now, fourteen months into the job, Mr Windsor is wide-eyed and innocent – just the way Griffin Cox likes them. Decent people are so much easier to manipulate. They expect the best of everybody.

'I said – is that helping?'

Cox's voice, rising from the floor. Eloquent. Precise. 'It is, yes, thank you, Mr Windsor.'

'It looks bloody uncomfortable,' he says, garrulous as always.

'I have to sleep on the floor now and again when I visit the in-laws. Always wake up feeling like I've been stepped on.'

Cox files the information away, making a mental note in the big red ledger that he visualizes in his mind.

In-laws. So . . . he must be married. No ring, though. And why the floor? Religious parents, perhaps? No congress under their roof? Or perhaps a too-small house. Better yet, a too-fat wife . . .

Cox will enjoy finding out the answers in the weeks to come. And when he knows everything, he will work out how best to use them to his own advantage. It is a game he never tires of playing. It is not as much fun as murder, but it passes the time. Cox is always involved in a game of some description. His recent presence here is part of a game he has come to think of as his *grand design* – his 'grand plan'. He experiences a sudden warmth, low down in his belly, as he permits himself to think upon the game in which he is currently engaged. The pieces he has crafted, manoeuvred, placed where they should be, employing the infinite patience of a man who has learned to truly savour anticipation.

He becomes aware that he has neglected his visitor. Offers up an inoffensive reply.

'I'm not a stranger to discomfort, Mr Windsor. Delightful as I find my accommodation, I will confess to occasionally feeling a little short-changed in terms of luxury.'

A little laugh at that. The sound of Mr Windsor making himself comfortable in the open doorway.

'We'll have to see what we can do about that,' he says; his manner that of somebody with a pint in his hand and one elbow on the bar. 'Maybe bring in a big feather bed, eh? A couple of sheepskin rugs. Perhaps a chandelier.'

'That would be a tad incongruous, but certainly appreciated.'

'Aye,' says Windsor, as if he knows. 'Incongruous as fuck.'

Silence for a moment. Then Mr Windsor clears his throat: his standard *amuse-bouche* before serving up a meal of bad news.

Cox's mind sprints through the possibilities. Trips, painfully, upon the least palatable of likelihoods. The course. The writer. The reason for the whole damn game.

'No room at the inn, this time, Cox,' he says, sounding genuinely sorry to deliver the tidings. 'No VPs allowed. Too much of a risk. To you. To the tutor. It's a no-go.'

Silence, from the floor. He digests it. Refuses to allow any hint of dissatisfaction show in his posture. 'I did say that I was willing to attend upon my recognizance.'

'Yeah, she said something about that. I don't think she knew what it meant.'

'That I would be accountable for my own welfare, sir.'

'Yeah, but y'know. This is prison. And you're a VP. And they sort of, well, hate you . . .'

Cox opens his eyes. Sits up without bending his knees: a vampire rising from a casket. He angles his head, and smiles at the young man; his keys hanging from the chain at his waist, utility belt cutting him below his lumpy gut.

'I don't think they hate me, Mr Windsor. I believe they hate the part of themselves which finds its likeness in an image painted by my detractors. They do not know me, as it were. They know only of my crimes. And of those crimes, I remain entirely innocent.'

Mr Windsor gives a shrug: an infuriating gesture. Cox's grand plan is a series of tiny, incremental half-steps and thus far, every one has gone the way he has desired. He cannot be refused a place on the Creative Writing course. Everything that comes next is dependent upon him securing a berth in a classroom with Rufus Orton, the mid-list novelist tasked with helping borderline illiterates learn how to weave literary gold.

He lays back down, lest his face betray the sudden fleeting twitch of desperation that clenches inside him. He puts his arms back out to his sides. Breathes.

'What's the theory, then?' asks Windsor. Behind his glasses, his brown eyes give the room a quick sweep. Sees nothing to concern him.

It's a single occupancy cell, like most of the rooms on the Vulnerable Prisoner wing. Cox is the only inmate to keep his accommodation immaculate. There is the air of a monk's cell to the small square of pale blue brickwork. His bed is neat enough to pass a military inspection – the sheets pulled tight enough to bounce and catch a coin. His paperwork and court documents are kept in black, lever-arch folders on the little wooden table by the windows. The wood gleams, polished as if it were a walnut credenza. On it sits a small wooden radio and an individual coffee maker. These items are his luxuries. He is permitted a television, but declines the privilege. He has entertainment enough in the books that take up the entirety of the inside of his wardrobe, stacked so neatly that they need to be levered out with a toothbrush. His few clothes are laid out neatly at the foot of his bed. He does not disturb them when he climbs beneath the covers. He is a small man. Five foot four. He's lost an inch or two since turning fifty. Can feel gravity pulling him down. He fancies he'll be dwarf-like by the time they let him out. Can see himself, wizened and grey. Wonders, idly, if he will still be fit enough to do what he enjoys. Whether there will be any possibility of securing work as a department store elf at Christmas. He fancies not. He'll be on the Sex Offenders Register until the day he dies.

'The theory, Mr Windsor?'

'How does it work?' he asks, more slowly, as if Cox were simple.

Cox rises again, reluctant to appear rude. He keeps his face inscrutable. It takes little effort. He has features that are hard to read, and even harder to remember. He has a gift for anonymity. He has cultivated a truly homogenous, unremarkable appearance. Anybody asked to describe him would struggle to offer up any more than the fact he is short, with greying brown hair. The rest of his face may as well be a blank piece of paper.

'We lose an inch in height every day, Mr Windsor. That's gravity, pulling us down. Compressing us. Pulling us home. If you lay down it acts the same upon your skeleton. Drags you back into the shape you are meant to be.'

Mr Windsor sucks his lower lip, interested. 'Read that in a book, did you?'

Cox permits himself a smile. He is always polite with the wardens, even when they wrong him. His skill, his *gift*, is in appearing harmless until it is too late to react to the danger. 'I did, as it happens. You'll be amazed at the knowledge you can pick up in books. They may catch on.'

'Don't read much myself,' says Mr Windsor, as if such an

admission were not shameful. 'Couple of thrillers on holiday. Can't concentrate though. Sends me to sleep.'

'I'd be glad to lend you something to start you off,' says Cox, companionably. 'Reading is one of the true pleasures. The prison library is tolerably stocked, if it does cater a little too brazenly for those interested in what I would term as the "lowest common denominator". But Miss Morrow, the librarian, is very good at finding the more difficult to locate titles. Educational textbooks. And my own little library is yours to peruse.'

'Those?' asks Mr Windsor, nodding at the shelves and openly laughing at the very idea. 'Had a gander. Bloody gibberish. Can't even read the names. Is that one about a hippo, or something?'

Cox doesn't turn around. 'St Augustine of Hippo, Mr Windsor. Saint Augustine, native of what we now call Algeria. His *Confessions* is an autobiographical tome detailing the sins of Augustine's youth and his conversion to Christianity. It is considered the first western autobiography, and has now influenced religion and philosophy for more than one thousand five hundred years.'

'Not about a hippo, then?' asks Windsor, despondently. 'You like all that, do you? Foreign languages, and stuff?'

'Latin, Mr Windsor. The building blocks of our own language. Winston Churchill declared that to learn Latin should be considered an honour, and Greek a treat.'

Mr Windsor gives a polite smile. Glances around again at the meagre possessions in the monk-like cell. Unlike the other cells on the wing, there are no photographs. No posters. No letters from home. The only decoration to the room's austere walls is the large wooden cross on the wall above the bed. It is an expensive piece: nineteenth-century and patterned with geometric parquetry: rectangles of overlapping inlaid rectangles of expensive wood. It is the only physical reminder of the life that was taken from him when the judge sent him down. There was a time when Griffin Cox was the very epitome of sophistication. Wealthy, by many people's standards. His was the life of a true Epicurean. He indulged his senses in the cool, vaulted palaces and frescoed vaults of olive-skinned dealers in objects of desire. Ate well. Ate sumptuously. Lost great chunks of reality gazing into the immortalized brushstrokes of Old Masters long dead. The cross on the wall hangs as a reminder of both penance and contrition. He grieves what he has lost, and chastises himself daily for allowing himself to be caught.

'I've got a Latin tattoo, actually,' says Mr Windsor, still conversational. '*Dulce periculum*. You know that one?'

Cox pauses, sensing an opportunity. He runs the next three minutes through in his mind: a chess master playing fifteen moves ahead. Fights the urge to grin as he realizes what an opportunity he has been handed.

'Oh, Mr Windsor . . .'

Cox does not yet admit it to himself, but he is losing his ability to rise above prison life. His mood is beginning to darken. There seem too many miles to traverse between now and his release date. He is not accustomed to a downturn in his spirits but if he does not find some source of entertainment, perhaps even of hope, he fears that he will soon be indistinguishable from the other, unimportant convicts within the great Victorian walls of HMP Holderness. And the writing course is the fulcrum where Cox will insert his lever; moving the earth, and his place within it, forever.

'Oh goodness,' continues Cox, looking momentarily shocked. 'Why on earth would you allow that?'

Mr Windsor looks at him, surprised. 'What? Means "danger is sweet", mate.'

Cox shakes his head. 'Mr Windsor, I'm afraid you've been the victim of a terrible practical joke. *Dulce periculum* means, well, perhaps I shouldn't say. The periculum refers to a part of the anatomy, Mr Windsor. An area one might refer to as intimate.'

'What? Balls? Arse?'

'I believe you would refer to it as the, ahem, bridge between those two locations.'

Mr Windsor's eyebrows shoot halfway up his forehead. 'Bastard!' he says, with a hiss. 'Are you sure, Cox? Are you winding me up? Because I paid nigh on two hundred quid for that and it's right across my bloody shoulders . . .'

'You're most welcome to do your own investigations, Mr Windsor,' says Cox, not letting his amusement show in his face.

'But I do know my Latin, sir. My tutor was a remarkable man. Relative clauses, conditional clauses, the conjunctive and disjunctive. I can recite much of Ovid's *Ars Amatoria* from memory, though there is a copy on my shelf if you wish to peruse it . . .'

'Bastard,' hisses Windsor, again. He slumps, crestfallen. 'You think anybody will know? I mean, who speaks Latin?'

Cox feels a familiar despair settle upon him like snow. It has ever been thus. He has always been surrounded by cretins, halfwits and those for whom the accumulation of knowledge has always seemed less important than maintaining the continued bliss of their ignorance.

'Your secret is safe with me, sir,' says Cox, lowering his voice. 'My mind is a repository of secrets and unspilled truths, sir. My word is my bond.'

He holds the younger man's eyes for a moment. Waits for the moment of realization to penetrate the mush of his brain. Watches it happen – a rock thrown into a still pond.

'I'll know it was you, Cox,' he says, attempting to threaten. 'If people start shouting that I've got a sweet *peri-fucking-neum* or whatever you call it, I'll know it was you.'

Cox looks hurt. 'Sir. You are the officer I respect most on the wing. I'm hurt that you would even think I would betray a confidence. You can rely on me to say the right thing to anybody who even asks.'

Windsor eyeballs him for a moment. Searches his face for any sign of threat or duplicity. Sees none. Visibly relaxes. Cox watches the internal battle, and fights the urge to let his enjoyment show. By tomorrow, Windsor will have double-checked Cox's translation and discovered that the prisoner had been lying. The words translate exactly as Windsor had requested. But everybody on the wing knows that Cox is a Latin scholar. Windsor's protestations about the correct translation would count for nought when the men on the landings were whipping themselves into a frenzy of laughter and see who could outdo the others in coming up with the most stinging barbs about his 'mistranslated' body art.

'The course, sir. You're one hundred per cent sure that they can't find the space this time around? *Per cent*, as you know,

meaning "out of one hundred". It's Latin. Amazing how much
it bleeds into our day-to-day lives, isn't it?'

Mr Windsor probes at his gums with his tongue, considering
his options. Then he gives a tight smile. 'Let me see what I
can do,' says Windsor, and hurries away.

Cox lays back down on the floor. He permits himself a
smile.

'*Ad astra, per aspera*,' he whispers, for his own amusement.
Through difficulties, to the stars.

SEVEN

Only one windscreen wiper works, and it makes a noise
like a seagull in distress as it screeches across the dirty
windscreen of the 1978 Mercedes 450SL that used to
be Rufus Orton's favourite possession, and which is now worth
less than the monthly premiums on the insurance policy he
hasn't renewed since 2016. The rain isn't coming down particularly hard yet, but the dark clouds are hanging low: dirty great
hammocks of grimy sailcloth obscuring the flat fields of
Holderness and making the Gothic bulk of the prison look like
something from a Christopher Lee movie. It's a tall, imposing,
red-brick affair, rising out of the billiard-table smoothness of
the East Yorkshire landscape. It has the look of a medieval
fortress – behind the barbed wire and crenelated walls, soldiers
in chainmail might well be stirring vats of boiling oil and
nocking arrow to bow string.

Rufus sits in the driving seat, sweating wine and whisky,
clothes damp, fringe sticking to his forehead like the casually
draped wing of a seabird. He's late. Hungry. Jittery. He needs
a piss. He doesn't smoke anything other than the occasional
joint but right now he'd love a cigarette. There's a nervous
energy coursing through him – he'd be jiggling his feet up and
down if he could trust the car not to stall.

A tall man in an ugly luminous jacket lopes across the car
park, head tucked into his collar and a soggy dog-end sticking

out above his zip. He could be staff, a visitor, or an inmate hurrying back from a disappointing escape.

Rufus winds the window down, feeling the cool air and mist of rain seize his face like a damp fist. His words trip out too fast, as though his tongue has split in two.

'Sorry . . . mate, mate . . . hi, can I park here? Yes hi? I got so turned around. The one on the road that I passed, that's not this one, no?'

Rufus considers this sentence as the man looks at him as if he might be simple. He grimaces. Tries again. 'This is HMP Holderness, yes? I'm supposed to be teaching a class?'

The man considers the car. Ignores Rufus's question. Kicks the front tyre and wrinkles his nose. Rolls the dog-end from one side of his mouth to the other and back again. 'Would be a nice motor, that, if you took care of it. Give you a ton for it, here and now.'

A laugh escapes Rufus's lips. He feels a little manic. The journey was hellish. The tyres are completely bald and he skidded half a dozen times on the dark country roads before he made his way to the motorway, and then he found himself in nose-to-tail snarl-ups from Castleford all the way to Goole. The car is too much of a classic to have a functioning radio so he's had nothing but his own thoughts for company. He'd hoped that sighting the Humber Bridge would inspire some poetry in him: briefly fancied himself a Larkin or an Armitage. He'd felt nothing. The best he could come up with was the vague suggestion that the strings of the bridge with the sun at their back looked a bit like an egg-slicer and an organic yolk. He couldn't imagine Radio 3 being interested any time soon. Then it had just been muddy water and warehouses, bleak utilitarian flats and houses and chain stores and budget hotels. On, feeling the country grow thinner as it neared its most easterly point: great cargo ships and ferries to his left, a sprawl of cemetery and lorry parks to his right, then he was drifting into the misery of HMP Holderness and watching the sky grow dark as his mood.

'Sentimental value,' says Rufus, recovering himself. He's actually tempted, but he can't risk selling the old beauty. He doubts he'd be able to find the paperwork and it last had an

MOT about three years ago. 'Thanks though. Anyways, can I park here?'

'Dunno,' says the man, shrugging. 'May as well. What they going to do?'

Rufus considers this. Swings the big old car in a wide arc and squeezes into a space between a powerful Japanese motorcycle and a small silver Toyota. Reaches into the back seat and grabs his battered old satchel. He chucked a couple of his own books in before leaving the house and has a few old copies of *Writing* magazine to flick through before the afternoon session. Figures there'll be some exercises in there he can pass off as his own.

'Reception's that way,' says the tall man, who is still waiting in the rain, sucking on a vaping machine. He points with his foot, one hand in his pocket. 'You'll want to lock your car up properly. Full of criminals, this place.'

'Yeah? Even in the car park?' Rufus smiles, expecting to see it returned.

The man just gawps at him. 'Aye,' he says, as if Rufus were a little hard of thinking. 'Even out here.'

Rufus checks that he's locked the car, then jogs, painfully, in the direction of the big archway, where big wooden doors occupy the space that would once have housed a portcullis.

'Bloody hell,' he mumbles, as something hot twinges in his side and the muscles in his calves do their best impression of old knicker elastic. He needs to get into shape, he knows that. Some mornings he wakes to the sound of distant church bells and ice cream vans, only to trace the high metallic tinkling sound to his own strangled breathing. Were he to take up mud wrestling, the mud would definitely win. There was a time when he told people his body was a temple, which is why it weighed the same as the Taj Mahal. He doesn't make jokes about it any more. Nobody gives him their attention for long enough to reach the punchline.

He arrives in reception short of breath and uncomfortably damp. Finds himself in a dismal room with a low roof. There's a reception desk to his right where two women in white shirts and blue jumpers sit behind big screens. A lumpy, bearded man in glasses lounges on the desk, arms folded. He looks like he's in a bar, trying to get a better view of the spirits. There's a row of lockers off to one side and a wall covered with old photographs of the building in decades gone by. Only the hairstyles have changed. The building in which he finds himself is every bit as bleak and forbidding as it would have been when it was still a place of execution: when men and the occasional woman would be led across the courtyard for an appointment with a trapdoor and a knotted rope.

Rufus crosses to the desk, his cords making a shushing noise as they rub together at the thigh. Three pairs of eyes swivel towards him. He picks the ones that look most awake. They're green, and belong to a young woman with a round face and a general air of friendliness about her. She's freckly, with glasses and simple gold studs in her ears, and up close he can see that she has combed talcum powder through her hair rather than wash it. Wonders if she rose late, or just couldn't be bothered. Files the question away for later. They can dissect it in class: aspects of character and flawed perception.

'I'm due to be teaching here,' says Rufus, trying to catch his breath. 'I'm late, I think, though I can't remember what time we said. Annabeth. Erm, Miss Harris. Mrs, maybe, I don't know . . . never asked . . .'

'Definitely a *Ms*, that one,' says the man beside him. He has blackheads on his nose and beneath the thin white material of his shirt he's covered in coiled black tattoos. '*Mzzzz* – that's how you say it, isn't t? Like a mosquito against a window. Going to stay that way, I reckon. Of course, they're all allowed to get married now, aren't they? Lasses and lasses, lads and lads. What next? I've a plasma screen with surround sound that I bloody love. Reckon I should pop the question?'

Rufus processes the officer's words and finds himself rumpling his features in distaste. 'Wow, that's extraordinary,' he says, as sarcastically as he can. 'To fit so many prejudices into one sentence – your parents must just drip with pride.'

The young woman on reception laughs and the male officer returns her smile. He hasn't taken offence. Clearly sees himself as a wind-up merchant; somebody who likes a bit of banter and believes everybody should be able to handle a bit of leg-pulling in the workplace.

'Ignore our Antony,' says the receptionist, fumbling with a name badge and checking the time before scribbling something onto an official timesheet. 'Anybody who turns him down for a drink is automatically a lesbian. Which, if we're honest, means everybody who works here. He thinks I'm a lesbian, and I've been with my Johnny since we were at school.'

'Proves it,' says Antony, smirking. 'Started too young to know any better and now you're together out of habit. Come out for a drink with me, I'll show you a different way to live.'

Rufus sizes him up. He doesn't see himself as a physically able man, but he still has the broad back built up during his days on the university rowing team, and he's had his nose broken and fingers trodden on in rugby matches countless times. He isn't afraid to say what he thinks, and he thinks that 'our Antony' is a prick.

'Told you before,' says the receptionist, brightly, as she hands Rufus a name badge. 'She's focused on her career.'

Antony snorts, disgusted at the idea. 'Needn't worry so much about it. The rate the newcomers are jacking it in, she'll have her pick of the jobs even if she never gets any better at it. Bloody fast-tracks, coming in with their degrees and trying to show us where we're going wrong. I mean, why pick this bloody place? It's an embarrassment to tell people you work here. My mate at Full Sutton reckons this was like her third or fourth choice but they couldn't find room for her at Frankland. Lucky us, eh?' He looks Rufus up and down. 'What are you then? Writer or something, is it?'

'Or something,' says Rufus. He gestures at his bag. 'Do I leave this here? Take it in?'

'Metal detector and a search through that door,' says the receptionist, still all smiles. 'You're going to the education centre. A lot of halls and a lot of locked doors, so Mr Womack will meet you at the family area, just down the way there. Don't listen to Antony. Annabeth is an absolute star.'

'Wouldn't know,' sniffs Antony. 'Too good to come out with the rest of us. Bloody hermit, that one. Can't answer a simple question. I mean, you've got to know your colleagues, haven't you? Know they're on your side. Know what they're about. I reckon she's a do-gooder. Worked for that charity, my mate said, but he's full of shit too so I can't swear to it . . .'

Rufus holds up a hand as if directing traffic. 'Antony, can I stop you there?' he asks, cheerfully.

'Yeah, what?'

'No, that was it. Just wanted to stop you.'

He enjoys the giggle from behind the desk as he walks away, bag banging on his hip, and a certain pep in his step.

Annabeth sounds *fascinating*.

EIGHT

Annabeth watches Karen talk. She knows she should probably listen to some of the words as well, but experience has taught her that the prison librarian only requires the occasional nod, grunt or elongated vowel to feel as though she is engaged in dialogue rather than a monologue. It has always struck Annabeth as deliciously ironic that such a chatterbox could ever excel at a job so inextricably linked with the word '*shush*'. She doesn't look much like a stereotypical librarian. In the picture books that Annabeth read when she was young, the librarians were stern, austere characters; bony yet limp; all cardigans and spectacles; a name badge pinned to a twinset. Karen is the opposite. Big and bubbly, curvy to the point of roundness, she could pass for a sketch on a saucy postcard if she showed any flesh whatsoever. Instead she wears a loud, floral-print dress and a huge fisherman's jersey, baseball shoes and tights thick as fur. There are cat hairs on her shins. Biscuit crumbs upon her chest. Round, jolly face made owlish by large circular glasses. She's useless, but pleasant with it.

They are sitting in the office at the rear of the prison library: a cramped space full of books and files; three boxy old computers whirring on cluttered desks and posters taking up every inch of wall space, advertising different government initiatives or bookish promotions, competitions or suggested revenue streams. Karen Morrow is head librarian, which means she has one junior member of staff. She's been in the job for years and doesn't appear to have lost any enthusiasm for the job. She's a fizzy, ebullient soul and today, anxiously looking up at the clock and pulling endless panicky faces, she is vibrating as if plugged in to the mains.

Annabeth, sitting on one of the dusty swivel chairs and leafing through a self-help book, looks up when she realizes that the rapid-fire talk has briefly halted. She becomes aware of other sounds. The rain on the roof; the heavy footfall of staff in the administration offices upstairs; the distant clatter of cooks and helpers beginning the process of preparing lunch for eight hundred inmates and staff. She looks up. Cocks her head.

'He really is cutting it fine, Annabeth,' she says, playing nervously with one of the gaudy strings of beads that hang at her neck. 'Maybe we should call him? Should we call him? We should. Definitely. Yes, we should call him.'

Annabeth glances at the clock. It's a little past nine thirty a.m. He's late, but not by much. The attendees haven't even begun arriving yet.

'He'll be at reception,' she says, placating. She spins a little on the chair, swiveling left then right. 'He's a creative sort, isn't he? You know artists and writers and such. They're as bad as professors when it comes to getting their shit together. Head in the clouds.'

'Head up his backside, more like,' says Karen, making herself laugh. 'My book group gave up on his last one, did I tell you? Just pretentious drivel. I swear, I won't be caught like this again. Any book that has the word "ambitious" on the cover is unfit for human consumption.'

Annabeth smiles, politely. She'd like to tell her that she's wrong – that *RedGreen* is, in fact, a masterpiece. She'd like to tell her that the only reason she didn't enjoy it is because she isn't clever enough to understand what he was trying to say. She could say this, and so much more. Has a pre-prepared speech for just such an occasion. She isn't sure how or when she would get the opportunity to deliver it to the critics who universally panned Orton's magnus opus, but she finds it pays to be prepared.

'It's a challenging book, definitely. Maybe not my favourite. But it blew me away in places.'

Karen wrinkles her nose. 'I always try and read the full longlist but I couldn't get through it. No story, was there? Just a lot of lyrical meandering. If you ask me, he's gone off the boil, though I won't be saying that when he shows up.' She looks again at the clock. 'If he shows up.'

They sit quietly for a moment, experiencing the silence in different ways. Then there is the sound of chains and keys and the turning of the big iron lock in the double doors beyond the office walls. Lights flicker on, illuminating the half dozen stacks filled up with crime novels, thrillers, science fiction and biography. It's a warm, ambient sort of space. Colourful pictures on the wall and soft chairs around circular tables. People tend to respect the libraries in prisons, in Annabeth's experience. It is a sacrosanct space, like church or the gardens. They provide some semblance of peace in an environment where such a commodity is in short supply.

'Oh thank goodness . . .'

Quiet voices, growing louder. Mr Hale, a tall, thick-set, old-school warden. Fifties now, but still the military bearing. Grey moustache and bristly crew-cut. Seen it all, done it all, wouldn't been seen dead in a T-shirt.

'I should imagine they'll be skulking in the office,' says Mr Hale, passing the glass partition that affords the library staff a view of the main body of the book repository. 'Ah yes, here they are.'

'You, my friend, are an absolute superstar.'

Behind him, Rufus Orton. Tall. Rumpled. Elegantly shambolic. Thick dark hair sticking up at the front, as if somebody has run their fingers through it. Blue pullover, hanging poorly: a hole at the elbow and one collar of his polo shirt sticking up through the zip-up neck.

'And here we are, Mr Orton,' says Hale, as Annabeth gets to her feet and Karen wobbles herself down from the desk. 'Thought I would save you ladies from having to come all the way over. Gave me a chance to pick his brains, a little.' He turns to Annabeth, shaking his head in admiration. 'Done well here, Harris. Best of luck with it all. If Suggs gets up to mischief I won't be far away.'

'We meet at last,' says Orton, and squeezes past Hale's bulk.

Karen reaches him first, grinning and gushing and talking so quickly that it's not so much a sentence as a sneeze. He looks past her. Catches Annabeth's eye.

He looks older, in the flesh. Not old. She knows from his Wikipedia page that he won't be fifty until next year. But the stubble on his cheeks is greying and there are deep grooves in his cheeks. Even so, his blue eyes sparkle.

'Not late, am I?' he asks the room in general. He edges past Karen. Swings his battered leather satchel off his shoulder and slumps down on the edge of the nearest desk, toppling a pile of books. He makes a face, embarrassed with himself. Reaches out to start tidying them and Karen tells him to stop. Annabeth notices he is wearing soft cords and hiking boots. Holds back a smile as she clocks the odd socks. She wonders how much of this is an affectation; whether he saw Hugh Grant play the bumbling Englishman one too many times, or if he has been like this all his life. He certainly seems genuine. She can imagine him attending dinner parties at the homes of directors, photographers: dipping aubergine crisps in roasted red pepper hummus with old school friends called Aubyn, Barclay and Euripides. Knows that he will have at least five or six Pippas in his phone.

'Annabeth! We meet at last. Goodness, what a cheerless place! Well-run, you can see that immediately, but frightfully dispiriting. George here was telling me it has its own ghost. How fascinating, and what a boon for our lessons. Do you want to tell me how you'd like to play things or shall we just busk it? I'm rather excited about all this. I did Northallerton when I was starting out but this seems a different kettle of fish, if you'll excuse the cliché. Actually, remind me of this when we put the punt in the water, would you please? Origins of the word "cliché". Past passive participle, borrowed from the French and not given back, early nineteenth century, I think. Same period that gave us "saboteur" – the act of throwing a shoe in a loom . . .'

Annabeth realizes she hasn't spoken yet. Puts out a hand. Orton shakes it, miming seriousness. She fancies he would have offered a hug were he sure of the rules.

'You talk as you write,' she says, shaking her head. 'Your

messages, not your books. It's like there's fireworks in your head.'

He grins, delighted. 'I did warn you. They do say that listening to me talk is like getting molested by a thesaurus.'

'Do they really,' asks Annabeth, retrieving her hand.

'No. They just say I talk a lot of bollocks.'

'Then you'll be right at home,' butts in Hale, and gives a barked laugh as he raises a hand in farewell and stalks back out towards the doors.

Annabeth keeps her eyes on Orton's as Karen fusses around him, procuring pens and blank paper, exercise jotters and printed worksheets. Annabeth pushes her hair behind her ear. Gets a fleeting whiff of woodsmoke and tobacco. Expensive soap.

'It's nice to meet you in person,' she says, quietly, as Karen momentarily disappears and bustles off towards the noticeboard at the back of the library. 'She was flapping.'

'I was here in plenty of time. Got chatting to a lovely young lady on reception.'

'Neck tattoo?'

'Yes – Frida Kahlo and arum lilies. Not a reader, apparently, though still intrigued to meet a writer.'

Annabeth rolls her eyes. 'I rarely get the chance to use the word "incorrigible". Thanks for the opportunity.'

He doesn't smile as she had expected him to. He seems to have exhausted his supply of froth and frivolity. He's turned inwards, darkness in his eyes, as if something is troubling him. He presses his lips together in a bloodless line.

'Are you all right?' she asks, her voice soft. 'Are you OK with this? If it's the VP, I can still say no. I only said yes because a colleague wore me down. I didn't think you'd mind. One peep of trouble and he's out.'

Orton shakes his head. Wrinkles his nose: a child sniffing something unpalatable on a proffered spoon.

'Bit nervous, truth be told,' he says. 'Never very good at getting the rough boys to like me. All seemed very different in my imagination. Rather shitting the old plus-fours now I'm here.'

Annabeth reaches out. Squeezes his forearm. He's strong. Beneath his soft cords and rugger-bugger wardrobe, he's made of teak. 'I'll be here the whole time,' she says, and as she speaks she wonders just what she would really like to happen next.

'You're littler than I thought,' he says, looking her down and down. 'The uniform suits you. Not everybody can shine in polyester.'

Then Karen is back in the doorway, holding out a pristine copy of *RedGreen*. 'Would you mind signing this please, Rufus? I adored it. I'll only forget to ask if I don't ask now. Then we'll get you a coffee and crack on, yes?'

He looks momentarily pained. Then he's back in what passes for character: humble and blushing and fumbling about on the desk for a suitable pen.

Suddenly, she's worrying. She feels like she's about to throw a lamb to the wolves.

Wonders what it says about her that she rather wants to know what he will look like when they tear him apart.

NINE

He enjoys making an entrance.

There is something delightful about seeing the heads turn in his direction: big meaty necks rotating like doner meat on a spike. Eyes widening. Hackles rising. It makes him feel as if he is a star taking his turn on the stage: perhaps an A-list singer making an impromptu appearance in a village pub.

Of course it only takes a moment for things to turn. Once they realize who he is, what he is, things quickly sour. The air fills with that certain, indescribable something. It's primordial: an ancient impulse to fight or flee. He likes watching them make their connections. Sees them remember who they are, and how they are supposed to feel about him. He is Griffin Cox, pervert and killer, even if the courts have never proven it beyond a reasonable doubt. He is the man that the cops call 'evil' and whom prison rumour has transformed into the very devil.

The other players in his performance are all ready. All waiting.

Sitting at their desks like schoolboys, with their plastic beakers of water and their felt-tip pens. Men with bad posture and spread legs, lounging in hard chairs or leaning forward on folded arms. The youngest, maybe twenty-two. The oldest, white hair and pale skin, maybe eighty, and not long for the world. Cox surveys the room in a glance. Takes them all in. Karen the librarian, ditzy and distracted; all wobbly flesh and flashy colours. The writer, out of place and staring around him like he's on safari. And Miss Harris, professional and focused. She has gone out on a limb to accommodate his request. Were he the sort of man to remember a favour, she would've earned herself a place in Cox's good graces. But Cox has no good graces. He remembers slights, not courtesies.

Then it begins.

'Are you fucking kidding me? What in God's name is that dirty evil bastard doing here?'

'I swear to God I'll tear out his eyes . . .'

'He's not on this course is he, miss? I'm not breathing in the same air as that murdering bastard.'

He stands in the doorway, all innocence. Mr Windsor lingers in the hall, trying not to meet anybody's eye. Miss Harris has been lumbered with this, all so the inmates of HMP Holderness don't begin to think he has a tattoo congratulating himself on having a sweet perineum.

It's Suggs whose voice carries the most weight and venom. Suggs who is going to ensure whether the sessions are a success, or the scene of a riot.

Miss Harris stands, cool and casual. Gestures for Cox to come in and take the seat near her own. Cox nods his thanks. Walks, head down, to the plastic seat by the wipe-clean desk, his back half-turned to the rest of the room.

She gives Suggs her attention. 'Settle down, Suggs, we are all going to play nice. Cox has had his request for inclusion granted and I have sworn that you can play nicely. I know you were very keen to participate in all this, so let's not spoil it, eh?'

'But he's a fucking nonce!' spits Suggs. 'He's a VP! We shouldn't be anywhere near the sick fucker . . .'

Cox turns and examines the squat, brutish man who so objects

to his presence in the drab classroom down the corridor from
the library. He knows very little about him, but feels as though
he knows his type. Suggs is a criminal, but in his own
mind, he's not a bad guy. He's a veritable Robin Hood. He
believes himself to be several revolutionary steps up the ladder
from the sex offenders, grasses and paedos who people the VP
wing. He feels it is his duty to kill or maim such men, so his
gaggle of brats on the outside never have to be exposed to such
ugliness. Cox has never considered engaging such a man in
debate. He has never vocalized his opinion that it is men like
Suggs who create men like him. It is the alphas, the big silver-
backs, oozing testosterone like blood, who feed the demon in
him. Men like Thomas and Rory, the popular boys at school,
who saw the weakness in Cox and chose to exploit it for their
own gain. Men who wielded their masculinity, their sexuality,
their fertility, like a weapon. Men who raped him not because
they found him attractive, but because they knew he wouldn't
like it, and wouldn't tell.

'I'm sorry, Miss Harris. Perhaps this wasn't a good idea after
all. Mr Suggs here clearly has some poetry in his soul and it
would pain me to deny him the opportunity to get in touch with
his repressed sensitivities . . .'

Suggs springs up, fists clenched, shoulders squared. 'What
did you fucking say to me?'

Cox turns away from him, catching the eye of another
inmate. He gives a wink. The man, forties and shy, gives a little
smile, then looks away, flustered.

'Steady, Suggs,' says a large man, seated at the next
table. He's a big lad. Older than most of them. Red-faced and
bearded. He's quiet, but his voice carries an authority. Suggs
sits down, grumbling to himself. Cox wonders if this is Callan.
He's heard the name but not yet had the pleasure of meeting
the man. He was an armed robber, on the outside. A good one
too. Only got caught because one of his crew gave him up when
cutting a deal with the police. Callan had to spend a lot of
money to get access to the grass. Paid a computer wizard to
alter the database so there was no mention on either of their
files that they should be kept in different jails. Then he had
himself transferred. Was waiting for the grass in his own cell.

Beat him to death over the course of nine hours. Cox wishes he had such useful contacts. Were he the sort of man to have dabbled in organized criminality, escape would not prove difficult. A rope over the wall, a mobile phone in a friendly rectum, and he could be a free man within a week. But Cox has no such contacts. This is why escape is going to be all the sweeter.

'You're welcome to leave, Suggs,' continues Miss Harris, holding his gaze. 'It would be a shame, but we can all just about muddle along without your contributions. It's just, I've seen your letters of complaint about the staff and canteen, and I know you've got a lovely turn of phrase. "Twatwaffle", "cock-blanket" and "sphincter-bandit" are all particular favourites . . .'

Titters, from the group: pressure escaping from a valve.

'That's not fair . . .' begins Suggs, looking petulant. He's probably thirty. Muscled, tattooed and pretty damn fond of himself. He dresses much the same inside as he did before he was convicted: grey jogging suit and flashy white trainers. He's got tramlines shaved into his short hair and the blood-speckled rash on his neck suggests that he's fighting a daily battle against the thick dark hair that sprouts out of him like an animal pelt.

'Excellent, thank you, Mr Suggs,' says Miss Harris, taking control. She pushes herself away from the desk and walks to the front of the classroom, where the writer is standing, tight-lipped, a little embarrassed smile on his face.

Cox considers him. Knows him. Knows him all the way through. Posh boy. Sensitive. Wordy but useless. Hopeless romantic and a true mishmash of arrogance and self-doubt. Cox has to stop himself from smiling. Congratulates himself, silently, instead. He's chosen right. Rufus Orton couldn't be more perfect if Cox had written him himself.

Miss Harris flashes a smile at the writer. Cox sees something in the glance. Something that makes his pulse quicken.

'So, this is Mr Orton . . .'

'I'm fine with Rufus, actually,' says Orton, pulling a face. 'Mr Orton is my father.'

'And Mr Orton, or Rufus, is going to be helping you learn how to write creatively. We are very lucky to have him here. He's won lots of awards for writing and is one of my own particular favourites. So, give him your attention, listen to what he says, and please don't dick about.'

Orton stands up, smiling widely, as if he's just been welcomed on stage at a literature festival. Pulls a hardback book from the satchel at his feet.

'Well,' he says, brightly. 'Where do I begin . . .?'

Miss Harris takes her place by the door. Stares at him in fascination. Devours him.

Oh yes, thinks Cox, settling back. *This is going to be so much fun . . .*

TEN

I t doesn't take Rufus long to find his stride. He stumbles a little while introducing himself, as if he isn't quite sure which level to pitch his message at, but Annabeth enjoys watching him expertly tune himself in to the correct frequency. She fancies there's a little battle taking place inside him about which level to pitch at. Whether to impress these new associates; to come across as humble, blokey; one of the guys. But as soon as he begins to talk about books and the art of storytelling, his enthusiasm is infectious. His hand gestures become more animated, his voice full of passion and positivity. It's like watching an evangelist. She can imagine a gospel choir arising behind him, silky robes and big hair, as he somersaults and backflips his way through a rousing, triumphant codetta.

'I hear people tell me they don't have the time to write – then they tell me what they love to read. So, there's the decision first off. Do you want to continue adoring other people's work, or is the need to create your own more pressing? Do you just love stories, or do you need to tell your own? That's the first question. Because if you have time to read, you have time to write. If you have time to watch TV, or play some game on your phone, or hit the gym or play five-a-side with your chums, then you have the time to write. But if you don't have an absolute and all-consuming desire to do so, then don't do so.'

Clayton Mings, a shoplifter from Newquay who stole a doctor's briefcase while off his head on spice, tentatively raises a hand. He's a scabby specimen; flaky skin and misspelled tattoos, but he'd been one of the first to put his name down when Annabeth first posted the notice on the library wall. He wants to write children's books, so he says.

'Yes, mate,' says Orton, making guns with his hands. He's bringing a lot of energy today. Annabeth wonders if he will sustain it, or drop before lunch.

'What if you really want to write but you can't work out which of your ideas you should be working on? Like, I've got this one story . . .'

'Aw here we go,' grumbles the man to his right. Ibrahim Curtis, a drug courier from Malton in North Yorkshire, is Mings's cellmate.

'Don't start,' mutters Mings.

'He'll get to it. You've always got to make it about you . . .'

Annabeth lets them grumble. They bicker like a married couple but it never goes further than that. She catches Orton's eye and is delighted to receive a fleeting wink. He's enjoying himself.

'. . . every bloody night he's whispering to himself like he's praying, but nobody prays about dragons and goblins, do they? I mean, that's not what you want to hear when you're on the bottom bunk and your new padmate's talking about exploding planets and upside-down volcanoes and shit . . .'

She tunes them out. Uses the opportunity to scan the room. They're listening, there's no doubt about that. That, in itself, is a victory. Everybody is staring at Orton and a couple of the inmates are even suppressing the urge to raise their hands or shout out. They remind her of children, in many ways: over eager and desperate to get it right, but afraid of their own baser natures. She wishes she had been in the job years back, when prisoners were given access to endless courses and educational facilities aimed at helping them use their time inside wisely. There's no funding for that now. When she proposed bringing Orton in as a visiting creative writing tutor, she'd had to make a pitch outlining the investment-to-outcome ratio of the sessions, and even then, she'd known herself to be fighting an uphill battle. The accountants in the education department had told her the whole thing was a non-starter. She had to go above their heads to make it happen, applying to a charity on the outside for the funding to host the sessions, and promising to promote their involvement in an article with the local newspaper and the prison magazine. Even with the funding in place she had to get tough with a few people to make sure there were enough attendees to not look stupid. She'd all but bullied one or two into attending, convincing them this would look good at their next parole hearing, and promising them that going to sit in the classroom and listen to a visiting author would be like spending the day in a comedy club. She's finally starting to relax.

'. . . and "what if" are the most fascinating, inspirational and exciting words in the English language. What if, tonight, you could hear what was being said in the cell next door? What if you could witness the home lives of the officers? What if, you woke up tomorrow and you were a cockroach – that's where all literature, all stories, begin to smoulder . . .'

'I'd love to hear what was going on in Miss Harris's room, Rufus!'

'I'm sure you would, Swifty! Wahey!'

'OK, OK, settle down . . .'

As she scans the room, she becomes slowly aware that she is, herself, being surveyed. She feels the strange prickling hotness of being the subject of somebody else's attention, as if in the glare of a hot bulb.

Slowly, she turns herself into the full glare of the gaze. It's Griffin Cox. He's looking at her. Looking past Orton and considering her as if she were a painting on the wall of a gallery. He keeps turning his head this way and that, trying out different angles, staring into her as if trying to see every individual brushstroke and whorl.

Annabeth looks away, instinctively. She can hold the gaze of any prisoner on the main wings but she feels like a timid little girl when confronted with the very worst of the VPs. She sees so little of what they portray to the world: sees only the fibrous, worm-eaten thing that lives inside their flesh. She never wants to work on the nonce wing. Doesn't trust herself around people like Cox, even while she tells herself that she must be professional and that no one abuser can serve as a proxy for any other. He is not the man who did those things to her. None of them are. That man is gone, just like the one who tried to take her child. She had to lie to even secure her place on the training course. Had to tell them she'd never been in trouble with the police or been the victim of any acts of criminality that could have provided an ulterior motive for her application. She guards her confidences fiercely. Cocoons her past. And yet the way Cox looks at her, it is as if her every sin and secret was carved into her flesh.

'. . . the book that's out at the moment, *RedGreen*, is essentially about a feeling of intense, concentrated empathy: a character who feels in several dimensions all at once, who hears in colours – who looks at a sharp object and can feel it manifesting physically in needlepoints down the backs of her legs . . .'

Annabeth gives Rufus her attention again; turning her back on the blowtorch attentions of Cox's dark, staring eyes. Facing away from him, his glare becomes a feeling on the back of her neck: the slow, stalking footfalls of an ice-cold spider. She feels the hairs stand up on her arms. Feels suddenly cold, uncomfortable, as if her hair is being pulled at the roots; as if there is something grating, inexorably, into the soft parts of herself. She tells herself to ignore him. That she's an adult, a mother; a prison officer tipped for a bright career. She's dealt with him, and his type, before. But the fear is real. He doesn't look at the person she portrays at work. It is as if he is looking at the person she was, years ago, when those things were done to her, and she had to fight back. She has the sudden and absolute feeling that he knows. That he has seen what she has endured. Seen what she has done.

'. . . of course, character is everything. There seem to be authors today for whom the notion of somebody's character is their hairstyle and the model of their car. I, for one, would hate to be reduced down to something so fleeting and incidental. Character is so much more than that. Look at Holden Caulfield in *The Catcher in the Rye*. Sensitive, intuitive, appalled by the ugliness of the world, and yet his manner is jaded. Cynical, even. That is a human being, not a character in a book. We are all inconsistencies and doubts, poor decisions and temper tantrums; moments of kindness, moments of weakness, peculiar, trivial, selfish . . .'

Annabeth wants to listen. Wants to lose herself in his enthusiasm for his subject. Cox is spoiling things for her. Baiting her. Goading her, without saying a word. She wants to yell something at him. To tell him to pay attention, or to stop bloody staring, but she doesn't want to interrupt Orton while he's in full flow. The rest of the class seem to be going with him, appreciating his passion for the subject even if not fully understanding what he's talking about. She takes the opportunity to throw a savage glare at Cox. He's not even looking. He's eyeing Rufus, with the rest of them, doodling something on his paper without a care in the world.

'. . . we're talking a conflation of the senses – so the things you see are felt on your skin. Imagine that. Just imagine what Julietta experiences every single day. If she sees another person's injuries, or sees them caressed, or touched, she feels that on her own skin. Every single day, she sees something that triggers waves of pain, making it very hard for her to participate in what we think of as reality. She can't watch violence, for example. To see torture is to experience torture. And yet when she watches something positive – she'll watch ballet, and feel as if she is pirouetting. It's uncontrollable. It's called "mirror touch synaesthesia". And in essence, the whole book came about because I thought "what if?" . . .'

He stops for a moment. Becomes aware of himself. Gives a self-deprecating little smile and pushes his hair out of his eyes. Flicks a look at the clock.

'Golly, I do prattle on, don't I? No wonder the critics say that I'm somewhat fond of myself. Perhaps if we stop for a moment and I can let you all have a turn – learn a little about you, so we can come up with some exercises that will be of particular use—'

'I've got a question.'

Heads turn, noses wrinkle. It's Cox. He puckers his lips, using forefinger and thumb to wipe the edges of his mouth. He angles his head, a bird hearing a worm.

'Well, there'll be plenty of opportunities, but sure, if something's just occurred—'

'Do you feel what your characters feel? I read that for a character to be authentic, to be believable, there must be some element of lived truth within them. Some part of the author. Each character, from the smallest cameo walk-on to the main series protagonist and antagonist, they are all elements of the author's inner life. I ask, because I read your third book. I was drawn very much to the housemaster character. Mr Deacon, I believe. Weak. Vulnerable. Cruel. Perverted, in the eyes of some. Rent asunder by the conflicting urge to coddle the boys in his care and to bend them to his will; repelled by his own reflection apart from when he is involved in acts of brutality with a victim. It was, I confess, quite harrowing. Where, might I ask, would such a character come from. And do you feel the same affinity for the abuser, as the abused, in that passage. I ask, essentially, whether you wrote those scenes while curled in a foetal ball, or tumescent with unspent vigour.'

There is a pause as the rest of the class digests this. Orton gives a quiet laugh. Callan leans to the younger inmate to his left, and whispers, none-too subtly, 'Tumescent means "hard-on".' Suggs, hearing this, gives a disgusted groan.

'Miss. I can't be sitting here listening to this – why's he even here, why's he fucking here . . .?'

The rest of the class joins in, turning on Cox and demanding to know why he's being a prick. It's almost as if they are embarrassed to be shown up: humiliated by any notion of association with such a vile specimen.

'Sorry, mate,' says Swift, a middle-aged accountant who broke his neighbour's leg with a golf club when he made an inappropriate remark about his wife. 'Just ignore him, he'll slither off back to the VPs at lunch . . .'

'It's fine, it's fine,' says Orton, keeping it light. He gives Cox an appraising glance. Smiles, as if enjoying the sudden intellectual challenge. 'Cox, was it?'

'Yes, Rufus. And may I say, I thought the use of the phrase "plummy, tortured and toothless" was particularly unnecessary. Some of these critics are just out to make themselves look good.'

Orton sticks his tongue in his lower lip. Closes an eye. Nods. He understands, Annabeth can tell. This is the battle that will set the tone of what's to come.

'Well, Mr Cox.'

'Griffin, please . . .'

'Well, Mr Cox, I admire your question. I admire the frankness of it, and your own courage for asking it in such an environment. And I agree, yes, that every character should contain an element of the author, however vile that character may be. Characters need to be multi-dimensional. They need to have a believable psychology. I believe that most everyday people can conceive of truly terrible deeds and perhaps even the reasons behind them. That truth feeds into the character and informs their actions. The skill to being a functioning member of society is in not giving in to such impulses.'

Annabeth wonders if she should jump in. Wonders why he can't see the trap he's walking into, so wide-eyed and innocent he should be wearing a red cape.

'A little harsh, Rufus, wouldn't you say? You're essentially saying everybody has the same base impulses but only the weak-willed give in to them. Brave words, in a room full of convicts.'

The eyes turn on Rufus. He swallows. Flashes a smile. Looks to Annabeth for help. She begins to stand.

'The last thing I am doing is passing judgement on anybody in this room. I've made it my business not to enquire about the past misdeeds of anybody here . . .'

'You'll have heard of me,' boasts Hawkes, an energetic young car thief from Warrington. 'Stole a fucking baby, didn't I? Nicked a Cavalier from a petrol station forecourt and didn't know there was a nipper in the back 'til I was forty miles away!'

Laughs all round, as if this could have happened to anybody. Suggs doesn't join in.

'You'll know Cox,' he says, his voice cutting through the hubbub. 'Kiddy fiddler. They reckon he's done loads of them. Be a cold day in hell before they let him out. Coppers are back every few months trying to get him to admit to this and that. Dirty bastard. Somebody should fucking shank him.'

'That'll do, Suggsy . . .'

Cox puts up his hands in surrender. Sits back. Licks his lips. He's enjoyed himself.

Rufus breathes out. Annabeth tries to catch his eye, to check he's OK, to see if any of the past few minutes has rattled him. If it has, it doesn't show.

'So, before we have our little break, I'm going to tell you what we'll be up to. Just to get a sense of who we all are, the different energies we're all bringing, I want you to complete a simple writing assignment. Just write about a safe space, OK. Somewhere that, in your mind, you would associate with comfort. I understand that your present accommodation means the task could be considered a little cruel, but I'm presuming that you spend a lot of time thinking your way out of these walls. Creative writing starts with creative thinking. So, let's take a few moments just to chat, run a few ideas around with your chums here, and then we'll start writing, yes? You all have pens, paper . . . good . . .'

Annabeth breathes out, relieved. At once the room becomes alive with chatter: men knocking about bawdy jokes about feeling comfortable with somebody's legs wrapped around their face, or feeling at their best propping up the bar in the White Horse. She is about to use the hubbub as a cover to chat with Rufus, to see if he's doing OK, when she notices him walking over to Cox. He leans down. Whispers in his ear. Stays there, bent over, for several moments. When he straightens up, there is a red welt on the back of Cox's wrist. Though he tries to hide it, pain is etched on his face.

Orton turns away from him as if nothing has happened. Smiles, as he witnesses the class engaging in the topic. Seeks out Annabeth and catches her eye. Gestures at himself, with a mock arrogance, that says, 'I did this'.

She looks back to Cox. He's looking at the back of his wrist. Staring at the livid red welt as if not quite believing it.

And he is smiling.

Grinning, inanely, as if listening to a joke nobody else can hear.

She crosses to his table. Looks down at what he has doodled on the paper.

Feels her heart clench; her insides turn cold.

He's drawn a snow globe.

'Like it?' he asks, his eyes hypnotic, his face inches from hers.

And she is eighteen, again. Bloodied and weeping, trapped beneath the unmoving bulk of the man she has just stabbed through the neck.

ELEVEN

They're looking at him as if he's about to sing. Eyebrows up, pencils poised over clean, lined pages. Christ, if he'd known criminals were this eager to learn, Rufus would have sacked off universities and their lifeless, dead-eyed English students years ago. Sure, Karen the librarian is busy scribbling something more important than he is on her big A4 pad, but everybody else wants to know what Rufus Orton – a man who went from a rising star to yesterday's darling without noticing anything very much in-between – is about to say. He likes it. Likes it a lot. He'll hate himself later for basking in such unmerited adulation, but for now, he just likes having an audience.

They've had their coffees. Had their biscuits. He didn't get a chance to chat with Annabeth as she was off doing something in the offices during the break, but she arrived back just as the second session was about to begin. He's glad. This is the bit he prides himself on. He might be shit at almost anything, but he knows he puts on a good show.

'*Character's* not a difficult area to get right, provided you're even slightly interested in human beings,' he says, perched on the edge of the desk and addressing his comments to the room in general rather than a specific student. The last thing he wants is to make anybody uncomfortable, though he wouldn't object to another opportunity to butt heads with Griffin Cox. He feels him on the periphery of his vision, sitting there and giving off a fog of bad energy: a compost heap on a hot day.

'If you've had one meaningful conversation in your lives, you can create characters who are fully formed: real people, with flaws and dreams, regrets and secrets. It's like building a snowman. You start with a snowball, and you roll it and roll it and it becomes bigger and more human until soon you're looking at something that deserves a face and a name. Watch.' A smile, to the group: a clown about to twist a balloon into a rude shape for the children. 'I'll show you.'

He glances at Annabeth. She's staring at him as if studying a painting.

'I'd like to introduce you to somebody,' he says, smiling. He shifts his position and waves into the empty air to his right. 'This is John,' he says.

'You're off your box, mate,' smiles Mings, with a grin, and is shushed at once by a hard stare from Callan: his eyes looking like they could cut a hole through a bank vault.

Rufus rubs his hands together. Presses on.

'I won't ask you to say hello because he can be a bit shy, can John, and he has a tendency to blush when he's anxious. It's a bit of a disability. He's got Irish blood, you see, on his mother's side. A tendency to freckle in the sun. Sweats a lot so he's always paranoid that he's giving off a bit of a whiff. Over-compensates. Splashes on the aftershave until it's a bit overpowering. Big brown eyes that make him seem a bit soft – the sort of chap who might like to stay out of trouble rather than throwing himself in. Clever lad, is our John, though he doesn't push it forward. Big reader. Loves the poetry of Seamus Heaney and can recite it from memory, though he's got nobody to recite it to. Lost his wife, God rest her. Three months after the honeymoon and the doctors told her that she wasn't going to make it to their first anniversary. Broke John, so it did, but she was determined to make the best of her last few months. Told John to take out the biggest loans he could so they could have the holiday of a lifetime. Sad thing though, John's credit rating was shot to shit. His dad – bit of a wrong 'un. Been using his boy's name to swindle credit cards. So John couldn't give his dying wife what she wanted . . .'

'Poor bastard,' mutters Mings, at the front of the room, and nobody takes the piss.

Rufus alters his posture. Enjoys knowing that everybody here is now emotionally invested in a fictional character he's making up as he goes along.

'But John here had a friend, who had a friend, who knew

somebody that could help him out. Said he could have ten K
in his pocket within the hour. No contract. No further discussion. No details about repayment rates or deadlines. Just a
gesture that could enable John and his missus to make some
memories before the end. He took it, of course. Took the money.
Booked a break. Cruise to all the lovely spots his wife had
dreamed of. Gave her the trip of a lifetime. Came home
three weeks later to find that he had missed the first repayment.
There was interest on top. Interest on top of that, too. His pal
didn't want to take his calls. And then there was a guy on his
doorstep, wanting to explain the gravity of the situation . . .'

Rufus gives a theatrical shift of position. Points to the empty
air to his left.

'Come on, I'm not doing all the work here,' he teases. 'Who's
this chap?'

There is much shuffling and sitting up straight. He can hear
dormant imaginations being stretched like tight hamstrings.

'Doesn't have to be a chap,' says Callan, with a shrug. 'A
collector's a collector, and blokes aren't as likely to take a
swing at a lass, in my experience. Good enforcers, women.' He
glances at Annabeth. Gives a little nod of respect. 'Worth their
weight in gold.'

There are titters and assorted respectful chuckles from the
group. Annabeth smiles. There's something delightfully sincere
about it: a guileless moment of pure pleasure that makes him
want to know her better. What had the bloke said on the walk
across from reception? A bit of an enigma, our Annabeth. He
finds himself wondering whether it would take a tiresome
amount of unpicking for her to unravel. Dislikes himself for it
at once.

'OK, we have a lady on his doorstep,' says Rufus, standing
up. 'What's her name?'

'Nicola,' shouts Suggs. 'Never met a Nicola who wasn't a
bit nuts . . .'

'Jasmine,' says an older inmate: lank grey hair dangling down
to dandruff-speckled shoulders. 'Posh lass gone bad, maybe.
Did a bit of kick-boxing when she was at boarding school and
when her dad lost all his money she joined the Army. Got an
injury and the pension wasn't what she expected so she's

teaching fitness full time but doing some collecting on the side . . .'

Rufus claps his hands, grinning. 'She sounds superb, sir. Top of your head or somebody from your own circle of friends?'

'Bit of both,' he shrugs. 'Lass at our local I've never spoken to, but I've looked at her plenty. Tried to work her out.'

'Awesome,' says Rufus, and looks around for the whiteboard, paper and pens. Flips over to a clean page. Starts to scribble illegible notes.

'We happy with Jasmine?' asks Rufus, to the room in general. 'Anybody got another idea? Does the name make a difference? Do we have a different idea about somebody called Shaniqua to somebody called Agnes? Does the name inform the character or does the character inform the name?' He looks at Annabeth. Smiles, bringing her in to the discussion. 'Annabeth,' he muses, then looks around at the inmates, pretending to have slipped up. 'Sorry, sorry, don't know if they know you have a first name. Miss Harris. What do you think? Would you be the same if you were called Pauline? Sharon? Moon-unit? Let's imagine you're called Morgana Morningstar, or Raven Beachbuggy, or somesuch. Would you still be working in a prison? Would it be an act of rebellion against the Bohemian parents who saddled you with their hippy beliefs and tree-hugging claptrap?'

To Rufus's surprise, Annabeth doesn't return the smile. Just gives a tight-lipped shake of the head – an instruction to move on.

'So . . .' he mumbles, trying to recover his thread. He hadn't meant to upset her. Begins to worry at once that he has gone too far. Decides to try and make her laugh. Nobody can be cross when they're laughing, he tells himself, as he so often does. He just needs to keep at it. 'So, yeah. This is character. This is all about how to make people more than one-dimensional cut-outs. It's about real people. Real lives . . .'

A hand rises. Griffin Cox. Rufus ignores him.

'So we're going with Jasmine, yes? OK. Tell me, what does Jasmine care about? What's the thing that excites her? What journey is she on, in life? What is she hiding?'

A young Asian man, short and bespectacled, is the first to

answer. 'Her boyfriend's inside. He's got debts. She's doing collections for some gangster to try and pay it off.'

Rufus nods, impressed. 'So in many ways she's in the same situation as our protagonist, yes? That might lead to an understanding. To empathy. A connection . . .'

'They're gonna end up shagging!' shouts out Suggs, and everybody laughs.

'The choice is yours, mate,' smiles Rufus. 'Story structure is a different thing entirely but if the characters are strong enough, people will invest in the story you want to tell. Like I say, human beings are fascinated by themselves. We go our whole lives with the one brain, the one genetic code. Are we made or do circumstances change us? Can bad acts be compensated? Can a good person be brought low by circumstances? Are there such things as good people and bad people? This is what a writer is out to investigate – to ask the question without the need for an answer. It's psychology, philosophy, sociology: it's acting and engaging with your own inherent schizophrenia all at once . . .'

'There's no way to say who's good or bad,' grumbles Mings, pushing a hand through his hair. In the weak light from the window, Rufus sees tiny scraps of skin rise up like flakes of snow. 'Like, that bloke you've just talked about. John, or whatever. I mean, how could he do anything else? The banks were the bastards for not giving him the loan. He had to go to a loan shark, didn't he? And if he ends up having to do a job or go on the rob or something, it's hardly his fault? But he'd still get sent down for it. Still have his life ruined for doing something that anybody with a heart would do. Still end up in a place like this . . .'

Rufus nods, understanding, and sees that the rest of the group are nodding in agreement. 'They ask if you have any mitigation,' says a tall man with a flat nose and home-made tattoos on the backs of his hands. 'Every time, you get your chance to explain. But the explanation doesn't mean anything if they take it as an excuse. You still get done for stuff, no matter what.'

'My pad-mate in Frankland was there for knee-capping his best mate,' says a broad-shouldered black man who hasn't previously spoken. 'Best mate had shagged his wife, got her pregnant, sent her to some doctor he knew to get rid of it, and the doctor bodged the job so badly she couldn't have kids. So my pad-mate done him. Took his kneecaps off with a golf club. His mate took it as well. Accepted he had it coming. Police still ended up involved and my pad-mate got eight years. Eight fucking years! Like, he was the bad guy! I mean, whose rules are these?'

Rufus stretches, glancing at the clock. It's been a good session. He wants to wind them down a little before lunch, but the discussion is becoming a little animated as the group share similar stories of injustice. He glances at Annabeth. She's glaring at Griffin Cox, who still has his hand up. To distract the class from their private conversations, he gives a theatrical sigh.

'You were after my attention, I believe,' he says, brightly. 'If you're after a lavatory break, we're almost ready to stop for lunch . . .'

'This Jasmine,' says Cox, drawing out each syllable, almost tasting each letter in the name. 'I think perhaps it is demeaning to suggest she would be imperiled into the situation by her love for another. Perhaps it is simply her choice – an opportunity to use skills otherwise dormant. If we are to imply that she is not a willing participant in the debt collection, I fancy it would be more potent if she had been forced into it for reasons of her own – perhaps for mistakes in her past . . .'

'Fuck off, Cox,' says Suggs, sourly, shaking his head as he remembers that he is sharing airspace with a specimen he finds repellent.

Cox turns to Suggs. Angles his head as if watching something fall from a great height.

'Perhaps,' says Cox, sucking on the thought, 'or perhaps she has a secret. Something she did that she can never escape, no matter how far she runs. Maybe, she is at John's door, doing this unsavoury thing, so as to safeguard her precious: to shore up the walls as they begin to crumble.'

'Whatever, Cox,' spits Suggs, pushing back from the table and scratching out the two sentences he has been jotting down on his pad in a spidery hand. 'You write your own story, you dirty bastard. Something about a nonce stuck between the people

who want to kill him inside, and those who want to see him
released so they can saw his fucking head off . . .'

Rufus holds up his hands. Glances to Annabeth for reassurance. She's not even looking his way – just staring off through
the small, dirty window, into a sky that looks as though its
colour has been slurped away with a straw.

'Shall we pause there?' asks Rufus, hopefully.

When Annabeth fails to reply, it falls to Callan, his big fists
on the table in front of him: silverback to his core.

'Aye, prof. We'll leave it there.'

Before he turns away, Rufus locks eyes with Cox. Looks at
the little lesion on his arm. Watches, mystified, as Cox takes
his pencil, and pushes it, ever so slowly, into the wound. A look
of ecstasy passes over his face, and then it is gone, and he is
raising his arm to his mouth, sucking at the droplet of blood
as if trying to remove venom from a snakebite.

'Jesus,' mutters Rufus, turning away.

And behind him, soft as rain: '*Sanguin Christi*. Amen.'
Blood of Christ.

TWELVE

'Thanks for this, Annabeth. Honestly. It's a privilege.'

She examines him critically, alert for any sign he's
taking the piss. Sees none. He's tucking into macaroni
cheese and a slice of fatty gammon, stopping every now and
again to take a slurp from his can of Sprite. He seems very
much at ease, suddenly. He's got the morning session out
of the way and has the look of somebody who has already faced
the wolf, and won. He has the air of somebody who knows he's
equal to the coming tasks. Despite the swearing and the steam
and the jangle of keys not ten feet behind him, he could easily
be sat at The Langham tucking into afternoon tea.

'A privilege, Rufus? You can't mean the food, surely.'

He smiles at that. 'It's perfectly edible. Nice, even, though
if you were one of my students I'd be appalled at such a vapid,

vacuous word. No, I mean the whole thing. Being here. Getting a chance to connect with people that perhaps I would never have spent time with if not for opportunities like these. It feels wrong to be paid for it, somehow, though that is, of course, no instruction to cancel the transfer . . .'

She smiles at that. It had been a surprise to learn that an author she considers a contemporary legend might be struggling financially. She had presumed that the royalties from his books would pay for at least two holidays a year, and that the advance on his next manuscript would have paid off whatever remained on his mortgage. The truth had struck her as deeply unfair. 'We're all skint,' he'd said early on in their friendship. 'Don't give creative people money. Ever. Asking your creativity to make money is a sure-fire way to rob it of its joy. Focus on the work, on the craft, on the delight of creating. Say "bugger it" to money as much as you can. Honestly, if you give a writer too much money, they spend it. Creatives don't live in the real world. Even when you have a big imagination, you can't conceive of everything going wrong!'

'I'm sorry I left you during the break,' she says, sensing the moment is right to make the apology for what must be the tenth time. 'I knew you'd be OK with Karen, and they'd all warmed to you, so I made a judgement . . .'

He waves his fork, carelessly, chewing politely through a piece of gristly meat. 'I said before, I didn't notice you'd gone. Honestly, we're bonding. I'm not expecting to get Valentine's cards, but I can see them listening, and wanting to learn.'

She nods, gratefully. Moves her meat and veg around the chips as if playing culinary Tetris. Tries not to think about what caused her to flee the classroom as if scalded. It's a futile effort. Griffin Cox is at the very centre of her mind. How could he possibly know? That's what she kept demanding of herself as she sat in the toilet cubicle and tried to control her breathing; to wash the blood from the walls of her mind. Could it be coincidence? An innocent doodle on a scrap of paper? A snow globe. Easy enough to draw. A peaceful, pleasing shape. Perhaps she had seen a poorly executed balloon and her own subconscious had turned it into something symbolic. She would so love to believe that. And yet Cox had put himself in harm's way to get himself on the course. Could she be the reason for his uncharacteristic enthusiasm for spending time with the general prison population? She scuttled back to the classroom without answers, determined to neither meet his gaze or acknowledge him again before the session was over. She has been successful, so far, though she feels a cold, creeping anger towards the man who has ruined her enjoyment of a day she has looked forward to so very much. They're halfway through the lunch session, and she has Rufus all to herself. She could be picking at the stitches of his fascinating mind; grilling him for insider tips and hidden truths. Instead she seems distant. Aloof, even. He keeps asking if she's OK. She likes being asked the question, truth be told. Close as she is to Ethan, her welfare is rarely enquired about.

'What's the story with that chap, anyway?' asks Rufus, neatly putting his knife and fork together and turning around to nod a thank you to the armed robber operating the till. The tattooed inmate gives a big gap-toothed grin in return, and throws up a thumbs-up. Rufus is smiling as he asks the question. He doesn't name Cox, but Annabeth knows to whom he refers.

'He shouldn't be here,' she says, shaking her head. 'I said no – I told you, didn't I? Then one of the officers he has a good relationship with laid it on thick. Called in a favour, and in a place like this, favours are important. So I said yes, and I don't think there's much I can do to go back on it. Let's be honest, he didn't do anything that would lead to a report. He's not going to get an adjudication for asking a question about the writing process, even if it was a bit off-colour. He's a game-player, I can see that. Loves winding everybody up then sitting back to watch what happens next. He's bored, I think. A big brain can wither in a place like this. Maybe that's why he wanted to come on the course – just to throw some petrol on the ashes of the other inmates.'

'Oh that's good,' says Rufus, enthusiastically. To her amazement, he pulls a slip of paper from his back pocket and a blue pen from somewhere under his jumper, and scribbles down her words. '"Throw some petrol on the ashes",' he mutters, then nods, satisfied. 'Lovely turn of phrase. Can I tempt you to write something this afternoon? I would love to hear the lyrics and timbre of your subconscious. I can tell from your emails, you have a gift: an ear for language. I promise, the only feedback will be positive . . .'

She scrunches up her nose, an embarrassed pre-teen. 'Don't be silly, I'm a reader. I love books and writers are like my rock stars but I wouldn't know where to start . . .'

'Rock stars?' he asks, wiping his mouth with a napkin. 'Not quite. It's a very solitary passion. You don't get big triumphant moments. It's mostly just you and the voices in your head. But if you've got a story in you, you should tell it.'

'No, like I say, I wouldn't know where to start . . .'

He looks at her as if she has said something ridiculous, and slightly sweet. 'Yeah, if only you knew a half decent writer and had time to sit through a creative writing course . . .'

She rolls her eyes. 'All right, smart-arse.'

He grins back, all twinkles and charm. 'Go on, tell me something. Anything. Something about yourself we can use as a springboard into your narrative. Annabeth, for example. Not a name I know. Were your parents looking for something unusual? Hippies seeking something less out-there than Zebulon? Is it a portmanteau of two other names? Come on, intrigue me.'

Annabeth breaths in. She'd like to close her eyes. Would like to open them again and find herself alone. She knows now what a bad idea this all was. Of course he would ask questions. Of course a student of people would need to dissect her inner world. She can't work out which of her lies to tell him. Amazes herself when she hears herself telling the truth.

'You couldn't accuse my parents of being hippies,' she says, looking past him. 'Last thing they'd want would be to be thought of as alternative. Proper upstanding middle-Englanders, my mum and dad. Volvo, golf clubs, neat lawn, two weeks in the South of France each summer. Home brew in the garage for Dad and a potting shed at the end of the garden for Mum.'

She glances at him, and sees she has his attention. He's nodding, as if she's telling the story the right way.

'Where did you grow up?'

'Little place near Cheltenham,' she answers, automatically, and has to fight the urge to bite down on her lip. She hadn't known until she spoke just how desperate she is to let the truth fly briefly free. She sees herself as a glass bottle: her truths smashing against their transparent jail, begging, manically, for release. She presses her lips together. Makes a show of looking at the clock. 'We should get back.'

He cocks his head, as if waiting for something. 'You haven't told me why you're called Annabeth,' he says, kindly.

She laughs at herself; a practiced gesture: making fun of herself for being so scatterbrained. His expression doesn't change. He's not buying the performance. He really does want to know.

'I was the third baby,' she says, unable to make light of it. 'Eldest was Elizabeth. Next down was Hannah. Nine and seven when they died. I was what the doctor recommended to help with their grief. The replacement baby. And just to ram it home, they slammed their names together. Made me.' She shrugs, as if she has been through this so many times she doesn't mind telling any more. 'Sorry to depress you. You did ask.'

He holds her gaze. She sees something there, for the briefest moment: a flicker of something that was not there before; as if something scaly and colossal has briefly disturbed the surface of a still lily pond, then slunk back to the depths.

'That's . . .' he begins, shaking his head.

She shrugs again, cutting him off. Stands up and heads to the counter so that she doesn't have to look at him any more. She's fought so hard for so long to keep her tears behind the bars of her eyes. She cannot let them fall now. Not when she needs her resolve the most.

She glances back, for a single heartbeat, as she orders coffees from the server. Glances over her shoulder, and sees him, hunched over his notebook, pen moving in a blur. She wonders how long it will be before she reads a book about a girl called Annabeth. A replacement girl. A smashing together of two dead sisters.

Knows, to her very core, that he will get it completely wrong.

She has never minded being Annabeth. Never objected to helping her parents get over their grief. It has never been that which caused her life to unspool the way it has.

No, it was Daddy's friend. It was Sandy Powell. The man who told her he loved her for who she was, and not what she had been created to replace. Sandy Powell, who persuaded his pal's twelve-year-old daughter that the things he did to her, the things he took from her, were things of beauty. Sandy Powell, who began raping her before she had started her periods, and who called her a lying little slag when she finally told her teachers. Sandy Powell, who got away with it. Who never served a day. Who got an apology from her father for the embarrassing fuss that Annabeth had made. Sandy Powell, who gave her a wad of notes, and told her to run. Sandy Powell, who threw her to the wolves. Abandoned her to a world of pimps and drugs and violent men. Men like Walter. Walter, with the jagged snow globe on his neck.

She blinks back tears. Swallows hard.

Walks back towards the library as if heading to the gallows.

THIRTEEN

GRIFFIN BOETHIUS COX

PART 1 OF RECORDED INTERVIEW
Date: 11.04.2021
Duration: 38 minutes
Location: HMP Holderness

Conducted by Detective Constables Ben Neilsen and Andrew Daniells

POLICE: This interview is being tape recorded. I am Detective Constable Benjamin Neilsen, here with my colleague Detective Constable Andrew Daniells. We are officers with Humberside Police Serious and Organized Crime Unit and part of the multi-agency task force investigating cold cases with the National Crime Agency. Could you please tell me your full name.

GC: Griffin Cox. Middle name Boethius, but I don't use it.

POLICE: Is it OK if I call you Griffin?

GC: I've been called much worse. But if we're getting familiar, I prefer Gary.

POLICE: Fine, Gary. In that case, I'm Ben, this is Andy. Can you confirm your date of birth for me?

GC: 19.02.68.

POLICE: And just to confirm, you're happy for this interview to be conducted without legal representation? You are entitled to have your solicitor present, but you have declined . . .

GC: No need to trouble him. He's expensive. Charges for 'thinking time' some months, if you can believe that.

POLICE: Free counsel can be provided if required, Gary.

GC: No, there's nothing new to talk about, is there? I've said it all before.

POLICE: You might be wondering why we're here . . .

GC: Not really. I watch the news. Read the papers. You're looking for that poor girl.

POLICE: Which poor girl, Gary?

GC: Bronwen. Bronwen Roberts. You're digging up the farm by the airport at Kirmington because somebody has told you that they were my accomplice in her abduction and murder, and that she's in a sinkhole under the asparagus. Am I right?

POLICE: And what would you have to say to that contention, Gary.

GC: I'd say it's very cruel on her family. They've clearly been through hell. I read an article in a magazine, years back, in which they spoke of their endless pain at not knowing if she is dead or alive. To give them these false hopes – if hopes could even be considered as the right word – seems an act of sadism. Or, if nothing else, the ramblings of a clearly degenerating mind.

POLICE: You've been questioned about Bronwen's disappearance before.

GC: Yes, among others. I seem endlessly popular among earnest young detectives trying to find a monster on which to pin high-profile cases. Unfortunately, I am never able to assist. Hard as it may be to believe it, Ben, I'm not the man you all imagine me to be. I made one mistake. I fell for an exceptionally talented and beautiful young woman and I believed that the relationship developing between us was more important than the age gap. I thought she believed it too. I feared losing her when she learned my true age and I wanted the time and space to convince her that love should know no barriers. If it were told about in prose, it would be a story of true love and passion.

POLICE: You abducted her, put her in the boot of your car, and were equipped with tie-wraps and tools, Gary. Hardly romantic.

GC: Depends on your vision of love, Ben. Even in Ovid's *Metamorphoses*, beauty can be observed. So too the sainted Lavinia, daughter of Titus Andronicus. I'm sure you're familiar with the texts.

POLICE: We know that you and Bronwen were in contact, Gary. You were a sponsor of the young musician contest that took place in Salisbury three weeks prior to her disappearance. We know you exchanged details. We know that you sent volumes of poetry to her home address and acted, to all extents and purposes, like a suitor.

GC: Truly, you are an oracle.

POLICE: We have a witness who places you at the

caravan park on the outskirts of Caistor, North Lincolnshire, the day before she was last seen by her father. That's roughly four miles from the family home.

GC: I told you all last time, I have an interest in church architecture. There's a church near there mentioned in Pevsner, and where Tennyson himself was a regular visitor. If you know the poem 'Claribel', then . . .

POLICE: We have another witness who claims that you made a telephone call to his home number at 1.38 a.m. in a state of some distress, raving about something having gone wrong, about making a mistake – begging for help.

GC: This is fantasy, Ben. The person in question, you'll have their phone records, yes? You can rule this in or out without difficulty, I presume.

POLICE: We've had some difficulty in securing said records, due to the time elapsed, but we believe the claims to be credible. Our witness has made it plain . . .

GC: Please refrain from calling him your witness. Use his name. We're talking about Wilson Iveson, yes? Elderly gentleman. The chap who has been looking after my property and my affairs since I was incarcerated. A man of eighty-six, with degenerating cognitive abilities and a recent diagnosis of pancreatic cancer, yes? Half blind, last time he visited. Barely recognized me. This is the same gentleman who claims I buried Bronwen Roberts in a farm beneath the flight path of Humberside Airport, yes? I fear, Ben, that if this were made common knowledge you might appear foolish and questions would be asked about use of resources. I really have nothing else to say on this matter, or any other unsolved murders or disappearances that you would like to throw at me. I was rather enjoying my writing class before you came and ruined the day, so I think I shall stop talking now.

POLICE: He says she was your one mistake. The others, he knows they'll never be found, and if they are, there'll be no trace evidence. But he made it quite clear that as and when we find Bronwen, we'll find you all over her. Inside her. Do you have anything to say to that?

GC: Oh Ben. What an imagination.

POLICE: We will find her, Gary. But maybe you're safer in here, eh? People like you don't always face justice in the courts. Sometimes they get a more traditional kind of retribution. Can I ask you about a man called Keith Van de Sande?

GC: A paedophile, yes? Killed by vigilantes of some kind? The latest of many, so I'm informed. But I am not a paedophile, Ben. I'm not a perpetrator of sexual assault. I am a victim of coincidence and ugly imaginings who is endeavouring to serve his sentence in peace.

POLICE: I can read a list of names, Gary. Adolescents with three things in common. They are all talented, some might say exceptional individuals. They are all missing, presumed dead. And they all came into contact with you at some point in the months before they were last seen. This won't go away, Gary. Help yourself. Clear your conscience. Do one good thing and give their families some answers. You'll feel better. How do you imagine there is any other way out of what's coming.

GC: *Aut viam inveniam aut faciam*.

POLICE: And what's that supposed to mean?

GC: Look it up, you halfwit.

*Latin phrasing later transcribed as a motto attributed to Hannibal: 'If I can't find a way, I will make one'.

FOURTEEN

It's late afternoon. The day has turned dark so swiftly that it is as if somebody has pinned a strip of sailcloth across the little windows at the back of the classroom. They can hear rain striking glass. Have switched on the strip lights overhead so they don't have to squint to see the whiteboard at the front of the room.

'. . . beaks on a coffin lid,' says Rufus, standing, wide-legged at the front of the class: a football manager addressing his players. He's riffing on ways to describe the sound. Seems to be enjoying himself immensely. 'Drawing pins falling on a table . . . An avalanche of coins tumbling from the pocket of an inverted corpse . . .'

Annabeth is weaving her way in and out of the tables, chatting with inmates, marshalling disagreements, offering words of encouragement where needed and the occasional command to shush when bursts of enthusiasm become too rowdy for polite company. She's listening to Rufus despite the hubbub around her and the static fizz in her head. Can hear every word, picture every scrap of projected imagery, even over the sound of her own panicked self-admonishments.

Why did you tell him, Annabeth? What is wrong with you? You're going to spoil it . . . The snow globe, Annabeth. How could he know? How?

The afternoon has gone well. Cox's absence has undoubtedly helped. Annabeth had felt her heart genuinely lift, cartoon-esque, when Karen welcomed her back from lunch and informed her that Cox had been called back to the VP wing for a previously scheduled conversation with his lawyer.

'He's asked for you to bring him any handouts, and has promised to catch up on whatever he missed,' said Karen, pulling a face that suggested she hadn't enjoyed his tone this morning. 'I've never seen that side of him,' she'd whispered, conspiratorial. 'He's very keen on the library, though sometimes I think he likes to request certain books just to make fun of the staff. He's had me searching the shelves and the database for books that turn out to be the Latin names for all sorts of venereal diseases. But he's clever, certainly, and he's helped a couple of other vulnerable prisoners with their reading and their letters home. I don't know, people are complicated, aren't they? Maybe he's not all bad . . .'

Annabeth hadn't offered any thoughts of her own. Just said a silent prayer of thanks that she wouldn't have to keep the peace.

Distractedly, she leans over the shoulder of Dougie: an inmate whose pencil is moving swiftly across the third sheet of lined paper. She can barely read his writing, but there's passion in his words and she doesn't want to interrupt his flow. She feels eyes upon her, and looks up to see Callan, the hard-case, watching her intently. He gives a nod, as if she's passed a test, and Annabeth cannot help but feel strangely pleased: the same feelings running through her as when she meets with her superiors and receives a few words of praise.

'You've never been so quiet, Suggs,' she says, lightly, giving him a moment of her time. He's been paying attention, asking questions; even offering up a story to the class about a supply teacher who loaned him a book when he was fourteen and for whom he reckoned he could have been persuaded to try harder at school.

'For my lass,' he says looking up, using his forefinger and thumb to wipe the dew drop from his nose. He gives a cheeky, schoolboy smile. 'Not exactly a romance but I'm trying to tell her how it feels being away from her like. I try and tell her on the phone but it's not the same, is it? I just get embarrassed and sad and pissed off and end up giving her jealous shit. Like people used to, when we was civilized . . .'

From the front of the class she hears Rufus clap his hands.

'Right, gentlemen. That was a treat to see.' He licks his index finger and holds it up. 'The air is bloody crackling with creative energy. Honestly, that was better than I could have begun to hope for.' He looks around the room, pulling faces as if he's teaching kids. Gets smiles in return. 'So, anybody willing to let the class hear what you've got to say? Remember, there's no right, no wrong, there's just words on a page. Some of you may have chosen to go your own way and written something that presently matters to you. The others may have done as I suggested and written about a safe place beyond these walls. Would anybody care to . . .?'

'Aye, I will . . .'

Annabeth is surprised to hear Dougie speak so clearly. Normally he's all mumbles and shyness.

'Excellent,' says Rufus. 'I applaud you. Which direction did you choose to go in?'

'I've written about life inside,' he says looking around him and seeing a largely supportive crowd. 'Like, how they treat us, how it's not what people think. How the screws fuck with you . . .'

Several pairs of eyes seek out Annabeth, who gives a good-natured shrug, as if he may well have a point. It seems to be the correct response, as everybody turns back to Dougie, who stands up holding his scribbled pages like a hymn sheet.

'I won't read all of it, like. Just the bit I want you to hear, y'know. Like, the blurb or whatever . . .'

'Get on with it, son,' growls Callan, and the younger inmate makes a great show of hurrying the hell up.

'. . . if people knew what went on in here they would lose their minds. Even those who say if you can't do the time don't do the crime – they wouldn't wish all these days and weeks and months locked up with rats and cockroaches and nothing to do . . .'

'Come on, Dougie – this is fucking Butlin's compared to Belmarsh . . .'

'Belmarsh? Piece of piss, man. Full Sutton, that's the one . . .'

'You're kidding me, they've got celebrity chefs in there sorting their canteen . . .'

'Shouldn't be giving out shit in front of miss, like that, she's OK . . .'

Dougie reddens. Throws himself down in his chair. Slams his paper down on the table and slams his head onto his folded arms: a toddler tantrum from beginning to end.

'Shall we leave it there?' asks Annabeth, seeking to end on

a relative high. 'Mr Orton will be back tomorrow and if you leave your notes and handouts at the front, he has promised he will go over them tonight in order to provide feedback for tomorrow . . .'

There are the garbled sounds of the session drawing to a close. Tables and chairs squeak across the cord carpet. Inmates stretch, extravagantly, and give each other nods of approval. This was OK. It was better than any of the alternatives. They've done all right all things considered.

Rufus approaches her as she's helping Mings find the lid for his felt tip. She knows it's up his sleeve and believes that given the right amount of cajoling, he'll miraculously discover its presence.

'Tomorrow?' he asks, wincing. 'I thought it was Thursday . . .'

Annabeth shakes her head, ruefully. 'No. Same time tomorrow. Is that a problem . . .? Ah see, there you go, Mings, isn't that a surprise . . .'

'Oh sod,' he says, looking pained. 'I'm dreadful. Truly. Such a mess of a human being. But, look, it'll be fine. I'm resourceful. A bed for the night, or a sofa, or a rabbit hutch . . . all are definitely within my skill-set to procure . . .'

The last of the inmates file out. They both get a couple of shouted words of thanks. She gathers up the cups. Listens as Karen bustles back in, jolly and windswept, asking whether the afternoon had been a success.

And she hears herself asking Rufus Orton, her favourite author, if he would like to stay the night.

FIFTEEN

Cox pushes himself back against the cold black railing: a bear scratching a tricky spot with a rough tree. He's trying to find the perfect spot to apply pressure. His back is agony. Pain is a constant companion but usually it is no more than a dull ache from which he can distract himself with activity or imagination. Today it feels as though somebody has inserted a chisel between his vertebrae and struck it repeatedly with a hammer. In Cox's case, such comparison is not a flight of fantasy. Though he has never experienced such an act of brutality, he has witnessed it up close. Has felt the screams reverberating through his own naked flesh.

He ruminates upon the day. Assesses his achievements and considers the moments that could have been improved. Cox is always seeking to be the best he can be. He has never imagined himself finished. Apex predators reach perfection before they cease to evolve and Cox, though he knows himself to be very dangerous, remains afraid of man's capacity for arrogance. He runs the day's events through his head over and over, each word perfectly recalled, each glance clear as if he were watching a recording. He traps a laugh behind closed lips as he remembers the look on Harris's face as she looked at his page and saw the item he had doodled just for her. Remembers with true pleasure the way he had steered the writer towards the cliff edge before allowing him to step back. Things had been going almost exactly as he had foreseen. It was the coppers who risked spoiling things. The coppers who turned up at reception and made swift arrangements with the wing governor to be granted access to an interview room, and Griffin Cox.

They had something real, this time. Wanted to talk to him about the one thing he'd always hoped they wouldn't: the thing that has kept him awake at nights and stamped great knots of tension into his lower back. They'd wanted to talk about his relationship with Bronwen Roberts. He does not allow himself to think upon her. Fast-forwards through his memory: the tiresome interview with the two cops. Detective Constables Daniells and Neilsen. A plump, friendly chap and a fit-looking, handsome guy with a shaved head and nice clothes. He'd given it 'no comment' in every language that he knew. Faced down their every attempt to persuade him to incriminate himself, from gentle persuasion to outright aggression. He hadn't budged. He believes he played things correctly, but he cannot help but replay the handsome detective's parting words.

'You'll be here forever, Cox. Here, or somewhere much worse.

They'll find her, and your DNA will be all over her. I swear, you're going to be here forever.'

Cox pushes back against the bars. Sucks his cheek. He does not doubt the police officer. They will find his first victim. They will find her soon. And there is a very good chance that there will be forensic evidence on her and in her that will ensure he is never released. But Cox doesn't plan to stick around for any of what is to come. Cox intends to be free before things get much worse, and certainly before the press start sniffing around.

Damn this back, he thinks, irritated. He intends to enjoy his first night on a proper mattress. Can already taste the *Tournedos Rossini* with rosemary-and-salt roast potatoes that he intends to devour with a deep glass of blood red Amarone. He won't let Bronwen Roberts tell him he can't have what he wants. He certainly didn't afford her that luxury at the end.

'Practising for the Olympics, Coxy? Or is this a suicide attempt? Never heard of anybody jumping off backwards.'

The voice belongs to Travis Parton, who has endured the nickname 'Dolly' for as long as he can recall. He's on the wing for amassing an unforgivable amount of debt to some of the hard cases on B-wing. Likeable though he is, he's due several serious kickings and he's reluctant to endure them. He'd rather be safe with the paedos and rapists than getting his cheekbones crushed to dust among the general population. He's not alone in that regard. The VP wing offers some form of sanctuary to those considered at risk of violence. Ex-cops, ex-wardens, grasses, informants, pad-thieves who've done the unforgivable and stolen from those with whom they share a cell. The sex offenders are a minority, but they are the ones for whom there is no hope of rehabilitation. They will never rejoin the general population. They will serve their entire terms in danger of reprisal. Most of the men inside have been victims of abuse themselves. Men like Cox will always be the focal point of their rage.

If Dolly has a problem with Cox, certainly he doesn't show it. If anything he seems a little in awe of him. Treats him like a minor celebrity, though whether he is awed by Cox's life of relative privilege on the outside or his connection to a string of unsolved but well publicized crimes, is open to debate. He's late twenties. Chatty. A cheeky sort. Hard to dislike. He has a tattoo on his neck that he swears is a flying eagle, though to Cox's eye, it resembles a dead chicken.

Cox lowers himself to the ground. He's on the landing, enjoying a change in air. He does not detest his cell the way some other prisoners do, but he takes pleasure in the rare moments between the evening meals and lights out, when he can stand on the passageway outside his cell and take a breath of bigger, bolder oxygen. The other prisoners on the wing are doing much the same, solitary men or occasional twos and threes, leaning on the railings and enjoying the peace. The men on the nearest wing are at dinner, now. There are no threats coming up from the floors below. No threats bleeding through the bars.

'Good evening, Travis. Are you well?'

'Aye, grand, grand. I said, are you practising for the Olympics?'

'Back pain,' says Cox, stretching lightly. He can feel a tingling in his fingers. Can barely feel his toes at all. It's beginning to concern him. He has never thought of himself as an imposing physical specimen, but he has always been wiry and quick. He does not feel old enough to be suffering from such unfair aches and pains. Not now. Not when things are moving in the right direction.

'My dad suffered with that,' says Cox, chattily. He stands close: nearer than Cox is accustomed to. 'Not my real dad, like. Mam's boyfriend. Was with us for years, off and on. Never called him Dad when he was alive. Seems wrong not to, now. But aye, he was a marmite to it. Had to lay flat on the floor at the foot of me mam's bed, which was a pisser for the Alsatian as that was where he liked to have a kip . . .'

Cox licks his lips. Twitches a smile. 'A marmite? Do you think you might perhaps mean "martyr"?'

He waves a hand, unembarrassed. 'Yeah, whatever . . . that weren't the point of the story. Anyways, he said acupuncture was the thing that worked for him. You heard of it? I can give it a go – finding the needles, like, if there's somebody you'd let stick 'em in.'

Cox hears himself laughing. Realizes that he must be feeling rather good, despite the pain. Normally he suppresses his mirth. At school, the prefects found his laughter amusing. So too his cries. His pitiful pleading. His laugh has long been a source of embarrassment: an odd tittering noise; as if speaking the words '*hee-hee-hee*' over and over again. Dolly shrugs, a bit unnerved by the sudden outburst.

'Wasn't easy,' says Parton, suddenly, moving closer. Cox feels the item he has ordered being surreptitiously dropped into the pocket of his leisure trousers. Slips his hand in after it to mask the bulge. His palm touches the back of Parton's hand. Rough, warm skin. A jolt surges through him; the electricity of connection, of skin on skin. Parton pulls his hand free as if it were in the mouth of a snake.

'It's appreciated,' says Cox, recovering himself. 'And you have more than repaid my faith in you. There may be other items to procure, in the coming days. I trust that you will be similarly proficient.'

'Aye, most things, mate, most things,' says Dolly, moving away from him. He gives a funny jerk with his head, almost butting the air, then turns on his heel and heads back down the landing. Cox watches him go. He understands the younger man's sudden sense of disquiet. Cox's skin is always damp and clammy. He does not so much perspire as simply ooze a kind of cold, briny unguent. He does not seep from his facial pores but the rest of his flesh feels as if it belongs to somebody long since drowned in dirty water.

Cox stretches his back again, then returns to his cell. He is keen to examine the item in his pocket, but there will be inspections in the coming hour. Interruptions. He will not have the blessing of the turn of the key in the lock until much later. Even so, he allows himself a moment: withdrawing the cool glassy object from his pocket and taking a glance at its firm yet fragile shell. He did not imagine it would cost him so dear to obtain the empty glass jar, nor the packet of sparkling dust within. Took time and resources to have hard money transferred to the young man's bank account. Worth it though he thinks, slipping the bauble beneath the clothes at the foot of his bed. Worth every penny.

He lays back on the bunk, staring up at the ornate wooden cross: the light catching the different sections of inlaid wood, lighting and darkening the pieces in turn. He is not a religious man. The cross is there to remind him of the need for atonement and the eternal glory of resurrection. He has fallen, but Griffin Cox will rise again.

To entertain himself, Cox searches the reference library in his mind. Finds the necessary article – the feature on the website, glimpsed once and filed away. It fills him with an obscene pleasure, as if each cell in his body were remembering the sensation of young skin. He fills himself up with recollections of the boy's young, taut skin. The hope in his eyes, and the way the light left them: pupils like ink vanishing down a plughole.

Reads every word in the pleasant darkness of his mind. Doesn't even have to touch himself to experience a release that makes him shake.

SIXTEEN

The clocks went forward a week ago and there's a definite trace of spring in the air. Annabeth enjoys the feeling of driving home in daylight. Paull is a couple of miles from the prison and the road drifts mostly through agricultural land: the topography paving-slab flat. She likes to buzz the window down and breathe in the smell of the turned earth; of low tide; of diesel and salt and the odd chemical tang of the refinery that looms over the landscape like a space station: twisted metal and flashing lights.

It's a little before seven when she pulls in on the main street by the water's edge. Rufus's car is poorly parked – one rear alloy having scraped the pavement and the front wheel half on, half off the kerb. Annabeth parks behind him. Checks her reflection in the pull-down mirror. She's been in the gym for the past hour and pulled on a pair of jogging trousers and a hoodie when she'd finished toweling off. The result is a face she recognizes from long ago. Without make-up, and with her damp hair pulled back in a ponytail, her features are frighteningly exposed. She's a little plumper, a lot more lined, but the woman in the mirror is not much different to the girl who screwed jagged glass into the throat of a man she'd tried to love. She closes the mirror before she upsets herself. She's never liked how she looks, but it seems important to her now that she reveal the truth of herself. She would rather give Rufus a glimpse of the reality than spend an age slapping on make-up and choosing outfits, only to look like a glammed-up stranger.

A deep breath, then out the car. Her skin tightens at once. Despite the washed-out blue in the sky and the raucous squawks of gulls fighting over scraps by the sea wall, the wind still cuts like a lash as it streaks in from the water. She puts her hood up as she walks past Rufus's car, holding herself tight so she doesn't shiver. She follows the line of the sea wall, scanning the horizon for any signs of life. There's nobody here. Won't be for a few weeks. She's glad. Autumn and winter are desolate times in little seaside villages, but she enjoys the solitude. She can walk for miles along the lip of the estuary, gazing out across the muddy water to the distant blur of Cleethorpes on the south bank of the river. She's solved the world's problems more times than she can count, losing herself in thoughts and ideas as she walks for miles in the general direction of the ocean. It won't change much when summer comes. Paull is not a holiday destination. There are no arcade games or beach huts or chip shops. But birdwatchers arrive in decent numbers, and there are no shortage of US visitors eager to see the old lighthouse or to tell the locals that their ancestors arrived here three or four centuries ago, heading for life in the New World.

Annabeth pauses, one hand on the door, then pushes into the warmth of the Humber Tavern. It's a pleasant, cosy pub. Wood floor, round tables, a dartboard and a log burner: the glass glowing gold. Not many in tonight, though there never are on a weekday. She gives the room a quick once-over and spots the broad back and thick hair of Rufus, spilling over the wood of a stool with one elbow on the bar. His hand is curled, protectively, around the circumference of a pint glass, supped almost down to the foam. He's in conversation with Fran, a young barmaid who's saving up to go travelling for a year before committing to a university. Annabeth doesn't think she'll actually embark on either adventure. Imagines she'll settle down and become a mum with a part-time job and a half-decent husband before she gets anywhere near an airport. She's seen it happen time and again. Seen people with all the possibilities open to them, settle for something mundane. She tries hard not to be resentful. Annabeth's life choices were limited, and she's doing the best she can with what she has left.

'Evening,' says Fran, warmly. Rufus turns. Grins, widely, as she approaches. She takes the initiative. Kisses his cheek. He smells like old books and the outdoors. Past his shoulder, she sees two familiar faces, both staff from the prison. Julie works in the education suite, and her husband, Mark, is Supervising Officer on B-wing, and technically, Annabeth's line manager. He's short and stocky, with grey hair shaved down to the wood, and an air of quiet control. Annabeth admires him, and likes it when he praises her for the way she's handled situations, or offered gentle words of advice on the rare occasions she has not performed to her best. He raises his bottle of Brown Ale in greeting as they lock eyes. Julie, seated across the table, turns round to see who her fella is making eyes at. Seems delighted to see Annabeth out on what appears to be a date with a handsome, if rather careworn, older man.

'Sorry I'm so late,' begins Annabeth, breathily, caught in what her mother would describe as 'a bit of a tizzy'. 'Getting out of the car park, and then the fuss on Hedon Road, and . . .'

He shushes her, as nicely as she has ever been shushed. 'Not a problem, not a problem,' he says, half standing, gentlemanly, as she levers herself into the chair beside him. 'Been learning a lot. Fran here is off to Machu Picchu, soon.'

Fran, who has ruffled blonde hair and a slightly vacant look about her, begins to giggle. 'Don't be mean! He's being silly, don't take any notice . . .'

'Fran wasn't familiar with the place, Annabeth. Believed it was a Pokémon . . .'

Fran giggles, as if she and Rufus have been making fun of each other for years.

'What can I get you?' asks Fran, making a face. 'Good to see you in. You don't do weeknights, as a rule . . .'

There was a time when Annabeth would have loathed the idea of her routine being so well-known to her friends and neighbours. Years went by when Annabeth and Ethan made it their business to never interact with strangers and to give as little away as possible to those who became their friends. Annabeth didn't know if people were looking for her, but she knew that she had to keep moving if she wanted to make sure her past didn't catch up with her. All these years later, she can't so much as pop out for a stroll without being asked about her son's prospects in his GCSEs or have it remarked upon that she'd been home late on Tuesday week. She winces as Fran starts pouring her a small glass of Chardonnay with a squirt of soda, even before she is asked.

'Nice place,' says Rufus, to Annabeth, as if she were personally responsible for its upkeep. 'Apologies for use of the word "nice", but it is somewhat apposite. Cosy. Welcoming. I could doze off under a broadsheet newspaper. And a very fine real ale.'

Annabeth raises her glass. Chinks it against Rufus's. She takes a sip and he downs his froth, then points at the empty glass. Fran takes a clean one from under the bar and begins to pour.

'You should have been in when the fireworks were on,' says Annabeth, remembering. 'City of Culture celebrations. People going nuts to get tickets and us lot up here seeing the whole lot across the river for nothing. Amazing evening.'

'I did some stuff for all that,' says Rufus, and there is a slight slur to his 's' that suggests he's a couple of pints past merry. 'Wrote a script for some mixed-media play they were doing in a warehouse. All very avant-garde. I can't even remember what it was but it paid OK.'

Annabeth shakes her head. Takes a swig of her wine. 'I don't remember your name in the programme,' she says, frowning. 'I'd have been there, if I had.'

'Ah, I wasn't involved as Rufus Orton,' he says, as if imparting a confidence. 'I was Simone Lewis, if my memory serves. Got the gig through a friend of a friend, who wouldn't know Rufus

Orton if they fell over him. I pitch for no end of work under a pseudonym. Makes it less dispiriting when people turn me down – it's not the real me, it's the avatar. I've told you before – I'll do what must be done to put food on the table.'

Annabeth lets her sadness show in her face. She'd like to put her hand on his forearm and tell him that he deserves to be sitting in a private members club in Soho sipping cocktails with the bigwigs, rather than stuck here, on the wild and windswept spur of East Yorkshire, with a prison officer who can never put enough miles between herself and her past. She makes a concentrated effort to change the subject.

'Was it OK, all told? The course, I mean? That unpleasantness with Cox this morning, I'll admit I was grateful he didn't make it back for the afternoon.'

Rufus licks his lips. Closes an eye to better see the memory. 'I was rather disappointed not to get a rematch. I do hope he'll be there tomorrow. An interesting mind. Not somebody I would ask to babysit, of course, but clearly very bright.'

'Good at rattling people's cages, certainly. Say the word and he won't be back tomorrow . . .'

Rufus looks past her instead of replying. Annabeth turns, aware of a presence behind her. It's Mark, bringing his and Julie's glasses back to the bar.

'Evening,' says Annabeth, smiling and a little flustered. 'Mark, this is Rufus – the writer who's been teaching some of our wannabe literary sensations. We were just talking about Griffin Cox, and saying—'

'All right mate,' says Mark, cutting her off and reaching past to shake Rufus's hand. 'She look after you OK? One of our brightest and best is Annabeth. I'll be calling her "Boss" before we're through, I promise you.'

Annabeth pulls a face, embarrassed. He's always saying things like this: implying she's going to the very top. She wishes she could tell him not to expect so much of her. Any higher up the ladder and she risks her anonymity, and it is her anonymity that keeps her the right side of the bars.

'How do you do,' says Rufus, earnestly. 'Yes, this fellow Cox, he was certainly making his presence felt this morning, asking one or two slightly lewd questions. Shame to lose him for the afternoon. Called to a legal meeting, or some such, I believe.'

Mark laughs: a harsh bark that sounds unpleasant at close quarters. 'Life's going to get very interesting for Mr Cox,' says Mark, conspiratorially. 'Two of Humberside's finest had him in the sweat room for nigh-on three hours this afternoon. They're digging up a great chunk of farmland over Kirmington way – right by the airport on the road to Grimsby. Got it on good authority that some young lass he picked up, years ago, is under the potatoes in Chappell's Farm. Must be twenty years she's been missing. Witness has come forward to say he helped our Griffin dig the hole. Old boy now, trying to clear his conscience. They must be taking it seriously if they're digging the place up, eh? Can't remember the name. Bronwen or Bryony or something. Either way. So if he's still fancying doing the course, I'd see if you can get him to write a memoir – save the coppers the bother, eh?'

There is a clink as the glasses hit the bar. Mark gives Annabeth's shoulder a squeeze. He seems pleased she's out with company. 'Nice to meet you, Rufus. Annabeth loaned me one of your books. Couldn't get into it myself but Julie loved it. Anyway, enjoy your night.'

Annabeth mutters some bland reply while Rufus does the handshakes and farewells. Her mind is racing. Griffin Cox is facing serious time. He's in the frame for an old, unsolved murder. He's gone out of his way to get on a course organized by an officer that he may know secrets about. Beneath her hoodie, the hairs on her arms begin to rise. She realizes that she doesn't know enough about this man; that she has allowed a serpent to slither into her and Ethan's Eden.

'You seem miles away,' says Rufus, quietly, so close to her that she jumps when she realizes he is near. 'Are you OK? I really do appreciate the bed for the night. I checked my messages by the way. Don't worry, I won't be a dick about it but you did say it was one a week for six weeks. I'm not going mad. But seriously, I'm very glad to be here.' He reaches out and puts his hand over hers. Cocks his head and finds her eyes. 'With you.'

She says nothing. Looks at her hand as if it belongs to

someone else. Slowly he withdraws it. Drains his pint. Picks up his satchel from the floor.

'Are you going to read their stories?' asks Annabeth, eager to change the mood. 'Have you had a look?'

He shrugs, a little put-out at her sudden coldness. 'That's a job for when I'm tucked up with a whisky. Do you have a liquor cabinet or do I ask Fran here to take care of my needs?'

Annabeth finds his gaze. Holds his hard stare. 'Scapa, isn't it? Your favourite? I bought you a bottle when you agreed to do the course. You can have it now, if you like . . .'

He grins: a boy who's been told he's going to the football at the weekend. 'Annabeth, you may be my favourite human. It might not last forever but for now, it's you.'

Annabeth returns the smile. Drains her wine. Considers her house guest.

I don't need forever, she thinks. *I just need now.*

SEVENTEEN

'. . . honestly, a really strange feel to it: like an inner-city estate just dropped off at the water's edge – 1950s houses just turned up on the shore one morning and wandered in and decided to stay. Really weird vibe to the place. If it was Sussex the houses would cost twice as much. It's seaside, but not seaside. It just happens to be beside the sea. It's not what you think of as English. Not a cricket pavilion and roses round the door kind of feel. More that kind of small-town-in-Lincolnshire vibe. Hint of violence lingering in the air even when everybody's laughing. People raise an eyebrow if you order an extra pint of milk – as if you're getting too big for your boots . . .'

Rufus looks up from the document in his lap. Peers at Annabeth over the top of his glasses. 'Some lovely phrases here, Annabeth. Very lyrical. Maybe a bit specific in your comparisons but there's enough about the atmosphere that you feel transported.'

Annabeth hides her smile behind her glass. She's drinking an apple brandy that came in a gift hamper she won in the Christmas raffle. It's OK; like cough mixture, toffee apples and distilled heartburn has all been swooshed about with a cinnamon stick. She's feeling light-headed and sleepy all at once. She has her knees drawn up beneath her and she can feel herself slowly sliding into a sleeping position. On the armchair across the small living room, Rufus seems largely unaffected by the fine Scotch he's been drinking since Ethan said good night and headed to his room. He'd seemed to take to Rufus. It had felt strange and rather wonderful to sit down for dinner as part of a trio. Out of politeness, her son had joined them at the kitchen table, dutifully forcing down some dry cottage pie. Rufus had declared it 'magnificent', though he'd been similarly gushing when he told her that the little two-bedroomed house was 'a genuine delight' so she knows that his seal of approval is a dubious accolade. Ethan had silently worked his way through half a bottle of ketchup in an attempt to make the dish palatable: loyal to the last. She'd been even prouder of him for the way he'd chatted with their guest. He hadn't acted like a child. Came across as a clever, thoughtful young man. They talked about politics, about belief; about books read and unread. Rufus had seemed genuinely sorry to see him say goodnight and head upstairs to play his games with his mates. It had been almost surreal for Annabeth. Uncalled, a thought had flashed through her mind: a vision of a life. Dinner at the table. Chat. Gentle affection. A kiss from her son, a manly punch on the arm from her gentleman, then an evening on the sofa, chinking glasses, talking about words, drifting into a warm torpor to the lullaby of his deep, mellifluous voice. She'd had to bite her own cheek to make the vision disappear. The last thing she needed was to indulge in fantasy, no matter how delicious it might feel. Still, the sensation lingers.

'This is good,' says Rufus, his voice strange. He has a pen in his mouth, clamped between his teeth, as he scans the final paragraphs of the passage she wrote, years ago, and which nobody else has ever seen. Come the morning, she will wish she had resisted his overtures, but he had seemed sincere when he said he would dearly love to read some of her writing. She'd found herself agreeing without really knowing why and had stuffed pages of old jottings and random scraps of poetry into his hands before she could talk herself out of it. Then she poured herself a drink and retired to the sofa, listening as he made enthusiastic noises: telling her, time and again, that she had the soul of a writer.

'Your heart is an inkwell, Annabeth. Dip the quill in it and whatever makes it onto the page feels real to the reader. Your descriptions are lovely, but I can see that you're holding back. You seem to be on the verge of exposing yourself in parts but then you hold back, or veer away, or spoil the power of it with a joke or a frivolity. This could be so powerful if you let yourself lower your guard.'

On the sofa, Annabeth raises her head. Gives a nod of thanks and hopes that her discomfort doesn't show. She picks up a scatter cushion and all but hides behind it, hugging it tight. Lower her guard? She could scream at the simplicity of the suggestion. For fifteen years she has had to watch her every minute gesture and movement lest she somehow incriminate herself or briefly expose her own true nature. For her entire adult life she has feared meeting somebody with enough empathy and insight to look into her eyes and see the truth. Has scared herself imagining locking eyes with one of the killers in her care and being met with a knowing smile. There are days when she feels she must have 'killer' carved into her forehead. And yet, nobody knows. There is nobody on her trail. The only person to have implied some knowledge about her crime is Griffin Cox. She suppresses a shiver as she thinks upon him again. Feels a sudden heat inside herself, low down: a twisting sensation, as if her innards are tying themselves in knots.

'I suppose I should let you get your rest,' says Rufus, making a show of looking at his watch. 'I'm going to have a gander at the hand-ins and call home, see what's going on. Am I OK to potter in the kitchen if need arises? Forgive me for how pitiful it must seem, but if I don't get a warm milk before I lay down then my acid reflux has me wishing an early death on myself.'

Annabeth grins, wildly delighted to know this little titbit

about a man who, until recently, was merely her favourite author. It feels positively surreal to have him here, confiding about his medical grumbles, asking permission to use her microwave.

'Please, help yourself,' says Annabeth, slithering off the sofa and making a show of standing up. 'If you hear anyone moving about, don't worry. It'll just be Ethan coming down for one of his fifteen bowls of cereal. If you need anything, knock on the door.'

He nods, grateful. Locks his fingers and stretches. Takes off his glasses and tucks them into the top of his shirt. 'He's a really good kid,' says Rufus, and seems to mean it. 'Not all teenagers are people you'd want to spend time with. It's pleasing to see somebody his age who doesn't mind demonstrating that they love their mum, y'know? I sometimes wonder if mine are a little spoiled. I love them, but they're hard to like. And you can see how proud he is of you. Has it always been just the two of you?'

Annabeth feels her insides clench. She searches for one of her pre-prepared answers and can't seem to find anything that works. Her mind is all static and drink. She has a sudden, mad impulse to grab him and pull his mouth on hers, just so he won't ask her any more questions. Instead she mumbles something about it being a story for another day, then offers a swift smile and a 'good night' before all but scampering up the stairs.

She stops on the fifth step, her heart pounding. She tells herself to go back. To grab a glass of water or make a show of locking the back door so she can try again. Kiss his cheek, say 'sweet dreams' and go to bed like a woman in control of her life and not somebody with a closet full of secrets.

There's a creak at the top of the stairs. Ethan. Bed-headed. Childlike in his pyjamas, too short in the leg. 'You OK, Mum?'

She tries to hold onto her strength: to tell him that she's fine, just tired, just a little tipsy. Tries to tell him not to worry about her and to go back to playing with his friends. He can read her too well for any of it to work. So he comes, quietly, down the stairs. Helps her up. Holds her to him and eases her up the last of the stairs and into her cold, dark bedroom. She loves the nearness of him: that smell of sweat and freshly-mown grass; sticky drinks and laundered clothes.

The lights flare. She's bone tired, suddenly. Needs to sleep. To rest. Everything aches. And yet as Ethan helps her slither beneath her quilt cover, she hears herself talking. Hears herself telling her son about the day, tears in her voice. Were there a mirror on the ceiling, she would see a little girl.

'. . . don't know if I can do it any more . . . the hiding, the lies . . . all that pain . . . I don't know if I can let it all back in, or stop the bad stuff spilling out . . . and he's too clever, cunning – like, is he playing a game with me . . . the drawing, a snow globe, I mean, it couldn't be clearer, and with these detectives asking questions, I mean, maybe that's his whole plan from the off, and I can't judge any more . . . even Rufus seemed to sense something, asking about your dad . . .'

She yelps as she feels his fingers squeeze her knee through the blankets. She hears her own muffled apologies. He has never allowed her to call the dead man 'Dad'.

He leans over her. Presses his forehead against hers: somehow trying to vacuum out the bad thoughts. Up close, their eyes are a mirror image. There is nothing of his father in him, and there has never been a day when she hasn't been attentive for any indication that he may be carrying bad blood. She is so grateful for him. To him. Feels better just for the nearness.

'It will be OK, Mum. I swear. This is what you wanted. This life – and it's a better life than you've ever had before. Just sleep, OK? I'll be here.'

She believes him. Lets herself drift away. Lets sleep engulf her like warm snow.

The last thing she hears before she drifts into blackness, is the soft snuffling sound of her son, stroking her hair and singing the same lullaby with which she used to hum him to sleep.

'. . . there was a crooked man, and he went a crooked mile, He found a crooked sixpence upon a crooked stile . . .'

And she sees him. Griffin Cox. Sees him digging, moonlight striking the silver of his spade. Sees a dead girl at his feet, and a tall man in a long black coat by his side.

Rolls over, and sees the newspaper clipping on the floor by the bed.

Gives herself up to the nightmares, and the dark.

QUESTIONS ASKED IN COMMONS AFTER CHILD KILLER MURDERED

By Press Association reporter Grace Hammond

March 13, 2018

POLICE have launched a murder enquiry after child killer Keith Van de Sande was found stabbed to death in woodland in East Yorkshire.

Van de Sande, 48, served 17 years in prison before his release on license last year. Unbeknownst to nearby residents, he had been living in a small cottage property near picturesque Hutton Cranswick.

Ramblers yesterday discovered his body in the thicket of trees near the village of Hutton. It is not yet known how long the body had been there.

The brewery rep was convicted in 2001 for suffocating 12-year-old Catriona Flynn, after she rebuffed his advances and threatened to tell her mother, with whom married Van de Sande was having an affair. Her body was later found in the cellar of the pub where she lived with her mother.

Questions are now being asked in parliament about the security and welfare of prisoners released on license. Van de Sande's death is the third high profile murder of a convicted sex offender within the past 18 months, following the unsolved slayings of Carl Kennedy, 50, and Fergus McVeigh, 68, who were both members of the same paedophile ring and jailed in 1998 for the murder of 11-year-old Thomas Laing in Dumfries, Scotland, three years before. Kennedy's flat in Stockport was deliberately set ablaze, while McVeigh, released two years sooner than his accomplice, was beaten to death at his mother's graveside: a cemetery in Consett, County Durham.

Police have warned the public that violence against

convicted sex offenders will be treated exactly the same as any other crime, and warned those who applaud the idea of vigilante justice to pause before inciting further violence.

The mother of Catriona Flynn released a statement through the family solicitor last night, saying: 'I do not believe in the death penalty but I was disgusted to learn that the killer of my child was walking around, living his life, while my darling daughter was robbed of her chance to become all the things I know she would have become. Keith Van de Sande was a vile, manipulative man who propositioned my child then killed her so she wouldn't tell. When he was arrested, police found 30,000 indecent images on his computer. He had us all fooled. I won't mourn.'

A spokeswoman for CXO, an organization set up to help care for ex-offenders, said that there were real concerns among their members that vigilante action was being tolerated by the authorities.

A spokeswoman said: 'These men all served their time and were released having completed their sentence. Their locations and identities were meant to be protected but there is a real fear that somebody in authority is leaking that information, and I believe we will see more incidents like these if the authorities cannot do more to guarantee the safety of those released back into society with little or no support network around them.'

Walker Denise Middleton, of Brough, told this news-paper: 'It seemed so unreal. We saw this training shoe sticking out of a thicket of thorns, and then my friend was saying that she thought there might be a body. Next thing we were looking at this man who had been absolutely savaged. It sounds silly, but I thought he'd been got by a wild animal. He looked like he'd been attacked by a bear.'

EIGHTEEN

DC Neilsen isn't the sort to let his emotions show, but the effort of talking to Bob Roberts is making him feel as though somebody is squeezing his throat with fore-finger and thumb. There's a haziness to his vision. He knows he won't cry – he's been a detective long enough to have learned how to hold back even the most insistent of tears – but he knows that when he gets back to the car he will sit quietly for a very long time.

They're sitting in the boxy little kitchen of Roberts' flat, just off the marketplace in the attractive Lincolnshire market town of Caistor. The strip light on the ceiling gives off an unforgiving light, illuminating a dismal space: stained carpet and damp-mottled walls. It's scantily furnished. Neilsen sits on a white plastic patio chair and Roberts is sitting on an upturned crate: the logo for Hull Breweries seared into the side. Some of the woodchip has been scraped off on the bare wall, revealing a floral print beneath, but whoever began the decorations clearly lost interest before making progress. There are dirty pots stacked in the sink and on the drainer and bin liners full of takeaway parcels and empty bottles are piled up in a shimmering black mountain by the door. There's a calendar from the Chinese takeaway pinned to the wall: the cover page showing November 2017.

'I wish you'd met her,' says Bob, in the raspy voice of somebody who had spent months not letting themselves cry. 'I wish *he'd* known her too. Not the girl he killed – the soul he took . . .'

Neilsen fights the urge to put his hand on Bob's arm. He doubts the old man would appreciate the gesture. He's too brittle to be touched.

'You're OK, are you, Bob?' asks Neilsen, wishing he knew the right combination of words to make some kind of differ-ence. 'People stop by? You're on top of the bills and stuff?'

Bob raises his head. He's been staring at the grooves in the coarse wood of the kitchen table. Considers Neilsen with eyes that have bathed in tears since the day his only daughter walked out the door. 'Bills and stuff? Yeah, I think so. Don't take much notice, really. Anybody wants to come cut me off they can do what they like. I just need a candle to read by. Bugger 'em.'

Neilsen gives a smile, grateful that Bob is trying so hard on his behalf. He knows the old boy wants to have a drink. He reeks of strong cider but can only afford to have two pints in the little pub across the road. He only goes for a bit of company. Then it's home via the convenience store, where he picks up whatever's on offer, toddles off home, and drinks until the screaming in his head falls silent. He'd been about to crack open a bottle of Sailor Jerry rum when Neilsen turned up, fulfilling a promise to keep him informed of any developments. The last half hour has been gruelling for Neilsen, whose own father passed away a year ago. He feels his absence every day. None of the platitudes offered by friends or family have done anything to make him feel better. *Yes*, he did have a good innings. *Yes*, he did live a good life. *Yes*, he did stick around long enough to see his son become an impressive, respected adult. Neilsen takes no comfort in it. He just wishes that he were still alive. Wishes they could argue about football, or politics, or roll their eyes in unison at something said by Mum or some prick on the telly. He just wants him back. And yet he knows his own grief to be a measly thing when compared to the colossal great avalanche of sadness that consumes Bob Roberts.

'I never thought she'd be there,' says Bob, quietly. 'Chappell's, I mean. I know that place. I'd have felt it, or something, wouldn't I? I drove past it four or five times a day for years – you think I wouldn't feel the tug of her?'

Neilsen doesn't reply. Bob has said the same thing half a dozen times already.

'Somebody playing silly buggers, if you ask me,' he says, scratching at the backs of his hands. They're rough, with sunken knuckles: a tell-tale memento of a long-ago broken hand. Bob was a man's man, before Bronwen went. Worked for the Yarborough estate: one of the handymen responsible for the general upkeep of the landowner's huge portfolio of rental properties. He worked hard, liked a drink, and doted on the daughter who came along just as the older kids were preparing to fly the nest. She'd been a surprise to Bob. Hadn't been to his wife, Jenny, who had decided several months previously that she didn't know what to be if she weren't a mother. Jenny has been dead nine years now. She never got to learn what happened to Bronwen. Bob has all but resigned himself to the same fate.

'Silly buggers, Bob?'

He shrugs. Wipes his hand across his mouth. There's a sound like paper tearing as his old skin rubs across his coarse stubble. It's hard to see whether he's still a big man: he's wearing so many shirts and fleecy jackets that he could be stick-thin inside a Matryoshka doll of clothes.

'People like the limelight, don't they? Like to stick their noses in. He was probably reading about it in a magazine or he listened to one of them podcasts or something. Thought he would help, even though he had nowt to contribute. I remember that Wearside Jack character – sent tapes to the bloke chasing the Yorkshire Ripper and sent them off on a proper wild-goose chase. Cost a few more ladies their lives. It'll be something like that.'

Neilsen wishes he were brave enough to ask Bob what he prays for. After all these years, there is still a part of him that believes his daughter is alive, and that somehow, she'll come home. The alternative is that she was taken. That she was hurt. That she was killed, and dumped. And despite the not-knowing, the inability to properly grieve, Neilsen isn't sure that he wants the search of Chappell's Farm to lead anywhere. He's learned to endure the feelings that eat away at him – doesn't have the strength for the truth.

'I met him today,' says Neilsen, licking his lips. He looks away before he has to meet Bob's eyes. Stares through the little window above the sink and watches a tall man with a little girl on his shoulders emerge from the pub and light a roll-up. Inhales, and holds it with such obvious pleasure that his feet seem to momentarily leave the ground. The girl on his shoulders slaps him on the forehead and they both start to giggle, happy in one another's company. Neilsen isn't sure if he's watching good parenting or bad.

'Met the guy who made the call?' asks Bob. 'The witness?'
Neilsen shakes his head. 'Griffin Cox.'

They sit in silence for a moment. Bob stares at his hands as
if reading a tiny manuscript scored into his old skin. Eventually,
Neilsen stands and crosses to the counter, where a thin plastic
bag does little to hide the bottles within. He removes the rum,
and searches the cupboards until he finds two mugs that will
just about serve as drinking vessels. On Bob's, the tragic
message: World's Best Dad. He pours them both a measure,
his own barely enough to wet his lips, then sits back down.
Bob wraps his hands around the mug as if it were a hot chocolate and he had just been fished out of a frozen lake.

'How does he look?' asks Bob, after taking a deep swallow.
'I can't picture him properly. Only met him the once, and he
weren't much of a thing. That's why I've never believed the
conspiracy theorists, see? Bronwen wouldn't have had her head
turned by a bloke like that. He was a nothing sort of a bloke.
And she was such a good girl.'

Neilsen nods. He doesn't want to say too much in case it
causes the old man more pain, but he fears that whatever happens
next, Bob is in for fresh misery. He's been drunk near-enough
insensible ever since Neilsen told him they were digging in
Chappell's Farm based on fresh evidence that she had been
deposited there shortly after she disappeared.

'Tell me again,' says Neilsen. 'The presents. The letters. How
was she when she received them? I mean, did she seem excited?
Secretive? Unimpressed?'

Bob stares past him, looking at a memory that causes his
hands to shake. 'We never took much notice,' he says, softly.
'Older parents, see? You let them get on with their lives and
hope they know what they're doing. She never caused us any
bother, and it wasn't that odd for stuff to arrive addressed
to her and not to me or the wife. Her older sisters would send
her stuff now and again, and there were people who'd seen her
give a concert or appear in a competition who'd taken
her address and were writing to her or sending sheet music or
something. She was a very grown-up girl. Of course, we teased
her now and again, joking that she had some mysterious
admirer, but she just laughed along and said we were silly.

Maybe I kept her too wrapped-up, you know? She was a bit innocent. We did everything we could by her – all the trips to music recitals and residential weekends and whatnot – it wasn't cheap. But maybe she missed out on getting that bit more streetwise. I don't know.'

Neilsen can see that the old man has asked himself over and over what else he could have done. Knows that he will die without ever getting an answer.

'The nightingale?' asks Neilsen, carefully.

Bob gives a snort of laughter: a dry little hiss. He shakes his head, still marvelling at the oddness of such a gift.

'There on the bloody step, wasn't it? Big black cage, all fancy wrought iron, twisted in on itself. Looked bloody spooky. And there's this nightingale inside. Pretty little thing, like you'd expect. And there's this card attached to the bars with a ribbon. Bronwen's name, written in this twirly calligraphy, and a little line of poetry, though it were written in foreign. You'll have seen it all, I shouldn't wonder. And the coppers have had the cage since day one. Never helped, did it? It was all we had, save a couple of fancy books she'd been sent. She'd burned the rest. Chucked it all in the fire. Wish I'd never told the police about that – as soon as I did you could see them writing her off as a runaway. Gone off to meet up with somebody, hadn't she? Done a runner.'

'And you don't think it was Cox?'

He closes his eyes. Takes a drink. Swallows, painfully, as if forcing down rising bile. 'Never even bloody occurred to us. Didn't even remember the bloke until we saw his face in the paper having nabbed that girl in York. I think that was what did Jenny in, you know? Miss her like anything but she'd have hated these past few years. Once it was in the papers – once people started mentioning Bronwen again – it was all too bloody much. I tried to help other people, y'know? Do something positive, talk with other families who've lost somebody . . .'

'This was with the Missing People charity, yes?'

'Aye, they're good. Lady who looked after me was the bee's knees. Nothing was too much trouble, and she were only a young thing. Wanted to get me answers, or justice, or at the very least some kind of closure. I still don't know if that's what I want. Some people, they say that getting the body back is the thing that matters most. I don't know. Makes it real, doesn't it? But if she's dead and gone, I don't want her laying where somebody else chose for her. I want her home.'

Neilsen finishes his rum. Reaches over, and gives the old man's arm a squeeze. There's more fabric than flesh.

'You think he did it?' asks Bob, and he could just as easily be asking whom Neilsen fancies in the cup final. It's a voice out of which all emotion has been drained. 'Cox. You've met him. Think she'd go off with him? Think he's a killer?'

Neilsen stands. Takes his mug to the sink and rinses it out, leaning over the dirty dishes in his expensive suit. He knows that he should soft-soap the poor old bugger: tell him that they're not pre-judging, and that all lines of enquiry remain open; making a lot of noise while saying precisely nothing. He can't bring himself to do it.

'I think he's capable, yes,' says Neilsen. 'I don't know why the witness chose to direct us to the field at Kirmington, but we're going to do our damndest to find out if they were telling the truth. Whether or not he hurt your daughter, I don't know. But I think he's hurt a lot of people. I think he might be one of the most dangerous people I've ever met. And I don't know how to explain what it is about him that made me feel that way. I just know that as soon as he walked in to the interview room, the air changed. You know how animals react before a storm – they sense the change in air pressure, smell the rain, or whatever? It was like that. Like he was dragging storm clouds with him.'

Bob nods, the action barely noticeable. 'If he did it – if he took Bronwen – you'll make him tell you where he put her, won't you? Even if you don't find her at Kirmington, you'll do what you have to make him say.'

'Everything within the law,' says Neilsen, automatically.

Bob looks past him, his haggard face giving a little twist of resignation. 'So, nothing, then. Christ, it must be a killer, being a policeman. You'd be more use without the badge, wouldn't you? Have more of a chance to do something that matters.'

Neilsen doesn't reply. Just nods to the old man, and makes for the door. Just before he turns the handle, he stops, and asks one final question. 'The nightingale,' he says, quietly. 'What happened to it?'

'What you'd expect,' says Bob, drily. 'What always happens to a solitary bird in a cage. Bashed its brains in against the bars, didn't it? They go mad, trying to get out – trying to find a mate. Bronwen cried like a baby about it. Watched the pretty little thing go mad in front of her. That weren't long before she went. She wouldn't even let us throw the thing away. We found it in the outhouse a day or so before she went. She'd spread its wings out and pinned them to this piece of wood, all fancy, like. Looked bloody creepy, like it was still alive. God knows what she was thinking.'

'And that went to evidence too, did it?' asks Neilsen.

Bob shakes his head. 'Went on the fire. I didn't want people thinking my girl was a nutter or anything. Doubt it matters now. I suppose it was pretty enough, what she'd done. Like, she was trying to keep it beautiful, even after it was gone.'

'What did she call it?' asks Neilsen, opening the door and feeling the cold air rush in.

'Phil,' says Bob, with a little laugh. 'Philo-something. Philomena, Philomela – you'd have to ask the wife.'

Neilsen doesn't turn around. Knows that if he did, tears would spill.

Walks into the evening air, and closes the door softly behind him, leaving the old man to his ghosts and his tears.

NINETEEN

She wakes to the smell of bacon, of coffee and burnt toast. Drifts, one-eyed and dozy, down the stairs, wrapping herself in a drab grey dressing gown; only noticing her bare feet and the chipped nail polish on her toes as she pushes open the living-room door. She pauses on the threshold of the living room, about to rush back upstairs, but she hears him shout through from the kitchen. She's been spotted.

'Oh excellent, you're up. I was about to come and make

noises outside your door. How did you sleep? I got a few hours
– must be the sea air. Hope you don't mind me fiddling about
in your kitchen but I couldn't think of any other way to say
thanks for your hospitality. I could have written a sonnet, I
suppose, but I don't know enough about you yet and the only
rhyme I can find for Annabeth is 'black death' and even that's
a stretch . . .'

She regards him through screwed-up eyes, pushing her hand
through her hair. He looks fresh as the morning dew. Showered,
shaved, comb-lines in his thick, swept-back hair. He's wearing
yesterday's clothes. She wonders what he slept in. Whether he's
wearing yesterday's pants and socks. Stifles a little giggle
as she chides herself for thinking it. He grins, widely, and holds
out a mug, steam rising above the lip.

'Did I have bacon?' she asks, drowsily.

'In your freezer. Cold water then the microwave and you're
good to go. Not exactly a survival technique but a thing worth
knowing.'

She slithers into the chair at the kitchen table. Glances through
the glass. The air looks cold: a muzzling rain blowing in
from the water; great concrete blocks of cloud and a dirty blue
sky. She raises her mug. Tastes good coffee: the posh stuff she
keeps at the back of the cupboard for best; whatever as-yet-
undiscovered form 'best' may take.

'Are you always this perky in the morning?' she asks, still
muzzy with sleep. She tries to wake herself up a little. She's
never been good in the morning but has always managed to
navigate the trifling tasks on a form of auto-pilot: dozily
grunting her way through her various ablutions until the zestier
aspect of her personality wakes up at a more civilized hour.
She struggled terribly when Ethan was small, trying to be the
best kind of parent she could be: doing things the way experts
advised. She would bumble through to his crib, stumbling on
toys, leaking milk, accidentally squeezing something fleshy or
scratching something soft as she tried to scoop him up for
comfort while still in the liminal space between awake and
asleep. Eventually she gave up on doing things the way the
experts advised. Shoved him in her bed and got in the habit
of feeding him without even waking up. She has never perfected

a similar technique for handsome, effervescent houseguests who want to engage her in conversation while she is still sleepy to the point of coma.

He plonks down a plate of bacon, eggs, white toast and spaghetti hoops. She burps last night's brandy and stifles it, hiding behind the mug. She's dry-mouthed and a little queasy but the food looks inviting. He hands her a knife and fork and she tucks in, losing her inhibitions and feeling better with each forkful. She feels absurdly pleased to observe that he has a tea towel over his shoulder. Feels even happier when he starts rinsing the plates under the tap, whistling to himself as if he's on holiday somewhere sunny.

'Spaghetti hoops?' she asks, taking a breather and a swig of coffee. 'You're a maverick.'

'I have this discussion a lot,' he says, earnestly. 'So much more appropriate than beans, I reckon. Less heavy. More complementary. Fewer unintended consequences. People are wrong to think otherwise. My daughters agree with me on this. Little else, but on this we are united.'

'Did you call home?' asks Annabeth, smiling.

'Briefly. Shonagh called me "a silly goose" which means she's not really cross at me. She doesn't sound so delightfully middle-class if she really thinks I'm an idiot.'

'Was she OK about the accommodation arrangements?' she asks, making a face that implies not all partners would be on board with the set-up.

'I declined to mention that,' says Rufus, picking up his own coffee from the counter and grinning boyishly at her before taking a slurp. 'To all intents and purposes, I'm staying in a delightful bed and breakfast by the coast. Lovely landlady, can't do enough for me, and a nutritious, delicious evening meal.'

Annabeth almost chokes on her laugh, eyes watering as she makes a raucous snorting sound. Embarrassed, fighting a cough, she drains her coffee, then makes a face at her guest. 'That's where the trouble starts, mister. One lie leads to another, and the next thing you're making yourself ill trying to remember them all.'

His face changes. Softens. He watches her for a moment. 'I appreciate it, y'know. To be so open. So honest. However much is fantasy, however much reality, I feel honoured that you'd choose to share it with me. I knew you had hard miles behind you but I had no idea. I just want you to know, you're a very impressive person.'

Annabeth stops, her fork halfway to her mouth. Suddenly she can't seem to swallow. Can't seem to remember how to talk. What has she said? What hidden truth had she dug up and thrown his way in the soft warmth of apple brandy and rare company.

'Sorry,' she stammers, her voice half-strangled. 'Whatever I was wittering on about last night, I was probably half-comatose, and . . .'

'No,' he says, shaking his head. 'I mean the piece you wrote. The snippet of memoir. I hadn't expected it. It really moved me.'

Annabeth screws up her features, confused. What had he read in her folder full of random jottings: of little pen-portraits and unfinished flights of fancy?

'Oh, I'm forever scribbling, like I told you,' she says, trying to sound casual. 'Don't take any notice of that, I'll probably have been trying to come up with a character or something . . .'

'No, it was in the pile of papers that the inmates handed in for overnight assessment,' he says, looking at her as if he's going to blame this amnesia on the early start and the brandy. 'I got to it about one-ish. Made a welcome change of tone from the other submissions. That Mings chap might have a future in how-to guides. If there's a market for pamphlets preparing you for prison life, he's going to be the go-to guy. I learned a lot. Didn't know you could make a curry in a kettle until now! And a prison toastie – that's a thing worth knowing, eh . . .?'

'Rufus, sorry, am I being daft here? What memoir? I didn't hand anything to you. I was overseeing everybody else – I wouldn't have had time anyway. I don't know . . .'

Rufus looks confused. Tells her to hang on a tic and brushes past her to the living room. Brings his satchel through and leafs through his papers. Finds the page he's looking for. One piece of lined A4. Two sides. Neat blue ink. Looks aghast at the title as Rufus hands her the loose sheet. The title is underlined with a wiggly line, running past the end of the final letter. A shark fin emerges from the waves beneath a crudely drawn but clearly blazing sun. She feels her stomach clench: wires in her bones suddenly humming with an electric charge. The handwriting is not hers, but the childish underlining is as familiar to her as her own signature. She's been underscoring titles this way since she was a child. Had even done so on her coursework during her training for the prison service. Had underlined the words 'Creative Writing Opportunity' in this very way when she first pinned the notice in the library. Suddenly she can hear her own blood rushing in her head. There's a prickling all over her skin: a mad energy suddenly grabbing her. She wants to run. To tear the paper into shreds. To sweep the plates and mugs off the table and scream until her throat is raw.

'"Living a Lie",' says Rufus, gently, reading the title over her shoulder. 'No, you're not, Annabeth. You've nothing to be ashamed of . . .'

> Looking back, the journey feels as though it were all inevitable. I don't think I managed to avoid a single cliché on the road from nice, middle-class girl to streetwalker and drug addict. Yet at the time, I didn't believe myself to be on a journey that so many others had taken before me. I thought I was taking virgin steps, moving forward into new experiences, meeting new people, putting myself further and further away from home. But there was nothing new about my situation. Nothing special about me. I was one of countless girls who ran away from home because the pain was too much to stand. I knew anywhere had to be better than what I was going through there. I don't know if I was right or wrong about that. All I know is that in the first few weeks of my liberation I was cold and lonely and hungry all of the time. Money that had seemed like such a fortune when I closed the front door and walked away turned out to be a pittance on the streets. I'm not sure I ever knew where I was going. Maybe I'd read too many books. I kept expecting to drift into a narrative that would offer hope. I think I kept looking out for the scenario or situation that would turn my life into a movie. I would meet somebody kind, or find a job, or be

given an opportunity. Maybe I'd even find love. What I found was a way to numb the pain. Drink first. Then cannabis. That led me into a new circle of friends. Friends who would let me sleep on their sofa or their floor and give me a few quid here and there. Then I tried smoking brown. Found a way to transport myself to a world where I wasn't full of shame and self-loathing every second. And then nobody wanted to give it to me for free. I only had one thing to offer, and I gave it gladly. Gave it to other people too, bringing the money straight back to my dealer. I didn't know he was my pimp until somebody else called him that. And that was my normal. My life. I look back and wonder when I could have taken a different path. Even now, walking these halls, looking at the men jailed for crimes often so much less than my own, I wonder whether I will ever escape the cell inside my head.

Suddenly she is out of her seat, clutching her hand to her mouth, pushing past Rufus and running for the living-room door. She feels sick all the way through. Cold and feverish and horribly, horribly scared.

She thunders up the stairs and into the bathroom. Slams the door behind her and vomits into the toilet, emptying herself, eyes popping, half weeping as she retches over and over.

When she is done she slides to the floor. Through tear-fogged eyes, she reads the story that Griffin Cox wrote on her behalf and handed in to be assessed.

There is no doubt in her mind any more. He knows what she did.

And there will be a terrible price to pay.

PART TWO

TWENTY

Cox was the first to arrive. He's already sitting in the classroom, arms clasped demurely in his lap, as the rest of the inmates troop in. Mr Windsor, who has lately developed an irritating habit of sniffing loudly then blowing out a kind of exasperated sigh, is standing by the small window at the back of the room. He's irritated, and Cox is enjoying it. Windsor has been tasked with overseeing the class today. Miss Harris will not be coming in. A sudden sickness, apparently. Cox had looked forlorn, genuinely distressed, when Windsor broke the news. Whatever could have caused that, he'd wondered, as he fought the urge to congratulate himself.

'You back, are you, dickhead.'

'Thought you'd been moved on, nonce . . .'

'Mr Windsor, he can't be here . . . he missed yesterday, just take him back . . .'

'Where's Miss Harris, sir?'

Cox sits silently, enduring it all. He keeps the same unreadable expression on his face. Despite being the centre of attention, he finds that nobody ever really looks at him. Only Callan, the big armed robber with blood on his hands, takes the time and trouble to meet his eye and gives him a look that says, 'I know what you are, and if opportunity arises, we both know what will happen'.

Karen bustles in behind the assorted inmates, reading out names. They drop into Cox's memory bank like coins. He wants to know everything about the people he surrounds himself with. Not because he has any interest in them, but because when he escapes, they will each face unpleasantness: endless grillings conducted in the furnace glare of suspicion that they were somehow complicit. He will enjoy that thought, when what's done is done. Will allow himself to picture their discomfort as he begins whatever life waits for him beyond these walls.

'Sorry, sorry . . .'

The writer appears in the doorway, damp and breathless.
Behind him, a tall officer, saddled with the unfortunate name
of Crippen, throws him a thumbs-up and peers into the classroom through the door.

'All right, sir!'

'Crippen looking after you, sir?'

'Where's Miss Harris?'

'Shut up, Mings, Karen just fucking told you . . .'

Cox stays silent. Knows what's coming. Keeps himself
completely inscrutable as Orton slips out of his rain-speckled
jacket and scans the room. His eyes fall on Cox. Something
ripples across his features: a cat momentarily showing teeth.
Cox feels the deep, warm swell of excitement. Feels his body
loosen, his insides become liquid. She knows, he thinks. She
saw it. Read it. Devoured it. And it's made her so fucking sick
at herself that she can't even bring herself to face him. Cox
knows from experience that people are at their most vulnerable
when they feel helpless. He is the kind of man willing to offer
help to those in need, for the right price.

Orton drags his attention back to the rest of the class. 'Sorry
I'm running a bit behind. Nothing to worry about. Engrossed
in your writing, that was the problem. Let time run away with
me . . .'

Cox watches, delighted, as Orton tries to find the energy to
sparkle the way he had yesterday. He tries to decipher the cause
of the air of sullen greyness that seems to linger about him like
mist. Could Miss Harris have confided in him? Perhaps Orton
had read the whole batch of offerings and congratulated her on
having the courage to hand in something so personal. Cox likes
the idea. If so, it will have played out exactly as he hoped. He
wants Miss Harris to feel as though her whole world is shifting
on its axis: as if the bones from her past are going to climb
from the earth and crawl towards her; skeletal hands clutching
at the legs of her dark trousers; yellowed teeth in defleshed
craniums leering, obscenely; dirt and worms and dried blood
spilling down ivory jawbones.

'Mr Mings,' says Orton, finding him at the second table from
the front. 'A superb piece of writing. Not precisely a work of
fiction but I'm just pleased to see words on a page. Fascinating

reading. Lots of trivia about prison life; the relationships between inmates; that sense of fear; the way the smallest thing from outside can linger in your mind – turn to anger . . . it's a good read.'

Behind him, Suggs jerks his head up. 'What fucking relationships between inmates? Is he calling me a bender? I'm not having that, no fucking way . . .'

'Settle down, Suggs,' says Windsor, from the back of the room. He's found himself a seat and is reading a newspaper, crinkled and folded so it's the same size as a paperback. Cox presumes he's doing the crossword. Fancies that the *Daily Star*'s tea-break quickie will occupy him for the day.

'All interactions between human beings are a relationship of one sort or another,' says Orton, quickly. He glances at Cox. Gives the tiniest shake of his head. Looks around at the others. There's something harsh and accusatory in his eyes. He doesn't seem like the posh, befuddled man who addressed them yesterday. He looks, again, like the man who leaned over Griffin Cox's table, and twisted the skin on his forearm with such unforgiving force that it had taken an effort of will to keep the benign look on his face. Cox has enjoyed seeing the welt on his arm slowly darken. It is a yellow-tinged smudge of purple today: the indentations left by finger and thumb looking like the wings of a butterfly. Cox had not anticipated that the writer would respond to his rudeness with physicality. It disquiets him a little. He knows what the coming sessions will bring. Knows every step on his path to liberty. Orton may prove a nuisance, but he needs the sessions to continue in order to give him access to Miss Harris. He fancies the right course of action will present itself before long. In his pocket, he can feel the glassy smoothness of his gift for Miss Harris. He will find the right moment to present it, he's quite sure of that. He has always thought himself somewhat charmed; his present predicament notwithstanding. All of the setbacks and abuses he has endured have been learning experiences when considered through the span of his life. Were it not for the unfairness, for the inequitable distribution of merit, he would have not been a target for those stronger than he. And had they not pummelled him so mercilessly, the part of him that now controls his every thought and deed may have lain dormant forever. And had he not allowed that ferocious beast out to feed upon that which it craved, he would never have discovered just what pleasures were there to be consumed. He is grateful for his beatings. They have made him the man he is.

'Away with the fairies, Cox?'

He looks up at the sound of his name. Orton is addressing him. He's smiling, but it falls well short of sincerity.

'Sorry, sir. As you say. Thinking upon other things.'

'I was congratulating you on your own piece of writing. An impressive feat – to transport yourself into the mind of another character – to look out through their eyes, to feel their pain as your own. I must congratulate you.'

Cox purses his lips, endeavouring to look bemused. 'You'll forgive me, but I believe you have me at a disadvantage. My own work? I haven't yet had opportunity to deliver you anything. I was called away to a legal appointment yesterday, and . . .'

'Bollocks you were,' spits Suggs. 'Don't be giving it that shit. We all know where you were, you nonce. My mate Rich was on his way back from an adjudication when he saw Laurel and fucking Hardy with the wing governor heading to the interview rooms and you'd just been dropped there, so fuck off if you think it isn't all over the wing about what they've got on you. They're looking for that poor lass's body! How many you got on you, eh? How many you put in the ground?'

The escalation is volcanic. One moment Suggs is at his desk, arms crossed, spitting phlegm-tinged invective into the grey air of the classroom, and then he is lunging across the table, hands outstretched, trying to get his fingers around Cox's throat.

Orton reacts before the prison officer. Lurches forward as Suggs pushes the tables out of his way, scattering other inmates, and leaps towards Cox like a basketball player aiming to slam-dunk. Orton grabs him around the waist, taking the momentum out of the dive, and the pair of them clatter into the nearest table in a tangle of arms and legs, paper and pens. Windsor pushes past the men in front of him, baton extended, but the explosion of violence has turned the classroom into a cage full of animals and suddenly men are taking the opportunity to settle grudges, to release their tensions, and in a moment Mr Windsor is on his back, boots thudding into his ribs.

Cox slips from his chair, boots already hammering down the corridor, shouts of 'code red, code red' bouncing off the walls. He glances at Orton, trying to hold Suggs flat to the floor as he squirms beneath him. Sees Callan step forward and press a big firm hand into Suggs's face, picking a side, making it plain to the screws who barrel through the door that he has had no part of the melee . . .

Cox slips, unnoticed, behind the desk at the front of the classroom. Slips the object from his pocket and tucks it deep into the folds of Orton's satchel. His fingers touch something long and sharp. Tests the tip with his finger and could almost laugh with delight at the sheer ecstasy of the discovery.

He stands. Sees the officers grappling with Suggs; sees the two spiced-up drug dealers who have been booting Mr Windsor in the guts. Sees Orton, anger on his face, pulling himself upright; two inmates checking on his welfare and saying they had nothing to do with this. Nothing. Nothing . . .

Nobody is looking at Cox. Nobody sees him take the pencil, turn the tip towards himself, and delicately probe at the soft flesh beside his armpit for the space where he is guaranteed to cause himself no real harm. He steels himself. Grits his teeth. Pushes the point through his skin as if sliding pieces of uncooked chicken onto a skewer.

It takes a huge effort not to cry out. He feels light-headed at once. It is as if he can feel himself turning grey.

It only takes a moment for one of the officers to notice.

'Cox. Cox is bleeding. He's bleeding!'

And Cox, theatrically, gratefully, slips to the floor.

'He's been stabbed! Code Red. Code Fucking Red!'

TWENTY-ONE

Neilsen didn't sleep much last night. After he left Bob Roberts, he walked around for a while, meandering aimlessly around the half dozen streets that led off from the marketplace like fingers from a palm. He sat for a while on the wall by the churchyard, staring at the gates of the grammar school where Bronwen had been a pupil. Sat there until it was too cold and dark to tolerate. Then he drove home; the static in his head louder than the music on the radio. He did an extra workout when he got home: pushing himself so hard that he'd ended up in a foetal position on the floor, every muscle cramping, every pore oozing sweat. Freshly show-ered, newly shaved, he'd sat up most of the night, his bare skin sticking to the leather of his designer sofa, flicking through TV channels in search of something, anything, to divert his atten-tion. In the end he'd texted an old flame, engaging in a steamy half hour of suggestive repartee, before finally dropping off into a sleep filled with visions of sinkholes and headless birds.

It's a little after lunch, and he's parked his VW Golf in the car park of the pub by the Humber Bridge. It's one of his favourite places to be alone. There are always a few vehicles spread out along the pitted tarmac: each containing a solitary individual clothed in their own existential misery. It's a place where people in search of answers can go and stare at the choppy brown water and wonder if they have the strength to climb up through the woods and take a swan-dive into the water, or whether they should just suck it up, hope for the best and continue buying lottery tickets.

Neilsen has been coming here more and more since his father died. Things that hadn't troubled him before are weighing on his mind. He's beginning to question his decisions. What was it Roberts had said? That he could do more good – do something more useful – if he wasn't a police officer? That had stung. It stings more the more he thinks upon it. He knows where such thoughts can lead and has always done his best to fight them, but he suddenly finds himself wondering whether he may have held himself to the wrong set of principles all of his life. Would he not be a better man, he asks himself? Would he not be of more use, more benefit, if he just grabbed Griffin Cox and shook him until the answers fell out? He knows that he will not allow himself to do such a thing, but it does feel unspeak-ably silly not to. He and countless other detectives are running around chasing hair fibres and skin cells and trying to trace thirty-year-old phone calls, and the man who could tell them everything is in a prison cell, smiling benignly at his occasional visitors and enjoying himself on a creative writing course! He can't help but think it would all be so much easier if he could just be allowed to bend Cox's fingers in the wrong direction and see who has the greater resolve.

He looks down at the sheaf of documents in his lap. They're print-outs of items held in the evidence store, and they're no bloody use whatsoever. He lifts the top sheet and angles it. It's exactly as Bob had said: a Victorian, wrought-iron birdcage with fancy filigree and a glossy wooden handle. The only finger-prints are those of Bronwen and her mum and dad. It's been independently assessed by an auctioneer, who identified it as a relatively mass-market product from the 1930s, selling for upwards of £300 as of 1998. Neilsen can understand why Cox is a beguiling suspect. He's wealthy. He's a collector of fine objets d'art. Even in prison he takes pleasure in the merest whiff of the sophisticated; the sublime. He is the kind of man who could woo a young, naïve girl with poetry and antique books. He's the sort of man who might send a nightingale in a cage: a sweet-sounding emblem, urging her to set herself free.

He scowls. Glances at the book on the passenger seat. *RedGreen* by Rufus Orton. He's read the first few pages and reckons that Orton is a good writer, who could probably do with thinking up a more exciting story with which to employ his formidable vocabulary. It's well written, and he likes the feeling of splashing about in a well-drawn world, but by Christ it's boring. He feels a momentary pang of jealousy as he flicks to the back of the book and looks at the black-and-white mugshot: staring into the eyes of a rumpled, once-handsome man, with dark eyes and the sort of floppy hair that he associates with cricket and Last Night of the Proms. He wonders, idly, whether Orton might be worth a little chat. Indulges himself in a daydream in which Cox, adrift in a warm sea of creative impulse, admits to his crimes through the medium of a short story. Considers having a chat with him and telling him about the kind of man he's teaching how to better realize his fantasies, albeit within the relative safety of a notebook. Could he perhaps steer the class in a certain direction? What was the name of the woman who'd organized the course? Annabeth, wasn't it?

Maybe he could get her on board. He'd have to get his thoughts in order – couldn't risk letting himself getting muddled. He realizes, with a sudden dizzying thump, that he has lost sight of himself. Doesn't know how to be a police officer when nobody knows what's right and what's wrong, and every crime comes with a sackful of explanations and excuses.

Neilsen switches on the radio, pissed off with himself. He doesn't know if he sees something of significance, or is making one up. He didn't like Cox, he knows that much. As he told Bob Roberts, there was something about him that made him feel unsettled: as if the air pressure had dropped and the atmosphere was crackling with impending rain.

Agitated, Neilsen flicks through the sheaf of papers, hoping to spot something that matters. He comes to a halt on a print-out of a photograph. Makes a mental note to enquire why the NCA can afford to use coloured printer ink when he and the rest of the CID team at Humberside Police can't request a new pencil without proving evidence that the last one has been worn down to less than an inch.

He looks at the grand frontage of Caldwell Hall – the image taken some time in the early 1970s, judging from the style and haircuts of the people in the foreground. It's an imposing red-brick structure, built in the early 1800s for a rich family from Leicestershire and set in some fifteen acres of grounds. Neilsen skims the details, printed off from a website run by the Society for the Preservation of Ancient Buildings and Monuments. It details 150 years of the house's history, but Neilsen will admit to not giving a damn about any of that. He starts to read from the section headlined June, 1963.

> . . . at which point the Hall passed to Arbuthnot Cox's only surviving daughter, Procne Henshaw-Cox. She had been living in Italy at the time of her father's death, but returned home to begin the lavish restoration of the house, which had fallen into some disrepair. True to her vision, Caldwell Hall was developed in keeping with her fascination for Italian Romanticism and Renaissance, when Classic art and literature was elevated to the status of the sublime. Chief among her achievements was the complete

transformation of the overgrown gardens and lake. Over the course of the next ten years, the overgrown gardens at the rear of the property were radically reshaped in the image of Verona's Giardino Giusti. As with the original, visitors can still see many items that were in vogue in sixteenth-century gardens: pots with citrus plants, statues of mythological figures, fountains, lemon houses, grottoes, grotesque masks. The lower garden is divided according to the *giardino all'italiana* style, into nine square sections, each symmetrical green room formed of box hedges and dominated by statues of Diana, Venus, Atalanta, Apollo and Adonis. The garden's main axis is formed of the cypress alley leading to the grotto and the mask, with the labyrinth on the right, while on the left is a French-style parterre, the citrus garden and the so-called *vaseria* where plants in their pots are overwintered. This part of the garden, with its rigidly geometric design and straight lines speaks to us of man's intervention, of order and symmetry. In contrast, the wooded part of the garden is deliberately conceived in order to astonish the visitor as he climbs its steep and shady paths. The rocky precipice, the grotto, the play of light and shade and perspectives are all created artificially to elicit feelings of admiration, awe and wonder in the viewer. A secret staircase concealed in the little turret dug into the rock face leads up to the highest point of the garden . . .

Neilsen stops reading. He knows he's out of his depth. He wonders who he might know who would be able to translate it all into something relevant. His sergeant, the cleverest man he knows, is up in his native Scotland with his family, and he can't think of anybody else who reads for pleasure.

He glances again at the book on the seat. Thinks again of Rufus Orton. Glowers through the windscreen before letting his eyes fall back upon the folder. He turns to the next page, and looks upon Procne Henshaw-Cox. She's dark-haired and dark-eyed, and there is an energy about her that comes off the page in waves. She has the most mesmerizing eyes he has ever looked into, even when pixilated and printed on plain paper. She's

wrapped in a length of shimmering golden silk: a crown of
berries, flowers and thorns twisted into her hair. At her breast,
a fat pink child, glorious white angel wings upon his back, held
in place by lengths of twine. He has one pudgy fist gripping
the strings of a small wooden harp. Behind her, sitting on the
bonnet of a yellow sports car, a tall man with red hair and an
Easy Rider moustache. He doesn't seem to notice that he's in
the photograph: stares off into the distance – coloured lenses
flipped up atop the frame of his spectacles.

Neilsen shakes his head. He will make no allowances for
Cox based upon the peculiarities of his upbringing, but he cannot
help but feel a surge of compassion for the boy. Everything he
has read or viewed about Cox's childhood suggests his mother
saw him as a prop in whatever fantasy she was acting out.

Remembering something of note, Neilsen flicks back to a
transcript of one of the first interviews with Cox, conducted
shortly after he was locked up for the abduction of the teenager
in York, and around the time he started coming to the attention
of various other investigative teams looking into historic disappearances. Neilsen finds the section he's looking for. Most of
the time, Cox answered the detectives with a polite obstinacy.
He'd love to help, but couldn't. Didn't know why they thought
he was guilty of such terrible acts; wished he could help but
had no recollection of ever meeting the individual whose tragic
disappearance pains him.

When they asked him about his childhood, he became more
animated. Spoke, fulsomely, about the joy of his earliest
recollections.

'. . . we make them well, the English. Eccentrics, I mean.
And yes, that would be a fine description of Mother, although
I was encouraged not to call her by such an outdated title. She
was Procne. Are you familiar with the story? Forgive me if I
suppose you aren't scholars. Daughter of King Pandion of
Athens, as I'm sure you will know. A woman of rigid principle.
Served her husband his own son for dinner when she learned
of his misdeeds against her sister. Quite a name with which to
saddle a child, but her own father was a trifle touched by the
old family curse. Always a little trace of madness in the family
line, I'm sure you'll have identified that. Procne was treated in

several sanatoriums in her childhood but only found the peace she craved when she came home and inherited the Hall. I like to think that motherhood also assisted in her finding some form of equilibrium. She took such pleasure in the sublime, detectives. Such true ecstasy in the radiance of the Classical era. She would weep – truly gush with tears – upon reading a solitary passage of Petronius or Sulpicia. She surrounded herself by beautiful things. She wanted to be graced by angels. It was a Paradise: a portal – a doorway to a different age, a better age. I was raised like a noblewoman's child; the progeny of an emperor or a Caesar. I believed there was the blood of the ancient gods in my veins and the passers-by and pilgrims who took up residence with us did nothing to tell me of the well-intentioned lie that had been woven around me. Reality hit hard when it came. But Procne, for all her eccentricities, created a better world for me to grow up in. I was nurtured in a time of wisdom, philosophy and elevated thinking, detectives. Whereas you were raised in Scunthorpe. Tell me, whose mother was negligent?'

Neilsen closes the folder. He has to admit, he has a point.

On the radio, Amanda from the BBC is telling her listeners that police are continuing to dig at an abandoned farm near Humberside Airport. A spokesman for the press office can neither confirm nor deny that the dig is in connection with missing schoolgirl Bronwen Roberts, last seen more than twenty years ago . . .

He's saved from giving it any more consideration by the sudden trilling of his phone. Answers with a forced jolliness, so that DC Andy Daniells doesn't feel mistreated.

'Andy, how's it going? I was wondering, do you think—'

'HMP Holderness,' says Daniells, breathlessly. 'There's been a stabbing.'

Neilsen glares out at the water. 'Cox?'

Daniells huffs a dry laugh down the line. 'There's blood on the ceiling, Ben. And some author's got himself caught right in the middle of it all.'

Neilsen looks at the book in his lap. Locks eyes with the photograph. Chews his cheek, and wonders. 'I'll meet you there.'

TWENTY-TWO

Annabeth is curled up on the sofa. Her phone is going crazy. Ringing. Pinging. Bleeping and *dingly-fucking-bingling* and generally doing all it can to get itself smashed to bits with a brick. One message. Two. Now a call. Another. Vibration after vibration . . .

She pulls the blankets over her head. She feels weak. Giddy. Sick. She can't face it. Whatever has happened since she phoned in this morning to say she wouldn't be coming in, and made her weak protestations to Rufus that he should just go, just leave her there, behind the bathroom door . . . whatever has happened since, she doesn't care.

She can only fool herself so long. She wriggles, hotly, damply, out from under the folds of the quilt. Locates her phone.

Urgent messages from Mark, her supervising officer. He doesn't care if she's bleeding from her eyes, she needs to get to work pronto. Her 'writing course' has turned to shit. Griffin Cox has been stabbed. Her writer friend has got caught up in a fistfight with an inmate. Mr Windsor has three cracked ribs and is missing two teeth. He needs her to come in, to get her story straight . . .

Beads of cold sweat stand out on her exposed skin. Icy water trickles down her back. She half chokes on a sob, and then she hears the bang-bang-bang on her door. Suddenly a child again, she wants to hide beneath the bedclothes. Wants things to go back to how they once were. Wishes it so badly it becomes a prayer.

'Annabeth. It's me. You have to let me in . . .'

Gasping for breath, half drunk on fear, she makes her way to the door and cautiously pulls it open.

Rufus is standing on her doorstep. There's a bruise on his cheek. His hair is sticking up wildly. And he's holding out his hand. Holding it up, like a waiter with a tray.

On his palm, cool and glassy and unmistakable, the object thrust into the folds of Rufus's satchel.

A little strangled gasp in Annabeth's throat as she realizes what she is seeing.

A snow globe.

At its centre, amid the glitter and snow, two figures. They are hand-carved. Beautiful, in their way. One is a fat man, on his knees. The other, a woman; perhaps still a girl. She is reaching up, something sharp in her tiny pink hand.

Rufus closes his fist around the glass. Shakes the bauble with a faint hiss of apology.

Opens his palm.

The snow inside the glass falls red.

TWENTY-THREE

She leans over him, her blue, latex-clad fingers probing the yellowing edge of the wound. Makes a little clucking noise. Pushes, firmly, against the puckered skin, held together by a lattice of stitches and gauze. Her hair, dark and wiry, tickles his bare chest. He gets a faint whiff of her. She smells old. Doughy. Near her mouth there's a lingering trace of last night's wine and the spicy red-pepper and hummus wrap that she had for lunch.

It takes Griffin Cox all of his considerable willpower not to retch.

'Hmm, not bad . . . some minor signs of infection . . . odd bruising pattern . . . unusual to see just one injury here – I believe the modern criminal favours a "typewriter" approach, multiple penetrations, not the one, deliberate . . . hmmm . . .'

Cox ignores her. Makes a great demonstration of biting his lip and holding back his whimpers. He can take the pain of the inspection, but it is his proximity to somebody whose very DNA seems past its sell-by date that creeps beneath his skin. He feels as though his personal space is being penetrated by somebody with the potential to drag him closer to the grave. He feels the same way about mature adult women as most people do about newborn children – albeit in reverse. Some sniff the crown of

a baby and feel enervated, regenerated: suffused with the fountain of youth. Cox sees mature skin as corrupt: decrepit; putrid.
Each breath in robs him of his virility. He lets out a low moan:
pitiful, weak. Is gratified to see her take a gentler approach to
his precious flesh. He doesn't want this monstrosity, this old,
wrinkled thing, poking at him as if he were a body on a slab.
Doesn't want to look into her brown eyes, or see the places
upon her chin and upper lip where she has failed to pluck errant
hairs; or to see the pores across her nose. He finds her repulsive.
Finds them all repulsive, truth be told; fears being infected by
their ugly, wrinkled decrepitude. She is the same age as Griffin
Cox, but around thirty-five years past her sell-by date as a figure
of desire.

'You were lucky,' says Dr Lechmere, straightening up. 'A
couple of inches to the right, and you're looking at a broken
heart.'

Cox makes an effort. Smiles, thinly, as if it is sapping the
last of his strength. He makes a show of reaching down to find
his pyjama top, fumbling feebly around in the blue-and-white
bedsheets to locate the hem of his cotton shirt.

Dr Lechmere turns and addresses the two men behind her.
Wing Governor Laiquet Hussain is a decent, quietly efficient
chap from the Midlands whose broad Birmingham accent
disarms those inmates who expect his skin tone to directly
impact on his personality. Dark hair, dark eyes, thick black
beard, he would be a Home Office pin-up for diversity if he
could stand the incumbent government and if he hadn't made
a name for himself publicly criticizing the underfunding that
has left his prison dangerously underfunded and understaffed.
Behind him hovers Inmate Wellness Liaison Simone Greaves.
She's all affectation. Perm, headband, glasses, anorak, trainers,
stripy jumper and leggings that look as if they have been lined
with moussaka. She is a representative of the outside oversight
agency tasked with making sure no prisoner slips in the shower
or tumbles down the stairs more than once per sentence. Cox
finds it faintly absurd that the phrase 'do-gooder' has any kind
of negative connotation, but he cannot think of Ms Greaves as
anything other than a 'bleeding heart': arse-clenchingly saccharine
and systemically pious. She has a way of putting her head on

one side and asking questions in a soft, understanding voice that makes him want to slice her open and pull out whatever he sees first. He saw a picture of her once, front page of the *Hull Mail*, trying to block plans for a new incinerator. She had waged war on those who planned to damage the next generation's precious lungs. To Cox, she'd have emphasized her points more emphatically if the image hadn't shown her three quarters of her way down a Marlboro Red.

'They did a decent job,' says Dr Lechmere, referring to the emergency team who had looked after Cox as he lay on the classroom floor, and then sped him to A&E at Hull Royal Infirmary, where his wound was cleaned, stitched, and where he suffered the indignity of antibiotic shots to his rump. He was there under five hours. He's back at the prison now, looking feeble and weak on the slightly comfier mattress he has been furnished with for his brief stay on the medical wing. He's rather enjoying it. He has his own room, which is not a particular novelty, but it's cool, and quiet, and he's allowed to feel briefly like a victim, which is a rarity.

'Hear that, Griffin?' asks Mr Hussain, jovially. 'Survived, eh? Not quite fit as a fiddle but certainly not far off. I told you we'd see you well looked after . . .'

Beside him, Ms Greaves bristles. Her nostrils take on a double-barrelled-shotgun appearance. 'I think it's somewhat too early to make those kind of assessments, Mr Hussain,' she says, primly.

'Of course, Ms Greaves,' says Mr Hussain, with Herculean forbearance. Cox knows he's had a difficult day. Aims to wring the juice out of it in his own inimitable fashion.

'You'll be able to tell us what happened soon enough, no doubt,' says Hussain, with forced joviality. 'Of course, we're rather struggling to pin down precisely how the injury occurred, but once you're well enough . . .'

Cox makes sure his voice sounds sufficiently gruff and weedy: feels like somebody securing themselves a sick-day with a dose of feigned flu. 'Miss Harris,' he says, dry-mouthed and pained.

'Sorry, Griffin, that was just beyond me,' says Ms Greaves, who adopts the general air of somebody telling a dying loved one they are in their prayers. 'Miss Harris, you say . . .'

'Only one I trust,' he says, feebly. 'I don't feel safe talking to anybody. They all want to hurt me, I know that, but all I wanted to do was use my time properly . . . just try to write, to learn a new skill . . .'

'Steady now, Mr Cox,' says the governor, looking down at him and making every effort to seem concerned about his well-being. Cox has to fight the urge to throw him a wink and a cheeky smile. For now, Cox is a victim of attempted murder. It happened in the education suite, under the eye of one of his junior members of staff: himself currently in intensive care. There are rumours spreading through the prison like mist. Already three different officers have told him stories being spread among the inmates. Suggs claimed responsibility, at first, but backtracked when he learned how many years it would add to his sentence. Mings claimed to have seen Mr Windsor stab some form of sharpened screwdriver right into Cox's chest. Another, high on spice, claimed that Mr Orton had lost his patience with him and attacked him in front of everybody. HMP Holderness already has a reputation as an institution from another age. For now, Mr Hussain needs Cox to think of him as an ally, and that means swallowing his bile and pretending they are something akin to equals.

'Miss Harris,' croaks Cox, again. 'I'll talk to her. Please. She understands. I'll talk to her. My solicitor, if not. Has word reached him? Has he called . . .?'

'Don't you be worrying about things like that, Griffin,' says Simone. She manoeuvres herself past the silent bulk of Dr Lechmere and makes a show of filling up Cox's plastic beaker and placing it near the bed. 'If you decide to take this further, we will be on hand to make sure you are treated equitably . . .'

'You pronounce it in the French style,' says Cox, doxy and sore. 'There aren't many here who even understand what it means—'

'Miss Harris,' says Mr Hussain, cutting him off. 'Of course, Griffin – I shall arrange for her to come and visit you as soon as her next shift begins.' He turns to Simone. 'One of our brightest and best,' he confides, all smiles. 'Lucky to get her. Bringing lots of new ideas to Holderness. Rising star. A very understanding, fair officer. I have no doubt that had she been in this morning this whole unpleasantness could have been avoided . . .'

Simone Greaves gives a 'hurrumph' at that. Pulls a notebook from the pocket of her anorak. Makes a note, and jots down the time. Gives her attention back to Cox. 'We will be monitoring this situation. Anything you need, you have every right to contact my organization. Do not believe yourself to be anything other than a victim.'

'Thank you,' he growls, meekly. Starts to cough, and holds it back, out of politeness.

'Get your rest,' says Mr Hussain, and hustles the unwelcome visitors out of the small, cool room.

Alone again, Cox grins. Everything hinges on getting some alone time with Miss Harris. He had not known that Suggs would go for him, or that the writer would come to his aid. But he's known for weeks that he would have to endure an injury – a bad one – if he were to move his plan to the next significant step. He wonders how she reacted when she saw the snow globe. Wonders what she is feeling, here and now. Whether the bosses are pampering her, protecting her, hitching their wagon to a rising star. Or will they scapegoat her? Will they weave a mandala of interlinking lies and find a way to paint her as the rookie who vacated her post and allowed an infamous, suspected serial killer, suffer a near-fatal stab wound to the heart? He presumes the latter. He has been in prison long enough to have identified how things work.

He lays back on the cool pillow, ignoring the trifling throb in his chest. For the first time in forever, he can feel the cool, salt-flecked air of the Adriatic upon his face. Can summon up the taste of full-bodied wine and fillet steak: seared lightly on both sides and bloodily pink within. Can allow himself to imagine the sensation of warm, taut flesh against his own. He has fought the impulse to daydream; to fantasize, for fear of causing himself unnecessary agony should any of his steps towards freedom trip at an unforeseen hurdle. Now, he indulges. Permits himself a brief erotic projection. He has many miles to go before he rests, but he knows himself to possess the stamina for the journey.

Griffin Cox slips one hand behind his head. Slips the other down his pyjama trousers.

Pictures the deeds in which he will revel once the indignity of prison is behind him.

Closes his eyes, and thinks upon Miss Harris.

Thinks upon her son. *Ethan.*

Bites down so hard on his tongue that his mouth fills with blood.

God how he hopes it is a taste of things to come.

TWENTY-FOUR

'Keeping busy,' grunts Annabeth, lifting a vase from the mantelpiece and rubbing the varnished wood beneath with a yellow cloth. 'Getting stuff done . . .' she mutters, banging the thick crystal back down again like a gavel. 'Not thinking, that's the thing of it . . .'

On the arm of the sofa, Rufus Orton: a nobleman on a wooden horse, sitting for a portrait. Still as a statue, immortalized with a silly sad smile on his face. He looks as though he is waiting permission to leave.

'I mean, what does it look like . . . not going in . . . Ethan's home late, just getting on with the chores . . . daft bloody question for a man of letters . . .'

'But, is that what you need to be doing right at this moment?' he asks, tentatively, his words a pair of metal pincers tracing the line of a live wire.

'I don't know, Rufus,' says Annabeth, picking up a pile of magazines from beside the chair and shuffling them. *True Crime*; *Real Crime*; *Crime Monthly*: a blur of lurid colours. 'I don't have all the answers. I don't know what to tell you. And you're not taking any notice of what I say. So, I'm getting on with stuff. I've the car insurance to renew. I need to get the deposit together for Ethan's France trip. I've got to do a mixed wash. You're welcome to sit there and watch me do all these things, but I can't imagine it's much of a show . . .'

She's manic in her actions. There's sweat dripping off her forehead. Heat comes off her in waves, despite the chill in the room. She turns to Rufus as she talks and notices the hazy yellow light from the window illuminating the dust motes that hang in the air. She flares her nostrils, angry with the whole damn room. Starts swatting at the air, hands turned in: trying to scoop handfuls of dirt from the air.

'Are you practising swimming?' asks Rufus, cautiously. 'Seriously, can I get you some water? Do you need a sit down? A hug?'

She spins on her heel, eyes hard, teeth bared. 'Are you this hopeless at home? Christ, get me a drink if you want! Hug me if you want to take the risk. You weren't this bloody shy and retiring when you were raiding my cupboards for breakfast!'

Rufus opens his mouth to reply, then stops himself. Lowers his head. Picks something off the front of his cords. Nods, as if making a decision. Stands up and approaches her, arms outstretched, making his features soft. He looks vaguely imbecilic, as if he's trying out gestures he's only seen performed on the amateur dramatic scene. 'It's OK, Annabeth. You don't need to make me understand. I'm your friend. I care about you. Don't tell me, it's fine, but let me help you. Comfort you . . .'

'Fuck off,' she says, nastily, and it feels so good to say that she does it again. It fills her with something other than the creeping chill of panic: lights a fire in her. She sees herself: vest and jeans, sweaty and barefoot, slamming things around in her living room and bellowing obscenities at her favourite author. Likes what she sees. Suddenly likes being Annabeth.

'I'm in this too,' says Rufus, stopping in front of her. 'It's unnerving to watch, Annabeth. Disquieting, even . . .'

'Disquieting! Who says these things, Rufus? Who tells somebody they're feeling disquieted?'

Rufus considers it: angling his head as if draining water from his ear. 'Writers, Annabeth. People who can articulate themselves without smashing stuff.'

She glares at him, sick to her gut. Assesses him with eyes that seem to penetrate all the way through to the marrow in his bones. He's taller than she is and as her eyes travel upwards she notices all the imperfections. Sees the frayed collar, rubbed raw by the stubble on his neck. Sees the line of fat below his chin. The space by his ear where an errant hair curls out like a question mark. There is something in the flaws that she finds improbably endearing. She has spent months imagining him to be pristine and cognitively immense: that his every phrase and gesture would be the work of a dazzling mind. Up close, he's an ordinary man. He's baffled and scared and he doesn't know what's going on. For the first time, she wonders if this might at last be a safe place to deposit her secrets. His books have made it clear: his views on right and wrong, good and evil, crime and punishments, are far from fixed.

She raises her hand to her head. Wipes the sweat with her bare hand. Rubs at her arms. She feels all twisted up and directionless. Looks down at a sudden pressure on her arm and feels his warm, dry hand at her elbow. She flicks her head up. He's smiling, softly.

'Don't,' she says, and just saying the word causes her to fear a loss of control. Her eyes are hot: there's a stone in her throat. She can feel her lip quivering: a candle-flame near an open door. 'Don't touch me, I'm all sweaty, I must feel disgusting.' She stops, her nose running. Gives a silly smile, feeling the fury dissipate to be replaced by an overwhelming urge to be looked after. She wants to lay down. To have a blanket pulled up to her chin. To have her hair stroked until she forgets about Griffin Cox's gift. And yet she fights it. She despises this sudden weakness: this obscene need to be coddled like an infant. Would rather stamp and thrash and gnash her teeth than see herself mollified like some hysteric.

'Just sit down,' he says, gently, and steers her to the sofa. She hears footsteps, and then he is back with a glass of water. He presses the glass to her forehead, rolling it back and forth in the chilled sweat on her brow. Lowers himself until he is looking up at her, proffering the glass, insisting she take a sip, and another.

She's exhausted, suddenly. Her thoughts swirl like ash and ripped paper. She cannot get a hold of herself. There's a sudden ringing sound in her ears: high and obnoxious, like an electric charge being passed through wire. Her teeth hurt: her fillings seeming to leak a greasy, metallic taste into her mouth. It feels as though the temperature in the room is dropping through the floor. She can feel lightning in the air. Can feel the soft hairs on the nape of her neck begin to rise.

'Whatever it is you need me to say or do, I'll do,' says Rufus, softly, and it is hard to hear him over the low, thrumming pressure beating in her head. She tries to see past him: to see if the sky beyond the glass has turned purple. Thinks of Ethan, walking home. Can taste the nearness of rain.

'Not now,' she whispers. 'Tell them I'm not well. I can't . . .'

Rufus takes the glass and places it on the floor. Helps manoeuvre her into a comfortable position, as she slides into a foetal curl. She feels him stroke the wisps of hair from her face. Hears his knees creak as he stands and returns the glass to the kitchen. She feels drunk. Feels absolutely hammered, truth be told. Has done since he showed her the snow globe and her thoughts filled with Walter.

'He knows something about me,' she mutters, into the fabric of the sofa. 'It's a message.'

'Then you report it,' says Rufus, kindly. 'Tell your boss you've been threatened.'

'Then he'll tell,' says Annabeth, simply. 'He'll tell what he knows. And then I'm, not just out of work, I'm finished.'

Rufus doesn't reply. She keeps her eyes shut, drifting as if hanging on to a branch in a choppy sea. Part of her wants to shut down. Shut up. But God how she wants to tell him the truth: to finally unburden herself of the weight that she carries like so many twists of iron.

She shifts position. Opens one eye. Through the mist, she sees him. He's got his back to her, staring out of the window. She becomes aware of the drumming of raindrops: millions of hard droplets striking the glass. Feels the temperature drop some more. Sees him place his big hands on the windowsill, knuckles down. Can see him thinking.

'Don't tell me,' he says, turning slowly. 'I don't need to know. But he put this in my bag. He wound Suggs up until he went for him. I never saw anybody go near Cox, so whatever injury he sustained, it could only have been self-inflicted. Your Mr Windsor was neither use nor ornament but those injuries were bad. I don't know enough about the prison system to say whether this is all normal but it's not going to look good for the governor and staff, is it? A call to the papers . . . even a piece in the local rag will be enough to get the libertarians talking about prison brutality. And I say that as a bloody libertarian. But it feels like he's manipulated this. Didn't you say he shouldn't even have been there? On the course, I mean? And the creative writing – the one that made out it was by you. Christ, if he's doing all this just to get close to you . . .'

He stops talking. The room fills with the sound of raindrops: hoofbeats on metal. Annabeth stares past him, to where the snow globe sits, like a trophy, atop the little bookshelf. She swallows, painfully. She can feel Rufus's unasked questions darting about and around her: kite-ribbons slashing and cutting at her exposed skin.

She knows she has to get herself together. She's ignored all the phone calls. Switched off her phone. Doesn't want to be party to the inevitable. She has no doubt he will insist upon speaking to her. Has no doubt what he wants.

'Annabeth, how can I help you?' he asks, crouching down beside her. 'I can stay. I don't need to go back home, there's no bugger interested if I'm there or not. Tell me what I can do . . .'

Annabeth looks up at him. Sees the gun-dog earnestness in his features: the sad solemnity in his eyes.

She manages a smile, before she turns away from him, and curls into a ball.

Then, into the covers, she mutters one-word, barely heard, 'Leverage.'

TWENTY-FIVE

All in all, Rufus Orton is rather enjoying his little sojourn in East Yorkshire. It's been quite exciting. He doesn't know what he expected, but it wasn't this. Not sex criminals and classroom brawls, fistfights, beatings and coded messages. He's heard it said that it's never dull in Hull. He feels inclined to agree.

He's taken up a sentry position in the armchair, fingers drumming idly on the armrests. He hasn't helped himself to a whisky as he thinks there's still a slim chance that the next few hours will take him home, but he's experiencing the twitching thirst of a seasoned drinker who hopes the first sip of the day isn't far off. He shuffles his thoughts. Sucks his teeth. Stares through the window at the darkening sky and watches the rain. It's slowed down a little but there's still a menace to the air and the big front window is almost opaque with smeared raindrops.

On the sofa, Annabeth has been snoring, softly, for the best part of the last two hours. He pottered around for a while, making tea, opening cupboards, drying a few dishes on the drainer. He felt the soil in the pot plants and gave them a drink. Opened a few drawers in the kitchen. Admired the neatness. Papers held together with different coloured paper clips: bills, mostly, together with insurance documents, driving licence and the paperwork for her car. He cannot help but compare the order with his own haphazard kitchen. From the outside, he and Shonagh have the kind of home that those with a love of the countryside aspire to retiring to. It's a little tumbledown, but with plenty of character and a lintel above the door declaring it to have been built in 1729. He often hears the admiring superlatives gushed out by the ramblers who potter down through the woods that lead into the overgrown orchard by the back lane. When they find out it's home to a writer they positively explode with delight, as if having stumbled into a portal to a bygone age, when the tortured genius could scribble his prose by candlelight while downing claret and gnawing, menacingly, on the rind of a mutton chop. Rufus enjoys their imaginings – they fit neatly with the way he hopes to be viewed by literary historians of the future. But his reality is very different. Inside, the house looks to have been recently burgled. The table in the big farmhouse kitchen is positively groaning beneath the weight of unpaid bills and enforcement notices. There are too many empty bottles to fit in the recycling and he hasn't the heart to cancel his morning delivery of the *Guardian*, which are now stacked in great mouldy piles wherever he can find a space between the unwashed pots and the sticky, gleaming green glass. The flagged floor is mouse-droppings and cat-piss. Dried flowers hang from the eaves and beams, thick with cobwebs and studded with dead insects. His rocking chair – a salvaged maternity chair recovered from a jumble sale – is the only space unencumbered by any kind of grime, though there is a perfect arse-shape in the fabric that bears witness to the hours he spends there, laptop or paperback on his knee, writing, reading, watching porn or pretending to watch a documentary while working his way through old episodes of QI. He finds the neatness of Annabeth's little semi-detached almost erotically beguiling. Feels a certain something for Annabeth, too. She's certainly no beauty, but she has a face that would be handsome if not for the sternness about the mouth or the dark beneath the eyes. His wife, Shonagh, is without doubt the more classically beautiful, but it counts for nought when she is looking at him the same way other people may examine a slug making its way through their salad. They're almost separated. Not quite. Not officially. There's the girls to consider and they have to work out how to divide up the debts, but he spends most of his life in the kitchen while she is up and down the country bidding for work or delivering fabric samples – taking advantage of the credit card to stay in whichever three-star hotel allows her not to have to come home. The girls stay with friends more often than not: coming home now and again for a change of clothes. When they are home they ignore him. He doesn't take it personally. He remembers being a teenager. Adults are the enemy. Parents are uniformly sad, pathetic failures: killjoys and jailers. It doesn't matter that he allows them to do what they want. Doesn't matter that until they turned twelve they thought he was the coolest dad on the planet. Now, he's a sad bastard. Now, he's the guy who runs out of the house in yesterday's clothes to slash the tyres of whichever bailiff has just turned up to impound his car.

He rolls his shoulders. Feels a twinge. Somebody had given him a good boot high on his back during the melee in the classroom. He feels quite proud of the injury. Hopes somebody will want to see the bruise. If he ever went on social media anymore he would definitely tell the world what has happened to him, but he hasn't used any of the online platforms for an age. It all became too dispiriting. He allows himself a wry smile as the word occurs to him. Annabeth had really lost it when he spoke of feeling 'dispirited'. He'd liked the way she turned on him. There was passion there. Fire. And she can write. She has a creative soul, he can tell. He can't help wondering about the twists and turns her life has taken to lead her here. A prison officer at desperate, creaking HMP Holderness.

He looks across at where she dozes. Runs his eyes, soft as a fingertip, along her outline. Bare feet, soft, wrinkled soles, touching at the ankle. Fit, sturdy legs rising to a pleasing rump, then down to her waist and gradually sliding up over the curve of her shoulder and the pleasing messiness of her hair. Finds himself smiling. He considers waking her. Considers calling home. Calling Shonagh. Calling his agent just to see if they remember him. Thinks, briefly, about writing. He feels oddly inspired, though he doesn't really know how to turn the vague electric charge that pulses in and around him into something with a beginning, middle or end. Can't see a story. Perhaps the blur of a character, somewhere around the periphery of his imagination. Thinks of Suggs. Wonders if he could write such a man. Angry and bull-headed, indignant at the nearness of a nonce: the stirrings of a desire to write; to think different thoughts, to turn fury into words. Thinks of Callan. Grips at the fabric of the armchair as he pictures those cold, dark eyes – the way everybody did as they were told when he growled out the most monosyllabic of instructions. God how he would love to be respected like that. Sometimes he wishes he had spent his teenage years reading fewer works by Tolstoy and Thackeray, and devoted himself instead to learning how to kick the shit out of people. Perhaps he's been wrong about everything since day one.

He feels a sudden urge to scribble his thoughts down. He can feel the scratchy prickling of an idea. Wants to let the idea unroll like a ball of string. An exploration of modern masculinity. Were we all mis-sold on the desirability of sensitivity? Are we still our base elements? Is might still more attractive a quality than empathy? He feels quite fizzy thinking about it. There's a market for this stuff, he's sure of it. Last time he was in a bookshop seeking out and failing to find any of his own work, he had noticed that the bestseller list was groaning under the weight of semi-academic ruminations about who we are, how we are; ways to be happy or to live within the bubble of misery. He could do something like that, he's sure of it. He could talk to anthropologists; psychologists, scientists sifting through human genomes in search of that which connects us to ancestors and the animal kingdom. He could make it part memoir. Explain the miseries of being a poet; a sensitive empath with real feelings, real compassion, who listens and genuinely notices when a person has changed their hairstyle or done something different with their eye make-up. He's been the right kind of man and yet now, at forty-eight, he's less impressive to his wife than the great meat-headed debt collectors who bang on his door as if trying to enter Parliament. He needs a pen. Paper . . .

There's a little cupboard at the side of the armchair: a key sticking out of the lock. It turns under his fingers and he squats down, trying to keep the idea at the front of his thoughts while he rummages around for something to write with. There are lever arch folders inside. Big black ones, neatly labelled. Alphabetical order. Dates. Nothing to write on. He tuts, irritated, and is about to scurry through to the kitchen to continue the search, when a second impulse stills him. He wants to know what's in the folders.

He throws a look at Annabeth. Still asleep, breathing softly. Hears the creak of bedsprings overhead as her lad rolls over in his sleep. Realises he won't get a better opportunity than now. Rufus doesn't really have any moral compunction about going through her private things but he'd rather not be caught in the act. He pulls out the top folder. It's heavy. Opens it up and is greeted by the cover of a cheap gossip magazine. He frowns, puzzled. He understands that Annabeth likes things to be 'just so', but to punch holes in magazines and inset them into ring-binders is bordering on the obsessive. He leafs through it. There are more magazines beneath. Publications with names like *Closer*, *Life!* and *Pick Me Up*. The top magazine is dated April 2016. The last is January, 2018. He skims through the pages: cheap paper, grainy photographs, lurid headlines splashed across articles written in a first-person, conversational style.

Crosswords, competitions, recipes, a little celeb gossip. He can't help thinking that the reader gets a lot of content for sixty pence.

He stops turning the pages when he sees the fluorescent page marker stuck to the top right-hand corner of a seemingly random article. Flips the folder and spots several more little place-markers: yellow, pink, blue. Glances at the article she has considered worthy of re-reading. **GROOMED FOR SEX BY ONLINE PAEDO.** White letters on a red background. A picture of a teenage girl looking dejected and a mugshot of a plump, unattractive man. He flips on to the next story marked out by the thin, fluorescent Post-it. **HELP ME NAIL DAD'S KILLER BEFORE MUM LOSES CANCER BATTLE.** The accompanying picture shows a mother and daughter: Stacey and Louisa Defreitas. Both small, thin-framed, hard-faced, sitting side by side in a floral armchair with a photo album in their laps. Inset, a picture of a plump, jowly man: a hint of Mediterranean to his skin tone. Rufus makes a face. Chews his lip. He should probably put the folder back. He's a guest in somebody else's house. He shouldn't be rummaging around. What business is it of his if she has a folder full of junk articles? Maybe she's studied certain cases for a course, or has an interest in different styles of print journalism. None of his business, really.

He can't help himself. He walks through to the kitchen and locates the whisky bottle in the cupboard under the sink. Pours a quadruple measure into a half-pint glass. Settles back in the kitchen chair that allows him to see through the open door to where Annabeth dozes, and dreams. Starts to read.

There were tears in her eyes as she told me. She wouldn't let herself cry, but I knew she wanted to. I'd seen that look before, back when I was eight years old. Then, she had to tell me that Daddy wasn't coming home. Now, she was telling me that the cancer had spread and that she wasn't going to be around much longer.

I'm not somebody who wants sympathy. All of my friends know me as somebody who deals with whatever life throws at me. I'm one of those people who everybody thinks of as the 'life and soul' of the party.

But even when I'm laughing on the outside there's a

hollowness within me. You see, I'm the daughter of a murder victim!

I was just a child when it happened. My dad, Walter, was a kind man. A big man. He gave the best cuddles and treated me like a real princess. I was a proper Daddy's girl. He'd always bring me presents back when he went away to work and my favourite memory is of us sitting on the floor in my bedroom having little tea parties with my toys.

Of course, Dad was no angel. Mum always said he could be a difficult man to live with and I do remember he could get very cross if things weren't done just right, but he was a good provider and we lived in a nice house near Penrith in Cumbria.

Dad owned some properties and had a few different businesses in nearby Carlisle. One night in May 2006, he went out to go and look at an empty property he was thinking of investing in. I remember saying goodbye to him, getting a kiss on the cheek, then hearing him drive away like he had so many times. The next morning, I could tell something wasn't right. Mum was really jittery and nervous and kept running to the window every time a car went past. She started ringing people who Dad did business with. By the next day I had realized that Daddy hadn't come back. People were out looking for him.

I cried myself to sleep every night for weeks.

It was more than a year until Daddy's body was found. Somebody had slit his throat then buried him beneath the floorboards of a house where he owned a flat.

Life was very difficult for Mum and me after Daddy went away. He'd always been quite secretive about his business interests and suddenly we didn't have any money. We had to move in with my mum's sister and when Daddy's body was found we were suddenly getting calls from reporters and people were quizzing me at school and I became the daughter of the murdered man.

All these years later, the police are no closer to finding out who did it. We know he was seen in the company of a tall man the day that we saw him last, and that somebody had been squatting in the flat in the months prior to his disappearance. But we're no closer to finding out who did it.

I'm 22 now and am working as a nail technician. I'm pregnant with my first child and am hoping to marry my boyfriend this summer.

But Mum's cancer diagnosis has stirred everything up and we don't know how long she has left. I want to at least get her some answers before she goes to her grave not knowing what happened. All I can do is ask people to come forward with information and to pray, every night, that we finally get some answers. I'll be an orphan soon. Surely I deserve at least one bit of good fortune.

Rufus breathes out through pursed lips. Takes a slug of whisky. He can't say he feels any clearer about why Annabeth may have kept the article. Could she have been friends with Walter's daughter, Stacey? There's nothing to suggest so. An interest in the case? He doesn't know Annabeth well enough to say. He rummages in his pocket and finds his phone. There are a couple of new voicemails and an email alert but he ignores them and brings up a search engine. Double-checks the details and types in a string of keywords from the article. *Walter. Stacey. Louisa. Defreitas. Murder. Carlisle. Annabeth.*

There are reports about the unsolved crime in the *News and Star*, the local newspaper for Carlisle. A handful of pieces on the BBC website. A link to Wikipedia and a list of unsolved murders. He skim-reads a few. There's a byline on some of the newspaper stories. The same reporter each time the case is brought up. Ruth Baxter. He glances at the magazine article. Rotates it. There's a tiny credit in the bottom right-hand corner. Words: Ruth Baxter.

He finishes the whisky. Googles the journalist. Finds her Twitter profile. She's freelance now, and always interested in 'real-life' stories. The accompanying picture shows a bookish, smiling young woman with glasses and sensible brown hair. There's an email address attached. He closes his eyes. Drains the whisky. Puts her name into Google and finds her details on a freelance directory. It contains a mobile phone number.

Rufus looks to where Annabeth lays, still unawares. Experiences a moment of self-loathing, as he wonders what he is doing, or what he's doing it for. What had she said before she fell asleep? She needed leverage? Well how was he supposed to help her find that if he didn't know any of the details. Sure, this might have nothing to do with her current panic, but he can't be sure of that until he at least digs about. He's a writer, after all. He needs to understand people if he wants to think the way they do. More than anything else, he likes the feelings that are flooding him. He feels not so much like an author, but like one of the vastly more interesting people that he makes up.

He stands and moves to the back door. Opens it wide and steps out into the dark, damp air.

Dials the number, and closes the door behind him.

Ruth Baxter answers on the fourth ring.

'Mr Orton,' she answers, breathlessly. 'I'm so glad you called back! I really need to talk to you . . .'

TWENTY-SIX

When he closes his eyes, the rain sounds like fire. It's a crackling noise, something just short of static; millions of soft raindrops striking hard surfaces: the glass of the kitchen window; the closed door; the shed roof; the parasol in next door's garden; the damp wool of his jersey; and the unprotected skin of his face. He's going to get soaked. Going to go back in drenched to the skin. Will probably catch his death . . .

He doesn't know where the thoughts come from. Just knows that while he's considering them, some other part of his brain is sorting itself out, and limbering up to perform. It has always been this way. He opens his mouth, and somebody else takes over. He can busk and improvise like the finest New Orleans jazz band, leaving the part of himself that he thinks of as his true self, to ponder important things like the sound of raindrops.

'Yes, sorry about the delay,' says Rufus, licking his lips. Tastes whisky. Tastes rain. Stares into the darkness of the little garden, taking notes. Neat garden, mowed lawn, some bedding plants suffering under the onslaught; raindrops captured in the faint yellow glow given off by a neighbour's security light. 'I've got an awful line at this end, I just got the name and number. Ruth, yes?'

'Yes, yes. Ruth Baxter. Freelance journalist but there's no need to slam the phone down.' She says it with a smile in her voice – a line she must have used countless times. Her accent is broad Yorkshire. 'I've read one of your books, by the way. Belting stuff. Was is called . . . aye, *The Minotaur*, or something like that. About a scholar who gets obsessed with Ancient Greece and ends up locking his family in some place he's built . . . all wordy, clever, from what I remember . . .'

Rufus rolls his eyes. If people can't remember the title or the details of the plot he'd rather they didn't claim to know his work.

'Good, good. Long time ago, that one. I've written since, of course. You might like the new one—'

'Brilliant, brilliant,' says the reporter, brushing his words aside. 'Anyway, as I said, I'm a freelancer. Based out of Pontefract, if you know it . . . sorry, I'm just looking for the right notebook, you've caught me on the hop . . .'

Rufus listens to the muffled sound of footsteps and the hiss of muffled chatter. A door opens, then another one slams. The tone of the air changes. She sounds as though she's now sitting in a smaller space.

'Ruth?'

'Right, belting, belting. God, bloody awful weather, isn't it? My gran always said that you know you're getting old when your conversations turn to weather inside four sentences . . . right, so, am I right in thinking you've been doing some teaching at HMP Holderness?'

Rufus pauses, unsure whether to take the lead or see how things play out. He decides to play to type and perform his usual affable Englishman routine. 'Yes, yes I am, a real honour . . . not my usual environment but that's really rather what attracted me to the opportunity . . .' He hears himself begin a

long, rambling tangent. He didn't think there would be any
press interest in his presence at a prison, but hey, if she wants
to print something he's glad to be interviewed.

'Yes, belting . . . that's what I'd heard. And can I ask you
for your take on what happened during today's class? I understand you were involved in a violent altercation with an inmate.'

Rufus freezes. A strange iron taste fills his mouth and he
feels as though he has briefly ceased to function. He has to
remind himself to breathe. Christ, he doesn't need this. Doesn't
need his great comeback to be as a thug brawling with an
attendee at a creative writing session. He lets out a dry laugh.
It sounds hollow.

'Oh, the little set-to? Gosh, I'm sorry, Ms Baxter, but I fear
somebody's been pulling your leg. The sessions are going rather
well, actually. Really very rewarding. Of course, tensions run
high in any creative environment but as for a violent altercation,
well—'

'I'm told that Prison Officer Declan Windsor is in intensive
care, Mr Orton,' she says, still chatty in her manner. 'I've got
it on pretty good authority that one inmate went for another and
that you stepped in to restrain him. A mini riot followed
and Mr Windsor was set upon.'

'A mini riot? I'm sorry, I don't mean to be rude but who
told you this . . . in fact, where did you get my number from?'

She ignores the question. 'It all sounds a horrible experience,
Mr Orton. A line or two from yourself to explain how it all felt
and then I can leave you in peace.'

'Whom precisely are you writing this for?' he asks, still
sounding rather foppish. 'I mean, my days as a rising star are
long gone and your *Daily Mail* readers really won't give a hoot
if some prisoners have had a scrap, even if it is at HMP
Holderness. I mean, none of this is news—'

'I think you'll find that's not entirely the case, Mr Orton,' says
Ruth, with a grating note of jolliness in her voice. 'I'm given to
understand that a certain sex offender from the Vulnerable Prisoner
wing was allowed access to the class and that he was the intended
recipient of the violence. I also understand that he suffered a
severe injury by perpetrators as yet unknown. I'm further given
to understand that the VP in question was interviewed by two

detectives from Humberside Police in connection with a search for human remains currently taking place in a field in North Lincolnshire. You can see why I thought this call was worth making.'

Rufus feels the rain run down his face. Becomes aware of how cold he is. In the space of a few minutes he has gone from dogged investigator to the subject of an unacceptable invasion of his privacy. He feels himself growing angry, even as he tries to put the scrambled fragments of information together. He'd been calling about the piece she wrote on Louisa Defreitas and her murdered father. She had been ringing him in connection with the situation at the prison. Could it be a colossal coincidence or the result of two people pulling the same tangled thread from different directions?

'I'd love to be of help,' says Rufus, keeping his tone steady. 'Obviously I'm in a bit of an unusual situation. Really, the incident you're asking about was no worse than you'd see in a rugger match. I was barely involved. As to who hurt Mr Cox, I'm in the dark. It was all rather frantic, you see, and—'

'It was Griffin Cox, then?' asks Ruth, smoothly. 'Excellent, thanks. And I'm told it was a stab wound? He was taken to hospital and then returned to the medical wing, is that correct?'

Rufus tries to wrestle the conversation into different waters. 'I actually checked your name online before I rang back,' he says, impressed with the lie. 'You've written about a case I have an interest in, as it happens. Walter Defreitas? Killed in Carlisle, years back?'

There's a brief silence at the other end of the line. 'Defreitas? Yeah, I wrote what felt like the same story dozens of times when I was still at the *News and Star*. One of those weird ones that you sense the cops feel pessimistic about from the very start. What's your interest?'

Rufus pushes his damp hair back from his face. Wishes he'd brought the whisky out with him.

'Oh, it's a book I was considering pitching,' he says, breezily. 'Trying to get a character right. Young girl, loses her father, tries to make sense of it all but can't reconcile the daddy she remembers with the truth she discovers. I don't know if it will come to anything but I like moments of synergy. I saw the piece you wrote for one of the gossip magazines. Louisa's story.'

'Oh right,' says Ruth, enthusiastically. 'Aye, she owes me a few quid for doing the job of a journalist and PR department in one! Made her sound OK, didn't I? Wasn't easy. Creative writing? Jesus, try making Louisa Defreitas sound like anything other than a nightmare.'

'Oh really?' asks Rufus, smoothly. 'She came across as rather sweet. I was thinking of perhaps asking her if we should chat. She could be the clay I bake this particular character from . . .'

Ruth sucks her teeth as if she has burned herself. 'Oh no, save yourself. Honestly, she's not the goody-two-shoes I painted her to be. I'd chatted with her and her mum a few times over the years, just whenever it was a slow news day and I got one of my tame coppers to say they'd found new evidence or were following up interesting leads, that sort of stuff. They were always out for what they could get. To be fair, Walter did leave them in a right pickle but they were better off without him. Reading between the lines, the coppers were never going to bust a gut to catch whoever did him in. He was bad all the way through, and that's a quote I'd have loved to have used. When I went free-lance and I went through a rough patch I called Louisa up to see if she fancied doing a piece about the anniversary of his death or whatever we could rustle up, and she mentioned her mum's illness in passing, so we cooked up the piece. Fresh angle, and all that. Features editor at the mag took it off me. 50/50 split for Louisa and me. She wasn't even grateful . . .' She drifts off, as if remembering, then comes back with a little laugh. 'Wow, talk about losing the thread. How did we get onto the Defreitas family?'

'The art of conversation comes from letting it flow,' says Rufus, a smile in his voice. 'Writing dialogue is one of the hardest parts of being a storyteller. You should come to one of my classes – you've obviously got a gift with words—'

'Are you back home in North Yorkshire?' asks Ruth, sounding more businesslike. 'Only, there are a few things I'd love to chat about if you had the time and as soon as I'm back down the M62 I could pop over and see you. Maybe take a photograph.

"Heroic author saves dying guard". Works, doesn't it? Better than the alternatives.'

Rufus doesn't respond to the veiled threat that there could be far worse headlines in his future. He creases his brows, running her words back. 'Back down the M62? Are you at the prison?'

'No, not much point in that,' she says, testily. 'Hussain the governor has no interest in talking to me and I don't want to make things difficult for my source. No, I'm over in the land of the Yellow-Bellies. Half a shandy in the Marrowbone then I'll be over the bridge and home . . .'

'Kirmington?' he mutters, recognizing the name of the pub. What had she said about searching for human remains? His head is spinning. He doesn't know if he's the dog or the cat – just that somehow he's caught in a chase.

'Yeah, nice enough little place. Getting together some reactions from the locals about the police trampling all over the field by the airport looking for poor Bronwen. That's the story I was on – trying to get some info on the interview with Griffin Cox. Heard from a source about the fracas involving "a famous author", and wondered if there might be a yarn worth selling while I'm covering the Bronwen dig. Busy-busy, and all that. It's the freelance world – one minute you're twiddling your thumbs, next you're too swamped to breathe—'

'I won't be back, as it happens,' says Rufus, cutting her off. 'Staying with a friend tonight. I'm not really sure if there's a story here for you, if I'm honest. I mean, mention me if you wish, but I'm not famous, and if I'm honest I'd rather just leave the whole thing alone. I mean, I don't want to pretend I'm a hero. I just reacted – did what anybody would have done.'

'That's a perfect quote,' says Ruth, smiling. 'Just to check, you have two children, yes? And your wife, Shonagh, she's into art, apparently.'

Rufus doesn't want to talk about himself, or his home life, any longer. He wants to sit quietly in the half-light, and make sense of what is happening. He suddenly feels ludicrous. Preposterous. Silly. What the hell had got him trundling down this strange track? Why's he even here? He brought Annabeth the snow globe that somebody had hidden in his bag. She had named Cox as the likely suspect, and quickly degenerated into a frightened, manic wreck. He'd found a stack of articles in her cupboard while she slept. Read one and needed to know more. He can't seem to make sense of what he's learned, but he senses a connection. He wants to come right out and ask her – do you know a lady called Annabeth Harris? Do you have any idea why she has a load of articles about paedophiles and victims; missing teens and human remains? Do you know what hold Griffin Cox might have over her . . .?

'What's he like?' asks Ruth, lancing into his thoughts. 'Cox, I mean. What's he like, really? You know they say he's in the frame for God knows how many, don't you? I mean, maybe creative writing isn't what he needs – not unless it was some ruse to get him to open up and talk about where he put the bodies. That would explain why the coppers chose midway through your session to come and speak to him . . .'

Rufus forces a laugh. He can hear her journalistic wheels whirring. 'I think I should be off now, Ruth. If you could perhaps rustle up that number for Louisa Defreitas, that would be a help, and obviously whatever else I can say to help you I'd be glad to—'

He hears a door opening at her end of the line. The patter of rain. She's about to say goodbye.

'Just one other thing,' says Rufus, as a name pops into his head. 'Weird synergies, and all that jazz, but the story I read about the Defreitas family suggested he was no angel, even thinly veiled, and you said the coppers weren't bending over backwards to find him. Go on – I'm intrigued. What was the deal?'

There's a pause for a moment, as she considers the currency of information. 'I'll use that quote, if you don't mind. Doing what anybody would do . . .'

He sighs. 'If you must,' he mutters.

'Belting, thanks. But my copper friend with Cumbria Police, well, he's told me plenty. They had their eye on Defreitas for a while before he disappeared. Dodgy sod. Into young girls, or so they suspect. At the crime scene they found prints belonging to another dodgy bastard by the name of Mark Fellowes. They quizzed him but he was never a real suspect and by 2009 he was doing time for snatching a little girl from her garden. He's in HMP Wakefield or Frankland, can't remember which. But my source reckoned the pair of them were thick as thieves.'

'Fellowes,' muses Rufus, turning suddenly as the light changes behind him. He sees a shape through the frosted glass of the back door. Looks into the face of Annabeth's son, soaked to the skin and frowning accusingly at the man loitering in the garden. Wherever he's been, he doesn't look happy to have returned home to this.

Unaware of the interruption, Ruth continues to chat, warming to her theme. 'There was evidence that he'd had a girl staying in the crummy flat where his body was found. Somebody had done a clean-up job but there was blood staining the floorboards. Shards of glass that matched the wound to his throat. They wouldn't give it to us on the record but there was glitter in the trachea. You probably saw in the article Louisa talking about the presents he would bring back from his business trips. Couldn't confirm it, of course, but I should imagine they were considered as the murder weapon.'

'The presents?' mumbles Rufus, holding up a finger and grinning, madly, as Ethan angles his head, requesting explanation.

He tunes back in to what she is saying. Mumbles the words at the same time that Ruth tells him about the little treasures Walter Defreitas would bring home for his daughter. Makes the connection, and feels himself fill with something that is at once excitement and fear.

'Snow globes . . .'

TWENTY-SEVEN

Annabeth dreams.

Her mother, this time. She's sitting in a rocking chair on the porch of a little seafront cottage. Whitewashed, sun-bleached; sky-blue slatted shutters and window boxes full of purple pansies and yellow primroses. Annabeth doesn't recognize the house, nor the humps of soft sand and grass that shield it from the wind, but the sound of the nearby sea is familiar. It's rhythmic, like the crunch of hard cereal, or the springs of an old bed.

Annabeth feels a chill all over, as if rimed with frost, as she considers the woman in the chair. She's all hunched in on herself: timid, fragile, as if frightened of taking up too much space or of drawing too much attention to herself. She's holding something in her hands: pale wrinkled specimens the colour of seashells. Annabeth is at once far away and directly in front of her. She's looking at the pattern in the crocheted blanket which winds about her mother's legs so tightly she could pass for a mermaid.

'Look,' says her mother, in a man's voice. 'Look what you did.'

There's a little conch shell on her wrinkled palms; the pinkish blue of newborn flesh.

'Take it,' she's saying. 'He wants you.'

And now the shell is in Annabeth's hand. She's raising it to her ear. She's excited suddenly, excited to hear Daddy's voice. And then there is wetness at her temple, at her cheek, and blood is spilling from the conch shell to gush into her ear as if she were drinking from a chalice, and her father is telling her not to make such a fuss, and that it means she's a woman now, and women don't make a fuss, and not to go upsetting her mother . . .

She jerks awake, gasping for breath. Licks cracked lips and tastes sea-salt and iron. Smears the heel of her hand across her face. It comes away dripping. She's been crying. Tears have trickled from her closed eyes and puddled in her ear.

She rolls over, aware of the gloss of sweat that covers her. There's a blanket around her lower half. She crocheted it herself, years ago, when she was still trying to be a certain type of mother. Ethan still asks for it when he's feeling poorly. Tangles his fingers through the holes and feels some kind of comfort at being tightly bound.

She looks up at the clock. It's a little after nine. She swallows, painfully. Memories flood her; surging from the depths of her mind to the very forefront of her thoughts: marbles on a tilting tray. She looks to where she left the snow globe. There's nothing there. Sits up, panicking, shivering suddenly, and looks around frantically. She hauls herself upright. As she changes position she sees that the door to the little cupboard is ajar. She has to hold herself steady not to begin hyperventilating.

Unsteady, dizzy, she runs to the kitchen. The lights are on, and there's a faint smell of whisky and rain.

A noise from upstairs. Ethan. God she needs him now. Wants to hold him close and sniff his head and feel as though nothing else matters as long as nobody ever takes him away from her. She makes for the door that leads into the hallway and upstairs. Hears the muffled sound of voices. Recognizes Ethan. Hears somebody else, too. Deeper. A pleasing lullaby quality to the syntax. Knows at once that Rufus is upstairs, chatting with her son. He's not going to go. He's helped himself to her deepest secrets with no more care than when he had rummaged through her cupboards at breakfast time.

She starts up the stairs, head spinning. She should never have let him stay. She should never have allowed anybody close. She should have acted clueless when he showed her the snow globe – not started blundering around like a crazy person. And Christ, she'd spoken about it, hadn't she? As she was drifting off. Told her that Cox knew something about her past.

She reaches out, her hand on the wall, steadying herself. Tries to regain control. What could he know, she asks herself? Really, what could he know? She's never been so much as questioned about the death of Walter Defreitas. Sure, she has a file full of newspaper clippings and magazines but that doesn't mean anything more than an interest in criminology, her degree subject. No, Rufus isn't her problem. He might even be a friend. If he's stuck around and covered her with a blanket and is now entertaining her son, he's an ally, isn't he? It's Cox that needs to occupy her mind. Cox who has got himself transferred to the country's most notorious prison just because he knows something about an officer there. Cox who's being questioned about the whereabouts of missing teens. She knows what he wants. She's got the message.

She breathes in and out, counting down from ten. She can do this, she knows she can. There are protocols. Systems. People in her job have muck slung about them all the time. So what if he tells people that she was involved in a crime when she was still a teenager? She can deny it, laugh it off, and put it down to the ramblings of a vindictive prisoner.

But Ethan, she tells herself, and it feels as though her mouth is full of sand. Ethan is a walking DNA sample. Ethan ties her to Walter Defreitas. He shares half his blood, as grotesque as that thought feels.

She stays where she is, halfway up the stairs, leaning her clammy forehead against the cool wall.

Voices again, through the bedroom door. It takes a moment to turn the mumbles into recognizable words, but quickly she catches the right frequency and listens, cold iron chains twisting around her guts, as she hears her son talk about murder, and the man she left dead on the floor six-and-a-half months before Ethan was born.

'. . . put both names in together and see if there's any connection, and if that doesn't work I have a programme I can send them that will record the keystrokes and we can get in to it that way – I mean it's dodgy, but old people don't think to look for stuff like that . . .'

'She's not old, she can't be more than thirty-five . . .'

'Yeah, old, but I won't do it if you don't want me to. It's not hard. Same with spyware. You can bag yourself a subject through the camera on their computer. Watch them while they're working, or gaming, or wanking or whatever. You get some people who'll blackmail their victims into handing over thousands just so they don't release videos they've taken of them when they thought they were alone. It's ugly, really. I wouldn't do that. Not ever. But I know how . . .'

'Just try the name. Fellowes. Not sure if it's with or without an "e". Try both. Then see if there's a connection to Cox. Try "snow globe" as well. You're sure she's never said anything to you about all this? Griffin Cox, yes? I mean, if we can sort this out so she doesn't have to deal with it, you'll be son of the century, you know what I mean? Pass the folder over, I'll go through the mags and see if his name's in there somewhere, and . . .'

'Fellowes, with an "e". Yep. Sent down in 2009. No mention of a connection with Cox. Nasty case though. Mark Fellowes, forty-six, father of five, sentenced to thirteen years for a "terri-fying" abduction . . . befriended a nine-year-old girl as she played in her garden in Consett, County Durham . . . told her he had bought a present for his own daughter and needed an opinion on whether it was OK . . . creepy bastard . . . then grabbed her and drove her to an area of parkland . . . "sickening" assault . . . oh Christ, this bloke needs stabbing, Rufus, he really does . . .'

And Annabeth cannot help herself. She is sprinting up the stairs as if fleeing from fire. She's yanking open the bedroom door. Freezing on the threshold of the room. She's looking at the computer screens, filled with newsprint, with crime scenes, with photographs: a StreetView image of the house on Chatsworth Square; a grainy shot of a smiling Walter Defreitas; a snapshot of a tall man with dark hair being escorted to a prison van outside Newcastle Crown Court. Mark Fellowes. Walter's friend. The man she was supposed to be nice to on the night she spilled so much blood.

'Oh, you're awake, I wasn't sure whether to wake you or let you carry on dozing until morning, but Ethan and me have been having a bit of a dig around, and . . .'

She sees the open folder on Rufus's lap. Sees the snow globe, sitting there on her son's desk like a paperweight.

The person she thinks of as Annabeth disappears like smoke. And the person left behind lunges at Rufus as if he were an intruder intent on harming her son. She grabs a handful of his thick hair and brings her fist down hard on his jaw. There's a strangled yell of pain, and then she's hitting him again, again, and he's falling back off his chair, covering up, trying to grab her wrists, and she's screaming, telling him to get out, to get the fuck out, as her son yells her name and begs her to stop, to please stop.

He wriggles out from under her, bleeding, his face already bruising, his jumper ripped all down the front, slipping on the glossy pages of the magazines torn from their binder, and he's throwing himself for the open door as if fleeing a grenade. She claws at his back, skin under her nails, blood on her knuckles, up her wrist, in her mouth as she grinds her teeth and screams . . .

Ethan's hand on her shoulder, her name on his lips, and she spins around, face all spit and fury, and she's screaming at him, telling him he's betrayed her, that he's no right, no fucking right . . .

The slam of the door.

And she collapses onto the floor, all sweat and snot and tears.

Through the haze she looks at the images on the screen. Locks eyes with Mark Fellowes.

Folds her arms over her head, and weeps until she's empty.

TWENTY-EIGHT

Dorcas answers the phone with a sigh so extravagant that it sounds to her father as if somebody has put their weight on the bloated carcass of a corpse. It's not so much an outbreath as a one-note monologue; a passage of epic prose, richly seamed with eloquent insights into the manifold disappointments of her life in general, and her father in particular.

'For God's sake, Dormouse, breathe in, breathe in!'

She doesn't laugh. Doesn't respond. Rufus closes his eyes. Transfers the phone to his other cheek. It's less sore, though there's a little cut on his ear that feels unpleasantly sticky against the screen.

'I was just ringing to, y'know . . .' He stops himself, unsure how to finish. Why had he rung? What had he hoped for? She thinks he's a prick, he knows that. She's too busy for him. Got too much of her own life to lead. He's the pissed-up failure who can't even afford to buy credit for her phone.

'Don't call me Dormouse,' she mutters, over the sound of whatever programme she had been streaming on her laptop when she was rudely interrupted by her joke of a dad. 'I didn't even like that when I was five.'

Rufus swallows, painfully. He's got his back to the handful of other drinkers who are taking up space in the front bar. He's a bit embarrassed about the way he looks. The neck of his jumper is torn almost down to his stomach and he's missing the top four buttons on his shirt. The gammon flesh of his pudgy face is starting to darken and there's a crust of scabbed blood in his nostril that makes every breath smell of liver and iron. He's feeling pretty damn sorry for himself. Had rung his daughter in the hope she would hear the lament in his voice and offer some words of comfort. He feels sore, and ill-used. He can't say in good conscience that he feels angry at Annabeth but he wants to talk to her. To explain. He didn't deserve the fury she unleashed but he understands that he crossed a line and he wants to put things right. He's good at making allowances for people. He feels deeply put out that nobody affords him the same courtesy.

'You loved being called Dormouse,' says Rufus, petulant. 'God, I dedicated book three to Dormouse and The Bump! I started writing a children's book with that very name, for you and Millie, and—'

'I'm a bit busy right now,' says Dorcas, cutting him off. 'Reading for an essay.'

'Yeah?' he asks, brightening. 'Anything I can help with?'

'You always take over,' says Dorcas, with another forced exhalation.

'I won't,' he pleads, desperate to be useful. 'Come on, Dormouse, if I'm not good for helping my best girl with her English homework, what am I good for?'

There's a laugh in her voice as she replies. It's not a nice sound. 'I think you've answered your own question.'

He swallows, taking a moment to find the right words. Swills the last dregs of cider in the base of his pint glass then tips it down his neck.

'Where did it go wrong?' he asks, half to himself. There's a slur in his voice. He knows he's pissed, but usually he can hide it from all but the experts. Tonight, after an hour in the boozer, he's lost interest in putting on a show. Yeah, he's drunk. What of it? He's a grown man. He's achieved things. He's done what he set out to do and he's passed on his genetic material to two ungrateful and distant daughters. Can't he pickle his own liver if he wants to?

'Go wrong?' asks Dorcas. 'What's gone wrong? You're living

your best life, aren't you, Dad? Not much expected of you, really. You write and you drink and you get strangers telling you you're amazing. Mum pays the bills when you can't and she'll never leave you because she still thinks you're some sort of Dylan Thomas character and your personality is the price for your genius. You might want to be grateful, now and again, instead of making her feel like you've settled for her instead of spread yourself among the masses.'

Rufus turns and catches the barmaid's eye. Fumbles in the pocket of his cords and finds a few pound coins in among the shrapnel. Points at the cheap whisky in the optic and indicates he'd like a large. Business attended to, he lets his daughter's words sink in.

'She thinks that? Mum?' His mind fills with images: curled lip, angry eyes; the way she freezes when he forces himself to touch her. What on earth was she talking about? 'Shut up, she thinks I'm a loser. You can see it every time she looks at me!'

His words are a hose of petrol on a smouldering bonfire. The explosion takes his breath away.

'God, you're supposed to be good at understanding people,' shrieks Dorcas, real wrath in her voice. 'All those critics and readers who say you've got these great insights into human beings? They haven't a clue. You haven't a clue. Go and get pissed, Dad. You can't afford to get me credit for the phone, but it's amazing how you can always pay your bar bill. Jesus.'

Rufus feels himself growing smaller, as if viewed through a magnifying glass moving inexorably away.

'I love you,' he says, and it comes out in a rush. He feels hot tears pricking at his eyes. God how he wants her to tell him she loves him too. His head fills with shoplifted emotions: projections and imaginings of the parents robbed of their own darling adolescents. His whole self fills with horror and sadness at what it must feel like to lose a child. Worse, to have one taken. For a loved one to exist, and then in an instant cease to be. What could it be like to not know whether your child was alive or dead? Whether they were somewhere living some kind of life, however terrible, or if their pulse had long since halted. He can imagine himself tasting each breath in the hope of catching the faintest trace of a familiar exhalation. Understands the sorrow. The rage. What would a person do in order to find out the truth? How far would a parent go to learn whether their child still lived?

He hears Dorcas give the faintest little laugh. She's exasperated with him, sure, but at least he's hers to be exasperated with. He sees himself as an incontinent old dog, forever shitting on the new cream cord carpet. The laugh is the tickle behind the ear that tells him he's maddening, but still a good boy.

'I love you too,' she says, sulkily. Then: 'Don't drive. You sound like Captain Jack Sparrow. Wherever you are sleep it off. And tell Mum you love her. Night.'

Rufus looks at the phone for a full ten seconds after she's hung up, processing her words and looking for something he can shape into an amulet: a charm he can hold to keep him safe when the misery threatens to drag him down. Wordlessly, he takes his glass from the bar and slides the money across. Takes a gulp and feels the whisky burn as it scorches his sore throat: a peach-stone of repressed emotion all but blocking off his airways. He starts to type a message to Shonagh. Something poetic, he thinks. Something that shows she can still inspire him. Starts to think about the ways she makes him feel, deep down, beneath the endless layers of shared experiences and the drudgery of two decades of co-habitation. Has an image of a paper lantern. That soft, dusky glow: warmth and light, inviting but fragile; ethereal against the darkness. Wonders if he is feeling it, or imagining it, or plagiarizing it from something once read, and drains his glass before he can type a single word.

Tenses as he senses a presence behind him. Glances at the barmaid, who is staring at whoever is behind him. She likes what she sees, that's clear enough.

'Mr Orton?'

The voice has a local accent. Yorkshire, with a touch of something entirely unique. Rufus turns and looks into the handsome face of a well-dressed man in his thirties. He's wearing a silvery-grey suit over a white shirt and thin red tie, and it hangs the way it would on a model. He's slim, but he has the toned physique of an athlete. With his shaved head and angular jaw, brown eyes and perfect eyebrows, he looks as though he could be anything from a businessman to an enforcer for a drugs baron.

'Who wants to know?' asks Rufus, hoping that it will sound frivolous and charming.

The man doesn't smile. 'I do,' he says, and reaches into his back pocket. Dangles a plastic lanyard in front of Rufus's face as if trying to hypnotize him with a pocket watch. 'Detective Constable Ben Neilsen. Humberside Police. I think you and I could do with a chat.'

Rufus falls into character. 'Goodness! I'm, erm, well, of course . . . you'll forgive me if I'm a little startled . . . haven't spoken to a Rozzer since university – a little hoo-hah about climbing onto the roof of the bursar's office . . . high jinks, eh? Years ago now, of course . . .'

The officer watches the performance with a little twitch of a smile on his face. Rufus realizes he's not fooling anybody – just making a prat of himself.

'Your glass is empty,' says Neilsen, when Rufus rattles to a halt. 'Let me fill it up and we'll go have a sit down and a bit of a natter, eh?'

Rufus looks at the empty glass. Philosophically speaking, he's always believed that any glass which isn't entirely full, is perilously close to being empty. He nods. Changes his order from Bell's to single malt.

'Double,' he instructs, pointedly.

The detective nods. Looks him up and down. Clocks the cuts and bruises. 'You been in the wars, Mr Orton? Is that what Suggs did to you?'

Rufus doesn't even take the time to think about it. Lies as easily as blinking. 'Yep. Stinging a bit, but such is life. A few cuts and bruises never killed anybody though, eh?'

Neilsen stares into him, considering it. Shrugs, decision made. 'Depends where you put the knife.'

TWENTY-NINE

They take a seat at the back of the bar, shielded by the fruit machine and a little wood and glass partition. Rufus doesn't like to sit down when he drinks in public, lest he fall asleep and not wake up without the aid of a defibrillator. But though his experience of police interviews is minimal, he fancies he would be well served by co-operating.

Neilsen loosens his tie a fraction as he sits down. He's got himself a sparkling water with a slice of lime – a drink that Rufus fancies he could replicate by squirting disinfectant into a toilet bowl and flushing the chain. Rufus takes a small sip of his whisky. Realizes he's going to have to make it last, and discretely lets a little flow back into the glass. He feels like a philistine for treating a fifteen-year-old malt with such contempt, but he knows he's committed far worse crimes against decorum. Somewhere, Shonagh has a photograph of him lapping expensive champagne from a dog bowl. It might well have been taken at their wedding.

'Serendipity,' says Neilsen, his hands in his lap, his manner suggesting an almost Zen-like sense of self. He smiles, a pleasant sight, and explains himself. 'I'd feared having to drive over Harrogate way to track you down. Happy accident to find you're still the right end of the M62. Staying with Miss Harris, are you?'

Rufus makes a conscious decision to be honest for as long as it serves him well. 'Yes, Annabeth.'

'She not joining you for a nightcap?' he asks, his manner becoming more relaxed with each syllable. He alters his position, one arm thrown out across the back of the neighbouring chair.

'Helping her son with some work,' says Rufus, smoothly. 'I feel a bit of an intruder, if I'm honest. Will slip back after last orders. I'm never really comfortable in somebody else's house, but I've definitely had too much to drive home.'

Neilsen laughs, pleasantly. 'Definitely? There's a grey area, is there? How many units would you consider to be worth the risk?'

Rufus feels a little silly, but plays up to it. 'Good job I've nothing to hide – I'd spill my secrets in five minutes, wouldn't I?'

Neilsen gives what looks a little like a wink. Snaps his smile off as if flicking a switch. 'We'll see.'

Rufus plays with his glass. Doodles on the varnished table with the condensation. He can feel his hangover creeping in at his temples and the base of his skull – a horrible feeling when still unforgivably drunk. He stops being so genial. Meets the hard face with one of his own. 'So,' he says, 'what is it I can do for you?'

Neilsen takes a breath. Holds his gaze. Sips his water without looking away. Puts the glass down, then reaches into the inside pocket of his jacket, flashing a burgundy lining that complements the oxblood of his hand-stitched brogues.

'I understand there was an incident in your class this morning,' he says, placing his phone down on the table, face up. 'An officer was badly hurt. So too was another inmate. Word is that you took a few bumps and bruises yourself trying to protect a certain infamous inmate from being seriously hurt. Didn't work, for all your efforts. Stabbed with a pencil, or so I'm led to believe.'

Rufus nods. Shrugs. 'That's about the size of it. Not really what I signed up for. I had a few misgivings about it but I believe in the importance of creative writing – engaging with your own imagination, y'know? It's a big part of a life well lived. And I'll admit, I was intrigued. Bit of a reputation, Holderness, hasn't it? And of course, Annabeth has been a big supporter of my books.'

Neilsen nods, understanding. 'You were aware that one of your attendees was from the At-Risk wing, yes?'

'Sort of,' admits Rufus, sheepishly. 'I get a lot of emails. I'm not exactly Mr Organized. Annabeth said something about it but my only thought was the more the merrier.'

'Even if that somebody has abducted a child?' asks Neilsen, frowning.

'I wish I could give you some sort of deep and meaningful

breakdown of my core beliefs, I really do. But I just said "yes" because I tend to say "yes" to most things. It's actually easier than saying "no" and leads to more interesting situations. That probably sounds ridiculous to you.'

Neilsen shrugs, his manner a little too louche for Rufus's taste. He takes a sip of his whisky. Feels the burn and wonders where the hell this is going.

'I'm told there was some unpleasantness during yesterday's session,' says Neilsen. He adjusts his position slightly, flicking a glance at his phone. 'The gentleman in question was, in the words of one of the witnesses, "trying to wind you up". Asking off-colour questions. Generally making a nuisance of himself.'

Rufus puts his hands down on the grainy wood of the table, hears the clang as the barmaid calls last orders. Answers with a frown. 'I've had worse questions from little old ladies at Women's Institute meetings. It didn't bother me. Bothered the other chap though. What was his name? Suggs? But it was fine. Just added some heat to the blaze, you know?'

'Mr Cox is alleging that you responded violently,' says Neilsen, quietly. 'Twisted a big patch of his forearm while everybody was distracted. He has a nasty wound.'

Rufus feels heat start to prickle at his skin, the drink in his belly sloshing about and climbing up his throat. 'What are you talking about? That's not even remotely true. He did that to himself, I saw him do it.'

'He says you called him a nonce.'

'He what? When? How would I . . .?'

'And obviously with the situation developing today – the serious assault . . . well, CPS could even decide it's a case of attempted murder. As things stand, he's staying very quiet about what he saw. Can't seem to recall who did what. Only willing to talk to one officer, and she's not well enough to come to work. Your sainted Annabeth . . .'

Rufus sits forward, fringe flopping forward across his brow and sticking to his clammy forehead. He twitches his hands. 'Are you accusing me of stabbing him? Is he? That's mad. I don't know him from Adam! I saved him, if anything!'

'What a hero,' says Neilsen, drily. He takes a sip of his sparkling water. Cleanses his palate: the mention of Cox having left a sour taste. 'We have a mutual acquaintance, as it happens, Mr Orton. You and I, I mean. The reporter you chatted with earlier this evening. She's a good operator – one of those free-lancers who takes their job seriously and understands that "off the record" actually means something. She has been showing a great deal of interest in a case that you seem to have acci-dentally inserted yourself into. You'll be aware that we're searching an area outside Kirmington for the remains of one Bronwen Roberts, yes?'

Rufus drains his whisky, wishing to God there was another on the way. He'd like to rewind forty-eight hours and be back in his armchair, pissed and useless but largely harmless. 'Yes. The reporter, she mentioned it, I think.'

'Apparently you had an interest in a cold case. Walter Defreitas. That name rang a bell, you see, Mr Orton, because Defreitas was big pals with one Mark Fellowes. And Mark Fellowes is on the radar of the joint task force which is currently looking into a series of disappearances. Teenagers, as it happens. Similar modus operandi, similar victim profile. Can you guess which other of our mutual acquaintances is very much a suspect in these disappearances?'

Rufus lets his feelings show. Rolls his eyes like a child tired of being lectured. 'Would it be Griffin Cox?'

'Give that man a prize,' says Neilsen, pointing a finger directly at the centre of Rufus's chest. 'You know he's in prison for abduction, yes? Groomed a teenage girl online, made arrange-ments to meet, bundled her into his car and only got pulled over through sheer bad luck? You know that's why he's inside?'

Rufus nods, his head really starting to ache.

'He was in HMP Frankland for several years. On the VP wing. He was there at the same time as one Mark Fellowes.'

Rufus stares into the bottom of his glass. 'Right,' he says. Shrugs. 'And?'

'And if I were to put a load of names on a whiteboard and start drawing lines between them all, I think it would make for a very interesting picture.'

Rufus rewinds a little, plays the conversation back. Shakes his head. 'No, you've lost me. Why have you come out of your way to talk to me? What do you think I've done?'

Neilsen doesn't reply. Glances at his phone. 'You're an academic, aren't you? First class degree from Durham, yes? Tell me about Ovid. About Lavinia.'

Rufus wrinkles his face, unsettled by the change in tone. 'Ovid? What are you asking about Ovid for? And who's Lavinia?'

'*Metamorphoses*,' says Neilsen, enunciating every word. 'And *Titus Andronicus*.'

'They're different things, mate,' says Rufus, thoroughly baffled.

'They were mentioned by Cox. Examples of romance.' He looks uncertain. 'I'm sure it was Lavinia.'

'You might mean Philomela,' says Rufus, scratching his head and wishing he had the cash to buy a fizzy drink and a couple of painkillers. 'A true symbol of the destruction of something pure. A princess, raped by her brother-in-law. She had her tongue cut out so she wouldn't tell and was imprisoned in the woods. Wove her defilement into a tapestry that was sent to her rapist's wife. His wife baked his children into a pie in revenge and Philomela was transformed into a nightingale.'

Neilsen makes a face. 'And Lavinia?'

'Raped on her lover's corpse. Tongue cut out. Hands cut off and replaced with twigs. You said he saw these things as romantic? Was he just playing with you?'

Neilsen doesn't reply. Mulls it over, his face twisted in concentration. Rufus snaps. 'Look, my brain feels like it's full of spiders here. Just tell me, what's any of this got to do with me?'

Neilsen considers this. Stares past him to where the barmaid continues to throw admiring glances. 'I would be very surprised if you stabbed Griffin Cox,' he says, at last. 'I'd be very surprised if you had any agenda at all. But I do know that Cox knows he's on borrowed time. He's responsible for the abduction and no doubt the murder of several adolescents. He's done his time quietly but if we can charge him with even one of these missing persons cases, he's going to be inside until he's very old. I think that's unacceptable to Mr Cox. He wants out, that much is for certain. Myself and my colleague chatted with him yesterday and it was clear that for all his bravado he was definitely panicking about what we might have found at the field in Kirmington. The only person he would consider an ally has given a statement claiming that Cox called him the night Bronwen died and told him in a state of some distress precisely where he'd put the body. He's an old, old man who seems to be trying to clear his conscience before the end, but that hasn't stopped him taking a monthly salary to look after Cox's possessions and estate all these years. We don't know what other influence Cox carries, but he's not poor. And, not to put too fine a point on it, you're in something of a financial pickle, are you not? That car of yours? No insurance, no tax, no MOT. A man like Cox could solve those problems. Put a few quid in your pocket to help annoying evidence go away . . .'

Rufus locks his jaw, teeth clamped together. Glares at the detective. 'You're out of your mind.'

'No,' says Neilsen, as if holding a document proving that he is entirely sane. 'No, I'm following a thought to a series of intriguing conclusions.'

'This Mark Fellowes,' says Rufus, and as he shifts in his seat he realizes that the sweat on his body has turned uncomfortably cold. 'I can't see the connections there. What's he got to do with the missing teenagers? And how many missing teenagers are we talking about? What evidence do you have against Cox?'

Neilsen grins at him, seemingly pleased to have been asked. 'You're showing a lot of interest, Mr Orton. And obviously I can't share the details of an ongoing investigation.'

'So what do you bloody want?' he asks, bitterly. He pushes his hair out of his eyes. Watches his own reflection shimmer in the soft, intelligent eyes of his gentle interrogator. 'Tracking me down like I've done something wrong . . . making your accusations . . . messing with my head . . .'

Neilsen smiles. Glances at his phone. 'I want you to know you've got my attention,' he says, quietly. 'That's all. If you're thinking of doing something rash, I want you to be aware of the consequences. I want you to know what kind of man you saved today.'

Rufus pulls a face. 'So I saved him now, did I? Didn't stab him, and take his money to get rid of evidence—'

'I want you to read something that our mutual friend wrote,' says Neilsen, picking up the phone and tapping the screen with his long, nimble fingers. 'I'm sending you something that might make you think. And when you've read it, and digested all this, and had a little chat with Miss Harris, then maybe you'll consider doing your civic duty. You could talk to Mr Cox. Quietly. Confidentially. You could persuade him he has a friend in you. And you could perhaps get him to open up.'

Rufus is chewing his tongue, grinding his molars against the great dry slug in his mouth. How the hell has he found himself here? He's a writer of half-decent literature and a better-than-average creative writing tutor. He thinks of the snow globe. Of Annabeth's reaction to it, and to the picture of Mark Fellowes on her son's computer screen. Defreitas had an interest in teenage girls. He moved in the same circles as Mark Fellowes. Fellowes left prints at the murder scene. And years later, he shared a wing with one Griffin Cox. Cox requested a move to Britain's most notorious prison, not long after Annabeth appeared in the prison magazine. Could he have recognized her? He'd fought tooth and claw to get on the course. To be near her. Suddenly, he fancies he can see a picture, and it is all he can do to keep it from showing in his face.

Christ, he thinks, and his whole body fills with a quiet sadness. *You poor child.*

Neilsen stands. Takes his wallet from his back pocket and removes two twenty-pound notes and a tenner from his wallet. Puts it on the table in front of Rufus, and winks. 'After you've read it, you'll want to buy a bottle. Make sure it's the good stuff.'

He slides the money across the table. Drops a business card on top. Nods, and walks away. The barmaid traces his every step with her eyes.

Rufus feels his phone vibrate in his pocket. He does as he's bid. Starts to read.

At closing time, he buys a bottle of Glenfiddich and two packets of crisps. Goes to his car, and climbs into the back seat. Drinks, and cries, and falls into a sleep full of leering skulls.

THE STRANGE DISAPPEARANCE OF LUKE ASHLEY
By CrymeReport.com staff
February 11, 2012

In the time it takes you to read this article, three children will have gone missing from home. More than 300,000 children go missing in the UK every year. Not all return home. Some are never seen again. Others disappear for years at a time. For some families, the search for answers ends in grief. And for others, there are no answers at all.

Susan Westoby, 49, has spent the last six years hoping that her 'perfect son', Phillip, walks back through the door with an innocent explanation for where he has been since leaving the family home early one Sunday morning in June, 2007.

'I remember the last evening we spent together as a proper family unit. We were all together in the living room: me, his dad, his big brother and little sister, and it was one of those warm, nice nights where you have the window open and you can small the barbecue smells wafting in from other people's gardens. Phillip was sitting by the stereo with his headphones on, reading a graphic novel. I had my magazine. Dad and the other two were watching DVDs. It was a normal, pleasant evening. The next day everything changed. Our lives have never been the same since.'

Phillip is described as 'clever and kind' by those who knew him. A pupil at his local comprehensive in Carlisle, he was thought of by teachers as a pupil with the potential to reach one of the Oxbridge universities and he completed two GCSEs – in music and information technology – three years before his peers will sit exams, having been placed on a Gifted Student fast-track education scheme.

Since his disappearance, Susan has worked with charity organization Missing People to raise awareness of the number of young people who vanish without trace each year.

She believes that while many cases make headlines, others are quietly ignored by the media or dismissed by police as 'problem children' and 'troubled runaways'.

Police have been unable to piece together any sort of log of Phillip's movements on the day of his disappearance. Susan has turned detective in her effort to find witnesses.

'He was never the most popular kid in the class, but he had friends, or at least people he was friendly with. A neighbour saw him leaving the house and told us he seemed to be going to an effort not to make any noise, but that would be just like him on a normal day – frightened to wake his dad, who was going through awful problems with his back. After that, we have a vague sighting from an older boy who thinks he may have seen him hanging around by the phone box on the row of shops at the bottom of Chances Park.

'Phillip did have a mobile phone of his own but he was forever losing it, so whether he had it with him, we don't know. Certainly it hasn't been used. We've managed to get into his computer and talk with some of the friends he played games with through some sort of internet link-up, but it all goes over my head and the important thing is that nobody could offer any sort of help. One gamer he used to chat with suggested that he'd been going into a private chatroom online in recent weeks, but didn't know the name of it. The police were no help at all.'

Susan believes the charity has been a lifeline these past years. She said: 'They have volunteers and paid staff but everybody connected to it is completely focused on doing everything they can to help people like me. And there are so many people like me. Too many.'

The charity has helped Susan connect with the mother and father of Bronwen Roberts, who vanished from her home in rural Lincolnshire in 1998.

She said: 'That family has been through so much. It's

the waiting – the not knowing: the hoping for answers but the terror at what those answers might be.'

There is at least a little ray of hope for the Roberts family. A website set up to keep Bronwen's memory alive was recently contacted by an anonymous source claiming that Bronwen had been involved in a secret relationship with a family friend in the weeks before her disappearance.

Police initially dismissed the accusation as a cruel hoax by an attention seeker, but after the story was publicized in a national newspaper, a friend of Bronwen's confirmed that the 'clever, gifted and inquisitive' teen had indeed been secretly seeing a friend of her older brother – a student at the University of Hertfordshire.

A spokeswoman for Missing People said: 'We can't talk about that particular development but suffice to say that the family are struggling with some very conflicting emotions.'

A website set up by Susan Westoby was closed down last year when it became a target for vile internet trolls who taunted the family. The internet is awash with forums and noticeboards where users share theories and dissect his disappearance, along with so many others. There is a growing theory that some of the teens listed as missing in the UK were all victims of the same perpetrator or perpetrators, though police have been quick to deny any suggestion that there is an active serial killer at work targeting bright and naïve UK teens.

The spokeswoman for the charity said: 'That kind of gossip only hampers us and causes harm to those already under an obscene amount of stress and pain. We will continue to work with families and the police and do what we can to minimize the pain for those left wondering what has happened to those they love best.'

THIRTY

Governor Laiquet Hussain looks as though he has gone beyond 'tired' and has somehow transcended into a different reality. He looks as though he is fragmenting: his outline disintegrating into pixels and particles and mingling with the fog and dust and dandruff that makes up the grey air of his joyless office. Annabeth has never seen a man looking so thoroughly broken. His olive skin has taken on a waxy, bloated look that makes her think of drowned corpses. His eyelids are puffy, hanging low over his half-closed eyes like a rain-filled awning over a shop. He's wearing a clean shirt and a nice suit but it's a bandage over an infected wound. The room smells of unwashed skin and coffee breath. She wants to look up at the ceiling light: to check whether it would support a noose and take his weight. Fancies, given his current luck, that he would just end up on his backside covered in plaster dust and, quite possibly, a forgotten escapee.

'Please,' he says, squinting at some papers on his desk. He waves vaguely at a chair. 'Take a seat. Move any clutter. Burn it, if you feel the urge.'|

Annabeth does as requested, minus the arson. She's been in the governor's office twice before. On the first occasion, he was welcoming her and three other new-starters to HMP Holderness – telling them all not to believe the headlines about conditions within the jail, and that all he asked of them was that they be the best version of themselves. Nine weeks later she was here again, discussing a minor amendment she might care to make on a witness statement. Another officer had broken the eye socket of a minor drug dealer on C-Wing, and Annabeth had neglected to mention that the alleged victim had lunged for her colleague and struck him with a cosh. Annabeth had done as she was asked. She wonders what other moral adjustments she will have to make today. Wonders what Hussain will request of her, and how it will dovetail with

what she knows Cox will insist upon when she makes her
way to his bedside.

'Nasty business,' he says, licking dry lips. 'Did Cathy ask
you if you wanted coffee? Tea? Berocca?'

'I'm fine, sir.'

'No problem, no problem. Yes, as I say. Nasty.'

'So I'm told, sir.'

'He's OK, of course. Mr Windsor. Probably be back in a
month or so, provided that's what he wants.'

Annabeth can think of nothing to say. She doesn't see Windsor
as a great asset to the profession, but with staffing levels as
they are, she'd rather have as many colleagues around her
as can be found. She's the only one of the four new starters
who sat here on their first day who haven't already walked out,
citing stress or dangerous working conditions.

'You weren't in yesterday?' He eyes her, sleepily. 'Ill, I'm
told. Mr Windsor stepped in. You'll be able to provide a doctor's
note, I'm sure.'

'Yes sir,' she says. She's struggling to work out what to do
with her hands. She has them clasped in her lap, trying to
obscure the scuffs and bruises on her knuckles. She doesn't
want anybody seeing them, but she doesn't like seeing them
herself. She doesn't need reminding of what she did to Rufus.
Ethan isn't talking to her. She can't find the courage to ring
Rufus and apologize. Even to explain. She feels like she's
floating, somehow: as if she's tethered to reality by a fraying
thread and that if she doesn't keep concentrating, she could
simply drift away. She knows that she won't hear from Rufus
again. His car was gone when she woke in the early hours of
the morning. The house had seemed empty without him. He'd
only stayed one night, but he'd left some elemental trace of
himself: the way a house that has experienced great joy or grief
can provoke shadow feelings in its new occupants. She'd felt
him all around her: a big personality brought low by the violence
of a woman he'd thought of as a friend.

She'd set about tidying up. Put her folders back in the
cupboard. Tidied away the sticky glasses and folded the blanket
she had cocooned herself within on the sofa. Sat and looked at
the snow globe for an age. Then she had put on her uniform

and come to work. She has bigger things to concern herself with. Rufus was good company; she likes the way his mind works, but after what comes next, he'll be glad of the distance she has created between them. He won't want any part of the fallout that accompanies the denouement of Cox's scheme. She has run through endless permeations about what Cox will demand of her. All she's been through, all she's endured, and she will spend the next few months in debt to a monster. He'll want special privileges. Will want her to turn a blind eye to drugs; money; mobile phones – hell, he could tell her to bring him pornography and if she said no he would tell the world she was a murderer. He owns her. Her son is part made of a dead man's DNA. She can do nought but comply.

'Anything serious?' asks Hussain, concerned for her health.

'Stomach upset, sir. Had to wait the recommended twenty-four hours.'

'And you're OK now?'

'I wanted to be what help I could, sir.'

Hussain nods. His eyes slide shut. He gives a little shake of his head, and sighs. It seems to contain the ghosts of countless hopes. Annabeth scans the room. It's not a bad office. High ceilings, painted Racing Green. Long mahogany desk, made lopsided by the chunky computer at one end, shoved to one side to accommodate his sleek little laptop. There are citations and certificates in frames on the wall, and a framed photograph of Hussain shaking hands with Prince Charles, hanging wonkily beside a double-page spread in the *Hull Daily Mail*, profiling HMP Holderness's 'new' governor and his grandiose promises to make an 'excellent' prison within twelve months. It was written five years ago. The accompanying picture shows him looking two decades younger.

'I'm all for the ideas, of course,' says Hussain, with a slur that suggests he's not entirely awake. 'Creative writing? Wonderful. I've overseen a lot of similar schemes myself. Art. Woodworking. Mindfulness. I ran a meditation group when I was at Wandsworth. Obviously the current paymasters have different priorities to those who used to sign the cheques, but it's up to people like you and I to find ways to turn time spent in prison into time well spent, yes?'

Annabeth smiles, politely. She's heard him use the soundbite before. She feels a rush of pity for the man. He really did believe he could turn things around at Holderness. He really did believe that railing against Government would lead to public support and increased resources. Instead it made him a hate figure for everybody who thinks of the phrase 'bleeding heart' as an insult. Words that Annabeth hadn't used since school were thrown his way. *Wishy-washy. Touchy-feely. Namby-pamby.* The same papers that had criticized Britain's crumbling, out-of-date prison sentence promptly leapt on him for espousing the self-same complaints, wilfully distorting his views until the popular presses were claiming that he wanted paedophiles set free and for the victims of crime to feel sorry for the perpetrators.

'Could have happened to anybody, of course,' says Hussain, reaching behind him and picking up a folder from a pile behind him. He leafs through it, scowling one moment, nodding the next. 'You have a good record, Annabeth. We're very lucky to have you. I'm told we weren't your first choice but I'm glad we got you in the end. You've been a true asset. It's no secret that we have high hopes for you, if you stay in the service.'

'Thank you, sir,' says Annabeth, with as much enthusiasm as she can muster. She feels sick. Feels as though she has the word 'PSYCHO' carved into her forehead.

'You understand the bigger picture, of course,' says Hussain, smoothly. 'You've worked out there in the real world. You've life experience. You've got your degree and with a CV like yours – working for such a commendable organization before you came to us – well, the world's your oyster, really. Which is why I know you'll understand why I thought we should have this conversation.'

'Sir?'

He clears his throat. 'Mr Cox. You're aware that he suffered a nasty injury, yes?'

Annabeth nods.

'He's unclear of the details but has suggested that your writer friend might somehow be responsible for those injuries. He's suggested that Mr Orton had an agenda, and may even have deliberately inveigled his way into your good graces in order to abuse his power and to find opportunity to attack him.'

'That's absurd, sir,' says Annabeth, quietly. She looks at her knuckles. 'He's just a writer – a good one – who got caught up in something.'

'Of course,' says Hussain, and takes a swig of cold coffee from the mug on his desk. 'Prisoners will say anything, we both know that. But unfortunately, this incident occurred the day after Cox was questioned in connection with an unsolved missing person case. Cox's name is already out there as a person of interest to the police. There are websites and podcasts which don't hold back and which name him, quite candidly, as a potential killer. He's very much a high profile inmate, which is why he was always best served by remaining on the At-Risk wing. And yet he was permitted to attend a creative writing class with the general population. With Suggs, of all people. I understand that you were acting with the best of intentions but given the profile of this prison, and this prisoner, questions will be asked about your good judgement. It would be helpful if Mr Cox saw the merits in amnesia.'

'Sir?'

Hussain swallows, painfully. He looks one more bad shift away from stringing himself up. 'He's very fond of you, Annabeth. He says you are the only officer he trusts. He's asked for you, repeatedly. He believes himself to still be in harm's way and has told the overseers that he is too afraid to allow the medical staff at this prison to treat him for his wounds unless you are there to ensure his well-being.'

Annabeth feels the colour drain from her cheeks. Feels as though her throat has been cut.

'Ordinarily, such requests would be given short shrift, but in this instance I'm going to arrange matters so that you are his personal officer for the foreseeable future. He's requested that he be sent to segregation when he is well enough to leave the medical unit. We'll rearrange your shift pattern. The most important thing is that he feels safe. Feels protected. That he understands the harm it could do your career if he were to persist in making such half-formed accusations.'

Annabeth studies him as he speaks. She knows that he hates himself for putting her in such a position. She's a young, moti-vated member of staff who has just been told to go and be nice to a convicted predator with a skill for manipulation. She tries to summon some anger, but the squall of despair circling Hussain seems to suck the passion from her. She just feels desperately sad. Sad for all of them. She feels sorry for her boss. He's a good man, if such a thing exists. He just can't change the world. What matters to him most is keeping his job. Protecting his prison from more bad headlines. She blinks back tears as she considers how hard he will be hit by what comes next.

'Of course, sir,' she says, flatly. 'Thank you for the opportunity.'

He can't meet her eyes, even as he flashes his best fake smile. Looks down at her file, open on his lap, and makes approving noises.

'I'll walk you over to the unit myself,' he says, and the room is so silent she can hear the sound of him unsticking his tongue from the roof his mouth and swallowing.

'Sir?'

'Cox,' he says, quietly. 'He's waiting for you.'

Cox has moved from the bed to the small plastic chair at its side. He's fastened up his pyjama buttons wrongly, and the bandage covering his wound is peeking out from the great triangle of exposed skin. He looks just the right amount of pitiful. Anybody looking in through the reinforced glass would see a helpless figure. He's pale; his eyes seamed red and dark beneath, and with a day's growth of patchy grey stubble, he looks a lot more like a patient than a prisoner.

When he first began to suspect there was something unusual about him, Cox read a lot of academic textbooks on different forms of mental disorder. He read every book he could find on serial killers and investigative methods. He read books by criminal profilers and dry, academic tomes filled with case histories and insights. He read in the hope of identifying kindred spirits: of seeing himself reflected back among the endless pages of black ink. He found little that felt familiar. He doesn't particularly enjoy categorization. He knows he isn't a sex offender, though he will confess to an element of arousal during the deaths of his prettier victims. He feels no shame for it – the action is involuntary, and he has long since made the decision not to cheapen the experience of murder by turning it into an opportunity for sexual release. His pleasure is more tantric; more elemental. He folds the pleasure back inside himself and surfs the wave; existing in a state of residual bliss until the hunger for new experience begins to growl afresh. Nor does he see himself as a nihilistic beast: killing with a sense of futility and justifying his actions by pointing at the greater crimes of an unjust, hypocritical society. Cox is a believer. A religious man, in some sense. He finds the notion of God and devil infinitely more appealing than other explanations for existence, even while seeing in himself a perfect example of Darwinism. He has evolved into the perfect predator.

Checking that nobody is watching, he bends down, briskly, and picks up the two books that he has been ping-ponging between while waiting for the arrival of Miss Harris. One is Ovid's *Metamorphoses*. He has read it in three languages, but the English translation by Allen Mandelbaum is his favourite: unshowy and stately, seamed with the right amount of humour and violence. It never fails to leave him breathless. He is simultaneously reading *The Sociopath Next Door* by Martha Stout. When he regains his freedom, he intends to see out his years without drawing attention to himself. He studies the book as if learning a new language: assessing himself every few sentences to see whether he is guilty of exhibiting the signs guaranteed to cause alarm. He believes himself to be a psychoanalyst of exceptional insight, but he still isn't quite sure which label suits him best. He imagines a Venn diagram made up of at least half a dozen different circles, intersecting like petals of a flower with himself in the middle: a bee gathering pollen. He has elements of psychopathy, sociopathy, narcissistic personality disorder, dissociative personality disorder, depersonalization disorder and the comically named intermittent explosive disorder. He finds it ironic that the depression, anxiety, eating disorders and bed-wetting that plagued him as a child disappeared entirely as soon as he began killing people. He sometimes wonders whether he should write an academic tome espousing the psychological benefits of murder. He imagines there is a market for such a work.

There is a sound from the doorway. A changing of the lights.

The sound of a key turning and then the muted chatter of the hallway forms into decipherable words as two lots of footsteps make their way across the floor. He feigns sleep, the books in his lap. Makes himself a sculpture of somebody so pitiable as to barely register as human.

'Gary? Gary, are you sleeping? I've brought Miss Harris. How are you feeling? Can I get you some water, perhaps? Reading again, I see. Excellent. Good to see you haven't been put off, eh?'

Groggily, Cox raises his head. Looks past Hussain to where Annabeth stands. She's been crying. From the way she holds her hands he can tell she has suffered an injury. She didn't wash her hair this morning. There are fibres of wool upon her white shirt. Did she sleep downstairs, he wonders? On the sofa, under a blanket? Or did she and her friend enjoy one another on a patterned rug? He ruminates on this, and more, as he looks up at his heaven-sent angel and allows his eyes to fill with tears.

'I'm sorry,' he whispers, holding back the sobs. 'I'm sorry this happened. All I wanted was to write. To use my time properly . . .'

'I'll get you some water,' says Hussain, quickly; trying to exude compassion and understanding. He hurries away towards the door.

'You can stop that now,' says Annabeth, her voice thin: breathy.

He sits up straight. Wipes snot and tears with the back of his hand. Grins and shakes his head, almost in wonder. 'You got my message,' he says.

Annabeth nods.

'So you understand.'

She nods, lips pressed together. 'What do you want?' She looks sick just asking. 'Money? Phone? Drugs?'

He stares at the side of her face. Forces her to meet his gaze. Then he holds it until he sees the colour in her cheeks change from red to white, and the black dots at the centre of her eyes to dilate and swell: ink dropped in water.

He shakes his head, a little disappointed in her. 'Oh Annabeth,' he says, sadly. 'I want what everybody wants. I want my liberty.'

She looks at him, mouth twisted, already shaking her head.

'No, you can't expect me to do that, not even if you tell the world what you think you know . . . no . . .'

'Yes,' he says, almost regretfully. 'I wish it were somebody other than you. I have no interest in causing you harm, or ruining a career you have worked hard for. Nor do I pass moral judgement on the act committed against a serial rapist when you were a vulnerable child. But the walls are getting tighter around me. The idea of freedom has sustained me, but there are those who would do anything in their power to deny me. And so I must use what leverage I have.'

'I can't,' hisses Annabeth. 'I became a prison officer to help people . . .'

'Then help me.'

'You're a killer,' she says, then tries to snatch back the words when she realizes what she has said.

'Two peas in a pod,' grins Cox, then slips down into his chair, eyes brimming afresh, as Hussain comes back through the door.

'I can't . . .'

'John. 8:32.'

She stares at him, face bone white, confusion and sorrow in her eyes.

Cox looks up, wearing the tear-streaked face of the man he has spent these past years pretending to be.

'"The truth will set you free".'

THIRTY-ONE

It's a ghastly day. Although the fog has not taken this part of the east coast in its fist, the sky is a great smear of grey: the entire panorama made of damp pelts and dead rabbits. The chill air is speckled with a misty rain; a billion tiny raindrops hovering like flies in an atmosphere that reeks of spoiled crops and spilled diesel.

Rufus winces as the car grinds and bumps its way down the pitted farm track that leads to Chappell's Farm. He's not entirely

sure which village he has just passed through, but he had to
pause at a level crossing and call a bored-looking guard to open
the gates for him. He thinks he's somewhere between Barnetby-
le-Wold and Melton Ross but he wouldn't be able to swear to
it. There's a lot of green, beneath the grey, but not many people.
None of the houses match and the fields don't appear to
have any crops in them. He's already passed two abandoned
outbuildings and the rusting guts of a combine harvester.

He strikes a pothole. Pitches to the left. He curses and lets
out a groan of true pain. He woke with a hangover and all-over
achiness that made him feel as though he had slept in a suit of
armour, two sizes too small. His first instinct had been to secure
some fizzy drink and as many Ibuprofen as he was permitted,
then drive home in a state of near-terminal self-pity. Then it
came flooding back. Cox. Annabeth. Defreitas and Fellowes.
The journalist. The copper in the pub. Each recollection hit him
like a fist. The sun was only just rising – the sky streaked with
thumb prints of purple and pink, casting a metallic sheen to the
waters of the estuary. He'd wound the window down, taken as
many deep, cleansing breaths as he could without vomiting,
and driven away from Paull as if he were a cowboy riding
towards the line of the horizon. He got three miles before he
had to pull over and throw up. Managed another five, then saw
the glorious golden arches of a McDonald's, gleaming radiantly
against a backdrop of offices and retail parks. Two McMuffins
and a coffee and he felt as though there was a chance he would
be able to move his eyes from left to right without one or both
of his ears falling off. By the time the place started filling up
with other customers, he was borderline human. Was able to
charm a staff member into letting him charge his phone. Checked
his messages, and felt his heart sink as he realized Annabeth
hadn't reached out. He had a sudden stabbing pang of empathy:
a knowledge of what she has endured, and what she still may
have to face. And he had made a decision, even without real-
izing it. He wasn't going home. Wasn't drifting back to a life
that didn't need him. He was going to help Annabeth. And
perhaps – the thought slinking furtively around the periphery
of his conscience – perhaps he might help himself too.

There's an old folks' home up ahead on his left and a small

woman with long, straw-coloured hair is standing with her hands in her pockets beside a white Fiat 500. Rufus slows down. Reaches across and winds the window down.

'Ruth?'

'No, I'm your Tinder hook-up. Take your trousers off, I haven't long.' She grins as she says it, her West Yorkshire accent making it sound as though he is being propositioned by a lascivious coal miner.

'Are you jumping in, then?'

'Too right.'

She brings the ugliness of the day into the car with her: the wind scattering papers and her floral perfume doing little to disguise the stink of churned-up farmland. She clatters back into the seat, untangling her hair and rummaging in the pockets of her black coat. Retrieves notebook, betting-shop pen, a packet of cigarettes and a bag of mints. Dumps them all on the dashboard. She's a ball of energy, her movements feverish. As the sleeves of her jacket rides up he spots a semi-colon tattooed on her left wrist. He fancies she's probably more interesting than most of the subjects she writes about.

'Farm's yonder,' she says, lighting a cigarette with a cheap lighter and popping a mint into her mouth at the same time. Rufus looks at her, curious. 'They didn't have any menthols,' she says, as if this explains everything.

Rufus eases them forward, feeling uncomfortable. He's aware of himself, suddenly. Bruised. Dishevelled. Unwashed. He's never been overly concerned about his appearance but he's aware he's made the transition from looking like a novelist, to simply looking novel.

'Quiet,' says Rufus, looking out through the grimy glass. 'Thought there would be a load of police cars and a forensics van or something.'

'Nah,' says Ruth, winding the window down and blowing her smoke out. 'The way most police forces are staffed these days you're lucky it isn't just a bloke with a spade.'

'But they have such a huge area to search,' says Rufus, wishing she would either stop smoking or offer him one. 'Oh,' he mutters, as the road comes to an abrupt halt at a rusty metal gate. 'That didn't take long.'

Up ahead is the outline of a large, rundown farm: big, ramshackle barns rising over the remains of a neglected stable. There are grain silos off to one side, doors hanging open, rusted ladders dangling haphazardly from the metal gangway that winds around their outsides. The fields are overgrown. A decent sized mobile home sticks out from the open end of the nearest barn, surrounded by a huge wall of abandoned tyres and an avalanche of damp, mulched straw. It's thoroughly uninviting, but Rufus feels the hairs on his arms rise with something like excitement as he stares through the roiling mist.

'They can't have completed a search in that time,' says Rufus, baffled.

Beside him, Ruth gives a friendly laugh. 'It's not the way you see on telly, mate. Most of it is done by drone and geophysics, reading the landscape, placing thermal measuring implements. Cadaver dogs would be nice but I don't think they've got more than a handful for the region so I don't know if they were here. But to be honest, Ben tells me they were pretty sure where they were looking, and if they've done that and drawn a blank then they're not going to start digging up everything else on a whim.'

'But if there's the body of a missing girl, wouldn't it be worth any expense?'

'You're sweet,' says Ruth, chucking her cigarette through the open window. She gives him a once-over, frowning. 'You don't look like your picture. I read a bit on my phone last night. One of your books was down to ninety-nine p. Bit wordy, bit smart-arsed, but you're pretty good. My sub-editors would hate you though. Too much fancy stuff to cut out. You thinking you might write something on Cox, are you? I'd be glad to help, like. Not that I've got any sort of special insights, but I do know he's been on the radar of a few coppers over the years.'

Rufus isn't used to being hit with such a stream of questions. He pauses, gathering his thoughts, and she takes it as an invitation to carry on.

'Definitely dodgy, that's about as close to an outright accusation as I've ever got Ben to admit, but that in itself is enough to suggest you don't want him babysitting.'

'Ben?' he asks, bewildered.

'Cox, you doofus,' she says, laughing. 'No, Ben's OK. We had a thing, years back, but that's hardly an exclusive club for either of us. Been on the periphery of some big cases and he'd be a detective inspector by now if he didn't enjoy being part of the unit at Humberside. He said you and him had a drink last night. Cosy, was it?'

Rufus chews his lip, suddenly feeling a bit silly. He doesn't know why he's here. 'He basically warned me not to let Cox manipulate me. Buy me off, or whatever.'

'Whatever? I thought you were meant to be wordy!'

'I'm better written down.' He shrugs, and rubs at the sore patch of skin on his cheek.

'They'll be back later, apparently,' says Ruth, looking through the glass. 'I might have a potter around.'

'What, just go in, you mean?'

She smiles at him as if he were a baby. 'Yes, Rufus. Go and look around. Ben wanted to let me in yesterday but his boss is a right cow and wouldn't hear of it. I can make a few quid just from the pictures. And if you're writing a book . . .'

He frowns at her. 'Why do you think I'm writing a book?'

She shrugs, climbing from the car. 'Everybody is, aren't they? Anyway, you're more than welcome to tag along.'

He watches her light another cigarette then trudge off into the grey air, only halting briefly to find a safe place to put her foot on the rusty gate. Then she's clambering over and dropping down, plodding up towards the abandoned building, bag over her shoulder and the bulge of mints in her pocket.

'Oh bollocks,' says Rufus, and tucks the car in at the side of the road. Then he climbs out and trots, painfully, in the same direction that Ruth had taken. He clambers over the gate: cold, dirty metal unpleasant on his palms, and drops down onto the rutted track, jarring his knee. He feels a hundred years old.

'Ruth,' he says, into the gathering mist. 'Hold up.'

He half walks, half scurries towards the first of the buildings, hoping she'll be waiting for him. He can't see her. Can't hear her either. There's an ugly creaking sound coming from some-where nearby – metal on metal, a gibbet on a hinge – but the wide emptiness of the land makes it hard to follow the direction of any sound. He calls Ruth's name again and it's snatched away on the wind. He pokes his head around a crumbling brick wall and sees two rusty oil drums filled with brick and ash. A rotting bridle hangs from a hook. There's a plastic school chair off to one side, surrounded by cigarette butts. There are dirty mugs, unwashed plates scattered in among the mulch of hay and hard earth: sickle-like hoof prints hard-baked into the ground.

There's movement to his right.

'Boo,' says Ruth, and she appears at his side, a mint tucked into her cheek like a hamster. 'No bugger here. Pictures would be ace if I was a photographer but I can't make it look moody, just misty. Do you reckon you could stand facing off to one side just for scale, like. I'll send you a JPEG of the image if you cut me in to the royalties.'

Rufus feels the headache return with a vengeance. He needs to get his thoughts in order. He can feel the shape of a story that makes sense, but it's a vague, nebulous thing, just out of reach. He doesn't want to look at it too closely for fear of it delineating into something unequivocal. Right now, he thinks that Annabeth might have killed somebody who absolutely deserved every bit of suffering they endured. Somehow Griffin Cox knows about it – possibly from his association with Mark Fellowes at his last jail. He requested to be moved to HMP Holderness when he saw her in the prison magazine. He stops himself, cowling inwardly. How could he have made that connection? Sure, he could hear a story about a young woman having killed her abuser, but how could he then identify her as the prison officer busy running a creative writing course? He can't work it out. Thinks instead of Cox. Could he really be responsible for abducting half a dozen teenagers? Could he really have dumped Bronwen Roberts in a sinkhole on this farm? If so, why? He refuses to believe that people sometimes can't help themselves. Refuses to countenance the notions that killers are born, not made. He feels horribly ill-informed. He needs to understand Griffin Cox, if only to stop himself going mad.

'What brought them here in the first place?' asks Rufus, sucking his teeth in discomfort as the wind twists about him like damp rope. 'Why this exact spot? What's the connection?'

'His pal. Wilson something-or-other. Known him since he was a bairn. He was a general handyman for Cox's mum when Cox was growing up. Anyways, he's the one who spilled the beans. He's geriatric now but Ben thinks he might be clearing his conscience. Told a member of staff at his care home, and she got in touch with the police, and it's been getting bigger ever since. Made a full statement, claiming that he helped Cox put Bronwen Roberts down a sinkhole in the low field at Chappell's Farm. I doubt there'll be much left of her if it's even true, and he's not exactly a reliable witness, but if there are forensics then there's a chance it could lead to Cox.'

Rufus looks down at his left hand and realizes he's got a lit cigarette between his index and middle finger. He doesn't remember asking for it or being given it, but he raises it to his lips and enjoys every second of his in-breath. 'I don't know much about him, other than the fact he went to a posh school and was a bit chummy with a member of the Cabinet . . .'

Ruth pulls a face. 'He wasn't chummy with anybody. Had an awful time at school, which doesn't sound very good value for five grand a term. Very much a mummy's boy. It was just her and him, you see. Older mum, hadn't ever expected to be blessed with a child. They were living on savings, rattling around in this big old place down in Cambridgeshire. She was a funny fish, and I'm using that as a euphemism for "fucking nuts". We don't know who the father was, which no doubt wasn't easy to deal with back then. Old money, as it were. She doted on him. Had him believing he was somebody destined for greatness. Had him believing he was going to be remembered through the ages. Reality kicked in when he went to boarding school. Older kids used to dress him up as a girl and have him sleep in their beds, if you can believe that was allowed to go on. He was the designated "pretty boy" in the dorm. Must have messed him up, or at the very least, added another layer to what was there before.'

Rufus smokes his cigarette. Thinks of the small, inscrutable man in his writing group. Can't help but feel a surge of pity for the child he was.

'Mother had him thinking he was the new Renaissance – got him playing instruments and translating Latin and Greek texts when he was still a nipper. Went half-loony before he was five, opening the house up to all of the hippies and bohemians who wanted the Summer of Love to last for ever. God knows what he was exposed to.'

'And Wilson something-or-other?' asks Rufus.

'Father figure, I suppose. Lived not far off and was paid to keep the house shipshape. Don't ask me if there was something going on with him and Mum as I don't know. Either way, they were close. My source who went to prep with Cox – he reckons that Wilson was the one who put a stop to the bullies in the end. One of the ringleaders woke up to find a stranger in the dorm. He'd been tied to his bed and there was tape over his mouth. Told his pals that he'd thought he was having a nightmare: this grotesque thing with a hook nose and a gnarled back, sitting on his bed like a succubus. He tried to cry out but couldn't make a sound. Then the man leaned over him, took off the tape, and told him to open his mouth. Poor posh lad did as he was told. His visitor poured dirt down his throat.'

'Dirt?'

She shrugs. 'Mud. Sand. Ash. I don't know. But it nearly choked him. Visitor didn't speak other than to tell him to leave Griffin alone. Then he was gone.'

Rufus stares up at the clouds, hoping for a square of blue. Grinds out his cigarette. He's had enough. Wants to get home. Wants to put this whole silly game behind him.

'This Wilson – you think it was him?'

'Makes sense,' says Ruth, taking out her phone and snapping off a couple of shots of Rufus looking bemused. 'He's loyal enough to have looked after the old house all these years. Loyal enough to have visited Cox once a fortnight since he was arrested. Hasn't been to see him since he moved over to Holderness, but that's no doubt because he was ill. Must have come as a shock to Cox to find his old pal turning on him. Wonder what he did to deserve that?'

Rufus chews on his cheek, thinking hard. 'His connection to the missing teens,' he says, softly. 'Ben said they were all of a similar profile?'

Ruth nods. 'All relative innocents, if there is such a thing.

Clever, insightful, talented – not necessarily beautiful but certainly not tearaways.'

'And how did they come into contact with Cox?'

'In Bronwen's case, she took part in a junior music contest he was present at. Something of a Renaissance man, as I told you. His furniture company sponsored the trophy so he was on the panel of judges. According to the family, that was around the time somebody started to send her presents. Wrote letters. Sent her a nightingale in a cage, if you'll credit it . . .'

Rufus points at Ruth's pocket. Says nothing until he has another cigarette. 'And when she vanished?'

'They told the police about it. Police at the time were looking for a student – maybe a local boy she might have fallen for. It was a long time before anybody made the connection to the nice quiet man who'd met her at the recital. She was a flautist, you see. Cox too. Played as a child and kept it up through university. Even won a couple of scholarships to study in Italy under one of the greats. I think he'd hoped to go in that direction, but then his mother died and he lost the enthusiasm for it. Took a job with a family friend and rather drifted after that. But each of the cases that Cox has been questioned about involved somebody with a particular skill. Singer. Writer. Melanie Grazia, the girl from the boarding school – she was a dancer and we know he was at the school for a prize-giving at the same time she was involved in a rehearsal for a school production and could well have seen her. But it's all circumstantial. Hence the need for something solid. Forensics. A witness. A confession.'

'How did she die?' asks Rufus, turning his back on the bleak farm and beginning to head back towards the car. Ruth falls into step beside him. 'His mum.'

'She'd suffered a stroke about a year before she popped her clogs,' says Ruth, tactlessly. 'Wheelchair bound. Needed lots of help, apparently. He came home from Italy to care for her. She suffered a nasty tumble: wheelchair went down the steps out the back of the house. Lay there for hours in the fancy garden she loved: statues and sundials and stuff. Nobody could see her from the house. Died of exposure and head trauma.'

'And Cox?'

'The people who remember the funeral say he sang. Tried to, anyway. Broke down. Wept like it was a Greek tragedy, poor bastard. And then, like I say, he drifted.'

'I can see why the police like him as a suspect,' says Rufus, thoughtful. He shakes his head. 'But that's only because I'm viewing it through the filter of the notion that he's guilty of abducting and killing a load of teenagers. I mean, as you said, it's circumstantial.'

Ruth shrugs. 'Your mate Miss Harris would know better than me, wouldn't she? What's her name? What's her name again? Lillyanna, or Arrabella, or something, wasn't it?'

'Annabeth,' he corrects her, then pauses, one hand on the car door. Could it be that easy? Could Fellowes simply have remembered the unusual name? Mentioned it to his pad-mate in conversation. He can picture Cox, filing the name away. Seeing it in the prison mag. Setting his big old mind whirring. Would that be around the time Wilson last visited him? Could he have been telling him that he was ill? That he was going to clear his conscience and tell the police? Cox had requested the transfer, after all. Begged to be on Annabeth's course.

He throws the cigarette away and opens the car door. Is about to ask another question of Ruth when he realizes she's stopped, just in front of the gate. She's studying her phone intently, her lips twitching. She glances up: sees him watching.

'Can you drop me back?' she asks, urgently.

'Sure. Why? What's—'

'Cox,' she says, breathlessly. 'Cox has escaped.'

THIRTY-TWO

At the same moment that Rufus was taking his third bite of a sausage and egg McMuffin and wondering whether to throw himself in the Humber, Annabeth Harris was rushing from the medical wing at HMP Holderness to find Dr Lechmere. Griffin Cox had started fitting; his body convulsing;

blood running from his mouth as his teeth mashed down upon his tongue.

In the absence of the doctor – stuck in traffic on Hedon Road and listening to an operatic CD that drowned out the sound of her mobile phone – she located the resident nurse practitioner: an ex-Army staff sergeant named Matthew Keighley whose CV described a man of great experience with a commendable history of remaining cool in high pressure situations. His online employment history called him a 'robust and capable clinical thinker' and painted a glorious pen-portrait of the kind of individual tailor-made for dealing with such a set of circumstances as these. Nowhere on his application for the job did the word 'fraud' appear. Nor did 'chancer'. The phrase 'kept his head down and lucked his way through twenty-two years of service' was notably absent.

When confronted with the unnerving sight of Officer Annabeth Harris running into his little cubicle office and demanding he come and tend to a bona fide emergency, Keighley did what he had been trained to do in times of extreme crisis, and excused himself from performing any function that could carry even the slightest whiff of negative repercussions. He followed the rule book. He did what he had been told. He called an ambulance, registered the incident, amended the inmate's prison file. He didn't move from his chair: just stayed at his desk eating a multi-pack of donuts. It was left to Annabeth and PO Barry Lambert to wheel the gurney carrying the wide-eyed, trembling Cox down the sloping floors towards the maintenance exit and load him into the rear of the waiting ambulance; his right hand twisted shut as the paroxysms of pain gripped him like so many coils of barbed wire.

The paramedics checked his pupils, placed a breathing mask around his nostrils, and muttered in low voices that he seemed to have suffered a cerebrovascular haemorrhage and that his temperature was 'through the roof'. Annabeth and PO Lambert squeezed themselves in to the rear of the vehicle as the sirens wailed into life and the driver swung them through the big arched gates and out onto the rain-streaked country roads of Holderness. Lambert suggested they cuff him to the stretcher. The paramedic told him there was no way he was going to permit that. Lambert tried to get a signal on his mobile to update his line manager about the sudden development. Annabeth made a great show of doing the same – leaving a voicemail for Governor Hussain and explaining she had done as instructed and made sure she was on hand to provide a reassuring presence for their most high-profile prisoner.

The paramedic who tended to Cox did a professional job. He knew nothing about the patient in his care – just that he looked bloody awful and that his heartbeat was erratic and there appeared to be blood in one of his eyes. Annabeth filled him in on the patient history. He'd been stabbed the previous day – taken to hospital and sewn up. He'd complained of a high temperature and sickness in the night. He'd been given pain-killers but the wound smelled a little funny beneath the bandages and she was concerned that he had picked up an infection.

The ambulance was just passing the entrance to Hull's Victoria Dock estate when the miracle occurred. The ambulance slowed down to skirt the roundabout that turned left into the great tract of identikit new-build homes, rising from the broken foundations of the filled-in dock. The paramedic leaned forward and peeled back the bandage on his pale, bony chest. He leaned forward, examining the stitches and seeking any sign of the infection that the professional, halfway pretty prison officer had suggested. And then Cox opened his eyes. The transformation was sudden and absolute. The figure who, moments before, had seemed like somebody recently disinterred, had sprung with a strength and ferocity that came from somewhere deep within. His right hand, twisted into an unyielding claw, changed position to better grasp the canister of pepper spray upon his palm, and unloaded the stinging liquid straight into the hapless medic's eyes.

Later, the drivers of the vehicles that were near the ambulance, would tell police that the vehicle seemed to swing suddenly to the right, as if somebody had grabbed the wheel, and then barrelled straight towards the centre of the roundabout, crashing into the side of a Kingston Communications van, then rear-ending a Land Rover that had pulled in to the let the ambulance scream by. Moments later, the doors burst open, and a squat, plumpish man in a prison officer's uniform collapsed onto the road, clawing at his eyes. Moments later, a wiry figure, barefoot and wearing pyjamas, leapt down to the road, dragging a female prison officer by the hair; something sharp at her throat. He dragged her to the nearest vehicle: a red Suzuki Swift with white stripes up the bonnet and roof, and yanked the driver's door open before she had the presence of mind to lock it. He sprayed the driver straight in the eyes with the aerosol, then let go of his hostage for long enough to drag the driver onto the road and stamp on her head, twice, in quick succession. He pushed his prisoner into the driver's seat, and jumped in the back, pressing the shard of glinting metal back against her throat. Then the little car squirmed up the muddy bank round the waiting vehicles, and sped off into the maze of the estate, leaving only the scream of the siren and the desperate shouts of 'help me, help me' from the officer on the floor. It would be six minutes before the police arrived. They would find the paramedic unconscious on the gurney, eyes streaming, a great trench on his crown where he had been struck, hard, with the base of the small fire extinguisher from the shelf above the medication locker. They would find the driver sitting at the side of the road, weeping into his hands, blood streaming from his nose, having lost control of the vehicle the moment he heard the commotion from the rear of the ambulance. It would be four months before the detectives at Humberside Police would untangle the complex transactions and maze of accounts that had been used to disguise the £50,000 deposited in his account by one Wilson Iveson to make sure it was he who answered the emergency call to the prison.

It would be several hours before Annabeth presented herself at the doctor's surgery on the Victoria Dock estate, dripping wet and bleeding from a head wound, puking up sea water and mud and trying to tell the frightened receptionist to call the police, to call the hospital – to get divers in the water. He'd crashed through the sea wall, she said. He'd taken them into the water at forty miles per hour. The car was at the bottom of the river. As far as she knew, Cox was still inside. She'd only escaped because the windscreen had smashed when they hit the sea wall and she'd been able to drag herself free. Cox, who had taken the wheel once they were away from prying eyes, hadn't been able to untangle himself from the airbag before the water rushed into the car, and down his throat. She had no doubt he was dead. Dead, at the bottom of the river. And then she had crumpled in on herself, and begged those who rushed to provide blankets and hot tea and motherly arms, to ring her son. To tell Ethan she was so sorry. It was the only part of her story that wasn't a lie.

PART THREE

THIRTY-THREE

Rufus is sprawled in a sun-bleached wooden chair, tucked away in the overgrown garden at the rear of his home, attempting to allow an unfamiliar sunlight to undo some of the damage that his lifestyle has done to his face. It isn't working. He's just hot and sweaty and half asleep. He isn't normally fond of hot days: preferring to see the beauty in grey skies and bleak, zig-zagging rain. But the school holidays have filled the house with teenagers, and the only place he feels able to sit, and think, and drink himself insensible, is in the little tangle of wildflower-strewn grass between the courtyard garden and the orchard. It's a pleasant spot – the apple trees forming a lacy parasol overhead and the shadows moving with a pleasingly haphazard choreography. He has his eyes closed. There is a cigarette clasped between his lips: a dog-turd of ash threatening to tumble onto his stubbled chin. He's wearing a wrinkled linen shirt, shorts that won't fasten over his belly, and deck shoes with broken backs: his feet having stamped them flat. In the twists of bluebell, dandelion and cowslips that surround the rickety chair in which he reclines, hardback books form colourful stepping stones. Two wasps are slowly dying in the sticky residue of his home-made elderflower gin. He knows they will die happy.

'Not a bad spot, this. If I didn't know your financial situation I'd think you were doing well for yourself.'

Rufus sits forward, opening an eye like a dog asleep in front of the fire. He recognizes the voice. DC Ben Neilsen. He'd expected as much. He hasn't returned any of his phone calls or made arrangements to give a statement, as requested, so the handsome detective's presence at Rufus's home in North Yorkshire comes as no surprise.

'Pull up a tuffet,' says Rufus, grimacing as the sunlight makes his head spin. 'You want a drink? Do you like your elderflower gin with or without wasps?'

Neilsen stands directly in front of him, blocking out the sun. Rufus raises a hand to his forehead. He's sweating. Everything aches. He'd hoped vitamin D would be some miraculous cure-all but he just feels hot and tired. His thoughts seem to have been dulled by the sun. He wants to sleep. To roll into the soft grass and doze off with the smell of spring suffusing his senses.

'You didn't call me back,' says Neilsen, with a sigh.

Rufus looks him up and down. He looks like something from a magazine. He wears a light grey suit with a pale shirt and open collar. There's not a bead of sweat upon him and he looks as though he has just been professionally cleaned. Rufus would hate him for it, if he had any energy for the task.

'Your wife said I would find you out here. She didn't seem surprised to see me.'

Rufus feels ash patter onto his chin. Removes the dog-end and rubs his hand across his bristles. 'I don't think Shonagh has the capacity for surprise, Ben. I think the juice ran dry on that score a few years ago. Gave too many feelings away too freely, you see. All the good ones. Compassion, lust, sense of humour, creativity – let them gush when we first met. Now the barrel is empty. Still got a few kegs of bitterness and disappointment left though. She can spray that around like an elephant spraying water.'

Neilsen looks around and locates an old stone birdbath. It's heavy, but he picks it up without much effort and moves it nearer to where Rufus is sprawled. Sits himself down and peers at the books which surround him.

'You're re-reading *Metamorphoses*?' he asks, drily. 'Psychopath textbooks. *The Gates of Janus*? That's by Ian Brady, isn't it? Not exactly light reading, Rufus. Anybody would think you were studying for an exam. Heading on *Mastermind*, are you? Chosen subject: true evil.'

Rufus runs his tongue around his mouth, wishing that somebody, anybody, liked him enough to bring him a glass of water. He sighs, and tries to sit up. There's an unpleasant sound as he unpeels his sweaty skin from the wood of the chair. He laughs at the absurdity of it all. At the ridiculousness of the picture he must present.

'I spoke to Ruth this morning,' says Neilsen, conversationally.

'She was trying to get the address of a certain Wilson Iveson. Considering a profile, she said. Trying to drum up a piece about the man who helped create a monster. I don't think she'll get very far. He's properly gaga now, and that's a genuine diagnosis. We had a couple of local bobbies go chat with him at the care home. Barely knew his own name, poor sod. The idea that he'd be hiding Cox, or have anything useful to say – it's laughable.'

Rufus licks his dry lips. 'So you still haven't found him?'

'Divers have been down three times, but the currents there are erratic. It could be weeks or months before he washes up. Found the car, but no useful forensics. Found the spot where it went in, too. No tyre marks on the road or pavement. Didn't even hit the brakes before it left the road.'

'Good job you've got Annabeth's statement,' says Rufus. 'Would be quite the wild-goose chase if not.'

Neilsen nods, giving nothing away. 'Of course, we're still making enquiries. There's the chance that he got out. The chance he's out there somewhere. It would be nice if we had the manpower for a major investigation but resources aren't what they were. We're watching the ports and airports, just to be sure. He has contacts in Italy, as we understand it.'

Rufus nods. He's spent the past week familiarizing himself with Griffin Cox. He fancies he's better informed about the escaped prisoner than anybody on the investigation team.

'Naples,' says Rufus, smoothly. 'The Amalfi coast. You should see if your paymasters will fund a trip over there. Get yourself some Limoncello and a Marquette crucifix.'

'You heard about that?' asks Neilsen, picking a daisy and spinning its stem between forefinger and thumb. 'Got the pepper spray from another inmate. He'd clearly been planning this for an age. Spritzed himself with it to raise his temperature and look like he was dying. Chewed his own tongue. Not your friend's fault that she fell for it.'

Rufus stares down at the grass. 'I sent flowers. Haven't heard a word from her. Spoke to Ethan very briefly but he says she's too shaken up to talk.'

'She's gone to stay with family,' says Neilsen, pulling the petals of the daisy and scattering them like confetti. 'She's been through a lot. Hussain's replacement will be moving heaven and earth to keep her but I doubt she'll go back to work. Not after that.'

Rufus chews his lip. He wonders whether Neilsen is deliberately loading his words with sub-text, or if he's just imagining it. He'd like to be able to just speak honestly – to ask the detective if he knows about the snow globe, and Walter Defreitas. He just can't risk it.

Neilsen seems to read his mind. Cocks his head, and asks him direct. 'Do you think she was in on it? Annabeth.'

Rufus shakes his head. Makes a great display of being shocked to hear the accusation. 'She's a good person. She'd never help a man like that. He's dangerous.'

'He may be,' says Neilsen, cautiously. 'We don't know. His name has been linked to a lot of missing people, yes, but he was inside for one act of abduction. He served his time as a model prisoner. Only made his break after we ruffled his feathers. And as you've no doubt heard, the location was a lie. There's no body in that field. Wilson Iveson was either mistaken, or deliberately lying. Which means we're precisely nowhere. Bit dispiriting, if I'm honest. The charity provided the families with more closure than we have.'

Rufus narrows his eyes. 'Charity.'

'Missing People. At least they've kept the cases in the news – provided some comfort for the families. If Ruth's right and you're writing a book, that's where I'd start. All of the families we've spoken to have nothing but good stuff to say about their caseworkers.'

Rufus opens his mouth wide, trying to relieve the pressure in his jaw. His brain feels too big for his head, as if great globules of matter are about to start pouring down his cheeks like batter mixture. He rubs his eyes and gives Neilsen his full attention.

'Do you want this statement, then? I can tell you it pretty damn straight. He was just a bloke on the writing class. I didn't really take to him but I stopped Suggs hurting him out of instinct. I know nothing more about it than that.'

Neilsen plucks another daisy. Blows on the petals, his mind elsewhere. 'We can sort that another day. I came to let the car

stretch its legs. I know a woman who works at Swinton Hall
that I've promised to take for a drink. Just thought I'd pop in
to let you know I'm still around.'

'Good of you.'

'You'd be amazed the miles you put in in this job. Up to
HMP Frankland to see Cox's old mate, Mark Fellowes, couple
of days back. Wanted to check the visitor log, just belt and
braces stuff. Two-hundred-mile round trip just for a bit of due
diligence.'

Rufus feels himself being reeled in. 'Anything interesting?'

'Nah, not exactly Mr Popular. Nobody been to see him since
there was a meeting organized through the Victim Support
service. He agreed to meet with the sister of one of the girls
he was charged with hurting. I won't say he's a reformed character, because he's an evil fucking paedophile, but he had the
good grace to apologize. Held his hands up. Said he just couldn't
help it. Hated that part of himself and hated it even more in
others. Just rotten. Dead inside.'

'Horrible waters to swim in,' says Rufus, with feeling.

'My boss was all for sending me to chat to old Wilson, too.
Bloody miles though, isn't it? All that way? I mean, Ely's not
exactly a little jaunt, is it?'

'No, I suppose not . . .' begins Rufus, surprised to hear
Neilsen descend into petty griping. He isn't sure he even knows
where Ely is.

'Strange name for the place though. I mean, Prickwillow
Lodge? It's not ideal, is it? Not one you see online and think
"that's the spot for Grandad".'

'That's a cracker,' says Rufus, smiling. 'Really? Prickwillow?'

Neilsen nods. Throws the daisy into the long grass, and stands.
'I hope you and I understand one another,' he says, looking
down upon Rufus, and then at the books all around him.
'Sometimes I think that being a police officer makes it more
difficult to do some good than if I were just an interested
bystander. Anyway, good to catch up. I'd go and get some
suncream on and have a glass of water. Give yourself your best
chance, yeah?'

Rufus frowns, unused to being lectured by strangers. And
then his mind catches up. Wilson Iveson. Prickwillow Lodge.

Ely. He's all but drawn him a map and given him instructions. He's not just asking him for something – he's damn near telling him what to do.

Rufus reaches up. Extends a hand. After a moment, Neilsen takes it. Rufus's palm is warm and clammy. Neilsen's is firm and cool. As they touch, it seems for a moment as if something of one passes to the other.

'I might catch you later,' says Neilsen, with a slight smile.

Rufus nods. Licks his lips. Watches dandelion seeds pinwheeling, carelessly, through a shaft of sunlight. Wonders, for a moment, whether he is being given an opportunity, or thrown to the wolves.

THIRTY-FOUR

Prickwillow Lodge is a few miles outside of the pretty Cambridgeshire city of Ely. Rufus was almost within the city limits before he realized he'd visited the place before. There was a decent independent bookshop near the cathedral, and he had given a talk there one night, years before, when he was still being touted as the next big thing. He remembers thoughtful questions and good wine, and a night in a decent hotel courtesy of the publisher's publicity budget. It all seemed a very long time ago now. He thinks he may have been taken on a tour of the cathedral, but he could just as easily have read a book about it and imagined pictures that are every bit as clear as authentic recollection.

The old people's home is just north of a little hamlet called Queen Adelaide, backing on to the River Ouse. It's an impressive property: a grand, red-brick affair surrounded by landscaped gardens and ringed with a high wall that must be reassuring to the families of prospective tenants: uniformly run ragged by Grandma or Grandad's continued bids for freedom. Rufus has done his research. He knows that the house is a former hunting lodge converted into a statement home by far-sighted Victorians, and that it was converted to its current use thirty years ago. It's part of a chain now – the jewel in the crown of a property portfolio owned by a London company that has managed to steer clear of any bad press.

Rufus pulls in to a large, circular parking area, the tyres crunching over neatly raked gravel. The car broke down twice on the journey down but on both occasions he was able to restart it through sheer force of will. He isn't sure it will get him home again, but at the moment he doesn't really care.

It's a pleasant blue day: the sky smudged in places by tattered strips of cloud. The wind is harsh, when it comes, but Rufus is grateful for it. The journey down was hot and uncomfortable and his shirt is sticking to his damp skin as he stands, immobile, and tries to get himself together. He feels jittery with nerves, as if he's going for a job interview and knows he's already lied upon his CV. He's interviewed scores of people over the years – all in the name of research – but this feels very different. He doesn't know yet if he's researching a book, or trying to put himself at the centre of a story.

He grabs his battered satchel from the rear seat, locks the car, and makes his way past a large picture window to a big set of double doors. There's a mosaic on the floor: different shades of sepia and black artfully arranged to form an approximation of a church. Beyond that is the cool of reception, with its dark wood floors and a staircase that curves up towards the high ceiling. There are fresh flowers in a huge Chinese-looking vase on the reception desk and the buttermilk-coloured walls are hung with the kind of oil paintings favoured by people who use words like 'gelding', 'yearling' and 'cob' rather than 'horse'. They've got a George Stubbs air to them: glossy-coated stallions standing proudly in stables or in front of dusky, tree-lined landscapes.

'You must be Rufus.'

He turns at the sound of the voice. The woman marching towards him plays havoc with his sense of perspective. He can't quite work out how far away she is. She's tiny, but so round as to be almost spherical. It's hard to guess her age, but Rufus decides she's probably around fifty. She has long dark hair, nice blue eyes, and a face that goes from forbidding to beguiling as soon as she smiles. She's wearing a black suit over a cream blouse and he notices as soon as she gets close enough that safety pins have been discreetly employed to pick up any slack left by inexpertly-placed buttons.

'I'm Wendy,' she says, extending a hand. It's small and fleshy and there's a wedding ring on her finger: the only ornamentation other than the ruby-coloured nails. She gives off the scent of body spray, liberally applied. It makes him note the absence of other smells he had expected to assail his nostrils upon entering the lodge. He'd expected bleach and school dinners and the faint but unmistakable trace of funeral parlour lilies and ammonia. All he can smell is furniture polish, and Wendy.

'You're right, I must be,' says Rufus, taking her hand in his. He gets into character at once: the affable and bumbling English gentleman, delighted to have been given some of her valuable time. 'Lovely to be here. Lovely to be anywhere really. I have two teenage daughters so I'm forever looking for reasons to make myself scarce. Some days I pour the last of the milk down the sink so I've an excuse to drive to the shop.'

'I hear that,' smiles Wendy, grinning. 'I was saddled with sons. Three of them. The youngest is still at home and I can't see him leaving any time soon. Got it too good. The others come home when they're hungry or need their washing doing. I should say no, but I can't bring myself to.'

'You're obviously in the right job. You're a giver.'

She considers this. 'Either that, or I've raised three takers.'

Pleasantries exchanged, she rubs her palms together: the international sign language for getting down to business. Rufus reads the signs. 'So, as I said on the phone, this is rather a new direction for me. Your Mr Iveson – apparently he's the absolute authority, but I was warned that he's not always on the correct wavelength.'

Wendy nods, understandingly. Lowers her voice, even though there's nobody around. 'He's growing increasingly frail, I'm sorry to say. Has been for some time now. We treat the pain, but the dementia is quite far advanced and it's heartbreaking to see him not understanding what's happening to him. You don't want to keep reminding him, as you can imagine. Sometimes ignorance is bliss.'

Rufus softens his expression. 'There's nothing about getting old that I'm looking forward to. To think, all that he's done, all that he's accomplished, and now . . .'

'Indeed,' says Wendy, with a sad sigh. 'We have several residents with equally fascinating stories, of course. Ex Battle of Britain pilot passed away last month. Arthur, in the Feltham room – he used to play for Preston North End. Marjorie – she struggles to recall why she's here or whether it's breakfast or bedtime, but sit her at the piano and she can play like Liberace. It's fascinating to me – they're like these Russian dolls; different versions of themselves all the way through.'

Rufus makes a show of being impressed with the phrase, and mimes writing it down on his palm.

'I must admit, Wilson is one of our more – shall we say – enigmatic residents. He's been here for a little under four years, but he was really quite fit and active until the last year or so.'

'He's eighty-five, eighty-six . . .?'

'Eighty-six, I think. A proper gentleman, there's no mistake about that. Still insists on wearing a collar and tie and even though he can't get his feet into his shoes any more, he brushes his slippers with a wire brush as if he were blacking his boots for military parade. Hugely intelligent, which is why the deterioration is so sad to watch.'

Rufus nods again, wondering whether he has sufficiently ingratiated himself with Wendy to start asking questions that matter. A journalist would know, he tells himself. A copper. What are you, Rufus? What are you even doing here . . .?

'He gave some fascinating talks over the years,' says Wendy, smiling to herself. 'Not just here. Libraries, all the Women's Institute groups locally. Very much our Renaissance man.'

'Fretted instruments, yes?'

'That's his speciality. Violins, violas, guitars – things I hadn't heard of until he did his slide show in the lounge. He's lived quite the life. That's why I suggested it might be worth engaging him in conversation: if you get him on his chosen subject it's as if the fog clears. Otherwise it may be a wasted journey, as his other visitors have found out.'

Rufus keeps his face neutral. 'Does he have many visitors?'

'No family,' she says, sadly. 'The occasional old friend, or one of the volunteers from the local groups that come in and sit with our residents to help them feel less lonely. No, a confirmed bachelor, Mr Iveson. Quite the life, as I'm sure you'll know already.'

'Always happy to hear more,' says Rufus, hoping he sounds charming and fearing that he sounds like an idiot.

'He was quite the charmer, until he took poorly,' says Wendy, her voice not much more than a whisper. 'Always had little presents for the staff or would get the young ones giggling with some phrase in Italian or Latin or Greek. He once told me I was his Helen of Troy – a face that launched a thousand ships, though I probably spoiled it when I asked if that meant I had a face like a champagne bottle. But he could chat for hours if you showed an interest. Lived with a rather eccentric lady in the 1960s, helping her turn this big old stately home into a kind of bohemian paradise. He kept the house as a base after she died, while he was off buying his instruments and valuing them, giving talks, arranging insurance policies for their worried owners, that kind of thing.'

'Fascinating,' says Rufus, his mind whirring.

Wendy stops suddenly, her mouth clamping shut like a fly-trap. She eyes him, quizzically. 'The book you're writing – you said the central character is a collector? Rare instruments?'

Rufus nods, finally in his comfort zone. He can bullshit about books for ever. 'It becomes an obsession for him,' he says. 'He's a very remote person – emotionally distant – seeking out the sublime at the expense of the everyday. He's never really been there for his children, even as they've been jumping up and down for his approval. He has something of an existential crisis when he has a bit of a health scare – begins thinking about the choices he's made, about what he's leaving behind. When he suffers a stroke and can no longer take care of himself, his daughter and her son move in with him to help him, and the boy shows a real gift for music. It's a journey of explor-ation, really, and the instruments that line the walls are symbols of elevated sublimity versus grounded, primal, everyday forms of love. I can feel the story taking shape – I'm just woefully underprepared for the level of detail required to pass inspection when it comes to such a nice area as vintage musical instruments, and then my publisher told me about Mr Iveson, and well, I'd rather speak to the best.'

Whatever brief moment of doubt had scuttled across Wendy's mind appears assuaged by his story. She puts a fleshy palm on his forearm, just to reinforce the burgeoning bond between them. 'Sounds a wonderful book,' she says. 'Perhaps a little over my head, but then, I'm four foot eight.'

'You looked a bit worried there,' says Rufus, pushing his luck.

Wendy looks pained. Wrestles with her conscience and decides there's no harm in a little gossip. 'We've had a few unsavoury types over the last few weeks,' she says, and the word 'unsavoury' seems to cover a multitude of sins. 'One or two journalists posing as old friends. One even brought his so-called "grandson", if you can believe it.'

Rufus looks puzzled. 'What's the interest?'

'He was guardian to a man who did some very bad things. Stepfather, I suppose. I don't know the case myself but apparently there was some documentary about some missing people, and this particular man's name kept coming up, so a few reporters did some digging and found out that Mr Iveson looked after the house that the man still owns – the bohemian paradise I mentioned to you. I've seen photographs of the place and it's exquisite, it truly is. Of course, it's hardly Mr Iveson's fault if a lad he took in when his mother died has gone on to be a bad chap. You'll have heard about the prisoner who did a runner a few days ago from the back of an ambulance? Self-same gentleman. As you can imagine, we've had a few phone calls on that front too, and the police even sent a couple of officers. What did they think? That he was hiding in the conservatory behind a pot plant? Anyway, we've given people very short shrift. I'm just pleased you came to me direct. An author wanting to talk about violins? That'll make his day.'

Rufus gives a smile, hoping it reaches his eyes. He feels mildly pleased with himself for choosing to contact management rather than concoct some elaborate ruse to gain access to Wilson Iveson. But now he's secured access to the man who knows Griffin Cox better than anybody, he has no idea what to ask him.

'Anyway, I've been very rude. Can I get you something? Tea, coffee? Then I'll have Katrina take you up to his room. He's happier there than in the lounge. Listens to his music, sometimes an audiobook. Looks at his photographs, reads his old sheet music like he's lost in a good book. Don't let the sound of the oxygen canister upset you – it does take some getting used to but at present he's in no pain. And please, don't be upset if he ignores you or falls asleep. He's in a world of his own most of the time.'

'Coffee would be lovely,' he says, feeling a little sick. Questions line up like bullets but he's terrified of firing a single shot lest he somehow cause injury to those who stand behind him. He wishes Annabeth would answer his calls. He feels so damn lonely that this morning he took Shonagh a cup of coffee and a bacon sandwich, leaving them outside the bedroom door with a little twist of wildflowers foraged from the garden. He hasn't had any response yet. Feels a bit silly now, as if he's asked a girl out and been flatly rejected in front of his friends.

'If nothing else, do take a look at his albums,' says Wendy, leading him through to an office behind the desk, where a middle-aged and rather mumsy woman is reading a magazine and eating cold pasta from a Tupperware box. She blushes as he smiles at her, mouth full.

'His albums?'

'The photographs of the gardens he looked after. I doubt they're in such good shape now but back when it was a hippy paradise it was like something from another world. Like Ancient Rome, or Ancient Greece, or . . . well, somewhere ancient . . .'

Rufus stays quiet. Just opens his mind, and feels the oxygen of new ideas rush in.

In his eyes, on the black dots of his pupils: a pinprick of fire, glowing like liquid gold.

THIRTY-FIVE

Wilson Iveson's room is on the first floor. It's a pleasant, comfortable space and if Rufus were booked in for an overnight stay after an appearance at a literary festival, he would have no complaints. The Lodge has the feel of a country hotel: carrying an air of ubiquitous Englishness, from the heavy floral curtains to the elegantly potted aspidistras that bask in the sunlight on every sill. Rufus enjoys seeing grey heads turn as he and Katrina pass the conservatory: a sea of pink women and grey men, clad in pastels and sitting up in high-backed chairs, reading books, knitting or simply staring into the past with old, damp eyes. Katrina, it transpires, is even more talkative than Ruth.

She's in her late twenties, and not much taller than her boss, but whereas Wendy is made up entirely of overripe melons, Katrina is all breadsticks. She weighs about the same as Rufus's leg. She has black curly hair and glasses that sit in an odd place on her nose, bisecting her eyes and making her look quizzical and simple all at once.

'Not really an old person, if you catch my meaning,' says Katrina, conspiratorially. 'What I mean is, not all old people are nanas and grandads. They don't all go soft and carry toffees in their pockets and give you a quid that you can't tell your mam about. Some of them are just the same people they were when they were young, but with more wrinkles. Mr Iveson's like that. He was always a bit, well, aloof – like he didn't really want to be here but he knew he had no choice. I suppose when you've lived your life in a big mansion with its own lake, or you're swanning off all over the world all the time, this must all feel like a bit of a comedown, but we do try and make it nice for him. But don't get your hopes up. I brought a couple of those detectives to see him last week and he didn't even look in their direction. I don't think we've got him for long, if you'll forgive me for saying so.'

'Does he know about his stepson then?' asks Rufus, a little breathlessly. 'Apparently somebody he used to be guardian to has disappeared from prison?'

'Yes, all rather exciting, isn't it?' asks Katrina, beaming. 'The police I mentioned, well they mentioned it, but if he even knew who they were talking about he didn't respond. Poor old chap – did a good turn by somebody years ago and still getting bothered about it now.'

Rufus realizes he should probably feel a little guilty. Tries. Can't seem to remember which buttons to press, so just smiles: the very image of compassion and understanding.

'Here we are then,' says Katrina, and Rufus wonders for a moment if he's expected to leave a tip. They've come to a halt outside a wooden door. There are pictures in frames on the wall near the handle: mugshots of smiling staff members, clearly placed there in case the residents forget who they are or where they are and believe themselves in danger. 'Hello Mr Iveson, it's Katrina, we'll be coming in if you're decent . . .'

Katrina announces all this as she opens the door and enters the room: a little ball of sunlight flaring in a dark space. Rufus follows her in. She's at the window, throwing open the curtains to let in a shaft of yellow light and expose the collection of assorted knick-knacks on the windowsill. A jade bird, a black opera mask, a broken Grecian urn filled with dried flowers tied with red silk. Rufus takes in his surroundings as if drawing a slow breath. Fills himself up with it. The neat bed, with its heavy red-and-gold embroidered throw. The walls are a dull gold that reminds Rufus of Mediterranean beaches. The walls are covered in artwork; incongruous in thick gilt frames: lithographs and landscapes, portraits and monochrome photographs. There is a huge bookcase by the entrance to the bathroom: an elaborate piece of furniture that must have taken five men to carry upstairs. It's filled with textbooks, hardbacks and dog-eared notebooks, photograph albums sticking out at awkward angles and faded parchment scrolls half unrolled wherever there's space.

By the bed is a walnut writing desk with Queen Anne legs, decorated with photographs in silver frames. Rufus squints and makes out open collars, floaty dresses, sideburns and moustaches; daisy-chain diadems and bare feet tangled in wild-flowers and long grasses. Sees a young woman with dark hair and intense eyes, laid out Ophelia-like among great leathery waterlilies; a smiling child sitting on her stomach as if she were a canoe.

Above the bed, next to a Rococo mirror with a gold frame, is a large wooden cross. It's Neapolitan marquetry: glorious slivers of quality wood expertly interwoven and underlaid to create an effect of both iridescence and solidity.

Iveson sits in a high-backed chair. It's old and expensive and backed in a threadbare green embroidery. Rufus has only seen such pieces in museums before: usually taped off and monitored by officious volunteers. The chair suits Iveson perfectly. He too has a faded majesty: a careworn lustre. He's got the look of an antique vase that has been smashed and put back together.

He was never a big man, that much is clear, but the shrivelled husk that stares blankly past Rufus has the distinct air of a ventriloquist's dummy. His slippered feet dangle a good few inches off the floor, the legs of his dark suit rucked up to reveal bone-white shins, completely hairless: freshly laundered towels drying over a rail. His hands clasp the arms of the chair as if he expects it to levitate. He wears a patterned shirt: blue silk, decorated with twists of gold, and a tie with a large knot. His scrawny neck protrudes from the too-big shirt and makes Rufus think of Galapagos tortoises: wrinkled and comical. His hair is a reddish brown, swept back from the sides and teased into a wispy, off-colour meringue at his crown, failing to camouflage the mottled, red-veined skin beneath. His eyes stare past Rufus at nothing at all. His eyelids are so puffy that it's hard to tell if the lids are open, but Rufus can just make out the curved half-moons of white. His irises are almost invisible: just two vague insinuations of impermeable darkness.

Slowly, Rufus becomes aware of a monotonous tick: a tick-tock slightly too slow to be a clock. He traces it to an antique metronome atop the little shelving unit by the wardrobe. It's an irritating sound: a heartbeat counting down to some unwanted deadline.

Katrina's voice cuts through the silence, cheerful and jolly. She talks as if to a child.

'Rufus, this is Mr Iveson. I'm sure he wouldn't mind you calling him Wilson. Now, Mr Iveson, do you remember what we talked about? Rufus here is a writer. He's won awards and all sorts of stuff. He wanted to talk to you about music. Antique violins. All the things you did the slideshow about. Oh that was good. Not very funny but very informative. Will you be OK if I leave you to it?'

Rufus stands by the bed, waiting for a flicker of interest from the half-dead man in the chair. Receives none. Katrina looks at him apologetically. 'Keep trying, if you're not in a rush. He goes like this. Bit of a trance, I suppose you'd call it, and then he pops back and asks if we're using fresh herbs or dry ones in the risotto. You just have to roll with it really. Our ethos is not to do anything for our guests that they can still do themselves, but it's hard to know. Anyway, lovely to meet you. Will be passing by. I'll leave the door open.'

She pushes past him, still all smiles, and Rufus is left feeling horribly awkward. He doesn't know what he was expecting, but it wasn't this. He endures a sudden plummeting of his spirits. Is it possible he has completely misread DC Neilsen's intentions in coming to see him? He knows himself capable of seeing alternative narratives in almost all scenarios. Maybe Neilsen had told him where to find Griffin Cox's stepfather out of carelessness, and not with some tacit instruction to go poking around and find out what he, as an officer of the law, could not get away with. The more he thinks upon it, the more ridiculous he feels. He doesn't know whether he is seeing a pattern, or making one up.

Rufus walks to the window, his back to Iveson, and looks down into the pretty courtyard garden. There's an ornamental fountain spraying water into a green pond: a wheelchair-friendly circular path through an attractive arbor, lined with comfortable chairs and occasional statues. He can make out a bust of a Roman god, and a marble imitation of Venus de Milo. He plays, nervously, with the dried flowers in the urn. Watches as dead petals fall like snow.

'Sorry to be bothering you,' says Rufus, to the room in general. 'I heard you were quite the expert in old violins, is that right? That's a specialism and a half, isn't it? Have I heard right – the bow is often worth as much money as the violin itself? That's interesting. You were a valuer for Sotheby's, weren't you? Or was it Christie's? Saw the world, I'm told. Freelance appraiser? It's fascinating. I suppose I was rather hoping that I could pick up knowledge somewhat passively – that you would tell me interesting things and I could absorb it and see what comes out when I write. Or maybe I didn't. Maybe I wanted to see you and ask myself what I really believe.'

Rufus hears his voice get softer: hears the last dregs of verve draining away. He turns and stares at Wilson Iveson. Sees nothing to fear, or to pity. Sees nothing at all.

'Did you know he was going to do it?' asks Rufus, quietly. He leans back against the sill, feeling the dry petals tickle his back. 'Your boy. Griffin. Are you afraid of him, I wonder? Or was this all part of some grand idea?'

Rufus walks to the foot of the bed, and perches on the mattress. A smell of detergent and dry paper wafts up, and he wrinkles his nose at the thought of the tiny particles entering his nasal passages and climbing down his mouth.

'You told the police where to dig, I know you did,' says Rufus, softly. He lets his gaze linger on Iveson. Spies a gleam of metal by the chair: an oxygen cylinder – the clear plastic mask puddled on the floor like a dead jellyfish. 'Why would you do that? You've been looking after the house all this time, taking care of his assets, going to visit him. You care about him, that's clear. There's pictures of him right there by your bedside. So why would you send the police to that spot? She's not there, is she? So you either thought she was, or you were messing with somebody. I don't know if you were sending a message to Cox. Maybe you were. Was he upset when you told him you were ill? Was he worrying that he'd have nobody else on the outside to keep his secrets safe?'

Rufus pushes his damp hair back from his face. Scratches at an insect bite on his arm. He doesn't know what he thinks. He's heard of people who trust their gut, but Rufus's prime influence is imagination, and as such he can never work out whether he believes something or just thinks it will make a good story.

'It's a lovely place,' says Rufus, looking around. 'Don't imagine that I've got no sympathy for you, because I have. I have for Griffin too, up to a point. You like beautiful things. You both revel in things that are sophisticated and sublime. You're Epicureans. You're Renaissance men. And here you are, trying to cram a lifetime's work into a little single room, and Griffin has spent years in a variety of small rooms, shitting in a bucket and making do with memories and drawings. It's almost tragic.'

There's no response from Iveson. Wherever his mind is, it's a long way from here.

Irritated, Rufus walks to the bookcase and starts glancing through the titles. There are some exquisite tomes. Endless classics. Plays by Euripides, the letters of Cicero, the love poetry of Propertius; Augustine's *Confessions*: all eight books of volume one. Rufus has a writer's love of books and feels an irresistible urge to take one of the leathery works from the cramped confines of the shelf and to open it up: to inhale the dry musk of its pages. He doubts that Wendy knows the value of what she permits him to keep in his room. Wonders how many other, similarly sublime manuscripts might be piled up, untended, at the big stately home where Griffin grew up, and where Wilson Iveson built a garden to rival Verona's *Giardino Giusti*. He shakes his head, considering walking straight back out and driving home. He could find a little pub. Knock back a couple of shots. Call Ruth, the busy journalist, and let her do the job properly. Try Annabeth again, or maybe try leaving her alone. He could text one of his daughters, or apologize to his agent for whatever it was he said last time they had a chat.

His eyes fall upon the big photograph albums. They're stacked like towels: black leather bindings absorbing the light. He grabs the top one, and pulls. It's an expensive binder: soft leather, vellum or calfskin. He strokes it, enjoying the feel of the material against his fingers, then opens the volume at random. The images within are printed on card, and their edges have been pushed into little slits in the black crepe. There is no plastic covering. Rufus skims through the pictures. They are unremarkable snaps of a life colourfully lived. He sees Wilson Iveson as a boy: grey shorts, grey jumper, a thick mop of dark hair, standing in a dirty street, barefoot and holding a cricket bat. There is washing flapping on communal lines behind him, his eyes too dark to make out. Rufus skims through a lifetime of moments: the same young boy, sitting on the knee of a plump, elderly woman in a headscarf; a man on a ladder leaning against a pear tree in the background of a semi-detached house. Sees him, older still, dressed up as Puck in a performance of *A Midsummer Night's Dream*, barefoot and feathered legs, furry jerkin and a crown of flowers.

Rufus puts the book back. Picks up another, from further down the pile. Opens it and sees the piercing, melancholy eyes of Procne Henshaw-Cox. She's strikingly attractive: pixie-ish, with short hair and fine features; a neck as thin as a wrist and perfect décolletage. She has a waif-like quality, somehow ethereal; other-worldly. In the picture she is sitting on a low stone wall, legs crossed demurely at the ankle, shielding herself from the harsh sun with a parasol. A magnum of champagne is clutched like a club in her other hand. Behind her, a handful of stick figures work upon the grounds of her home: bare-chested, dirt-streaked men oversee the planting of a finger-straight poplar.

Rufus turns the page. Follows the development of the garden as it is transformed from wilderness to wonder. In each of the images, Procne serves as muse. The camera lingers upon her with a tenderness that speaks of true delight. She is smiling in only some of the photographs, but she looks upon the picture-taker with an intensity that causes the hairs on Rufus's arms to rise. There's a lustful edge to her gaze: a suggestion that the sun is lulling her into a state of torpid sensuality. And behind her, men in tight shorts, or floral trousers; men with moustaches and long hair, hefting spades, pickaxes, levering statues onto great granite plinths or raking perfect pebbles around the circumference of the water feature: three winged women holding trumpets and golden apples, captured barefoot; their robes bunched behind the knee to reveal young, shapely skin. Rufus has never before found carved stone so alluring. He looks for Griffin. Sees the boy in a handful of photos: a slim, pale boy, dressed like a Victorian: cloth cap, long cotton gowns, or dressed up as something from a Pagan festival: furry britches and fake wings, clutching a harp while topless women twist and writhe behind him, throwing their arms up to the glorious sun.

Rufus swallows. It pains him. He doesn't want to feel these things; doesn't want to think about the strange, sad life the little boy had who grew up to become what he became. He screws up his features, ready to slam the album closed and stomp from the room. Then he spies the peculiar object at the rear of the final photograph. It's a simple snap: showing the finished gardens in all their glory. They are indeed a wonder, a perfect imitation of a late Renaissance palace garden: the paths lined with cypresses; the waterways paved with lilies; the steps leading to a wooded area where a romantic little grotto sits invitingly, guarded by a sentry of alabaster Roman gods. At the very rear of the picture, the water disappears into a large pool, partly concealed by the buttress of a little humpbacked bridge. It's a dizzying image, as if the perspectives had been designed by Titian. The water seems to be flowing uphill in places and in others the steps seem to go up to an area that is below the level of the main paths. Rufus peers at it, trying to make sense. He fancies he can see a roof below the level of the footpath, rising from the water, but well below the level of the bridge.

Rufus raises the album until he is almost touching it with his nose. Slowly it swims into focus. There is a grotto: a strange little boat shed, almost completely submerged by the newly dug pool. The photo shows a blisteringly hot day – the water level no doubt lower than eventually intended.

He lowers the book, wondering at the significance. He knew already that Cox had grown up in a stately home – that his mother met her end in the glorious mock-Renaissance garden upon which she lavished her every moment's joy.

Rufus begins to return the book to the shelf. Stops, as surely as if he had seen a predator, as his fingers touch the rear cover of the album. Beneath the crepe paper, he can feel something. There is a thickness to the crepe that feels somehow incongruous – as if it were quilted with something unyielding.

He glances back. Wilson still stares at nothing.

Slowly, deliberately, he slides his finger around the edge of the strange protuberance in the fine paper. Creates something approximating a square. Shakes the album, as carefully as he can, and a set of Polaroid images slide free and tumble down to the floor.

Rufus curses. Bends down to retrieve them, stops halfway to the carpet, as the images take shape.

Sees them all. All Griffin's victims. Sees them bone white and naked: the only light in the dark, dark place where they have been mounted like statues. Sees youthful flesh turned the texture and colour of candle wax. Missing teens, taken, murdered, and metamorphosed into moon-bright figurines.

And then Rufus is falling forward, crashing down towards the photographs of the dead, plunging face-first into the scattered images of murdered girls.

Above him, Wilson Iveson: straight-backed, eyes wide, bringing down the oxygen canister on the back of Rufus's skull: again, and again, and again.

THIRTY-SIX

Pain.
Pain that sings.

It's the worst hangover he's ever had. Every cell in Rufus's body seems to be compacting at once: grinding against one another with saw-toothed edges. His head feels as though something hard and unyielding has been forcibly pushed into his skull. His back is pure cold agony: spinal cord taut as a guitar string, vertebrae bunched against one another like stones beneath the hull of a wooden boat.

He tries to raise his head. There is a moment's resistance. He feels the electric charge of panic before he can unjumble his thoughts. For an instant he feels bewildered, ill-used: has somebody glued him to a rough cord carpet as he slept? Then the memories fall: a blizzard of torn images. He knows himself again. He is laid on the floor of Wilson Iveson's room. Blood from a serious head wound has clotted beneath him, all but sticking him to the floor. He can hear something familiar: a noise like clucking birds in a farmyard, the dry rustle of a high wind through autumn leaves. He tries to swallow. Tastes blood. Lets red spit drool from his damp lips. Keeps his eyes closed.

Lets the sounds arrange themselves until they become a voice. Words. The dry, perfectly enunciated timbre of an old man speaking softly into a telephone.

'. . . don't have to say anything. I'm catatonic, remember, or near as damn it. They can draw their own conclusions. It doesn't matter very much anyway, I'm beyond the reach of any justice they see fit to dish out. I'll be in Elysium soon – walking the great halls with the sun on my face and an amphora in my hand. There will be no pain. Just pleasure, for ever more. I'll be waiting . . .'

Rufus knows he is in a bad way. He feels sick and dizzy and there is a strange scratching sound inside his head, as if crustaceans were suddenly unfolding themselves and scuttling around on the underside of his skull. He tries to open his eyes. Sees carpet. The leg of the dresser. Sees blood.

'. . . can't wait any longer. You have to say your goodbyes. You choose life or stay with the dead. There's a future out there. You've created something truly sublime. Let it be now. Believe in yourself. You have such reserves of strength. You can begin again. Be somebody new. He won't wait forever and I won't be here much longer. I don't think we'll talk again.'

Rufus hears something in the old man's voice: a slight insinuation of emotion; of tears. He is saying goodbye to the child he raised. Rufus becomes aware of a sour, smouldering anger in his belly. There is a tingling in his fingers, as if blood were rushing back into a dead limb. He forces himself to swallow the blood that pools in his mouth. Slowly, his movements almost glacial, he raises his head. Through the haze of his vision he sees Wilson Iveson standing by the window, staring out into the watery blue sky. The bloodied oxygen cylinder is behind him on the floor. In his left hand, he holds the framed picture of Procne: baby Griffin on her belly.

Rufus forces down the wave of dizziness that crashes into him: a great fist pummelling the side of his head. He focuses on the small, wiry, straight-backed man in front of him. He needs to get the phone from him. It will contain the number that Griffin Cox is using. Neilsen will be able to trace it. They can find where he has been burrowed in since faking his death and abandoning Annabeth to whatever fate decreed . . .

Annabeth.

Rufus grinds his teeth. He knows that to recover Cox is to ensure that Annabeth's past will be exposed. The thought pains him. And then he thinks of the photographs. The missing teenagers, taken, killed, transformed into some grotesque vision of beauty by a killer intent on preserving the sublime.

'. . . I think he's still breathing, but I need to recover my strength before I finish him. My hands are shaking. Talk to me. Tell me how they look. How they feel? Is it like flesh, or damp stone? Can you still see the lines of the muscle? What happens to their eyes, Griffin – are they dark holes, or pieces of coal? Do you remember the snowmen? Your mother would always . . .'

Wilson doesn't finish the sentence. Rufus lunges forward, head spinning, half-blind with pain and rage. Sees his own hands rising, the sudden change in colours as his vision fills with the old man, and then the crushing impact of the two of them smacking into the windowsill; the unmistakable sound of glass shattering as his hand closes on the old man's face and pushes it against the first hard surface he can find . . .

On his back now, face wet, blood on his hands, on his front, dripping down the collar of his shirt.

Footsteps. Bangs. Raised voices. The bang-bang-bang of fists on a closed door . . .

He looks down. The little telephone is still illuminated: a square of neon light on the embroidered rug. Beyond, a slippered foot, a patch of hairless shin; a body still as death.

Rufus closes his hand around the phone. Lifts it to his ear and feels it smear the hot, dark blood against his cheek.

'Magister,' comes the voice. 'Magister, what's happening? Did you do it? Is his head open? Can you see inside? What's in there? Touch it. Tell me how it feels against your fingers . . .'

From the recesses of his mind, Rufus registers the Latin word. It means 'teacher'. Suddenly he feels no anger. No pain. He's cold, and everything looks soft at the edges, and a beautiful perfect blackness seems to be filling the room, as if he were bathing in treacle, or oil, or . . .

'Ink,' he says, and smiles to himself, pleased at the neatness of the word. 'Bathing in ink.'

He briefly registers the sound of violence somewhere nearby.

Skin on skin. A fist against wood. The crash and screech of pain and impact. He doesn't have the energy to decipher it all. Just wants to rest. To let go.

In his ear, a voice. 'Rufus? Rufus is that you . . .?'

He can't place the voice. It isn't Griffin any more. It's beyond his reach: a voice at once familiar and indefinite.

As he gives himself over to whatever comes next, his final thought is of his wife. He registers a vestige of surprise. A feeling of warmth, and need, and comfort.

Fuck, he thinks, as he fades. *Fuck, I love Shonagh. I really fucking love her . . .*

And Rufus Orton comes to an end.

THIRTY-SEVEN

During his prison psychotherapy sessions, Griffin Cox used to relish the opportunity to fabricate memories. There was something delightful about watching the well-meaning psychologists try to comprehend a person who never truly existed. In their company he has been a victim of abuse; a foundling child taken in by rich relatives who made him feel like the cuckoo in the nest; a solitary carer for an unhinged parent – a spitting ball of repressed rage made manifest in one solitary act of uncharacteristic impulse. He takes pleasure in knowing that he remains a mystery, and that as of a few days ago, he always will. Nobody will ever poke around inside his brain again. Nobody will get the chance. For the rest of his days, Griffin Cox will be known as Pietro Giudicio. He will live in the little farmhouse five miles into the mountains above Ravello on the Amalfi Coast. He will make wine, grow olives, eat well. He will read. Make decorative tables. He will draw. He may learn to play one of the costly antique instruments that are stored in the temperature-controlled room beneath the old paper mill, through the olive grove at the rear of the main house. Many of his treasures have been transferred these past months. His guardian has ensured that the things that mean the most to him have already been shipped out, awaiting his arrival. His guardian is good at such things. He is a practical man: able to oversee the creation of a Renaissance garden; provide false papers; or conceal the crimes of a child even as they continue into adulthood.

His bond with Iveson is the only flesh-and-blood relationship that has ever truly mattered to Cox. He thinks upon it, for a time, wondering at the strange, cold, quiet feeling at the edge of his consciousness. Could it be sorrow? A sadness at the nearness of the old man's departure: the inevitable loneliness of true isolation. He ponders upon it, laying back upon wet grey stone, naked and streaked with filth. Thinks upon psychiatrists and counsellors. Smiles, as he recalls his more grandiose fabrications, half wishing he could risk writing some down and sending them to Rufus Orton – show him how creative his imagination can be.

Cox can see himself now, sitting in the padded chair in the peaceful little office, letting tears pour down his face as he told his latest counsellor about the man who hurt him at an abandoned train station in Derbyshire when he was eight years old, or being forced by bigger, stronger boys to hold a litter of feral kittens beneath the water in the lily pond, sobbing as he felt the fight go out of their fragile, helpless bodies. Such revelations were always warmly received by the psychotherapist. They would nod, understandingly, and make sympathetic noises as their pen moved over the pages of their notes and their eyes gleamed with excitement at the notion of being responsible for opening closed doors in their patient's subconscious. Cox has never shared his earliest memory with any of his doctors, for fear that they would read meaning into it, when none exists. He sees nothing of importance, no symbolism or emotional catalyst. In his memory, he is a little under three years old. He is sitting on a dusty wooden floor in a room with a high ceiling. There are flickering candles and a smell that is not exactly pleasant, but which makes his mouth water. His mother is nearby. The light in the room does not permit him to see her features, but the shadow in the corner of the room contains her vague likeness, and he can see the glowing tip of the nasty-smelling thing she holds between her lips. He is cold, and sticky, and

his skin feels odd: tight and uncomfortable; the feeling he gets
when she forgets to change his nappy, but all over him. And
he is scared. He doesn't look right. When he raises his
hands he is the wrong colour: the jolly pink of his flesh transformed into an ugly off-white. He keeps shivering, and every
time he does, he watches his skin disintegrate: tiny fissures
opening up in the surface of his flesh; his skin cracking like
the shell of a hard-boiled egg. And he is trying not to cry,
because his mother has told him not to. So too did the voice:
the voice that smelled of Mother, and which clambered hotly
into his ear even as the strange cold goo coated his skin. Don't
cry, he'd said. Don't cry or you'll spoil it . . .

Half a century later, Cox has long since filled in the blanks.
His mother had instructed one of her gentlemen to make her
son look angelic. And he, eager to please, had painted Griffin
with a thick, chalky paint. He'd told him not to cry so he didn't
spoil the effect. His mother wanted to see angels, and it was
Griffin's job to become a moon-white cherub. He cannot
remember whether he satisfied his mother. That part of the
recollection is curiously absent. But he knows enough about
Mother's whims to presume that he fell short of her expect-
ations. She wanted her son to be a Hercules; a Theseus capable
of negotiating the labyrinth and slaying the minotaur. She told
him daily that he was descended from the ancient gods, that
his absent father came to her as a bull; as a swan; a shower of
rain or a vision of explosive ecstasy. She told him that the men
and women who lounged and laboured and touched one another
in every corner of the house and gardens were servants, ready
to lay down their lives in service to a boy with the blood of
the deities in his veins. He grew up believing himself Almighty.
His descent from Mount Olympus was brutal and merciless.
When reality intruded into their bohemian idyll, when he was
plucked from their Eden and deposited at a boarding school, he
discovered himself to be anything but godly. He was weak.
Fragile. Feeble. He was not beautiful, as he had believed. He
did not have loyal retainers upon whom he could call. He was
a small, delicate boy with wet eyes and a weak chest and he
would spend the next years of his life being dissected; broken
apart and badly remade, by boys who preyed upon him for sport.

Cox looks away from the memory. He has spent too many years undoing the damage of his childhood to linger upon the memories now. He is in an ebullient mood. Has been for days. He's free.

He smiles as he says the word, slowly, inside his mind.

Free!

It has been several days since he told Annabeth to help him push the little car into the deep water of the Humber, down a patch of shingly mud on the joyless Victoria Dock estate. The days since have done little to sap his joie de vivre at finding himself outside the claustrophobic embrace of HMP Holderness. He had always imagined himself capable of escape should it be deemed necessary, but he still allows himself to enjoy the feeling of proving himself right. He feels a certain pity for Governor Hussain, who always treated him fairly, but he has no choice but to think of the soon-to-be unemployed governor as a casualty of war. They were closing in, pure and simple. If the police didn't find his collection, then some bloody journalist would, and even if no evidence could be found linking him to the abductions, he had begun to see the looks in the eyes of the other inmates. His future would be lifelong incarceration, or brutal death, and neither really appealed.

It was his Magister, his teacher, who had finally convinced him that liberation was not going to be achieved through conventional means. When Iveson was diagnosed with the cancer that has so reduced him, he made it plain to Cox that his death was going to change things for ever. Iveson has been the only truly loyal servant; guarding his home, his resources, his secrets, these long years. But Iveson has weeks to live, and in his absence and Cox's continued incarceration, the bohemian palace of his childhood will fall into ruin. The labyrinth of accounts that permits the upkeep of the property will be beyond Cox's reach. And when the house is seized by creditors, they will conduct a survey on the property and grounds. They will see the peculiarities. They will take soundings of the lake. And they will find the subterranean room where he has spent three decades turning beautiful, exceptional young men and women into works of art.

Cox sits in the company of the beautiful dead, and breathes

in so deeply that he feels briefly dizzy. His whole being fills
with the mingled aromas, sights and sounds. He feels high;
intoxicated, drunk on the sheer hedonistic pleasure of being
here, again: situated in the place to which he has returned again
and again these past years. His Magister has sustained him with
descriptions, of course, and he has been permitted to glance at
the occasional photographs when his legal team have visited
and slipped him the envelopes for which they have been quietly
but handsomely rewarded; no doubt telling themselves that the
contents are items of sentimentality rather than criminality. But
to be here, to be beneath the water, in the cool and the damp
and the slime-scented air, is to glimpse Elysium.

It was his Magister who discovered the tunnels when he was
making Procne's vision a reality. She imagined the *giardinera*
descending to a clear, silver-blue lake: neat stone bridges curving
in from each side to meet at an ornamental fountain topped
with a statue of David. And his Magister did as he was bid. He
drained the lake, and happened upon the network of secret
rooms and tunnels that had been flooded, silted over, and hidden
from view two centuries before. They learned that the rooms
were once a lower floor – a lower floor of a long-vanished
bridge that arced over the central span of the water in Jacobean
times. Griffin, still not much more than an infant, was made
privy to the secret. He was carried through the stinking silt and
foul-smelling water to explore the cool, dark place that nobody
knew existed. And he recalls his mother insisting that the secret
space be maintained. That its existence remain a secret. That
the little entranceway beneath the boathouse be concealed so
perfectly that none could stumble upon it. She never ventured
down – even before suffering the cerebral event that altered her
life and accelerated its end. Her Renaissance garden was barely
completed before her fragile brain tore itself in two and reduced
her to the pale, dead-eyed thing he tries not to let himself
remember. It is a comfort to him that she died looking at her
statues, in a place that mattered to her above all else. He does
not feel any guilt for his part in it. She had seen him. Seen him
pressing himself up against the exquisite alabaster Aphrodite,
tucked away behind the cypress trees at the entrance to the
wood. She had seen him pressing his adolescent self to a vision

of something perfect, something his mother held up as a trans-cendent symbol: a bridge between the heavens and earth. And despite the twist of her cheek and the lack of control of her facial muscles, she had twisted her mouth in a scornful sneer. She was laughing at him. She was amused by his pathetic, inexpert thrusts, banging himself painfully off moss and stone. So he had done what was necessary. He'd pushed her wheelchair down the path, and tipped her onto the wet earth. And then he had walked away, tucking himself into his pants unspent and staring up at the rolling black clouds.

Cox looks around him, basking in the absolute beauty of the objects before him.

There are nine of them. Seven girls. Two boys. Each were beautiful, in life. Exceptional, even. Pure, virginal, timeless, angelic . . . each had seemed like a gift from the gods. Each was perfect: exquisite blocks of marble which he could transform into something exquisite and eternal.

Cox first learned of corpse wax at the foot of his Magister. Iveson had discovered something long since dead in one of the chambers beneath the lake. Whatever it had been in life, in death it had been transformed into a wax effigy; a monster carved in soap and tallow. The process, the substance, is called Adipocere. A product of decomposition, it turns dead flesh into a soap-like substance. It develops in damp, alkaline-rich envir-onments and occurs when body fat is exposed to anaerobic bacteria. In the right light, in the right environment, it can resemble the surface of the moon. Crumb like, strange, haunting, it feels like soap. It can be moulded. It can be carved. Were one given to such acts of Baroque metamorphosis, one could take a human body, strip it, bind it, and shape it to one's will. One could expose it to the right bacteria. And over the course of many years, a human being could become a statue: a thing of beauty. Griffin Cox is such a man.

He lays on the cold stone, and stares. Truly, he has accom-plished something of merit and significance. He does not mourn the deaths of those whose lives he has claimed – only wishes they were still alive to see the breath-taking results of their sacrifice. He sometimes wonders how it felt for each of them to wake here, in the cold and the dark, tied and nailed and twisted into a position that would eventually become their own spectacular tombstone. He imagines they felt fear, though he struggles to imagine such a sensation. Cox hasn't been afraid in a long time. As soon as he started killing people and mounting their bodies in the dark place beneath the lake, all of his worldly worries went away.

Slowly, leisurely, Cox turns onto his side. There is moss and pondweed cushioning the rock beneath him. He's cold but the chill serves to make his nerve-endings more sensitive so he makes no attempt to dress himself. He lies still as the creations that surround him: winged furies; laughing nymphs; a mighty warrior in breast-plate, clutching a spear.

'*Omnia bona capient finem,*' he mutters, and the sound echoes back so that it feels as though his head is reverberating with a hundred whispered voices, all telling him the same thing. *All good things must come to an end.*

The thought truly dismays him. If there were a way, he would have his sculptures sent ahead to the new home, but the risks are too great. He knows that when he climbs back up through the trapdoor and into the boat shed, he will have to turn the sluice gate and allow the water to flood the chamber. He will have to leave his creations to the rising sludge. He will weep, perhaps, as he drives away; head shaved, a neat goatee beard, little round glasses and a scar upon his cheek: all affectations carefully chosen to make him appear as far from Griffin Cox as can be achieved. He feels excited at the prospect. It has taken an irritating amount of time to make the journey down to Cambridgeshire: a tiresome relay in a series of bland vehicles – their keys left out for him on the rear tyre – and staying in pre-booked, nondescript hotels. His first sip of red wine since his incarceration was a true disappointment. He had let it dribble from his mouth and onto the bedlinen as if it were inferior blood. But soon he will be in a country where pleasure is performed correctly. His life will be beauty, and experience: truly – a paradise worthy of Caesar.

He stands. Dresses himself. Wrinkles his nose as the inferior material of the shirt, trousers and bland tie touch his skin. It will not be like this for long, he consoles himself. Soon it will be silks and ermine. It will be marble and soapstone. It will be flesh, and wax.

As he turns to look one final time upon the soap-rimed, greasy statues, he sees a flicker of movement – something, or somebody is with him, in the dark, beneath the lake.

'Magister? Wilson, you shouldn't be here, what if you were followed – imagine if somebody saw you enter . . .?'

The voice rushes towards him like a gathering storm.

'Yes,' says Annabeth, emerging from the stone plinth beneath the mutilated remains of Luke Ashley. 'Just imagine.'

THIRTY-EIGHT

A nnabeth watches him, his face a smudge of dirt and slime but expressionless as a full moon.

'No,' he says, shaking his head. 'No, nobody followed me. I made sure.'

She smiles at him. There's no humour in it. 'And yet here I am.'

He stands up, slowly, unashamed by his nakedness. He's a small man but there's a strength to him: his limbs hard, roped with thick veins.

He glances at her right hand and Annabeth follows his eyes. Sees the long, lethal-looking boathook. She'd scooped it up from the boat shed as she made her way slowly and silently into the dark – fighting down her rising gorge as she saw what had been done to the young people who had suffered the misfortune of meeting a true personification of evil. Holds it like a lance, as she stares from Griffin Cox to the gallery of disintegrating flesh, and back again.

She has remained silent throughout his communion with the bodies of his dead. She has watched the rapture with which he has beheld the spectacle: the gallery of dripping tallow corpses mounted in a grotesque tableau in the long, gloomy passageway.

'I don't understand,' says Cox, frowning. 'You did as you were bid. You helped me. I wouldn't break our pact, Miss Harris.

Never. I don't know how you've found yourself here, or why, but you have made a very poor judgement. This won't end well.'

Annabeth smiles at him, something like pity in her gaze. 'You really did convince yourself you were in charge,' she says, quietly. 'Mark Fellowes told you what I wanted you to be told.'

He shakes his head. 'No. No, he hates you.'

'Mark Fellowes, your cell-mate in Frankland – I visited him with the restorative justice charity I worked with. He recognized me at once. He'd gone back to the flat, you see – after Defreitas tried to kill me. I think there may be some goodness in him, somewhere. He told me to go. To get out of there. He cleaned up. Put the body where it wouldn't be found until he was long gone. When he saw me, I thought it was over. All that I'd worked for, all the miles I'd put between myself and my past. But he recognized me as the girl who'd killed a bad man. I hadn't changed so much that he didn't know me. But the thing with Fellowes is, he owns what he's done wrong. We talked. And he told me about his cell-mate – this true work of evil, this monster, who knows where the bodies of all those missing people are.'

'No,' says Cox, again, stepping forward into the muddy earth with a squelch. 'No, he told me—'

'I don't know how quickly your mind is working here, Griffin, but in a moment you're going to see it all very clearly. I've taken more lives than you have. Defreitas was the first, my baptism, if you like, and it was many years before there was another. I suppose it was frustration that pushed me into it – frustration at seeing good people in pain. Men like you, they're all about power. About control. About causing maximum suffering and pain. And all those years I worked with the missing persons charity, I couldn't get past the idea that those who know where a body is buried should be made to give up that know-ledge. That somebody should do something.'

'And that somebody is you?' asks Cox, and there is scorn in his eyes. 'You became a prison officer just to get close to people like me?'

'No, you were just the most difficult to get to. By the time I realized that you were guilty of all the crimes you're linked to, I'd already put plenty of recently released cons where they belonged. Opened their throats, usually.'

She stares at him, her voice amplified by the low brick ceiling of the chamber. Watches him form the pieces into a coherent shape.

'You wanted me to come to Holderness? You wanted me there so you could help me escape.'

She nods: a teacher pleased with a student. 'Go on.'

'But you needed me to feel I was in control. I was the one manipulating you . . .'

'The families deserve to know what happened to these children. I needed you to lead us to them.'

Cox chews his cheek. 'And now?'

Annabeth shrugs. 'You're not going off to your new life, Griffin. We're going to have to leave you here.'

The killer looks at her with something like admiration. 'You keep saying "we",' mutters Cox. He looks around slowly. The water only reaches his ankles, but further down the chamber slopes and deepens and opens out into the body of the lake. But there is no way in from the water itself. The sluice gates are down and have been for decades. There is no way in save for the twisty passageway that winds down from the boat-house. The effort of bringing his prizes here has half killed him before now. The climb is exhausting, even without the encumbrance of a struggling adolescent across his shoulders. Annabeth must be tired. Afraid. But is she alone? If he were to rush her, there might be somebody more physically able standing at her side. He is so close to his goal. Has looked upon the fruition of his work and can almost taste the full-bodied Amarone that will be spilling down his chin within days. He can't permit her to stop him. Can't let it end here.

Annabeth watches as he weighs his options. In the silence, she hears a sudden vibration: the soft trill of a phone buzzing upon damp rock.

'You should get it,' she says, not unkindly. 'He'll want to know you're OK. You can tell him the truth, or let him live in ignorance.'

Cox reaches out. Picks up the phone. Listens to the breathy voice of the man who tried to stop him becoming the thing that he is.

'Magister . . .'

Annabeth listens. Lets him talk to the man who raised him: who saw the dark thing within him and tried to help him control it; the man who didn't even turn on him when he found the bodies beneath the lake and decided to help conceal his crimes rather than ensure he face justice for them. He owed the boy's mother that, didn't he? What is love if not doing that which seems unpalatable for the good of somebody else?

He looks at Annabeth. Realizes he has never really seen her before. For an instant, there is a connection, as if staring into his own eyes in a mirror. And then he takes his chance. Lunges forward, stepping into the shallows, sprinting through the tangle of weeds and dark water, as Annabeth raises the boathook like a spear, and launches it straight at Cox's heart.

THIRTY-NINE

The sudden tug; the sensation of being punched in the chest; the burning, searing pain, and he is falling backwards, turning, reaching out to grab for purchase and feeling his hand claw into the waxy, ruined flesh of the dancing nymph he created with the body of Bronwen Roberts.

He falls. Reaches out. Coughs blood, and slithers down into the water. He pulls himself up; the shaft of the boathook sticking from his gut; warm blood pumping onto his belly, and then he is looking at a new shape; a new apparition. He is looking at a teenage boy; fresh-faced, smooth-skinned – something very like madness in his eyes.

And then Ethan Harris is grabbing the shaft of the makeshift spear, and pushing it further into his guts.

Cox's vision becomes a mosaic; a mandala of random pieces and parts. He sees the water. Black coffee and quicksilver. His head jerks back as he feels a sudden urgency. He lurches forward, and then he is slithering down and into the water. The cold is agony. He cannot tell whether his eyes are open or closed. He takes a desperate gulp and chokes as water floods inside him. It feels as though there are hands dragging at the tails of his coat, at his floundering feet, pulling him down. He kicks desperately, reaching out with his hands, feels the toes of his boots catch the river wall. He pushes against the slimy surface but cannot find the strength to propel himself upwards. He reaches out, frantic, clawing at the water as if it were a net he could climb. Inside his skull it is all static and echo. For a moment he fancies that the water has taken on a human shape; that it has transformed into a pale and phosphorescent assemblage of limbs . . .

And now he is reaching out, encircling his hands around the corpse that eddies with each movement of the water. The arms are taut and elongated, bound at the wrists with a wire that eats into the puffy white skin. He feels himself go under again, as if there are weights tied about his ankles: hands clawing at his clothes. He kicks out, hearing himself gasp and spit, water in his nose, his mouth, his ears. He tips his head back. Tries to shout. Gulps down another foul-tasting mouthful of brown slime. Turns himself over and feels the body bounce against his torso. Instinctively he lashes out. Pushes the corpse away with hands that do not feel like his own.

Spears of torchlight cast distorted polka dots onto the surging surface of the water. He tries to focus on the light, his teeth chattering, fingers numb. He is shivering, fading, unable to tell his body what to do, and then it feels as if somebody is dragging at his coat, pulling him away from his anchorage at the wall, and he is thrashing wildly, certain that the corpse is reaching out for him like a siren. He feels the meaty impact of his fist hitting bone. His gorge rises as his fingertips rake through the rotten meat of the dead girl's flesh, as if pulling a rake through soft mud. He gasps, raising his hand high; an eager pupil, desperate to be picked: skin sliding free of muscle, tendon, bone . . . He tries to find something to hold. Clutches frantically at the dead girl's skin.

He can see his breath rising, drifting upwards through the dark, and as his hands fasten around some solid part of the corpse's remaining tissue, he feels a tug, as of a fishing wire snapping beneath the strain. The body rises up; seal-like, ascending in a spume of white-flecked spray. Cox looks into the empty eye sockets of the faceless corpse. Glimpses metal.

Cox feels a great sadness bloom inside him. Shivers, and blood runs into his mouth. Blood and dirty water, upon his lips, his tongue, his throat. He smells it. Rust and old machinery, raw liver and Irish stout. Smells iron. Smells blood.

He awaits the tunnel of the light: the triumphant song that will accompany his ascent into Elysium.

The silence is absolute.

He takes a great shuddering breath, eyes bright as alabaster.

And then the darkness closes over him like the mouth of a shark.

'Like ink.'

Ethan reaches down and picks up the phone. Hears the sounds of violence. The ragged breathing of a dying man. Speaks before he can help himself; before his mother can leap forward and knock the phone from his hands.

'Rufus?'

Then there is just the silence, and the bodies, and the familiar sound of Annabeth Harris sobbing to herself, quiet and contained, as she asks herself, again, how many bodies it will take to fill the void within her – how many she will have to kill before she regains that which was taken by a man who thought he could do what he wanted to her and who died without facing the consequences.

How many abusers will have to die?

She asks it of herself, as she has so many times. How many, before she stops being afraid.

The answer comes in a voice that is not her own: a white-hot sensation right inside her head.

All of them.

Every last one.

EPILOGUE

Detective Constables Ben Neilsen and Andy Daniells are standing in the courtyard garden at the rear of the big old hall where Griffin Cox grew up. His body was recovered last night from a hidden network of rooms concealed beneath the surface of the algae-covered lake.

Also discovered in the secret grotto were a grotesque collection of waxy body parts and defleshed bones. How he had come to meet his end remains the subject of speculation. Wilson Iveson is dead, and unable to offer any light in the darkness. Neilsen has hopes that Rufus Orton, should he ever wake, will be able to provide answers. He also hopes that he keeps his mouth shut about who it was who told him how to find his way to Iveson's residence, and who wound him up like a clockwork toy and let him skitter away down a dangerous path.

It was Neilsen who broke the news to Bob Roberts. Told him that they were all but certain they had found Bronwen. Bob hadn't spoken for what seemed like forever. Then he wanted to know if she had suffered. Neilsen hadn't the heart to tell him the truth. He'd promised it was quick, and painless.

'He's a fighter, I tell you that,' says Daniells, looking up at a mossed-over statue of a naked god of war. 'Your writer mate.'

Neilsen nods. 'His heart's beating. I don't know if that's the same as "alive".'

'He'll have a story to tell if he gets better.'

'Sounds like a good enough reason to come back, I suppose.'

They stand in silence, looking up at the grand frontage of the old house, both lost in thought. Daniells feels as though he has been involved in something significant, but the pictures keep distorting and reforming: clouds glimpsed through smoke. He knows that in Griffin Cox he has glimpsed evil, but he fancies that he has inhaled the faintest trace of something else: something older. He feels as though he has been dumb witness to an act of primal vengeance: or restorative justice.

He cannot define whether he believes Cox's killer to be on the side of the angels or the demons. In the elegant Renaissance courtyard, surrounded by Classical statues and figures from antiquity, within sight of the place where a killer was created and taken apart, he wonders, briefly, upon notions of heaven, and the certainty of hell. Decides, on balance, it's all still to play for.

'Shall we?' asks Daniells, gesturing at the path that leads up to the big front doors. 'She'll be going spare.'

The 'she' in question is the head of CID. She's outmuscled the cowering suits from the National Crime Agency. Her team's in charge now, and they're going through the big house one room at a time. It will take an age, but Neilsen is looking forward to it. There will be a sense of peace in following instructions. In being dogged and dutiful and thorough. He'll relax. He'll lose himself in the task. He might even stop thinking about what Bob Roberts had said to him as he was leaving.

You should tell her, too, he'd said. *She cared as much as we did. Would do anything to get justice for Bronwen. For us. She's quit the charity now, like, but I've got her number. Annabeth. She's a lovely girl. Best of all of us. Swore to God she'd get her back, whatever it took.*

Neilsen puts the thought to the back of his mind. He doesn't want to look at it closely. Doesn't want to think about the deal he's made with himself.

They set off towards the house. It seems to Ben that the sun shines brighter with every step.